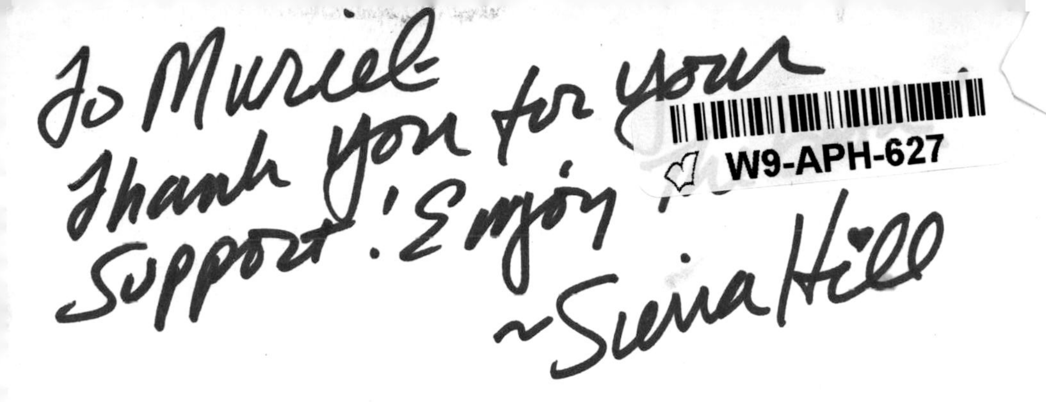

Physical Touch

Sierra Hill

Published by Ten28 Publishing

Cover Design by Dar Albert, Wicked Smart Designs

Edited by Stephanie Elliot

This book is a work of fiction. Names, characters, places and incidents either are products of the author's imagination or used factiously. Any resemblance to actual events, locales or persons, living or dead, is entirely coincidental.

Find Sierra on the web:
http://www.sierrahillbooks.com
www.twitter.com/sierrahillbooks
www.facebook.com/sierrahillbooks
ISBN: 1500157376
ISBN-13: 978-1500157371

TABLE OF CONTENTS

ACKNOWLEDGMENTS

My deepest gratitude to my college roommate and long-time friend, Sarah S., for providing me with the understanding of the complexities and mechanics of physical therapy. I know I took some extreme liberties in the characterization of the therapy scenes in this book and I've probably made the whole profession look bad. For that I apologize. But I'm ever-so-thankful that Sarah, who dutifully made it to her morning classes (while her lazy roommate stayed in bed), became the awesome physical therapist she is today. I love you, friend!

To my Zumba girlfriends (you know who you are). You're all such a blessing to me and an encouraging presence in my life. Thanks for believing that I could do this! And yes, I did include something about Zumba somewhere in the book.

Thank you to my writing heroines, the indie writers whom I admire and shamelessly relied upon for information on self-publishing: Lexi Ryan, Sawyer Bennett, J. Nathan, Angela Darling and Lauren Blakely. You are all amazing! I hope to someday repay the favor.

To my family. Mom, Dad, Jen, Mary & Burt, Nica, Steph and Caitlin. Thanks for your love and undying support throughout my writing journey.

To Stephanie Elliot, my editor. How lucky am I to have found you? Your knowledge, expertise and publishing insights have been invaluable. I'm so appreciative of your writing savvy and constant wit!

And lastly, to my husband, Steve. Without his encouragement, support, humor and understanding, I would not have been able to fulfill this lifelong-dream. Thanks for being patient with me, even on the days when I left my clothes in the washer and forgot to buy groceries.

CHAPTER ONE

Rylie Hemmons was typically in bed by ten on a weeknight, not in a crowded pub trying to socialize with people she didn't know. She had to keep reminding herself that she was there for a very good reason, otherwise she would have hightailed it back home to snuggle in her flannels and watch *Gilligan's Island* reruns on Nick at Nite. It was her friend Mark's farewell party that required her to forego her typical anti-social tendencies and attempt to behave like a normal woman her age.

The party was in full swing when Rylie joined the crowd at O'Leary's Pub, just after completing her daily five-mile run. The run had put her in a better mood, the increased endorphin levels mellowing her out so that she was ready to enjoy the celebration. True to form, socializing and idle chit-chat were never high on Rylie's list of favorite activities. The idea of having to talk with people who she didn't know and would never see again held little interest for her. And most times, she honestly didn't enjoy others' points of view. She had trouble keeping her mouth shut when she didn't agree with someone or felt they were just plain stupid.

She stepped through the crowd, narrowing in on Mark, and her other friends Sasha and Beth, who were huddled in a close circle, drinks in hand and already having a good time. She gestured toward the bar when she caught Sasha's eye, indicating her intent to get a drink. Her raven-haired best friend held up a nearly empty drink glass, signaling for another. Rylie frowned, knowing that by the end of the night she would either be driving Sash home or she'd pass out drunk at Rylie's apartment. Unless, of course, Sasha tethered herself to any one of these tall, handsome men, offering themselves up as good one-night stand. That was one thing Sasha never lacked in her life, and where Rylie could probably take a few cues from her daringly brazen BFF.

Rylie politely shoved and shimmied her way through a few groups of party-goers, making her way to the old wooden bar, scarred and pock-marked from years of use. She and her friends often hung out at O'Leary's at least one night a week; it was close to the clinic where they worked and always had good service, but she'd never seen it as busy as it was tonight. All of the bar stools were taken tonight, making it standing-room only.

Sidling up to the bar, she squeezed herself between two patrons; one was a man in a suit, his back facing her, talking to another suited man. On a bar stool to her right was a petite, fast-talking, high-pitched woman with curly, short blond hair.

Rylie took a calming breath and nodded to Skeet, the bartender. He smiled and walked toward her, a broad smile on his face.

"Hey there, gorgeous. Haven't seen you in a while. You want the usual?" Rylie's eyes widened in surprise. She hadn't realized that a) she was so predictable and b) he'd remember her drink order. Although she had gone out with him a few times before, they never made it too far in the romance department. She found him a little too interested in other women, and had the feeling he wasn't that into her. Not a biggie, since she wasn't looking for anything serious.

Rylie never felt she stood out in a crowd, especially when she was in the company of Sasha or Beth, who were both gorgeous and could flirt shamelessly with good-looking men. Rylie preferred to stand in the back, watching whatever game happened to be playing on the flat screen.

But she smiled at him, none-the-less. Skeet was pretty cute and had nice eyes and great forearms, which were on display in the tight black T-shirt he wore. Along with a full sleeve of tattoos crawling up his arm.

"Yeah, one Manhattan and also a Cosmo for Sasha, please."

As she waited for her Manhattan to be crafted, her attention was drawn to the conversation the two men sitting to her left were having. They were laughing and discussing a topic she was keenly interested in

– football. And not just *any* football, but her *favorite* football team, the Patriots.

Rylie leaned covertly against the bar, trying to look disinterested as she cocked her head toward them to eavesdrop on their conversation. Skeet returned with her drinks as she nodded her thanks, placing a twenty on the bar. Taking her first sip, she became more enthralled in their discussion. She knew it was rude to listen, to pass judgments upon men she didn't know, but it was inconceivable to her how these two seemingly intelligent men seemed clueless about the sport. How in the world could two grown men be so inept at understanding the basic elements of the NFL and season dynamics? As usual, her inner thoughts became louder and more aggressive, and within a few minutes of listening to them bash one of her beloved teams and players, she slammed her drink down on the bar and turned to give them a piece of her mind.

"You've got to be kidding me," she said, turning toward the man with the tailored Hugo Boss suit sitting with his back to her. "What kind of shit are you two talking about? The Patriots are going to kick ass this season. How could you be so lame not to consider the strength and absolute sheer force of their offensive line this year…any nimrod with a pair would know that."

The two men stopped their banter and turned to face her, the man sitting next to her swiveling around in the bar stool, looking incredulous.

Crap, did she just say that out loud?

Aww, hell. No sense going back now. She was about to continue to reprimand the two idiots when her gaze fixed upon the incredible pair of hazel eyes trained directly on her, which held an expression of both irritation and interest. Or maybe it was confusion over her lunatic rant. Either way, she felt a jolt of electricity run from the bottom of her toes to the top of her head, stopping only momentarily to leave a flutter of butterflies in her stomach.

Rylie immediately felt the red hot blush creep up over her face as she noticed the intense stare the man sitting closest to her was giving her. Eyeing her inquisitively, he allowed his gaze to leisurely run the length of her body, stopping at each juncture. And he made sure she noticed it. Was this a turn on or an insult? She wasn't sure, but it brought back the butterflies immediately. And more righteousness.

His thick, sandy-golden hair was textured and groomed perfectly, a bit longer on the top so that it flopped to the side across his forehead. Her first instinct was to run her hands through it to see if it fell back into its perfectly sculpted place. Just been fucked hair. That's what it looked like. His strong jaw had a hint of stubble, a five o'clock shadow that was a bit darker than the color of his sun-kissed head of hair. She tried not to consider how the rough texture of his beard would feel against her skin.

Holy hell, snap out of it, already.

His laughter came out in a booming guffaw and immediately brought her back to the two in front of her.

"Apparently, Jax, the lady doesn't appreciate our opinions on the subject matter tonight. Perhaps she'd be willing to educate us further on the merits of the Patriots over another drink." His mocking smile and raised eyebrows gave off an air of superiority that sent a quick stab of ire up Rylie's back. Feeling the heat rise on her face again, Rylie harrumphed and slammed back the rest of her drink.

Before she could respond with a witty comeback, his long fingers reached up to touch her mouth, wiping a drop of drink remaining on her upper lip. He touched his own mouth, his tongue reaching out to taste the remnants.

"Mmm…I like Manhattans."

Rylie stood in utter shock. Had he really just done that? What was this guy's deal, she wondered. His aggressiveness, partnered with her own socially awkward inclinations, drove her anger to a whole new level. It's one thing to talk about things you know nothing about, as this man obviously did, but then to have the balls to touch a stranger, like that, was not okay with her. Who did he think he was?

Stammering to find the words to say, Rylie backed up, feeling trapped and more than a little irate. "What the hell, buddy? You need a lesson in personal space, too? I think they teach you to keep your hands to yourself in second grade," she said with indignation.

"Hmmm…I clearly missed that lesson. Such a shame. But I'd be happy to get schooled if you're looking to act as my teacher."

The look in his eyes made Rylie shudder. There were deep, dark, tantalizing secrets hidden in those brilliant hazel eyes. And more lust than she'd ever witnessed in a single creature. The playfulness of his words with the intimate level of innuendo made her realize just how absolutely unskilled she was in the art of flirting. She now wished she'd taken more of an interest the many times over the years when she was witness to Sasha's skilled maneuvers.

She knew her hand was being forced and she had to make a choice. She could stand her ground and fire back with some snide remarks, which was typically her M.O., maybe even try to turn the tables on him. Or she could take her drinks and walk away, giving him less than the time of day.

Yes, she could do that, but it would be far less fun and wouldn't leave her with the satisfaction of knowing she put him in his place. She really wanted to fire one out, like one of those snarky eCards she loved. What she wanted to say was "I wish I had my duct tape. It won't cure your stupidity, but at least it would muffle it." She laughed at the thought, enjoying her own sense of humor. She had something to prove to this guy, even though she had no idea why.

He wasn't her type, even if she had one. He was far too arrogant and exuded too much cockiness for her temperament. Well, actually, that wasn't true. She liked a guy who could hold his own against her. That's what she found so appealing in this guy. He was so cock-sure of himself and the idea of knocking that sexy smirk off his face held an appeal all its own. She might just enjoy herself and play along. Why the hell not? She had nothing to lose.

Giving him a similar once over like he'd just given her a few moments before, she gave him a slow, knowing grin. "I think what you need is some remedial help. I'd recommend some Sports Center to start," she snapped. "At least it will give you a modicum of football knowledge."

The man nodded to Skeet who had stopped in front of them. "Please give the lovely lady another Manhattan. *Knowing it all* can make a woman very thirsty." He laughed, bringing the beer bottle up to his lips to take a drink. "I have a feeling I could learn a lot from you, *Miss…*" His eyebrows quirked up in question.

Oh, he wanted her name.

"*Miss* Hemmons," she said, a little snottier than was probably warranted. But it didn't help that he was clearly trying to get under her skin and aggravate the hell out of her. No way was she giving him her first name. She didn't have any intention of getting to know him further.

He held out his hand for introductions, which she shook. His hand was cool, strong and molded over hers in a possessive gesture. It was an immediate jolt to her system. She could feel the energy shoot through her veins, up her arms, straight to her chest where it landed in a chaotic thud. Rylie inhaled sharply and quickly drew her hand back, reaching for the edge of the bar to hold on to. She suddenly felt antsy and awkward, similar to when she was seven-years-old and had to perform in her first and only dance recital. The idea that she was so far out of her element, like a kitten in a lion's den. And that lion was ready to pounce.

"Well, Miss Hemmons. You seem to have proven your passion for the game, but I'm curious to see if you're willing to put your money where your mouth is?" he asked, leaning his elbow on the bar and sliding his hand up and down the beer bottle.

Rylie's head snapped to look at him, nearly spilling the new drink in her hand. His words were dripping with sarcasm and innuendo and his eyes were full of challenge. Did he know she could never back down from a challenge? That her own pride and stubborn nature had always pushed her into accepting any bet that was laid in front of her, whether she could win them or not? Growing up with an older brother had all but sealed her fate when it came to holding her own against someone bigger and stronger than her. She would never let any man make her feel less than him just because she was female, especially when it came to football.

She took a long pull of her drink, giving her time to think over her response. She was confident in her ability to beat him at whatever he was going to dish out, until she looked up at his face again and saw the heat in his eyes.

"Wh – what did you have in mind?" God, she sounded weak and pathetic. All her confidence went sprinting out the window. The gazelle being chased by the lion.

He laughed, a deep, throaty roar. His eyes roamed leisurely over her face. She gulped down her fear. "I bet that mouth of yours can do plenty," he said, his eyes landing on her lips, as his mouth turned up into a devilish smile. "But I'd like to see what that brain of yours can do. Are you up for some trivia?"

"Trivia?" she asked, her mouth hanging open incredulously.

"Yeah. If you think you can take me on, Miss Trash Talker?"

"Oh, I have no doubt about that. If the subject is football, you've got a deal. What's in it for me, Pretty Boy?"

She had no earthly idea why she was talking to this guy and participating in this ridiculous conversation. She was never interested in these cat-and-mouse games that people played in bars. The easy come-on's and stupid pick-up lines. This was *so* not her. Yet here she was, placing her bets on the table, feeling a surge of excitement from the exchange. And calling this man Pretty Boy. Where did that come from? There was no doubt he was gorgeous, even in his uppity duds. She didn't even think she liked men in suits.

His facial expression turned from amusement to something darker. He was still seated on the bar stool, but his face was about level with hers. He leaned in closer and his lips nearly touched the sensitive shell of her ear. "Let's just say I'll make it worth your while."

Rylie stood stock still, a little out of breath from his nearness. His broad shoulder had brushed against her breast when he'd leaned in and even through the material of her leather jacket and tank, her nipples responded immediately to the sensation of his touch.

"Hmm…so it would be a win-win for you, either way. The stakes aren't very high then, are they?"

"Good point," he mused. "I like my odds, though. In that case, what would you like the stakes to be?"

She hesitated, uncertain as to where to take this. She had to admit she was more than a little turned on by his overt aggressiveness, but she definitely didn't want it to extend past this point. She wasn't looking for a one-night stand or a quick *Wham-Bam-Thank you Ma'am*, no matter what kind of pull this man had over her. *Nope, not going to go there.*

So why she decided to say what she did stupefied her. "Tickets to an upcoming Patriots game."

He didn't appear the least bit fazed by her statement. He just held out his hand to her and shook in agreement.

"You're on, little Miss Know-It-All. Now, let's get this game started." He turned around to get his friend, who had since been chatting with a leggy, buxom blonde woman. As he did, Rylie noticed that her challenger, still seated, had a leg brace covering his leg. She hadn't noticed it up until now and he seemed oblivious to its presence. She'd have to remember to ask him about it after their little game.

His friend came around the bar stool and shook Rylie's hand. He was tall and lean, extremely handsome in a boyish way and impeccably dressed. He seemed genuinely friendly, unlike the shark-like demeanor of her opponent. "Hello there," he smiled warmly. "I'm Jackson. Pleased to meet you, Miss Hemmons. I understand I'll be the referee in your little trivia match against this jerk-off." He nudged his friend in the shoulder in a sarcastic gesture. Pulling out his phone, he entered his code and brought up an app. He turned his hand to show Rylie the display on his phone, indicating the sports trivia game they'd be using.

"Okay, who's up first?"

Her challenger lifted his drink in salute to Rylie. "Ladies first, of course."

She gave him a nonchalant shrug. *Okay, loser.*

Jackson thumbed through a few questions and selected the one he wanted. Looking up at Rylie, he asked. "Which Hall of Fame football coach started off his NFL coaching career with a one and sixteen record?"

Rylie couldn't help but smile. Little did they know that she was raised by her father, a Pittsburgh Steelers' fan. He taught her everything she knew about football and the history of the Steelers. Without hesitation, she gave him her answer.

"So easy," she said, shaking her head in fake disgust. "That would be Chuck Noll, Pittsburgh Steeler's head coach from 1969 to 1991."

Jackson looked up from his phone with amusement and glanced first at his friend, who was looking a bit dumbfounded, and then back to Rylie, who smiled smugly at them both. She knew she was right and did a little victory dance in her head.

"That answer is correct."

Her opponent, whose name she still didn't know, sat in stunned silence glaring at her, his mouth gaping open. "Well fuck me, you're a hustler. No way would any woman your age know that off the top of her head."

What the hell? Everything in that statement, along with his incorrect presumptions, brought Rylie's blood to a boil. He was an egotistical ass to have the balls to say that to her. He was obviously a poor sport and didn't like being shown up by a woman.

"Listen here, Pretty Boy," she hissed, shoving her pointer finger into his very hard, brick-like chest. "You're the one who started this game. So now that I know how you feel about women and sports, I will enjoy crushing your ass even more." *Punk*, she said under her breath.

"Well, well, well. I think someone has a chip on her shoulder. Let me just help you in lightening your load while I knock it right off." He took another swig of his beer and grinned over at Jackson. "Okay, Alex Trebek, give it to me."

Jackson cleared his throat. "All right. Which team holds the record for most Super Bowl appearances?"

With his face pinched slightly and his lips drawn tight, the man sat in quiet contemplation, fiddling uncomfortably with the tie around his neck. While still angry, Rylie felt something stir inside her as she watched him loosen his tie. She had an image of him yanking the tie off and wrapping it around her wrists to pin her down as he lay his body down on top of her. *Whoa. Stop it.*

"I'm thinking the Cowboys." His forehead scrunched up in anticipation, as he waited for the answer.

Jackson made a buzzing sound, indicating he was wrong. "Bah. That is incorrect, sir. Miss Hemmons, would you like to guess?"

Rylie knew the answer, but wanted to enjoy watching him squirm. She brought her finger to her mouth, gently patting her lips as they parted ever so slightly. His eyes seemed to want to devour her mouth. "Hmm…let me think…"

Her competition began humming the *Jeopardy* theme song as he leaned over her shoulder. "Hard one, isn't it?" he asked, capturing her hand and bringing it up to his own mouth, where he placed it to his lips and kissed.

Her eyes grew large, shock registering at his boldness. Creasing her brow, she yanked her hand back and rubbed it on her jeans, giving him an evil glare. He just grinned, his eyes pinning her in some sort of hypnotizing stare, making her feel a little weak and lightheaded. She needed to end this game as quickly as possible and get the hell away from this man.

"It's both Dallas and Pittsburgh. They each have been to the Super Bowl eight times. The Steelers won six championships altogether." She turned back to the bar and picked up her drinks, desperately wanting to make her get-away. "And with that gentlemen, I think you can pronounce me the winner of tonight's trivia."

She stepped forward, flipping her head back over her shoulder to give them a tight-lipped smile. "It's been real," she smirked.

Turning on her heel, she began to walk away, but decided to get in one last word. Smiling coyly, she glanced back at the men, who were staring in confusion over her departure.

"Oh, and Pretty Boy. Do me a favor? Never underestimate a woman again."

She heard a low whistle from behind her as she walked toward Sasha, who was standing in the center of the group, empty drink in hand, watching all of this unfold.

Sasha pounced the minute she was in earshot. "What the hell was that all about? It looked like you were going to get lucky with those two, at first, but now I'm surprised you didn't throw our drinks in their laps. What got you so riled up? Must've been interesting conversation."

Rylie handed Sasha her drink, shrugging her shoulders nonchalantly, her back toward the bar where they still sat. "Yeah, well, I should've thrown my drink at him. He was an egotistical asshole."

The rest of the night she spent drinking and talking with her friends, and occasionally she glanced over to the seat at the bar where the man was sitting. Each time she did, his eyes seemed to meet her gaze and she'd quickly glance away. At some point in the night she looked to find him speaking with her friend Mark and a woman, laughing at something they had said. Looking once again a short time later, she noticed he was gone. Feeling a bit relieved, but somehow disappointed, she left the bar around midnight to head home to bed, where she tossed and turned the entire night through.

Now nine hours later, Rylie only felt exhausted and temperamental as she entered the therapist lounge in the clinic, where Sasha glanced up from the computer screen and smiled.

"So glad you could join us today. I was worried you'd up and left us to go after that guy at the bar. Damn, from what I could tell, he was H.O.T. I'd never seen him there before. Did you get his name?"

Rylie shrugged off her jacket and hung it on the wall hook, crinkling her nose up as she spoke. "He was just an asshole who thought he owned the world. And didn't know shit about football, either. Complete tool." Even though she said the words out loud, something in the back of her head screamed, Liar! She had felt an instant attraction to this man; some visceral and nakedly instinctual reaction to his entire being.

"Too bad, because he was devastatingly handsome. And to my knowledge, you haven't had a good lay since…well, never." Sasha chuckled, sitting back down to peruse the stacks of files on her desk. "Oh well, can't go crying about your dismal love life now because we have a full schedule today, starting with your favorite patient, Miss Eugenia."

Rylie groaned in dissatisfaction as she obediently accepted the file she'd been handed. Starting out the day with Eugenia Bickford would be like pulling out her hair, strand by strand. To say it was a painful experience was an understatement. And Rylie wasn't sure she had the patience for her first thing this morning. Seeing her expression of defeat, Sasha motioned to the kitchen area. "I already have the coffee brewed, so go get some and grab a banana."

Sasha returned her attention to the top folder on the desk and scanned the contents. "I also have the file on the new patient starting today. The torn meniscus and ACL," she said, reading through the medical details she'd received from the surgeon. "It happens to be one of Mark's patients. I hear they're friends from school and apparently he was even at the party last night. Mitch Camden is his name. He just had the arthroscopy last week and Mark referred him to us to continue his physical therapy," Sasha stopped for a second to regard her friend who had just finished her first cup of coffee. "And Ry, with my current workload and patient levels, I need you to take this one."

There was no way Rylie could ever say no to Sasha. She owed her too much for all she'd given her over the last five years, the least of which was her friendship. Before meeting her, Rylie had had very few female friends or any female influences, for that matter. She had grown up a tomboy, raised by her emotionally distant father and wild older brother. And her mother...well, she hadn't seen her since she was four years old. The only women in Rylie's life up until college were the few women her father, Dan, had dated during her adolescence. Other than that, she relied only on what she learned through TV and movies on anything that the world considered to be feminine or girly.

And Sasha was the epitome of girly. She was a tried-and-true fashionista, who taught Rylie the fine art of designer clothes shopping and apparel. At age twenty-eight, Rylie had finally traded in her sensible sports bras for Victoria's Secret lace push-ups and her canvas Converse for Kate Spade's. Even the occasional Badgley Mischka heels could now be found in Rylie's closet thanks to her best friend. Sasha was a fierce flirt to boot, who enjoyed her men and flings as much as she did a fine bottle of champagne. It was Sasha who had coaxed Rylie out of her introverted shell, bringing her along to parties and clubs and introducing her to her own group of close friends. The time she'd spent with Sasha over the last five years had given Rylie the opportunity to see the world through a woman's eyes, not through two opinionated jock men who had raised her.

The one thing that hadn't changed was Rylie's innate ability to hold her own against any man in a game of Texas Hold 'Em, a beer drinking contest, or a fantasy football league. Only now, she wore 7 For All Mankind jeans and lace panties to do it.

"Don't even mention it. Of course I'll take this one," Rylie said, reviewing the notes on the patient chart. "ACL and torn meniscus are a piece of cake. He'll be out of here in less than eight weeks."

"Excellent – that's what I'd hoped you'd say. I know some of your other clients can be a bit challenging."

"Hey, what are friends for? Plus, you're my boss, so I kind of have to do what you say, right?"

"True. Very true."

Rylie smiled, feeling her mood improve slightly. As she began in on her second cup of coffee, Claire, the receptionist, popped her head in around the door corner.

"Rylie, your nine-fifteen and nine-forty-five appointments are here. I'll have Mr. Camden complete his new patient paperwork and show Ms. Bickford back to the whirlpool." Before she exited the doorway, Claire said softly so as not to be overheard by anyone but the two in the room, "Just a word of warning, Rylie. This guy is *GQ* hot."

"Thanks C. I'll be right up." Turning back to Sasha, she sighed, shook her head and grabbed the files. "Well, off I go. See you around lunch time."

Heading out to the front reception desk, she barely rounded the corner when she stopped dead in her tracks.

Her heartbeat spiked. Her muscles tensed. And her mood grew dark.

Seated in the waiting area, leg straight out and confined tightly in a knee brace, a pair of crutches lying on the floor next to him and wearing a smug look she wanted to smack off his gorgeous, arrogant face, was none-other than Pretty Boy from the bar.

Shit, she thought, *so much for piece of cake.*

CHAPTER TWO

Mitch wasn't happy about spending the next seven to eight weeks going through the boring and painful experience of physical therapy. He was a man of little patience and the thought of having a therapist tell him what to do and how to do it was unnerving.

Throughout the last ten years, Mitch called the shots and told others what to do. He was tough, both physically and mentally, building his business from the ground up. Camden Ventures was his dream, born in his college dorm room his senior year at Yale. With a love of the outdoors, coupled with a desire to build eco-friendly construction, he made his business proposal to his father, leaning on his financial backing and business savvy. His father, Mitchell Sr., who loved the idea and knew his son would find a way to get him the return on investment, gave him a proud pat on the back and the one million dollar capital investment needed to get the business up and running. Mitch tripled the money within a year. He'd done it with hard work, dedication and a risk-taking mental fortitude. No one told him what to do, pushed him around, or got in his way.

He hadn't expected his annual ski trip to Solden, Austria to do just that. Smack in the middle of the Kendall project, he had already been laid up for a week after the arthroscopic surgery on his knee and was still having to walk around on crutches like an invalid. He had no time to be hobbling from one place to another, much less spend two hours a day in a therapy clinic being bossed around like a child by some doctor-wannabe.

As he finished up the patient paperwork he'd been working on, he lifted his head just as she rounded the corner. If it wasn't Little Miss Trash Talker, in the flesh. *Well, well, well.*

He wasn't all that surprised to see her, it just wasn't the time or place he had intended. Last night after meeting the little spitfire, he had grilled Mark about the auburn-haired beauty, who so callously kicked his ass in football trivia.

He was immediately intrigued by her spunk and taken back by her quick wit. No one to be trifled with, that's for certain. She was a challenge to his ego and seemed to be resistant to his blatant charms. That rarely happened. In fact, had it ever happened?

Hell no.

So he was in a bit of a shock when she just upped and left him hanging there, without her number or a way to contact her again, immediately immersing herself with a group a friends the remainder of the night, giving him no chance to seek her out again. But that didn't stop Mitch from getting the low-down on Rylie Hemmons.

And now here she was, walking toward him looking equal parts confused and appalled, appearing stuck between bolting out of the room and charging at him at full steam. Instead, she surprised him even more when she straightened her shoulders and stepped forward, her expression turning uber-professional, extending her right hand in greeting.

"Mr. Camden. How very nice to meet again. I now can call you by an actual name," she said, shaking his hand firmly. Quickly dropping his hand, he noticed her hand tightly fist into a ball. He smiled at her unintentional, but very visible, outward response to his possibly unwanted appearance in her clinic.

"I'm Rylie Hemmons, your physical therapist. I'll be responsible for your recovery and therapy over the next few weeks. Why don't I give you some time to finish your paperwork and then you can go change. There's a locker room right over there." She pointed toward the wall near the front and then paused for the briefest second to give him a once over, taking in his sharply tailored, gray Giorgio Armani suit. He let her have her moment, knowing most women liked a man in a fitted suit. But judging from her blank facial expression, she seemed to be somewhat annoyed by his attire. Maybe she secretly wanted him undressed and on top of her. Now that would take his therapy session to a whole new level. And she could put her sassy mouth to better use than she did last night.

As his mind raced back to their brief encounter the night before, he thought about how hot she had made him standing there reading him the riot act. Very similar to the way she was looking at him now.

"I'll be with you in about thirty minutes, after I finish up with my other patient. I hope you are ready to give this your best effort, Mr. Camden. You only get out of it what you put into it."

"Oh, don't worry about that, Ms. Hemmons. I plan on putting a lot into it."

Mitch could tell he'd flustered her by the openly suggestive innuendo in his response, when her mouth opened in a surprised gasp. He thought she'd even blushed, but couldn't be sure as she stomped back into the other section of the clinic to work with her other patient. He would've expected a snide come back, just as she'd given him last night. He liked that about her. She spoke her mind. She was tough, but extremely easy on the eyes.

Lifting his head from his nearly completed paperwork, Mitch noticed how exquisite her long legs looked in those tapered pair of jeans. He watched as she bent over to assist an elderly woman out of a mechanical contraption. Holy hell, her ass was firm. He imagined how it would feel under his palms.

Hell, he was getting hard again. He could feel himself lengthen and strain against the zipper of his pants. He had to get a grip. He wasn't some horny teenage boy, for God's sake. His non-existent sex life over the last two weeks was obviously affecting his focus.

Had it not been for his accident, he would have had an amazing fucking weekend in Austria, literally and figuratively. The sultry redhead, Angela, whom he'd dated a few times before the trip, had pouted and massaged his leg in the lodge as they waited for the helicopter to take him to the hospital. He had been in agonizing pain as they sat on the lobby couch of the luxury ski resort. Pressing her breasts against him, she had the gall to ask if he'd mind if she remained there and went to the spa while he went to the hospital. It hit him then that she was using him just as much as he had planned on using her that weekend. Go figure. Tit-for-tat.

A week later, his thoughts a thousand miles away from Angela what's-her-name, he now had a case of blue balls over a tight-assed therapist who had a penchant for picking fights. And it turned him on, even in his current condition.

Finishing his paperwork, Mitch glanced toward the receptionist whose fingernails were loudly and rapidly clicking the keys of her computer. She looked up at him.

"Are you all finished? I can come get it from you," she smiled politely, brushing down her skirt as she got up to step around the desk. She looked at his leg and eyed him curiously. "How'd you hurt your knee?"

She took the clipboard and pen from him and began twirling it between her brightly painted fingers. She looked young, maybe twenty, wearing a floral print baby doll dress that showed off her tanned legs and oversized tits. For some reason, he was reminded of the classroom scene in *Indiana Jones* where the young female student flirted with Professor Jones. He might not be a teacher, but he knew a come-on when he saw it.

So unlike what he saw last night from Rylie. She was anything but vamped-up flirtatious or coy. She didn't try to come on to him, or use her sexual charms to get him to buy her a drink. In fact, she seemed oblivious to her sexual potency or how much she affected him. She was a ball-buster, giving back even more than he dished out to her. She had a quick wit, wasn't afraid to show him up and was smoking hot. And all he thought about last night was his missed opportunity to get her into his bed.

But it looked like his luck had turned around. Maybe having knee surgery wouldn't turn out as bad as it seemed.

Mitch smiled back to the receptionist and began to tell her the story of his trip gone horribly wrong. He'd soon finished reciting the weekend adventures that led to his accident and excused himself to go change into his rehab wear.

Stepping out of the locker room, his attention was drawn to Rylie's response at getting a very motherly hug from the elderly woman she had been working with earlier. He stood back to lean against the wall, casually admiring his new therapist as she assisted the woman in a walker to the front desk.

Her figure was tall and lean, her jeans hugged every tight curve. With long legs that expressed a level of athleticism, it wouldn't have surprised him to find out that she had been a track star or volleyball player in college. Fit and trim, but not with the hard edge that some female athletes could possess. And judging from her behavior last night, she had a competitive spark that could surely ignite things in and outside of the bedroom. He was beginning to reconsider his aversion to this therapy thing. It could definitely have its advantages.

"Mr. Camden…are you ready to get started with me?"

Mitch nearly choked. *Yes, you could say that.*

He pushed himself upright and bent down to pick up his crutches. He hefted his arms over and on to the crutches and nodded his head in her direction.

"Lead the way," he said, following her into the room that resembled a mini gymnasium. "And please, call me Mitch. We'll be working closely together over the next few months; we might as well be on a first-name basis."

He saw her consider it for a moment and then, as if it pained her to agree, she acquiesced. "All right…Mitch," she drawled, placing her hands on her hips to stress the point she was about to make. "You can call me Rylie or Ry. But don't think the lack of surnames is going to get you off easy. I work my patients hard because that's the only way progress can be made. You'll need to put in the effort and not screw around. If you want to be successful in your recovery, then you have to do what I say and as often as I say. Got it?"

Wow. She was a tough one. No nonsense. No bullshit. He wasn't normally one to give up any sort of control. Not in the boardroom or the bedroom. But for some reason, the idea of Rylie taking control of things seemed to be a pretty good trade-off. He wanted to see where things would go from here. He just might like it.

"Aye, Aye, Cap'n," he clipped, giving a quick salute. "I have to admit I like the idea of getting off easy, and I'm warming to the thought of you telling me what to do."

She scowled and her eyes, the color of melted chocolate, glared daggers at him. Truth be told, he was waiting to get slapped. He may have just crossed the line. Instead, she doused his thoughts of carnal knowledge with two words. Ice bath.

"Are you kidding me? You want me to get in that tub of ice water?" Mitch spat out the words and then immediately realized his mistake. He clamped his mouth shut as he noticed her stare, an unspoken, *You're going to start that shit already*? look.

"Uh, sorry," he graveled. "Okay. How do I get in this thing?"

She shook her head. "I'll help you."

Her hands moved out to grab his crutches, setting them down on the floor to the side of the tub. Reaching toward him, her arms extended around his back, shifting his body weight onto hers. She locked her arms around him in a bear-hug grip, her head turned to the side and resting against his chest. Mitch's entire body tensed, uncertain of his reaction to her closeness and her touch. His chin rested on the top of her head as he breathed in the scent of her hair. Vanilla and a hint of honey. Sensual and soft invaded his senses. As her hands made their way down his back and under his bottom, they agilely guided his leg over the side of the tub, helping him to sit comfortably on the ledge.

With nowhere else to place his hands, he draped his arm around her neck and clung to her. Feeling vulnerable and weak, Mitch cursed himself for having to rely on this beautiful and sexy woman to assist him into this contraption. It certainly didn't help his ego.

"I think I need to prepare you…this is going to be extremely cold. We'll need to work up to this, so for today, let's try for a minute." As she said this, Mitch was lowered into the forty-degree pool of ice-cold water.

"Mother of God, this is freezing! Are you trying to get me back for last night?" he growled, his voice shaking from both the emotion and the frigid temperature. His body convulsed and goose bumps littered his arms, legs and torso. He turned to her in time to see the wicked smile quickly vanish from her mouth. She sighed.

"I think I mentioned it was cold. Believe it or not, I'm not trying to get you back for anything. This is a normal part of therapy and there is a science behind the healing power of ice. The cold temperature decreases the inflammation and swelling in your muscles and joints. With all of the trauma your knee has had, we need to kick-start the rejuvenation process. After your surgery, lactic acid begins to crystalize around the joints and the ice helps to shock it." She moved around to the back of the tub and pulled out an oversized towel. Moving behind him, she handed him the towel and placed her hands under his arm to hoist him up onto the step again. Although his torso and below felt like a frozen human Popsicle, the feel of her against him sent heat waves coursing through his body.

"Okay, let's get you dried off and warmed up so we can start your exercises."

****

By the time the hour-long appointment was up, Mitch had begun to perspire and beads of sweat clung to his skin. His breathing was erratic and choppy and his attitude surly. Rylie had expected this to happen, as it did with most patients on their first visit.

Rylie had seen it all with a myriad of clients who had come and gone and wasn't surprised by the shape Mitch was in by the time he finished up. It was her job to find the individual limit for each patient and learn when she could push for more and when to give it a break. Observing Mitch over the last hour, it was clear he had the physical endurance and stamina, but she hadn't had time yet to assess his motivational energy.

When it came to therapy, it was easy for many patients to quit too early on, as the pain and fatigue of the work could become overwhelming. Her job was to be a cheerleader, a mechanic, as well as a psychologist to enable their continued progress. And it didn't surprise Rylie that Mitch might try to impress her with his ability to work through the pain.

What did come as an unexpected surprise were the jolts of electricity that erupted through her body whenever she made contact with his. Being physical with others, whether it was men or women, young or old, came with the physical therapist territory. It was what she did for a living and she was supposed to be immune to it. And yet she had never before experienced such an instant and intense heat from another human being. This worried her. This could be a problem.

And that problem was a solidly built, very handsome man who was now lying supine on her exam table, an ice pack fitted around his left knee. Rylie had excused herself to her office under the guise of updating her progress notes while he iced and recovered from the exercises.

In truth, it was she who needed time to recover. Her chest felt tight, as if someone had punched her with a twenty-pound medicine ball, limiting her ability to take a breath. Was that her heart racing so fast?

The moment she had made body-to-body contact with Mitch maneuvering him into the cold tub, it had sent her heartbeat skyrocketing.

He smelled delicious, of soap, spice and musk. An all-male scent emanated from his entire being. She could feel the strong, sinewy texture of his back and the thick muscular legs as she positioned him on the tub bench. And his chest, the soft tufts of golden-brown hair peaked through the top of his T-shirt, flirting with her nose as her face was pressed against his chiseled torso.

She was barely able to concentrate as he leaned against her, pressing his weight and his lower extremities into her. She could feel his length pressed into her belly and wondered what he would feel like to be buried inside her.

She shook her head clear as the sounds of the timer jarred her back into reality. She couldn't hide out in her office forever. Grabbing a few pamphlets and instruction sheets, Rylie went back out into the clinic gym to finish up her session with Mitch.

"I have a new nickname for you," he said, grinning like the Cheshire Cat, as she sidled up to the exam table. "You want to know what it is?"

"I don't know. Do I? How appropriate is it?"

He laughed. "Oh, I think it's quite appropriate under the circumstances," he said, his voice husky and serious. "From now on I'm calling you Ice Queen…IQ for short. Because even if you don't openly admit it, I know you're trying to freeze my balls off on purpose." He shook his head, handing her the icepack that had been wrapped around his now frozen knee.

"You really have a low opinion of me. Honestly, if I really meant to freeze your balls off, the icepack would have been placed a bit further north," she said, stifling a laugh. "Now, let's talk about the exercises you need to do at home before your next visit."

"How do you know Mark?"

Her head popped up from the table, her eyes wide in surprise. "What...excuse me? What do you mean?"

"The party last night, Mark Olsen's going-away party. You two obviously work together and he talked about you, so I'm naturally curious about the type of relationship you have with him."

Rylie stood there bewildered as to how he got onto this topic. What business was it of his how she knew Mark? *The gall of this guy.*

"What exactly are you implying?"

"I was curious if you're sleeping with him or anyone else for that matter?" Mitch leaned back on the table, his arms placed casually up behind his head, his bum leg draped over his other, looking sexy and pleased with himself.

"What business is it of yours?" she huffed. Rylie could feel her face turn bright red and her hands trembled. "*Mr. Camden.* I am your physical therapist. I am here to help you get back up on both feet – literally. I am not here to cure your curiosity on my personal life."

"So you've slept with him. Say no more."

"Good grief, I have not slept with Mark!" she said, louder and with more intensity than she meant to. She took a quick look around the room to see if anyone had overheard her outburst. Luckily no one seemed to notice. "Not in the past nor ever in the future, for that matter. We went out once or twice a long time ago, but decided we're better off friends." She couldn't believe she just told him that. This man was trying her patience.

Mitch chuckled. "I know. He told me that when I asked him about you last night. I just wanted to hear you say it."

"Wha? –You schmuck! You goaded me into telling you and you already knew the answer? You have some nerve," she fumed, trying to contain her frustration and regain her composure. What was this guy's deal? He was exasperating. She needed to get the ball back into her court.

"Well, how do *you* know Mark? Have *you* slept with him?"

His laughter was a loud boom, a commotion that now had heads turning to see what was going on. Swinging his legs around to the side of the table, he grabbed hold of the crutches that were leaning against the wall. Then he reached out and tweaked her nose. She pulled her head back at his gesture.

"As a matter of fact, I haven't slept with him either. But don't hold that against me, I'm sure he's a really nice lay. Mark's family and mine go way back. I've known him since we were kids."

"I see." She paused, considering how to ask the next question. "So, you asked Mark about me? Why?"

"After our encounter at the bar and your flippant departure, I wanted to know who you were. I figured you were there for Mark's party, so he knew you and he'd give me the details. I like to know in advance about the women I slee – uh, work with."

Rylie was all at once confused, flustered, angry and yet, intrigued, as to why Mitch would want to find out more about her. She thought back to the previous night and their limited exchange and conversation. She didn't think she threw off any vibes indicating her interest. Her flirting wasn't over-the-top and she certainly didn't come on to him like most other women likely did. Although he was forward, he didn't seem to show any further interest in her after she left him sitting at the bar. If he had, why didn't he come talk to her again? Before she could consider that possibility, she knew the answer to that. She had shut him down with little room for reopening that door.

"Well, you apparently got the details, so let's move on to what's next for you. Why don't you have Claire schedule your next appointment. You'll need to continue to do your home exercises daily and come in three times per week."

"Yes, about that. I've arranged for in-home PT from here on out. I have an extremely busy work schedule and that will just make it a whole lot more convenient for me. Mark said this clinic offers those services."

"Sure, of course," she said, handing him the folder of instructions and leading him to the reception desk. "I'll just get the name of your in-home therapist and send over my progress notes and eval forms, along with the recommendations for needed equipment."

Mitch stood at the front desk looking at her as if she were an alien, his brows furrowed. Balancing himself on the crutches, he took out his wallet and handed Rylie a business card. She accepted it suspiciously, uncertain as to its purpose.

"That has my home address, along with the security code to my entry gate. Apparently you seem to be missing a relevant piece of my therapy requirements." Smiling that devilish grin, he placed the wallet back in his pocket. "Ms. Hemmons…I've already arranged for *you* to be my in-home therapist."

Rylie blanched.

Mitch pushed the automatic door opener with his crutch. Turning back to see her still standing there, unmoved, he winked.

"See you on Friday, IQ."

CHAPTER THREE

"What in the hell did you get me into?" Rylie practically yelled when she and Sasha were finally in the back office for their lunch break.

Rylie had been so amped up and agitated over the previous several hours, she couldn't contain herself any longer. She'd confronted Sasha with what she felt was her erroneous decision of offering up Rylie to make house calls for her new patient. She wasn't certain if she was upset with Sasha for not telling her in advance about this twist or if she was pissed that she heard it directly from Mitch. Or just the sheer fact that she felt like an idiot for not knowing the plans.

"I can't believe you failed to mention this little tidbit of detail to me when you so casually gave me Mitch Camden as a patient this morning. How could you do that to me?"

"Rylie, calm down. Honestly, I don't see what the big deal is. I just forgot to mention it this morning. I'm sorry you feel slighted, but why is it such a crisis situation for you? You've done in-home therapy for other patients in the past. How is this any different?"

Rylie had moved from the doorway into the room and plopped down on the small beat-up leather couch. Her response to this situation did seem a bit out of proportion, considering it wasn't her first in-home client she had assisted. She had others over the last few years and it never bothered her before. But that was before him. Her concerns were obviously geared toward how this particular client made her feel. And she didn't like it. She didn't like feeling that way at all.

Trying to explain her emotional predicament to Sasha would be futile and could possibly jeopardize her professional credibility. She didn't even know what she was feeling. She felt stupid and immature. She had worked too hard to lose her shit over a physical attraction to a man who was just a player, anyhow.

"I'm sorry, Sash. I didn't mean to overreact."

"Hmm…that's exactly what you're doing. It just seems over the top for you." Sasha sat down next to her friend, handing her half of her tuna sandwich. "What exactly is the problem?"

"I don't know. I can't explain it, but the man gets under my skin. He annoys the hell out of me. He says things that are…" Rylie paused, trying to find the right word to describe the agitation he created in her.

"Are what?" Sasha asked curiously, folding her legs underneath her bottom and taking a bite into her sandwich.

"Flirtatious, for one. It's like he's just trying to get a rise out of me. And you know I can't hold my tongue to save my life." Taking a napkin Sasha had just handed her, she wiped off the crumbs that had spilled down her shirt. "He just…drives me crazy. Everything from him is innuendo."

Sasha got up, taking the trash over to the wastebasket at her desk and threw it away. "Oh, I see. He's getting a reaction from you because you're trying too hard to resist his charm."

Rylie snorted at her friend's wholly inaccurate analysis. As if she thought Mitch had any charm, whatsoever. "Whatever. The guy's a total player and I'm not falling for anything he's dishing out. I just don't know if I want to continue to put up with his antics. What if you move him to Carmen?"

Carmen Flores was another therapist, but part-time and only had a handful of clients she saw weekly due to her family commitments. Rylie knew immediately after making the suggestion that it wasn't a solution. Carmen would frequently trade patients with Rylie based on their scheduling needs and demands, but just the thought of Carmen touching Mitch brought a foreign stab of jealousy to the surface.

Although part of her rebelled against the idea of continuing to work with Mitch, the other half wanted to be near him. She didn't want to admit it to herself, but she liked the feeling of butterflies that arose from every single touch and point of contact she'd had with Mitch. It might be torture or career suicide, but she knew she couldn't walk away. Plus, she was great with these types of injuries and would have a sense of satisfaction by getting him back to fighting form.

Sasha moved to her desk and pulled up her scheduling assistant in her laptop. "Listen, I can see if we can get Carmen assigned to him, but it may not be for a few weeks. Can you handle it until then?"

It was Sasha's concern for her friend's well-being in that moment that overwhelmed Rylie to the point of tears, and she wasn't a crier. It made her feel like a spoiled, tantrum-pulling twerp. Rylie, not normally prone to physical expressions of adoration, bent down to hug her friend around her neck.

"If I haven't told you lately, you're an amazing boss, Sash."

Sasha glanced up in surprise at Rylie's PDA, obviously unaccustomed to that type of response from her. "Well aren't you just the kiss-ass today. I should really milk this for all it's worth and make you buy me dinner tonight. Or better yet," she grinned, "Neiman's is having their fall sale, and I'm in desperate need of a new Tory Burch handbag."

"That sounds just riveting...NOT. How about we go out this weekend after we see Mark off to Africa. I'm exhausted from being out late last night and tomorrow night I'm going over to Dad's for dinner and football. You're welcome to come over with me."

"I'll take a pass on that one, too. Maybe I'll swing by Mark's to see if he needs any help packing tonight. That reminds me, are we driving together to the airport on Saturday?" she asked, taking a sip of the herbal tea she'd just brewed.

"Yeah, I'm teaching my self-defense class at nine and then I'll come pick you up. Sound good?"

"You bet. And I'll be on pins and needles waiting to hear how the Friday session with Mr. Charming goes," she quipped, heading out toward the clinic gym.

Giving her a mocking shove, Rylie followed her out the door. "You bitch, don't make me regret what I said earlier."

****

Thursday nights during football season were spent at her dad's house where Rylie, her dad and older brother Dylan would root for their favorite teams, eat nachos and pizza, drink several six-packs, and generally banter with each other over their fantasy football wins and losses for the week. Rylie always enjoyed this time with her small and uniquely male family, joking and cavorting as one of the guys. Male bonding, with a little estrogen thrown in the mix.

Just after leaving the clinic Thursday evening, Rylie stopped off at the liquor store to pick up her favorite snacks and beer before heading to her childhood house. The store was packed with jersey-clad football fans, all of whom had similar ideas on pre-game libations. Her day had been much less stressful than the previous one, only because Mitch hadn't been scheduled. While her caseload kept her extremely busy, she still found time to think about him. And that pissed her off.

She hoped that an evening of football would calm her nerves and keep her attention on something else for a while. Heading back to the refrigerated section of the store, she opened the cooler door and pulled out a case of Heineken. Just as she was about to turn back around, a voice from behind caught her off-guard, nearly making her stumble head first into the cooler.

"I didn't expect you to be a beer drinker," came the low, silky baritone. "But Heineken's a good choice."

Rylie regained her balance and swung around, gripping the sides of the case of beer, as if holding on for dear life.

"What the…how the?" she stammered, clearly at a loss for words to see Mitch standing in front her. "Are you one of those stalker patients already? You know, I had a feeling about that." Letting the door close behind her, she tried to step forward and around him, but was blocked.

Mitch didn't budge, his crutches planted firmly on each side.

"It does appear that way, doesn't it, IQ?" He responded with a sexy laugh. "Is it so strange to run into your clients outside of the clinic?"

Mitch shuffled and turned to his left to let Rylie get around him. "But for the record, I'm just here picking up some things for the game. Looks like you might be doing the same thing," he said, gesturing to the beer she was holding, or maybe her Patriots jersey. Rylie stood, gripping the case of beer in her hands, a bit of the deer in the headlights thing going on.

Mitch cleared his throat. "But, since you're here, could I ask you to do me a favor?" He gave her a pleading look. He may have even batted his eyelashes at her.

Rylie eyed him suspiciously, unsure if she should say yes before knowing what he wanted from her. Knowing him, it would be something sexual, no doubt. She looked over his shoulder past him to the right and then the left, returning her gaze back to him slowly. "I don't know. What kind of favor?"

He gave her a low chuckle. "Well, I'm sure I could think of a few, but in this instance, I failed to consider how I'd manage to carry the items I need in my current handicapped state." He gestured down to his crutches. "If you could help me pick up the things on my list, I'd be more than happy to throw your beer and chips on my bill."

Feeling like a bitch if she left him to his own devices, Rylie reluctantly gave in to his plight. "Sure, okay. But let's make it snappy, I have someplace to be. So, where's the list?"

"In my iPhone…which is in my front pocket." He raised his eyebrows, as he gestured with his eyes down to his jeans.

A strangled noise erupted from the back of her throat.

"Nope. No way am I going there. Get the list out yourself." She shook her head in disgust and waited for him to comply.

"What, no helping an invalid? Fine." Mitch reached into his pocket and pulled out his phone and entered the code to bring up his

Notepad. Handing the device over to her, they proceeded around the corner to the wine aisle.

A quick glance down at the list had her questioning her limited knowledge of wine. His first three listed were French Bordeaux from some winery called Chateau Margaux. She had always been a beer or cocktail drinker and didn't know a thing about wines. Walking slowly so that he could keep up with her, they rounded the corner and he pointed to the two bottles he wanted. Grabbing them off the shelf, Rylie noticed the price tag in big, red digits. *Twelve-hundred dollars*?

She turned her head back to him, letting out a tsking sound. "You know what they say about men who drive sports cars and buy over-priced wine, right?" she quipped, uttering a hmmph of disgust and placing the bottles in the cart she'd acquired.

"No, as a matter of fact I don't. And who says I drive a sports car?"

"Just a hunch. You look and act like the type. Pretty Boy's who try to impress."

"Oh really? And what type are you, IQ? The "all men are pigs" garden variety woman?" He was pushing her buttons and she knew it. Rylie could once again feel the blush creep up over her face. She'd not let him get her riled up. She would remain in control. Keep her cool.

Her hands gripped tightly around the cart handle, she turned to face him with the intention of giving it back to him. Instead, it struck her how handsome he was, staring down at her with that sexy five o'clock shadow and intense hazel eyes. Just how he looked when she met him at the bar on Tuesday night, which shot sparks of electricity through her body. The color of his eyes were enhanced by the green T-shirt and gray cashmere crewneck sweater he wore, paired with worn jeans. She had to look up to meet his gaze, even though she was five-foot-eight, he towered over her. She thought he had about six inches on her, which did not improve her level of confidence when he stared, giving her a look that told her he'd easily throw her over his shoulder and carry her off to his bed.

"As a matter of fact, I don't think that. I've lived with my father and brother who were always respectful to women and they didn't feel the need to impress women with the money they could throw around."

"Is that what you think I'm doing, trying to impress you? You must have a very high opinion of yourself. If you recall, I came here with the list already written and no way of knowing I'd run into you. And what's so wrong about enjoying good wine? I'm sure you have favorite things you'll spend good money on. Now, if we can move along, you have somewhere to be."

Well, she felt like an idiot. She didn't know why she made such a big deal out of his purchases or why it bothered her so much. So what if he dropped a grand on a bottle of wine? She knew for a fact that Sasha would easily spend five-hundred dollars on a pair of heels or a handsome sum on a Hermes bag. Why she got so agitated over Mitch's spending choices was a mystery to her.

Moving back down the aisle, she grabbed another bottle, this one a Chateau Lafite Rothschild Pauillac 2006. The last item on the list was Magnums.

She was no wine connoisseur by any stretch of the imagination, but she knew a Magnum was a very large bottle of wine, but she didn't know what kind he was looking for or which aisle to locate it in.

Rylie extended her arm to press the phone into Mitch's chest.

"A little help on this one," she asked.

Mitch's mouth pressed up into a playfully naughty smile, lighting up his eyes with mischief.

"You want me to explain *what* they are or *how* they're used? Because I'd be happy to demonstrate if you need a visual explanation." His body shook with laughter.

She was perplexed. What did he mean? She looked at the list again and then back to Mitch, his face lit up with mocking interest. Finally getting it, she gave him a shove, sending him off-center and unsteady on his crutches.

"Oh my God…whatever, you perv. I do not need any demonstrations, thank you," she shuddered as if shaking off the thought. "You're on your own for this one. Do they even sell condoms at a liquor store?"

A low bubble of laughter rumbled from his throat. "Of course they do. Too much wine often lends itself to too much of something else, which may require precautionary measures. But let's not worry about those now," he winked, putting the phone away. "We'll revisit it later in case the need *arises* in the future."

Rylie felt the heat rise from the very depths of her core and she had to concentrate on breathing. Was he planning on getting lucky with someone tonight? And was his innuendo aimed at getting her in bed someday? Good Lord, she needed to get away from him and fast.

She rolled her eyes, turning toward the front of the store. "Whatever. We've got your goods, now let's get out of here." She headed to the open register and began placing the items on the counter.

"So where is it that you'll be heading tonight?" he asked nonchalantly, pulling his wallet out of his back pocket. "Got a boyfriend you'll be enjoying your Heineken with?"

She blinked at him, resisting the urge to make up a story about her body-building fiancé who was waiting at home for her this very minute, or tell him the pathetic truth about her non-existent love life and the embarrassing reality of her weekly football ritual at her dad's house.

"I don't see how that's your business," she blurted with indignation. "Didn't we cover this yesterday? All you need to know is I'm going to enjoy my beer and some football tonight. And if you're lucky, my team will win so that I'm not in a pissy mood tomorrow for your therapy session." She smiled when she saw his eyes flicker with a realization that her mood could bring about all sorts of difficulties for him. She could definitely make this work to her advantage.

"In that case, IQ, I do hope your beloved Patriots win with a very large margin so I don't face the firing squad tomorrow."

Taking the brown paper sack the cashier shoved in her direction, Rylie turned to hand the bag to Mitch, who was already heading out the door. Why was he leaving without his stuff? "Wait, where are you going?"

"Out to my car. I assumed you'd finish the job by delivering it for me."

She grumbled, fighting the urge to kick the floor like a two-year-old. Fine, she thought. I can just drop the bag in his car and get the heck out of here. She followed him out to the parking lot, the late afternoon sun still high in the sky and casting shadows on the row of cars. She watched him walk toward an old beat up Dodge Caravan and she inwardly laughed at her own guffaw. Here she assumed he was a sports car guy, when in reality he drove a mini-van. She chuckled and he turned his head back to her.

"What's so funny, IQ?"

"Oh nothing. I just didn't peg you for a family car kind of guy."

His face held a strange expression, as he rounded the vehicle. As she came up behind the van, it was then that she noticed a sleek, yellow, two-door Tesla Roadster Sport, parked in the spot next to the Dodge.

She about dropped the bag on the pavement. This was one of the most expensive, all electric sports cars in the world. This gave her two new insights about Mitch Camden. One, he must be incredibly wealthy, because no one earning less than a million a year could afford this car. And two, he liked speed and adventure. These cars, she'd learned from her brother, could hit sixty miles per hour in less than four seconds flat.

And the third thing she potentially learned about this gorgeous man. Well, it could go one of two ways. He might own a car like this because he was extremely eco-conscious. Either that, or he had a serious complex. As in, little dick complex.

"Sports car. I knew it! Trying to make up for a lack of something, Pretty Boy?"

"I've never heard any complaints about my lack of *anything*."

Hmm. Whatever, Stud Muffin.

Mitch opened up the passenger side door and held the door so Rylie could place the bag on the seat. She leaned in and carefully set the bag on the floor. Shifting herself up right, she turned around and came face-to-face with Mitch, who now was just inches of her. One step closer and he would have her pinned against the doorframe.

Her breath caught and a warm tingle shot up her spine. He was too close. Way too close. Totally in her personal space. She willed him to move. Instinctively, her hand rose to place it on his chest, presumably to push him away. His hand shot out and grabbed her wrist, yanking her toward him.

Breathe.

"I'm glad I ran into you, IQ," he whispered into her ear, his hand dropping her wrist and moving to her face to brush a loose strand of hair behind her ear. "I appreciate your assistance and hope I can reciprocate in the very near future."

Rylie's hand remained on his chest. She could feel his body heat and the beating rhythm of his heart. She meant to push him away, to maneuver around him and place herself a safe distance from him. But her hand somehow had a mind of its own and stayed there, enjoying the texture of his soft sweater and the marbled feel of his chest. In fact, the other hand joined in on its own volition. His lips quirked up, apparently showing his approval.

She had just opened her mouth to say something and without warning, his mouth was upon hers in lightning-fast speed. He placed his hands on the sides of her face and tilted her head, allowing him to gain access to her lips. He gently pried her lips open, rubbing his tongue sensually along her bottom lip. Rylie's mind rebelled, but her mouth betrayed her, giving in to the suppleness of his kissable lips. Her first instinct was to push him away and knee him in the balls, but the feeling was so intense and pleasurable, she gave in to the feeling that she was floating.

His chin scruff grated against her lips, excruciatingly erotic. His tongue began a full-on assault, tangling with hers in rapid fire bursts and her own tongue gave in to the seductive dance. She couldn't think. She couldn't move. Her brain told her to get the hell away, but her body wanted more. Craved more.

Her hands moved instinctively around his neck, and she shoved her fingers into his thick mane, pulling him in closer. She heard him groan. Or was that her? She didn't know, as she was lost in a trance of ecstasy. He deepened the pressure, changing up the pace to a slower, more rhythmic cadence. His tongue probed deeply, exploring the hot crevices of Rylie's mouth.

Her vision grew dim, as her eyelids closed, her head tilting back even further. Mitch's kiss grew sharp and punishing, pleading with her to give in fully. The kiss was filled with lust, hot and needy. His right hand slid down her neck and he pulled his lips away from her mouth, placing them just below her ear. He skimmed his tongue down her long neck and then began to suckle the sensitive spot at the base.

She forgot all time and space, making a free fall with every hot kiss he bestowed. She hadn't realized it, at least consciously, but something deep within her had wanted this since she met him the other night. Everything in her lit up with his touch. She felt a stab of electricity pulse through her, the heat pooling between her legs, and her breasts waiting to be touched and caressed. Her body curved into his, as his hard length pressed against her belly. She was quickly losing control of her senses, giving in to the pleasure he evoked.

Shit. What the hell is happening?

The thought hammered into her brain, bringing her back from the haze of pleasure she had been submerged in. Without thought or hesitation, Rylie drew back sharply, slapping him hard across the jaw. He staggered back, protesting with a groan as she pushed him out of her way, nearly sending him to the ground. He rubbed his jaw as his face reflected a look of bemusement. Remembering her case of beer, she picked it up and ran to her car, leaving him gaping at her sudden departure.

Opening the door and jumping into the driver seat, her hands trembling with adrenaline, she fit the key into the ignition and turned on the car.

Rylie had never before run from anything or anyone in her life, but all she could think of at the moment was flight – getting the hell of out there and putting as much distance between her and Mitch Camden as possible.

Her heart pounded as if she had just run a marathon and her thoughts clouded with the reality of what just happened. She was just kissed, deeply and satisfyingly, creating an insatiable need within her that she'd never known was there. And it was planted there by one of her patients. Something against all of her rules and moral conduct and an action that could never, ever, happen again. She wouldn't let it. She had more control over herself than this, Rylie chastised herself, as she pushed the accelerator to the floor and sped off.

CHAPTER FOUR

Mitch was both amused and a bit dazed, and slightly pained, as he rubbed the spot on his jawbone where she clocked him, reflecting on what just occurred. Had Rylie really just run off like a frightened schoolgirl? Come to think of it, this was twice now she'd run off on him. That was a first for him and it put him in foreign territory.

Most women he'd charmed over the last fifteen years would have eagerly followed a kiss like that with a trip to bed, allowing him easy access to their carnal pleasures. No chasing required. And he'd never been with a woman who reacted so instantaneously with that much passion, returning his kiss as sensually as Rylie just did, just to turn so cold so quickly on him. He was left there in a haze of confusion, standing there looking like an idiot with an unsatisfied erection.

Mitch had no clue what was going through Rylie's mind when she took off. All he did know was she was pure passion, bottled up in a package made for pleasure. Her kiss was like warm honey, hot and sweet. The heat that emanated from her body and scorching kiss was enough to drive him over the edge. It was all he could do to control himself and not reach out and caress every part of her body, starting with her luscious breasts. He felt her nipples harden as they pressed up against his chest, her breasts full and ripe. All he had wanted was to throw her T-shirt over her head and take one of her firm breasts into his greedy, wet mouth and relish in its erotic luxury. Damn the parking lot!

Wanting nothing more than to drive after her, Mitch instead hobbled into his car and cursed, turning to drive in the opposite direction. He was due at Jackson's home a few blocks away and was already fifteen minutes behind. During the drive, he quickly collected his thoughts and his breath resumed to its normal rhythm.

Mitch reflected back to the passionate exchange just minutes earlier and his sheer surprise to Rylie's immediate and fiery response to his kiss. What he'd half expected to get was a fast punch in the gut, or even worse, his balls. Instead, he was caught off guard by her intense physicality and heated desire. He had wanted to kiss her sassy mouth since the night in the bar, when she was spouting her wisdom on football history. She was sexy as hell and it turned him on. But he didn't have a chance before she left him hanging, leaving him and his invalid ass to dream about her. He had hoped he'd have the chance again, but didn't realize it would be so soon. Never one to forgo a second chance, Mitch found the opportunity and took it.

Now armed with this newfound knowledge of her feisty temperament and fiery physical touch, Mitch was eagerly anticipating his appointment with Rylie the next day. He chuckled, thinking of the way she sprinted back to her car and peeled out of the parking lot, like a bat out of hell. His appointment could turn out to be very interesting. Interesting, indeed.

Pulling in to the driveway, Mitch turned off the car and grabbed his crutches, honking the horn to alert his friend of his arrival. At the front door of his Spanish-style Colonial, Jackson Koda emerged from the house wearing a 49er's jersey and jeans, sans socks or shoes, making his way to the driver's side of Mitch's car.

"Took you long enough, ya gimp. These things putting a crimp in your strut?" Jackson joked, motioning to the crutches and slapping Mitch on the back as Mitch rounded the side of the car. "How ya doing, hop-a-long?"

"Why don't you stop being a dickhead and help a brother out here."

"Touchy, touchy. Are you sure you don't need a psychologist instead of a physical therapist, you puss?" Grabbing the bag from the car floor, Jax shut the car door and lead the way to his front porch.

Opening the door and stepping aside, he let Mitch enter first, following close behind him.

For a bachelor, Mitch was always impressed with Jax's skills in decorating. To the point where he razzed him on a regular basis for his 'feminine instincts'. Muted colored walls allowed for his bold taste in artwork to capture the warmth of his large first floor entry and family room. A Spanish tiled floor and kitchen, with a wine bar area next to the TV room. Mitch and his buddies spent a good deal of time at Jax's, watching football and soccer, playing billiards in his downstairs man cave, and hosting plenty of pool parties out back, where there was never a shortage of women.

Mitch and Jax had never had much trouble in that area, dating back to their sophomore year in college, when they met and became friends. It was Jax who helped bring Mitch's business plan to fruition, being the financial wizard behind his investments. Jax was the Eduardo Saverin to Mitch's Mark Zuckerberg, minus the Facebook technology or the legal woes that drove the Internet moguls apart. Where Mitch went on to get his Master's in Business, Jax became an attorney, and after passing the bar, he joined his friend as his counsel, a man he trusted with his assets and his life's work.

Mitch and Jax were night-and-day different, but their friendship had endured over the years and continued to grow stronger. Mitch relied on Jax to keep his investments and projects on track and could count on him to give him the truth, even when he didn't want to hear it.

Plopping down on the plush brown leather chair and propping his leg up on the wide ottoman, Mitch grabbed the remote to turn on the game. The New England Patriots, whom he had thoroughly despised until now, were playing the Philadelphia Eagles. Tonight's game winner became even more of an interest to Mitch, as he was curious as to the outcome of tonight's match-up. There was nothing more he'd love to do than to give Rylie a little grief tomorrow if her favorite team lost against their opponents. It might be sacrilegious to root against the home team, but it would be a hot button for a certain beautiful therapist. It might put her in an even feistier mood with him tomorrow, which he hoped he could use to his advantage to draw out that hot response again. If she got that worked up over a football game, imagine what she'd be like in bed? A tiger, to be sure.

Mitch was lost in his thoughts when Jax set down a bowl of chips, a beer and the open bottle of wine on the table next to him.

"Did you hear me?" Jax asked again, as he got comfortable on the sofa across from the flat-screened TV wall, opening the cap on the beer bottle.

"No, sorry, I was thinking about something else. What'd you say?"

Jax shook his head, squeezing a small crevice of lime in his beer before taking a swig. "I asked how the knee's doing? Do you think you'll be ready for our mid-winter ski trip to Telluride in January? Or should we head to Cabo instead?"

Mitch knew his friend always preferred the warmer, tropical climates to snow any day of the week. In a sense, he didn't blame him, considering the women were bikini-clad on the beaches of Mexico versus the fifty layers of clothing they wore on the ski slopes. His friend wasn't quite the adventurer that Mitch had become and typically enjoyed a more low-key vacation, where he could read and enjoy the local art scene. Jax was bookish and serious, both in business and his art and hobbies, but never dull. Music was one of his other pastimes. He'd often find a local pub on their trips where he'd spend hours listening to the local musicians, buying them drinks after their gig and getting to know them personally. Had Jax not gone into business with him, Mitch could have easily envisioned him being a talent scout or agent to up-and-coming musical talent. He certainly had the ear for it and was always on the lookout for something new.

"Therapy is okay, better than expected. Looking forward to more of it."

Jax nearly spit out his beer. "Let me get this straight. You're happy about physical therapy? Jesus, you're a sadistic one," he said incredulously. "I know you believe in all that "no pain, no gain" bullshit, but PT for a torn ALC is no Disneyland, dude, and you're acting like it's a walk in the park. I want whatever pain meds you have."

Mitch grinned at his friend and he raised his eyebrows in exclamation. "Truthfully, the therapy is hell. But the therapist? She is fucking heaven."

Describing to Jax that Rylie was his impromptu *Jeopardy* opponent from the bar, he went on to share the story of him running into her at the liquor store and their little make-out session in the parking lot. While he did provide his opinions on how gorgeous she was and her mean left-hook, Mitch failed to describe the sharp electric currents he felt when he touched her or the severe stabs of desire that coursed through him in her presence. That was not something he was ready to share with his long-time friend, as he himself didn't even understand what it meant. All he could think about, though, was how to find ways to experience more of it.

With the Patriots up by ten at the half, Jax and Mitch sat down over pizza to discuss their newest and by far, largest, business project to date. They were nearly six weeks into the planning for the Kendall project, employing over sixty subs to build a one-hundred-and-twenty-million fully sustainable, eco-friendly, nearly carbon-neutral and completely green complex.

Jax pulled out his tablet and began crunching the numbers, looking through the various contracts that were already signed and the several that were still in the hopper. He then pulled up his calendar and reviewed the various meetings they had scheduled in the coming weeks.

"So how's this therapy schedule going to work out for you? We have Jensen coming into town Monday and Albertson & Tully site visits in Miami the rest of next week. You good with those plans or should we consider moving the dates back?"

Mitch shook his head as he finished his pizza and poured another glass of the Pinot. "My therapy sessions are scheduled three days a week and if need be, I'll take the therapist on the road with me when I travel. Shouldn't be a problem or cause any delays."

Jax looked up inquisitively. "I've never heard of a traveling physical therapist," he questioned.

"The clinic owner is a friend of Mark's, so if necessary, I'll pull some strings. I will not let this be a problem," he said, pointing to his knee, "Or interfere with our business. Got it?"

If it was one thing Mitch did not look kindly on it was interferences and disruptions. His life was a well-oiled machine and he ensured everything worked like clockwork. That's one of the reasons why he'd never settled down. Not only were relationships a hassle, but they caused too many unnecessary distractions. From the moment he woke in the morning, which was generally five a.m., his life went according to schedule. It was orderly, efficient and thoroughly planned. Routine in his day-to-day life allowed for more spontaneity in his personal life, which is where he wanted it. He got satisfaction in that, and it was never difficult to find a willing woman to hang on his arm for a few weeks, but never long enough to get close to. He wouldn't subject himself to loss and heartbreak again. Getting close required opening his heart. The loss of his brother taught him one thing: never let someone in and you won't get hurt. His close relationships now consisted only of his friendship and partnership with Jax, as well as his mother and father.

As if right on cue, Mitch's phone rang indicating Mitch Sr. on his display. Clicking the button on the earbud still lodged in his ear, he answered with a brusque greeting.

"Hello Son," came the rich baritone of his father. "Did I catch you at a good time?"

Mitch laughed, wondering what his father thought he would be doing on a Thursday evening or who he thought he was with. "I'm just over at Jackson's watching a little football. What's going on?"

"Ah, good, good! Do give Jackson my regards, we haven't seen him in ages. Listen, Son, I wanted to talk to you about this upcoming benefit your mother and I are hosting next month. It's for the Doctors-Without-Borders charity your mother co-chairs. It's going to be quite the soiree and she wanted me to see if you'd be willing to escort Betsy Stanwood's daughter, Eleanor. It would mean a great deal to your mother if you would."

Mitch tried to picture Eleanor, or Elle, as she liked to be called now, but could only drum up images of the chubby, pimple-faced adolescent he remembered being forced to play with when he was twelve. He even recalled the nickname he'd given her at the time – Ellie Smelly. Not only did it rhyme with her name, but she always seemed to be a bit malodorous, leading him to believe she didn't like to bathe. He shook his head at the memory and the girl he hadn't thought about for over twenty years.

"Dad, I do have a pretty good track record for getting my own dates for these types of events, if that's what you're worried about." His father chuckled on the other end of the line and then gave a brief sigh before responding.

"I have all the confidence in your abilities to garner your own dates, Son. It's your mother and her friend Betsy who are concerned for Ellie. She went through a pretty tough divorce recently and needs a little pick-me-up. Surely you can be a gentleman and support her this one evening. For your mother's sake, if nothing else."

Mitch groaned inwardly at his father's mention of Eleanor's situation. There was nothing fun about an evening with a recent divorcee. For all he knew, she was probably still in the "all men are assholes and deserve to die" stage. Not a classification he ascended to.

And then there was the guilt he'd feel for not doing this favor for his mother. A no-win, impossible situation.

Mitch rolled his eyes and inhaled, trying to find his Zen, wanting to appease his parents. They'd always been there for him, even in the aftermath of his brother. He was all they had now and it was his responsibility to be there for them in whatever capacity he could be.

"Sure, Dad. Tell Mom I'll attend the gala and will be happy to provide my escort services to the embittered and spiteful."

His father let out an audible sigh, but he could feel him smiling through the phone line. "That's my boy. I knew you wouldn't let us down. I'll give your mother the good news. I'm sure she'll make all the arrangements and will send you the details. Just make sure to mark the date on your calendar, and don't forget to wear a tux." He paused momentarily, a muffled sound of his hand covering the receiver, obviously confirming with his mother the update. Mitch heard a few questions lobbed out by his mother in the background and then his father came back on the line.

"Say now, how's that knee of yours? Your mother wants to know if you need any help? You know we're just a hop, skip and a jump away. By the way, will you still be on those crutches during the fundraiser?" Mitch chuckled over his father's concern. He knew his parent's loved him and had his best interests at heart, but he also had been brought up to respect appearances and never to embarrass the family. A cripple on crutches at a charity gala they were hosting would certainly raise questions, sending the gossip mill swirling.

Confirming that his therapy was going well and he had plans to be back in fighting shape in a few weeks, he informed his father that they should have no concerns about his well-being or future participation in their rent-a-date. With a sound of relief, Mitch Sr. bid his son goodbye and suggested they lunch when he returned from Miami. Accepting the offer, Mitch said goodbye and ended the call.

"Did I hear you mention a date to a fundraiser? How the hell did they rope you into that?" Jax asked good-naturedly, stealing a look at his friend, who was polishing off the bottle of wine.

"I have no earthly idea," he said, shrugging his shoulders in a perplexed gesture. "I guess a family friends' daughter is on the prowl after divorcing and needs a stud date to my parents' charity event."

"Huh. I guess your parents figured my social calendar was already booked, being the stud service that I am, so they called you in to sub," Jax joked smugly. "Plus, with you in less-than-stellar physical form these days, they felt compelled to help your dating life out a little." He flashed a toothy smile in his friends direction.

"Listen, *Mr. Stud*...you and I both know my dating life is in no need of any help, with or without crutches."

And it was with this thought that his mind went back to a certain hot and feisty therapist that had occupied his brain for the last two days. With his appointment set for tomorrow, he had to figure out a way to play up his pain and vulnerability with Rylie so she'd be compelled to cater to his physical needs. He'd have to remember to keep it light and casual, knowing her propensity to run away like a timid colt ready to bolt out the gates when he tried getting too close.

Mitch tried to pinpoint what it was about this woman that had him wound so tightly. His natural proclivity was to gravitate toward women who oozed sensuality and were overtly sexual, giving into his demands and requests, when and how he wanted them. His sense about Rylie was that she could bring a man to his knees and have no idea how she did it. She wasn't coy or conniving; she didn't use her body as a vehicle to capture his attention – although it did, every time he was with her.

Rylie was just unique. He liked her spunk and her sassy mouth. She had an innocence about her, but covered it with her sharp tongue. And damn if he didn't want to endure the sweet torture of that tongue of hers again someday soon. Someday very soon.

CHAPTER FIVE

Rylie was beyond flustered and extremely keyed up by the time she made it to her dad's house for the game. So shaken, in fact, she had taken several detours around her childhood neighborhood and was purposely twenty minutes late to arrive, allowing herself time to cool down and figure out what the hell just happened.

One minute she was dutifully picking up some beer and the next thing she knows she's being erotically kissed by one of her patients – a very sexy and virile patient – in the middle of a parking lot in broad daylight. How did she let this happen? Rylie had never allowed a man to rattle her like this, but something about Mitch Camden had her throwing caution and her restraint to the wind.

Rylie's track record with men was not as illustrious as Sasha's or Beth's love lives. For them, it was a revolving door of regular lovers and adoring boyfriends and even an occasional stalker or two, at least for Sasha. They normally fought men off in droves. For her, being "one of the guys" was more of the norm; a much less complex ritual due to her frequent outings with her brother, Dylan, and his buddies. But to actually take time to flirt with any particular male, or act girly, was not a fond interest of hers. If a guy liked her, it was because of who she was, not because she tried to impress with make-up, clothes or accessories. Not that there was anything wrong with that, but it just wasn't her style. She figured her lack of boyfriends and dates was in large part because she didn't do what most guys expected. And honestly, she was never willing to give the time or energy to try and fake it.

Rylie, of course, had a few boyfriends along the way. Two to be exact. Boys, rather than men. She found that turning friendship into a physical relationship could happen, but it never brought out the fireworks for her. Intimacy was difficult for Rylie. The armor that protected her heart after her mother broke it had walled off any real prospects of a loving and trusting relationship.

Rylie started dating Tim Small, her chemistry lab partner, in her senior year of high school. They dated a few months, gotten to second base and even went to the Senior Prom together. But by graduation, it was apparent their chemistry really didn't extend past the lab. Parting friends and with no hard feelings, Rylie went off to Boston College and focused on her studies. She was the first one in her family to attend college, on a full- ride volleyball scholarship, making it nearly impossible for her to find time for anything other than her academics and sports. Extra-curricular relationships were off the table. Until she met and began dating Erik Merrill, a fellow collegiate athlete and star swimmer for the school.

Tall, extremely fit, good-looking and similarly focused on the prize, Rylie and Erik found an easy companionship during the year and a half they dated. He was a year ahead of Rylie in school and his plans to go into the finance business in New York after graduation were discussed regularly. She was aware of his future prospects and the offers he'd already received after he'd completed his internship and had been excited for him. She thought the world of him and knew he'd accomplish his goals, but had never pictured herself with him in that future, even though she lost her virginity to him. So it took Rylie utterly unawares, when upon his graduation, Erik felt compelled to immediately propose. And she immediately shot him down.

She remembered the day out in the quad, looking down into Erik's face, who was kneeling in front of her with a black velvet box in his hand. She could see the genuine confusion in his features and the wet tears building in his sweet, brown eyes. She took his hand in hers, turning his palm up to return the box.

It had been like a ball out of left field. Love? Did she love him? She tried to remember if she'd ever said it back to him when he professed his love for her. She liked him. Enjoyed his company. Found him attractive and interesting. But love? That seemed out of her grasp. An elusive state, creating a vulnerability she wasn't willing to commit herself to. She couldn't love. Her heart didn't have the capacity to return that level of emotion.

Rylie was wracked with guilt, but was nothing if not honest. She let go of Erik's hands and brought her eyes to his. "I'm truly sorry, Erik."

Two days later they had parted ways, he a little less amicably than her. He'd accepted the job offer in New York and left almost immediately. Rylie heard through some mutual friends that he ended up marrying a budding young artist he met in the Village a few years later and now lived happily in Connecticut, with two kids and the requisite Volvo SUV.

She smiled now, thinking how odd it would feel if she'd had been in love with Erik and ended up his wife, now the mother of his children. She tried to picture it, but always came up with an empty canvas. That wasn't her path and so she'd chosen to remain dedicated to her studies, even though she endured a dry spell in the man department while she completed her program and Master's in Physical Therapy.

While her friends tried in vain to get her to let loose every once in a while, Rylie took her education seriously and didn't spend much time partying or looking to hook-up with strange guys in bars. Although, after meeting and becoming close with Sasha and Mark, who both seemed to make it their life's mission to bring her out of her shell, she had begun to journey out on a regular basis to O'Leary's Pub, where Rylie finally let the flirty, tattooed bar manager, Skeet Smith, take her out a few times.

Skeet was so utterly far from her typical taste in men, it was almost laughable. But who was she to resist a blue-eyed, long blond haired Motorcross rider? Rylie found Skeet to be exciting and adventurous. She really couldn't count Skeet as a boyfriend, per se, since they had officially only gone out on two dates, but she did enjoy going to see him compete in his off-road races. She liked his fearless and fun-loving character and his strong competitive nature. And she did learn something very valuable from Skeet, even after he quickly hooked-up with a long-legged blonde named Demi, just after their second week together. Rylie had become fascinated with motorcycle riding and the rush it brought out in her, so Rylie had asked him to teach her how to ride.

Nothing could have prepared her for the thrilling excitement and adrenaline rush that overcame her on her very first ride. On their last day together, Skeet took her on a thirty-mile ride across the countryside, enjoying off-road scenery and the back roads splendor. The wind at her back and the trees scrolling by, Rylie felt like she was in her element. She would always be grateful to Skeet for his instruction and she never had any hard feelings, or even strong feelings toward him. He was still cordial, and even a bit flirty with her, when she hung out at O'Leary's.

Now that she thought about it, Rylie realized she'd never experienced anything close to the same feelings and attraction that she had with Mitch to the other guys she'd been with. In just these few short days with Mitch, his touch and his kiss, and his nearness, had electrified her in a way she'd never known before, making her body ache for something unnamed and nothing she did could make the feeling go away. He made her want him and it pissed her off to no end.

Rylie was still angry when she walked in the front door of her father's house, her brother Dylan running up to grab the case of beer out of her hands.

"That's five dollars you owe me, sis. Brady just threw an interception caught by Davis on the Eagles. That's my guy!" he gleefully exclaimed, doing a little touchdown tippy-toe dance in the hallway. Rylie scowled and shoved him out of her way.

"Whatever. Go gloat someplace else. I need a beer."

Rounding the corner into the kitchen, she heard the noise from the TV in the great room and saw her dad and Jason as they both jumped out of the seats in elation over a first down. Dylan shimmied up behind her at the counter and placed the beer down.

Eying her sheepishly, he nudged her with his shoulder. "Whoa. What's gotten under your skin? You're not usually a poor sport over our fantasy league. Everything okay?"

Feeling ashamed over the unwarranted abuse, Rylie shook her head and started unloading the bag he'd placed on the counter in front of her.

"Yeah – didn't mean to bite your head off," she muttered apologetically, handing a beer over to her solemn-looking brother. "You're right. I'm just having a bad week, with some difficult patients and with Mark leaving soon. I'm not handling it well."

Dylan reached over to his sister and gripped her shoulders, giving them a tender squeeze. The Hemmons' were not a people prone to physical or emotional displays of affection, but Dylan was more of the softie of the two siblings. He'd always tried to be both a protector and supporter of his little sister, especially after their mother left. Rylie leaned into him and bent her head toward him, just reaching his shoulder.

The Hemmons' family were taller than most and Dylan came in at a little over six foot-three. With his broad shoulders, short, wavy chestnut colored hair and intense green eyes, Dylan had made many a woman swoon over the years. Separate from his competitiveness and stubborn streak, Rylie understood that underneath the bluster of a big brother, Dylan was relatively reserved, which she felt prevented him from having a deep, intimate relationship over the years. Go figure. Sibling similarity. The strongest female relationship he'd had, Rylie knew, was with her, even though he brutally picked on her since childhood.

There were times, though, that he could be a pretty great guy. And now was one of those moments.

"Don't let it get to you, kiddo. You're a good person and a great therapist. Don't let them get you down. And Mark is only gone for a year. I kind of envy the guy. It's cool that he's going to Africa and putting his mad doctor skills to good use." Ruffling his sister's hair, he picked up the bowl of chips and beer and headed in the direction of the great room. "Now, let's go watch some football. And you still owe me that five dollars." He winked back at her as he made himself comfortable on the couch next to Jason, where the three men focused their attention on the game, leaving Rylie to her thoughts.

Rylie joined them for the remainder of the night, watching from the edge of her seat as the lead exchanged several times between the Pats and the Eagles. Fumbles, penalties and an injury that sidelined one of her fantasy football offensive men put her fifteen dollars down by the end of the evening, but her team still squeaked out a win. Feeling triumphant, she jumped up and down and issued high fives all around.

"My guys have a shot at another Super Bowl title this year!" Rylie grinned broadly, as she turned and caught her dad frowning. She reached over to pat him on the back.

"Come on, old man, don't be such a spoiled sport. You knew the Pats were going to take Philly, you're just too stubborn to admit it."

Dan Hemmons was a burly man of sixty, strong as an ox with a mouth like a sailor. Probably where she got her potty-mouth, she mused. Her father worked hard as a laborer in the Philadelphia area for twenty years before he moved his family to the Boston area to open his own electrical company. Rylie was still very young and it was just about the time his wife, Ginny, had up and left them, citing that it wasn't the life she had intended on living. She left everything behind, including their broken hearts.

After serving time in the Marines, Dylan returned home and joined his father in running the company, helping to move it into a profitable business. Dan and Dylan were a force to be reckoned with and blew their competitors out of the water with their shrewd business sense and attention to detail. Customers loved the father/son team for their honesty and humor. They had both tried to coax Rylie into joining the family team as their office administrator, but that wasn't what she wanted to do. She knew that she wanted to help others in their rehabilitation. If she couldn't mend her own broken heart from the persistent, aching hole, she could at least help others heal their bodies.

Dan grumbled at the loss, lowering his head in a sign of defeat. "My team has forsaken me. Why, oh why? What did I do to deserve this?"

Rylie laughed at his dramatic delivery. "Oh good Lord, Pops, you're sounding like a Jewish mother. Oy vey. Let me help you clean up the kitchen."

Rylie turned and moved into the small kitchen area that had remained untouched since they moved back in the early nineties. A small, scratched dinette table that was on its last leg sat pushed up against the wall, a few old decorative plates hung on the papered walls. With only room for two in the kitchen, Rylie and her dad stood at the kitchen sink, hand washing the bowls and utensils, since Dan had never even bothered to retrofit it with a dishwasher.

Handing Rylie a glass to dry, he glanced over at his daughter who was looking out the window, deep in thought.

"What's on your mind, Pip?"

He hadn't used her childhood nickname since she was in high school, but it was the only term of endearment that had been used regularly when she was a little girl. As a five-year-old, Rylie's hair had been a bright red hue and she wore her hair in the only style she knew how to manage – pigtails; thus the Pippi Longstocking reference was born. Pip for short. Her dad had joked that while her red hair had darkened to an auburn color with age, the ginger temper was still ever present.

Rylie tried to keep her voice even, clearing her throat before she spoke. "Nothing. Why do you ask?"

Dan stopped to turn and look at his daughter. Taking a deep breath, he looked into his daughter's deep brown eyes and sighed. "Jesus, kid. I don't know much about women, but I do know that when they use the word 'nothing,' it's most certainly 'something.'" He tweaked her nose. "My God, you look so much like your mother did at this age. Sometimes I just can't get over the resemblance. She was so beautiful," he sighed wistfully. "You are so beautiful."

His compliment made her sad and her first reaction was to lighten things up, trying to avoid the inevitable of going down memory lane. A very long and unhappy lane, as it were. "Geez, Pops. Sappy much? The Eagles lose and you get all teary-eyed on me?"

Rylie knew her father loved her and Dylan, but he'd never been one to verbalize it or show it in a form of physical affection. That just wasn't the M.O. for Dan Hemmons. But he did his best to create a home where trust and support were the foundational elements, tending to their basic needs. There was nothing that he wouldn't do for his family. For that reason, she always held her dad up on a pedestal and was always trying to find ways to make him proud.

Over the years, through both high school and college, Dan Hemmons never once missed a volleyball tournament or game. He was front row and center when she graduated Magna Cum Laude from Boston College, a big smile plastered on his wrinkle-lined face. And although he never expressed it, Rylie was acutely sensitive to his desire for her to someday settle down and raise a family of her own.

She smiled at the thought of him someday tossing a football around in the backyard with his grandson or maybe even building a fort and playing tea party with a little girl. Her smile faded quickly, knowing it wouldn't become a reality anytime soon. Neither she nor her brother were anywhere near that stage in life yet – both single and unattached.

Her brother was a playboy, with a track record in the dating field a sorry state of affairs and her lack of current prospects abysmal.

As if sensing the direction of her thoughts, Dan broached the subject he rarely discussed and normally steered clear from – with a ten-foot pole. "Anyone new in your life these days?"

She sighed, shaking her head in dismay. Looking back up at the man that raised her, she smiled. "Pops, if there were, do you think I'd even dare mention it to you and Dylan? There is a proverbial shotgun cocked and loaded, times two, in this household." She bumped his shoulder with hers.

"Eh, come on now – we're not that bad. We just don't ever want you to get hurt again," he paused, looking away quickly. "That doesn't mean we don't want you to try. You're a beautiful woman, Rylie Ann. It surprises me you don't have anyone special in your life yet."

"Thanks, Pops. I just haven't had a lot of time or luck recently. But I'm sure it's true what they say…it'll probably hit me when I'm least expecting it."

****

Later that night, Rylie lay in bed feeling keyed up and restless, thinking about the next day ahead of her. Kicking off the covers, she padded over to her bedroom window and opened it up, letting the fresh air into her small corner room. The fall night was cool and crisp, a perfect New England evening. She could hear the breeze blowing through the old maple tree just outside her third story apartment, the leaves silently making their way down to the earth floor. She loved this time of year, with the hot summer long forgotten and the brutally cold winter months not yet in sight. The beginning of October could still produce beautifully sunny days, like today, with temperatures in the low-seventies during the afternoon and mid-fifties in the evenings.

With the window cracked, she heard some neighbor's dog barking down the block and the sounds of a few cars traveling down the street. Climbing back into bed, she pulled the sheets up to her chin and stared up at the ceiling. She couldn't shut off her brain or the thoughts of how her traitorous body reacted to Mitch's kiss earlier in the day. Six hours had already passed and yet her pulse still raced at the memory of his tongue playing with hers and the sweet mixture of headiness and exhilaration as he pulled her against his hard body.

She cursed at herself as she flipped over, trying to get comfortable, willing herself to go to sleep and forget about his damn mouth. As her eyelids finally closed and her breathing returned to normal, her last thought as she fell asleep was the feel of his hand gently brushing her cheek.

CHAPTER SIX

Mitch woke to the sound of a soft whimper coming from the warm body that lay next to him on his King size bed. He rolled over and his hand instinctively went to her belly, prompting an immediate response of a big wet kiss planted straight across his nose.

His voice was higher than normal. "Hey there. How's my girl, today?" His question elicited yet another wet kiss and a whimper. The three-year-old German shepherd yawned broadly and scooted closer to Mitch, thumping her tail ferociously against the mattress. "Good morning, my sweets…let's go get some breakfast, shall we?"

The dog excitedly jumped off the bed and ran to the hallway, looking back at him with her big brown eyes. Barking once, she ran down the stairs and sat at the bottom, waiting anxiously for Mitch to come after her. Grabbing the shirt he'd carefully laid across a chair last night, he slipped it over his head and laughed at the sight of her, panting and whining at the bottom of the stairs. "Just a minute, Karma. It takes me a bit longer than usual these days."

Reaching for his single crutch, he saw her nose go down to her front paws, heaving a big sigh. "I know, girl. Life's rough – for both of us."

Once downstairs and their morning routine accomplished, Mitch pulled out his iPhone to check his messages. Five-thirty a.m. and he had already received seven emails from vendors and clients and two texts from Jackson. He shook his head, wondering if the man ever slept. Jackson was the only person he knew that could live on only four hours of sleep a night. All-nighters in college were nothing for Jax, who could go until four a.m. and still ace a test in his eight a.m. class the following morning. Just the thought of an all-nighter made him groan, feeling older than his thirty years.

Opening up his calendar, his phone chimed with the little reminder notification of his eight o'clock conference call with Stanley Jensen, whom he'd be meeting with the following Monday. He was hoping for some good news on his upcoming project in Miami.

Scrolling down the day's events, he came to his next appointment – his nine a.m. session with Rylie. He rubbed a hand over his day-old stubble and contemplated her mood today, given their most recent exchange.

Mitch couldn't quite place the feeling that overtook him last night or why he felt compelled to kiss her so impulsively. He certainly hadn't planned it, but when he saw her bent over his car seat, with her perfect ass lifted high in the air, his thoughts were so primal that it was only on instinct that he had to touch her. And knowing what he now knew of Rylie's response, his hunger was far from satiated. His dick twitched at the memory.

Looking back at his calendar, he considered rearranging his day to get some additional work done at home before heading into the office at noon. The rest of his day was to be spent in meetings and reviewing the plans and proposals required to ensure the Kendall project would remain on track.

There was nothing that he wouldn't do to see this building project come to fruition. He was mentally prepared to complete the pinnacle of his career in record time. He all but assured Jax that his physical condition would not interfere with his progress, but there was a small, nagging question at the back of his head that made him wonder if it would slow him down. He quickly pushed that fleeting thought out of his mind and got ready for his morning.

****

Rylie started off the day like most days with a four-mile run along the Charles River. Cambridge was a beehive of collegiate and professionals and she loved the atmosphere of the university town. Being a bit more sleep deprived than usual from her sleepless night, she stopped by The Cambridge Cup, just on the outskirts of Harvard Square, to grab a large Americano on her way back to her apartment. Hoping both the run and the caffeine kick would do the trick, she headed into the shower to get ready.

Forty-five minutes later, Rylie was heading west on the Massachusetts Turnpike, toward the suburb of Newton. The twenty-minute drive was devoid of any major traffic at this time of day, as most of the commuters were heading east into the city. It had been a while since Rylie had ventured out of the city and into the suburbs. Sasha's family lived out near Waltham, but she hadn't been to visit them since the previous holiday season, when Sasha dragged her to one of their lavish Christmas parties. She loved Sasha and her zealot approach to finding her a match, but her attempts to set her up with men from her parent's country club were not amusing.

Turning off the exit for Newton/Watertown, she turned south on Chestnut Street, heading into neighborhoods heavily lined with hundred-year-old maples and classic brick Tudors and Colonials that had been built in the eighteen-nineties. Coming to the intersection of Chestnut and Commonwealth, she turned right and followed the road for another eighth of a mile until her navigation system told her to turn right at her final destination.

The entrance of the long wooded drive was enclosed by a large wrought-iron security gate. Rylie pulled out the card Mitch had given her and punched in the five-digit code. Settling back into her driver's seat, she took a deep breath as she watched gates slowly open, parting before her like the Red Sea. Shifting out of neutral, she slowly accelerated, making her way through the lush grounds.

From both sides, colorful oaks, birches and maples enveloped her, hugging every inch of the curved driveway. The morning sun was sprinkling its rays through the trees, glimmering off the dewy autumn leaves. It could only be described as picturesque. Pulling to a stop, she placed the car in park and got out of the car.

In front of her stood a two-story white Colonial, the front entryway book-ended by white pillar columns. To the left was a stand-alone three-car Carriage garage, Mitch's bright yellow Tesla sitting idle in front. Stepping out of her car, she placed her hand to shield her eyes from the direct sunlight, as her mouth gaped open at the opulence of the historic home.

Good Lord, this man has money.

Grabbing her bag and purse from the backseat, she closed the car door and headed up the five steps to the front porch.

Reaching the door, her mouth suddenly dried, her throat constricted, and anxiety riddled her body. How would he react to seeing her after what happened the day before? Should she apologize for slapping him and acting like a complete dimwit? Would he try kissing her again? How should she act toward him now? Laugh it off as if nothing happened at all?

This is nuts.

Rylie took a deep inhale and slowly let it out, readjusting the strap of her bag on her shoulder. Counting to ten, she grabbed the front door knocker and made her presence known. Waiting for Mitch to answer, she turned around to look across the front yard. A fountain stood in the middle of the lawn, a small path carved around it, two benches on either side. The landscaping was absolutely beautiful. She wondered how many landscapers it took to maintain this type of beauty. These types of homes were surely only pictured in *Architectural Digest.* What in the world did this man do for a living, she thought, just as door opened to produce the man in question.

Rylie stood there, staring into his gorgeous warm eyes, unable to say anything, shifting awkwardly from side to side. Every sexual feeling that she had tried to banish from her mind since the previous night came rushing back the minute he smiled and said hello.

His shoulders, broad and strong, took up the majority of the doorway as he assessed her standing in front of him. "Good morning," his smile was warm, with a hint of lust. "Welcome to my humble abode. Please come in." Mitch stepped aside to usher her into the entryway, gently pressing his hand to her lower back. A thrill shot down Rylie's spine.

Two steps into the grand two-story foyer, she heard what sounded like a thunderous freight train coming toward her, full speed. A panicked squeal escaped Rylie's lips, just as a seventy-five pound furry creature came hurling at her, taking her not only by surprise, but knocking her off her already unsteady feet. The force of the dog's greeting sent her bag and purse toppling off her shoulder and down to the black and white checkerboard marble floor. She landed against something hard, as well. Mitch's chest.

"Karma – off. Now!" Mitch bellowed, swinging his body around, just as Rylie landed against his chest. His arms came up around and under her arms, the single crutch falling with a loud crack to the floor.

The dog, reluctantly obedient, planted her butt down to face a bewildered Rylie. Karma let out a loud whine and licked her shoes before laying her head down at Rylie's feet.

Letting out the breath that she had been harboring since knocking, Rylie began to laugh hysterically – the tension releasing with every breath. She bent at the waist trying to stop her fit of laughter and regain her composure.

"That's quite a welcoming committee you have. I can only imagine what your security guard would do if I weren't an invited guest." Bending down to pick up her bags that had been displaced in the commotion, she readjusted as she straightened, flipping her long, silky hair out of her face.

"Are you okay? Karma isn't normally quite this…exuberant with her greetings," Mitch said in an apologetic tone, admonishing his dog's behavior. Taking a step forward, he gestured to his dog, now sitting obediently and panting at Rylie.

"Rylie, meet Karma. Karma, meet our new friend, Rylie." The dog raised her paw in greeting. Rylie giggled, reaching out to shake hands with the beautiful dog.

"Now that you've both been properly introduced, I'll put her outside so she's out of the way. I'll be right back. Come on in and make yourself at home."

Rylie watched as Mitch and the dog walked through the foyer and down the hall toward the back. To her surprise, she admired his backside, his ass looking perfect in shorts and the black T-shirt that fit tightly across his shoulders and back. Rylie sighed as she turned her attention to the meticulously appointed surroundings of his home. So very different than her father's house, or even her little studio apartment. There were no garage sale end tables or Ikea furniture in this place.

Looking in the direction the pair had headed, she could see an entire wall of glass – floor-to-ceiling windows flooded with incoming sunlight, providing views of a stone patio, in-ground pool, screened porch and pool house, as well as the stunning wooded property.

To the left of the grand foyer was a library, complete with beamed ceilings, dramatic bay windows and mahogany paneling. To the right, through white-trimmed, glass paneled doors, was a sitting room with beautiful white millwork wainscoting, an exquisite Persian rug in the middle of the room and a romantic hearth and fireplace. A large cherry wood desk sat in in the middle of the room. She could envision a shirtless Mitch leaning back in the leather chair, reviewing some important paperwork that he'd brought home with him. *Where on earth did that come from?*

Shaking her head clear of her R-rated thoughts, she looked up and was in immediate awe over the curving white spindle staircase that wrapped around the second floor, exposing a chandelier she'd only once seen its equal in a Ritz Carlton hotel. This house, in a neighborhood like this one, had to be worth close to four million, she speculated.

Glancing back down the hallway, Rylie heard Mitch calling her from the kitchen area. Adjusting her bag strap over her shoulder, she moved in the direction of his voice. She found Mitch standing in a state-of-the-art kitchen that Martha Stewart herself would covet. Martha would no doubt also swoon over Mitch, who was looking incredibly sexy in his T-shirt and sport shorts. His biceps strained generously through his tight sleeves, a pattern of light hair covering his long, muscular arms.

Mitch stood at the counter with a coffee mug raised. "Coffee?"

"Oh, no, thanks. I've already had my fill for the day. More than one cup of coffee gives me the shakes. But I'd love some water, though, if you have some." *That was a dumb thing to say – of course he has water! Idiot.*

Mitch chuckled, as he grabbed a bottle of Evian out of the commercial size fridge, placing it on the counter in front of her.

She took it and looked around the room. "Thank you. This is a really beautiful house you have. It's rather large, though, for one person. You don't live alone, do you?"

"Of course I don't," he stated matter-of-factly. Rylie's heart deflated as the words rang in her ear. She hadn't considered the possibility that he might be married or have a live-in significant other. God, now she just felt like a floozy for the feelings he elicited with their kiss yesterday. And what an ass – how dare he kiss her like that when he was with someone. What a player! Just as well. She didn't need anything from him, anyway.

"Oh, I see. Your wife?"

The coffee Mitch had been pouring into his cup nearly slipped out of his grip, sloshing coffee on the counter. "Wife? No, I'm not married. It's just me and my girl here."

"Wh? Who?" Had he mentioned a woman before now? Who is his girl? Oh dear, did he have a child?

He chuckled at her seemingly dimwitted response. "My dog…you know, the one who just slobbered all over you? Karma's been with me since she was eight-weeks old and I got her when I still lived in the city. I knew a dog her size needed some space to run, so I found this place a few years ago in the hopes that someday I'll fill up the bedrooms with more than just dog toys."

Relief flooded through her like a dam that had just broken wide. He didn't have a live-in lover! Or offspring. Just the dog. She sighed, overcome with a happy satisfaction that he was single. Not that his relationship status meant anything to her. She wasn't planning on kissing him again. For real. She smiled, glad to know the kiss they shared didn't make her a home wrecker or a Jezebel.

Mitch glanced up to see a wide grin emerge over her face. "What did I say that has you so amused, IQ?"

Feeling the heat rush to her face, she quickly recovered by taking a sip of water and averted her eyes from his, which were at this moment boring a hole in hers.

"N – nothing. I was just thinking about that big dog of yours as a puppy. She must have been a handful. I never had a dog growing up. My dad didn't have the time and my brother and I certainly weren't able to take care of one." Stopping herself before she could say more, she noticed how Mitch was looking at her and realized to her embarrassment she had probably shared more than she should have. Damn her socially inept self.

Mitch had by now sat down on one of the kitchen bar stools and was watching Rylie intently. "Please, go on. I'd like to hear more about that." he encouraged, his finger fiddling with the handle of the coffee cup. His lips turned up into a bright smile, showing his incredibly white teeth and a small dimple appeared in his chin. She was curious what the little cleft indentation felt like, catching herself before she reached over and placed her finger in his dimpled chin.

"My childhood was pretty boring," she mumbled uncomfortably, pushing her hair behind her ear. Talking about herself or her past was not something she cared to do. Secrets had a tendency to reveal themselves when that happened and that was not something she wanted to divulge. "How about we move on and get working on that knee."

Before he could protest, Rylie opened up her pink nylon gym bag and pulled out several elastic bands, weighted balls and leg weights. "Where would you like to get down to business?"

As soon as the words were out of her mouth, she already anticipated his likely response. His eyes flicked up and a lopsided grin overtook his face.

"Well, IQ, given that we're in the privacy of my own home, we can get down to business anywhere you'd like," he laughed, his grin beaming wider. "But seeing as you and I may have different versions of what that business entails, I suppose we could head downstairs to my home gym."

Rylie was glad she had some time to compose herself as she followed Mitch down a hallway and then down a flight of stairs into his finished basement. She was mad at herself for getting so easily ruffled by his comments. She had grown up with a brother and his friends, for God's sakes. It wasn't unusual for her to hear crass or sexual innuendos coming from dirty-minded men. In fact, she normally joined right in without any qualms with a few "*That's what she said*" retorts. But it made her jumpy and itchy coming from Mitch. She snarled at her own stupidity.

At the bottom of the stairway, she turned to see once again, the entire back wall of the basement was floor-to-ceiling glass windows, leading out to the patio and pool area.

Stopping in the center of the room, Rylie surveyed the large workout area, complete with all the standard gym equipment – treadmill, elliptical, rowing machine, a full rack of free weights, Physio balls in various colors and sizes, a hanging boxing bag and several mats. A door was open that led into what looked like a shower facility.

Catching the direction of her interest, Mitch explained. "There's also a massage table in the room to the right, a steam room and an infrared sauna room."

She gulped and raised her eyes incredulously at him. "Impressive. Where's Inga, your Swedish massage girl? She off today?" Although she was kidding, there was a distinct possibility he did have his own personal masseuse.

He laughed. "Yep – I told her to take the day off. One beautiful woman fawning over my body today is all my ego could handle."

She blushed as Mitch stared intently at her. "Do you really have your own personal masseuse? Never mind, don't answer that," she said with a hint of disgust when she saw his expression. "I don't even want to know."

"You're not jealous, are you?"

"Pfft. I'm not here to win a contest over who provides the better service. It's all about your recovery."

"Mmm-hmm. So you say…" Mitch moved toward Rylie, his hand brushing lightly down the side of her bare arm. His touch nearly brought her to her knees. His head bent, leaning down with his lips hovering near her ear. His breath was warm and had a hint of coffee and mint toothpaste. "But if there were an Inga, you'd win hands down."

Caught off guard by his blatantly bold compliment, she pulled back from his touch, trying to busy herself with getting acquainted with the equipment.

"I see you have a pool. Have you been using it since your surgery?" Rylie asked, as Mitch shook his head in response. "Swimming and water therapy are great ways to get exercise and to strengthen the muscles in the knee. It's no impact on your joints and is quite soothing. At your session on Monday, if the weather is nice, I can show you some great underwater exercises."

Mitch looked like he was about to say something else, but instead just replied with a "sounds good."

Over the next forty-five minutes, Rylie had Mitch on the floor doing a series of range and motion leg exercises, some weight bearing and others not.

"This is to keep the blood circulating properly and to restore muscle mobility," she had explained as she instructed Mitch through each exercise. She then had him using an elastic band, which he wrapped around the ball of his foot, to pull his knee up slowly toward his face, to increase his range and motion.

All throughout the exercise regimen, Rylie continued to provide educational insight to Mitch as to the purpose of each exercise, helping him learn the proper procedures and precautions so that he didn't further injure his knee. She also instructed him on the daily exercises he was required to complete in between their three weekly appointments.

Once over the initial reminder of the kiss they shared and the briefest of touch's earlier, Rylie felt comfortable in their conversation, which seemed to flow easily between them. She'd been curious as to how Mitch injured his knee, so he shared the story of his ski accident and his love for adventure and sporting activities.

As he was in the midst of a rep of leg lifts, he asked Rylie what prompted her to become a therapist. She used her stock answer, avoiding the true depth and meaning behind her career and profession.

"I wanted to help people recover from traumatic experiences and injuries. I found it helped me when I recovered from my…accident, and I appreciated the process of therapy."

Eying her speculatively, he looked for her to continue. When she didn't, he asked. "Accident, huh? What happened?"

"Uh…I fell." Quickly looking away, her eyes left his face and landed on a spot on the floor.

"I see – so you're a klutz," he chuckled, getting a small smile from her. "I better keep all sharp objects out of your way, then." He joked, but didn't pursue it further.

Feeling uncomfortable with the topic and where the conversation had headed, Rylie had him finish the exercise before deciding that a break was in order. Knowing that she had worked him hard and pushed him to his limit for the day, which she could see written all over his face, she decided to do some isometrics and massage work.

Holding out her hands to help pull him up to a standing position, she motioned him into the massage room. "Let's put that massage table to some good use." His face lit up with her recommendation.

"It's not what you're thinking."

"How could you possibly know what I'm thinking?" He teased. "Get your mind out of the gutter, young lady." Making a tsking sound, Mitch wagged his finger at her. "But I was hoping you'd get me on the table – sooner rather than later."

"Ugh. You better be careful, otherwise I might just recommend that icy cold bath again. That's what I do to all my bad patients." She snickered, seeing his face tense up into a worried plea.

"Okay. Okay. I'll try to be good. But I can't promise for how long." He raised his hands in surrender and winked.

Rylie assisted Mitch up on the massage table and had him lie down on his back. Rolling up a small towel she found under the table, she placed it under his knee.

"I'm going to be doing some light massage work around the tissue, to keep the muscle warm and pliable. Let me know if any of it hurts or it's uncomfortable."

Reaching out with both hands, Rylie placed her hands on his quad muscle, just above his knee and the incision site, and began to knead it gently. His breath caught and he jerked slightly, then settled his head back down against the pillow. She had him start out just doing modified leg raises and then used some massage techniques in between reps.

Rylie had done this hundreds of times with a variety of patients, young and old, male and female. It was routine – an ordinary hands-on therapy technique. But it had never felt like this. His quadriceps muscles were firm and large, her hands looking small and dwarfed against them. Rylie's fingers moved in a circular motion around the kneecap, plunging into the tissue and muscle. Her fingers were on fire from the heat projecting from his skin, an electric current shooting through her nerve endings. She bit down on her lip, which began to quiver, just as the rest of her body similarly responded. She had to look at the wall to keep her eyes off of his gorgeous body and the hard shape of his erection against his shorts. She tried to think of something – anything other than how he felt under her fingers.

His voice was deep and gravely, as he looked down the length of his body and up to her eyes, meeting her stare.

"I think I might need that ice bath, after all," he said, grabbing her wrist and pulling himself up onto his elbows.

"Rylie…" His voice shook in uncertainty and was laced with a vulnerable plea. She stopped the movement of her hands but stayed where they were. Their eyes locked.

"This is…you are…God – you are driving me crazy."

He let out a breath and at the same time let go of her wrist. His legs swung around the edge of the table and she staggered back and out of the way to make room for him. He paused there momentarily in thought before reaching out to grab her arms and pull her in between his opened legs, until she was just inches from his mouth.

His eyes roamed her lips, as she licked them and they parted in anticipation. "I can't be good any longer. Tell me to stop right this second and I will. Otherwise...I'm going to kiss you."

He was giving her an out and she knew it. She saw it in his eyes, the desire and the need. The same way she felt. Her body was an incendiary device, ready to detonate at any moment. She understood that there were lines that she couldn't cross – her personal life could not bleed over into her professional. She took an oath when she became a therapist that her conduct would always remain professional and would not obstruct the patient/therapist relationship.

But that was before she ever felt anything quite like this. She stood there, trapped between his legs, frozen in the strong hands that were gripping her arms. Her mind warred with her body on how bad of a decision this would be and all she could mutter was "Yes."

"Yes, what?" he demanded.

"Yes, I want you to kiss me…but –"

Before she could finish her thought, Mitch wrapped his arms around her waist and pulled her body flush against his. His lips found her mouth and willed it to open for him. His tongue darted in, probing deeply, exploring the depths of her sensuality. Rylie's body shifted closer and she tentatively nudged her hips against him, bringing out a heavy groan of desire from deep within Mitch's chest. Her warm mocha colored eyes darkened with pleasure at the greedy sound, giving her the confidence to continue feasting on his mouth, devouring his taste and the feel of his lips on hers.

Reaching up to his face, her hands cupped his cheeks, the feel of his beard stubble stinging her palms. Snaking them back behind his head, her fingers threaded through his hair, encouraging him even further.

His hands suddenly moved under her to cradle her butt and with a powerful motion, he hoisted her up to straddle his lap. Her legs bent on each side of him, where she nestled against his arousal, which was pressing hard against her own most sensitive spot, burning through the fabric of her jeans.

"You feel so damn good," he growled, releasing her mouth and trailing his wet lips across her jaw and down her neck. Rylie arched her neck and angled her head back, giving him more access, as he continued to plant searing kisses down to the delicate part of her throat, just above the collar of her buttoned shirt. He was ravenous, unyielding and so damn appealing.

Rylie began to feel the tight knot begin to burn down from her belly into her core. A tingling sensation unlike anything else, screaming for release from the exquisite tension. Mitch's hand moved out from underneath her cradled ass, to work its way slowly up her waist and side, until it reached the pinnacle of its destination. His thumb grazed her nipple, which upon its command tightened into a hard peak. She let out a lusty moan as he continued to circle and court the hardened flesh with his fingers. Her breasts swelled in needy response.

She was wild and hungry, wanting him to touch more of her, waiting for the moment when she'd feel his hands run across her naked breasts and he'd take them between his lips and suckle them until she was mindless and bucking against him. It had been so long since she had felt this way or had a man touch her in this manner. She felt a spark had ignited a long, dormant flame and she was ready to burst.

A bark in the not-so-far-off distance and a loud ringing sound from the front door had Mitch reluctantly dropping his hand from Rylie's breast and mutter a curse to whomever had interrupted them.

Momentarily disoriented, Rylie was confused as to why there was the sudden departure of his hands and lips from her body.

Shifting her off his lap and on to the table beside him, he reached over to grab his crutch. "It appears I need that cold shower after all," he grimaced, as he pushed himself off the table, landing his feet in a soft thud on the floor.

"What? Where are you going?" she asked breathlessly, her swollen lips aching to be touched and tormented again. She felt the acute loss of his body and shame washed over her, dousing her with the realization of what they had been doing.

Mitch sauntered to the open doorway when he stopped to turn around and look at Rylie, who was now readjusting her blouse and angrily folding the towel.

"I was hoping I'd get to find out how wet I made you," he shrugged, a slow, sexy smile drawing across his face. "But business calls. I'll have to wait until next time to find out. Until then, you can let yourself out the back door here, the path will lead around to the driveway. Have a good weekend, IQ."

A rush of embarrassment flooded her face. Shame and guilt penetrated her thoughts. Rylie felt a rage and anger – mostly at herself for her own uncontrolled actions and reaction to his touch – come boiling up to the surface. He had dismissed her so casually, after what they had just done and the intimacy of it all. She had let her guard down and opened up to his touch and he was walking away like he wasn't affected at all by what happened.

All her frustration came barreling out in an angry squeal. "You ass! There won't be a next time, I can promise you that."

Rylie stood up to follow after him, but he'd already made his way out of the room and up the stairs. She heard a boom of loud laughter echo down the stairwell and his smug response.

"We'll see about that."

CHAPTER SEVEN

"I don't give a good goddamn about your delayed shipments, Joe. This delay is unacceptable and creating a logjam for everything else we have planned." Mitch expelled a loud exhale in his response, leaning back in his leather desk chair. "Get it the fuck together or I'll find another vendor. You got it?" He hung up the phone and cursed again.

From the hallway, a low whistle came from Jackson who leaned against the doorframe wearing an amused smirk. Stepping into his office, he closed the door behind him before sitting down in the chair directly across from Mitch.

Jackson crossed his leg over his knee and his hand came to his pant leg, brushing a speck of lint from his tailored suit pants. He lifted an eyebrow. "Problems?"

"You could say that. The shipment is stuck somewhere out west and was supposed to be delivered to the site tomorrow. Joe doesn't think we'll see it until mid-next week, but can't even fucking guarantee that." Mitch swiveled around in his chair to face the window and jammed his hand roughly through his hair. "Have they ever heard of contractual commitments? Hey, wait, you're a lawyer," he said with a sarcastic snarl, turning back around to face his partner. "Why don't you do something about this and earn your wages for the day."

Jackson leaned back comfortably in his chair, shrugging his shoulders. "As your legal counsel, I will gladly advise you on any business and legal matter and can review the contract again for any penalties associated with delayed shipments," he said thoughtfully. "But I don't think your little outburst has much to do with Joe Simpson and the shipment." He paused for emphasis, gaining his partner's attention. Mitch glared at him over his desk.

"Oh yeah? And what exactly do you think has gotten me riled up then, oh wise one?"

Jackson casually examined his friend, giving a discerning assessment. "I think your bitchy mood has a helluva lot more to do with a certain therapist you may have seen today." He brought his hands up behind his head and clasped them together. "But hey, that's just my attorney's best guess. I'm no fucking mind reader or shrink, for that matter."

Mitch glared at his partner and flipped him off before turning back around to look out the thirtieth floor window of the Prudential Tower, overlooking Boylston Street below. His friend knew him too well and it pissed him off. These types of hassles, like the delayed shipment, typically didn't faze Mitch or get him this agitated. The truth of the matter was he was frustrated and keyed up. He wanted something, or someone, he couldn't have. He was not a patient man and when he wanted something within his reach, he found a way to get it. His current physical condition, notwithstanding, didn't help matters much, either.

He felt limited. Held back. He hated feeling weak and lacking control over any situation.

Mitch experienced the same feeling earlier in the year, looking down at the throngs of people on the street, both runners and spectators alike. The Boston Marathon was an event unlike any other in the city that brought an energy and vitality to the normally dry financial district. It brought together a connection and a bond, not just of those Bostonians, but anyone who shared the living, breathing kinetic spirit of the marathon. But that essence turned into something much darker and sinister when the bombings occurred.

As usual, Mitch was at his desk working and on the phone that morning when he looked down at the street, the blast sounds registering in his ears, rocking the building and bringing a plume of dust and smoke up the building's exterior. Unable to comprehend what had just taken place, Mitch took immediate action and made his way down to the scene to seek out and assist anyone who needed help.

What he found when he made it to street level was mass chaos and sheer terror. Hundreds of bodies lay injured up and down the block, where minutes before two pressure cooker bombs had detonated in an act of senseless terrorism. A young boy, maybe twelve or thirteen, had been knocked back against the building rubble, his arm partially mutilated from the blast. Mitch saw him the moment he came running out of the building's front door, his disheveled body covered in soot, dirt and blood. He hovered over the boy, who was silent. No sounds, or screams or even cries coming from his catatonic body. He just lay there in a traumatized state, rocking back and forth.

Mitch began to triage and comfort the only way he knew how and waited for aid. He ripped off his suit jacket and tie and wrapped it securely around the boy's arm to stop the bleeding and shield him from seeing the extent of his injury. He pulled the boy into his arms and held him around his small shoulders, as silent sobs came pouring out of the thin body. He wasn't sure how long they sat there like that before paramedics rushed in and whisked him away, but in that time, he lost his faith in humanity. He had been brought down to the lower depths of hell, when a young boy could be torn apart through such an evil act of hatred. Mitch's view of the world became even more tainted and torn. If he had been devastated by the loss of his brother before, his soul was completely lost and shattered now as a result of this act of terrorism.

Now, even seven months later, the day's events were still etched deeply in his memory, the anger still festering under the surface, especially in his current state of frustration. His guilt and hatred over the deaths and injuries of so many innocent victims. The loss of his younger brother, who went off to fight a war and never came home. A brother whom he should have been able to protect. He had failed him, just as he'd failed that young boy.

His mood darkened even further, the tight lid that had kept his feelings about his brother's death from creeping open, inch by inch, as they threatened to slay his heart again.

His brother was two years younger and had been his best friend through childhood. Matthew was impish, and a bit of a dare devil, creating chaos and mischief at every turn, making Mitch's work as his older brother all that much more difficult. It was during Mitch's sophomore year in college when Matthew informed him of his plans to join the military, throwing Mitch and his parents in a tailspin over his brother's decision. It weighed heavily on him, Mitch's grades plummeting that first semester after Matthew's deployment to Afghanistan, his ability to concentrate on schoolwork completely thwarted by his powerlessness to protect his brother from such a distance.

"It appears you might need a drink," Jax said, interrupting Mitch's tormented thoughts. "Let's say we call it a day and start the weekend early. I've got tickets behind the Sox dugout for tonight's playoff game, so let's head down to Fenway early and have a few beers."

Mitch appreciated his friend's positive spin on life. Even when he was in one of his darkest moods, Jackson could always find a way to lift his spirits and be the glass half-full kind of guy. The Yin to his Yang, the Dumb to his Dumber. Jackson had been there for him when he and his parents had learned of their family's devastating loss and never failed to provide an outlet. A distraction. A deep trust and comfort that he had lost with the death of his brother.

"The dugout, huh? How'd you score those gold-plated treasures?"

"Remember Jenni Schmidt?"

Mitch had to sort through the number of women he met on a monthly basis that seemed to flock to his handsome and charming friend. He was drawing a blank on this one.

"Remind me again?"

"The art dealer. We met her at the exhibit last month. We've hung out a few times and it just so happens her uncle works for the Sox and offered up the tickets. Unfortunately for her, she's out of town at another art show in New York this weekend, otherwise she would have been my date. Instead, I'm left with your ugly ass to tag along. And believe me...I would definitely prefer Jenni's hot little ass sitting next to mine over yours any day."

"There's nothing wrong with my ass," Mitch balked, making an act of turning his head to mockingly grab his butt. "You're just jealous of my perfect David-like gluteus maximus."

Jax snorted as he stood up. "You just keep thinking that, my friend."

Five minutes later, they had decided they'd get changed and head down to the pub before taking the T down to Fenway. The idea of catching the game and a few beers had already lifted his mood and Mitch was excited to see the Red Sox pull out another win in the post-season, and maybe even take a pennant. Possibly another World Series.

Ready to close up shop for the day, he glanced once more at his Inbox. A new email from Sasha M. Lee, MD caught his attention. Clicking the email to expand the view, he read through the professionally written correspondence.

To: Mr. Mitchell Camden
From: Sasha M. Lee, MD, Lee & Associates
Date: October 8
RE: Change in your therapist

Dear Mr. Camden,

Due to a scheduling change, I'd like to inform you that Rylie Hemmons, MPT, will no longer be available. Effective immediately, your new therapist will be Carmen Flores. Carmen has over twenty years of experience and is a highly regarded physical therapist.

As we have previously arranged, Carmen will continue to provide you with your in-home services, so there will be no interruption in your schedules or create any inconvenience.

Thank you for your continued patronage.

Best Regards,
Sasha M. Lee, MD
Lee & Associates

WTF?

Mitch all but roared as he read and reread the email. What in the world was this all about? This couldn't possibly have anything to do with what happened between them, could it? Well if it was, this was a ridiculously childish thing for Rylie to pull.

There was no doubt in his mind that they had a powerful attraction, which he felt instantly when he met her at the bar the other night. And that heat seemed to only intensify and gain momentum the more they were together. He could only describe it as a hungry desire. Was it possible that she didn't feel the same way? Was that the reason she withdrew so suddenly? Was she just trying to get back at him for leaving her wet and unsatisfied?

Mitch felt a sharp pang of regret. Maybe he had brought this on himself, given how he had left things earlier in the day. He certainly hadn't meant to leave her high and dry, given the compromising position they had both been in when the doorbell rang. He had been caught off guard, and more than a little surprised, by her physical reaction and response to his kiss. He'd wanted to keep tasting her, run his hands up and down her beautiful body before their little interlude was interrupted. It pissed him off to have to leave Rylie in that state of desire. In his own state of desire – he was hard as a rock. Damn, if he could just go back in time. She was so warm and tasted like sunshine on his tongue. He wanted more of that feeling. More time with her, to devour her. That girl made him want to be a better man.

Each one of her touches blazed through him. They turned him into the equivalent of the Greek god Dionysus, making him burn with ecstasy. He wanted – no, had to – experience more of her. This would not be the way this would end, not if he had anything to do with it. And when Mitch wanted something, he got it. He would fight this and he would win. He would get what he wanted, come hell or high water.

Without even a second thought, Mitch began to type out an email response to Sasha Lee. To say he was demanding or unrelenting in any of his pursuits was an understatement. Mitch would not be deterred and would use his power and influence to see that his wishes became reality. Every facet of his life was governed by this personality trait. Some people, like his mother, found it to be 'willful.' His father was glad to see him put the family gene to good use.

It took less than two minutes for Mitch to write out a terse reply and hit the Send button. Feeling more in control of the situation, he closed his laptop and headed downstairs to meet his friend for an evening of beer and baseball.

****

Rylie's nightmare started just as it always did. It's a warm summer night, just after dusk, as she's walking through Boston Common. The breeze blowing gently at her back, the stars up above peeking quietly out from under their bluish-black blanket, she shrugs off her backpack to remove her jacket, revealing a green tank underneath. Hefting the bag back over her shoulder, she is aware of male voices coming up from behind her. She turns her head slightly to the left to peer behind her, but sees no one. Her pace quickens.

The hairs on the back of her neck begin to prickle.

The next thing she knows, her bag is being savagely ripped from her arm, the strap catching in the crook of her elbow. She tries to free herself, but she stumbles instead. Trying to regain her balance, she looks up into a face that is shrouded by a black hoodie. A noise from her other side causes her to look in that direction, another hooded head and face. A dark pair of menacing eyes glare from under the baseball cap. Then a low, dangerous laugh escapes his lips, which are turned upright in a threatening smile. His hot, vile breath comes out in a rage of sound against her ear.

"Don't move, or you'll die."

The kernel of panic rises from the pit of her stomach, a volcano of hysteria lodged in her throat, choking her from the inside out. Unable to formulate a word or a sound, she lays there in silent fear, terror stampeding through her veins. Her father had taught her what to do in a situation like this, but nothing would come to her. She felt panic-stricken and paralyzed.

The bigger one is now on top of her, pinning down her arms. His fingers pull at the strap of her tank, yanking it down past her shoulder. Her skin crawls. She wants to gauge his eyes out, but she can't. She struggles, pushing her shoulders off the ground, but he takes her head in his hands and slams her back down.

It momentarily goes black, the world around her. And then she hears a ripping sound. She blinks, trying to refocus, but her head hurts. She feels something warm in her eyes. It's blood. *Oh my God, I'm bleeding.*

The man is breathing hard and his rough, sweaty hand begins to grope at her breast. His touch is rough. Criminal. Sinister. She hears him cackle. She hears the word *No* being repeated over and over again. Is she saying it out loud? His face comes down to her body, his wet slobbering tongue inching over her flesh, tasting her. Groping her. Ruining her. She feels the man on top of her grind against her, his rigid body rutting hard against her. She hears him groan and then from far off in the distance, she hears shouting. Someone calling out.

The second man is whispering in a harsh, nervous tone. "Fuuuck, man. Let's get the hell out of here. Just get her fuckin purse."

Another loud sound, this time closer. A whistle, like the sound a referee makes. The man on top of her curses and pushes himself off, but not before his tongue darts out and licks her cheek. "Next time, pretty baby. Next time."

The two hooded men look around, grab her bag and take off, leaving her momentarily frozen, chills skating down her shaking limbs. She is now surrounded by other voices...helpful voices...covering her naked and bruised body.

Are you okay?

Someone call an ambulance.

Her head's bleeding.

Sweetie, it's all right. You'll be okay.

But she knows that's not the case. She will never feel okay again.

Rylie jerks out of bed, the sweat clinging to her, sending hot and cold shivers down her spine. Her entire body is a live wire – humming with electricity, her hands balled into fists. She's shaking uncontrollably and her hair is matted against her forehead, her T-shirt and shorts soaked through. Flipping to her side, she leans over to look at the clock on the nightstand. Four-thirty a.m. *Great.*

She had to be up and out of her apartment in three hours and she needed to get back to sleep, but she knew at this point sleep would elude her. Instead, she was drenched in sweat and wide awake – frightened and anxious. *Goddamn it. Those fuckers.*

Getting out of bed, she slipped off her shorts and shirt and found a new set in her bureau. She headed into the bathroom where she splashed some cold water on her face and grabbed a washcloth to wet and smooth over her forehead and the back of her neck. Slipping the tank over her head, she glanced up at her reflection in the mirror, letting out a curse as she gripped the sides of the sink.

When would this panic ever subside?

It hadn't dissipated in over five years. Only four people in the world, aside from herself, knew what occurred that night; her father, her brother, the beat cop who took her statement and Sasha. No one else was the wiser. Rylie made sure of that. There was no way she would ever let anyone look at her with pity in their eyes or offer up banal platitudes or sympathetic gestures like they did that night in the hospital. She had been mugged, attacked and beaten, left feeling violated and helpless in the heart of the city. It took everything from her, leaving her a withering mess.

And all she could do was swallow the fear and tamp it down. No use crying over it, because that would just be a travesty. There were few things worse than expressing your feelings in the Hemmons' household. And therapy or counseling? Don't even think about it. Even if her brother wouldn't have kicked her butt for showing weakness, there was no way Rylie would have subjected herself to having discuss the details of the attack with strangers.

So instead, and by accident, Rylie found a way to lose the victim mentality and take control of her fears. She learned, through a then-boyfriend of Sasha's who was an instructor, about a form of self-defense and martial art called Krav Maga, the same self-defense system that the Israeli Military used and trained their soldiers. At the incessant urging of Sasha, she attended Kip's class one Saturday morning. And as they say, the rest was history.

Blown away by the natural and effective techniques that Krav Maga used, including moves from boxing, Judo, wrestling and Kung Fu, Rylie found herself instantly enjoying the instinctual body movements and simple principles of the martial art. The fluidity of the moves, the concentration required, and the total body workout gave Rylie exactly what she yearned for – the control over her life. Without hesitation, she signed up for classes, fell in love with the sport and within a year, became a certified instructor.

Now she was teaching other young women every Saturday morning at the Cambridge Rec center, helping those who were like herself once – fragile, ashamed and afraid – learn to fight to win their freedom back.

Realizing that sleep at this point would elude her, Rylie reached for her laptop and placed it on her lap, as she got comfy in bed. Might as well do some web surfing – at least that could get her mind off her woes. Checking out the late breaking news for a bit, then moving to look at the Nike Outlet site for the newest running shoe, it only took her ten minutes before she found herself typing Mitch Camden in the Google search engine. 975,000 results. Hmm…okay. How about Mitch Camden, Boston? The first result that flashed up on the page was Camden Ventures. Clicking the link, she pulled up the Home page for Mitch's business.

Doing a quick scan of the contents and the current projects, she clicked the About Us page. It brought up two bios, including one for Mitch and another one for a Jackson Koda, Esq., the same guy that was with Mitch at the bar the other night. Nothing against Jackson, but she was far more interested in the juicy details on Mitch.

Rylie read through a brief description of his education and accomplishments, *very impressive*, followed by some comments about his philanthropy and charity involvements. For such an asshole, he certainly had a caring side, she thought, scanning the pictures. Clicking the photos page, her breath hitched as she landed on a headshot of Mitch. He was in a charcoal gray suit, white dress shirt and a deep green silk tie, that brought out the emerald flecks in his beautiful hazel eyes. *Damn, he was gorgeous.* Flipping through a few more, she saw pictures of him on various project sites, and what looked like a trip to Africa, where he was feeding a group of children.

In one particular photo, his golden smile lit up his face, his angular jaw transforming and softening his features. His deep hazel-green eyes, hooded by sooty, thick lashes, sparkled like sea glass in the sun. He had his arm around a young boy, who was maybe about five, and another man who was wearing military fatigues. Mitch looked gorgeous, his smile depicting a light she hadn't seen yet. And the other man he had his arm around had strikingly similar hazel eyes and a wide, perfectly straight smile. They all looked happy. She could see love and a deep bond between the two men. His brother? He had to be related to him in some way, their facial expressions and likeness too similar not to be.

In the few encounters and short time she'd known him, she'd never seen Mitch this contented. Sexy, yes. Incredibly handsome, absolutely. But she sensed something was missing right now. He didn't have the same gleam in his eye that he did in that photo. Interesting. She'd have to see if she could pick up on that if she ever saw him again. But that was unlikely, considering what she asked Sasha to do for her.

She must have been staring at his smiling face for five minutes and caught herself sighing as she continued to look at his full lips, upturned into his bright smile. Her body suddenly felt overheated, the memory of their kiss flooding back, spreading straight through to her core. Her finger came up to touch her lips, the memory of his lips skimming down her neck and his hands caressing her breasts. The warm tingly feeling invaded her body and she realized at that very moment that even the thought of Mitch turned her on.

She hadn't allowed anyone to touch her like that since before her attack. Five long, painful years of keeping her pain hidden and he was her first. And instead of repulsing her, bringing back horribly vivid flashbacks, Mitch's touch ignited her. It was pleasure and it was wrong, she knew it. But it felt right. It made her feel whole.

Rylie closed the website and sighed again. She didn't understand why she kept thinking about Mitch or worried about what occurred between the two of them. She shook her head, trying to clear her head and make herself forget. She had to remember that Mitch was just a playboy. She was a game to him. He probably got off on the chase and once he got what he wanted, she'd be erased from his thoughts.

It didn't matter, anyway, because come Monday, everything would be wiped clean. Mitch would no longer be her client to worry about, she made sure of that. She had beseeched Sasha to find a way to extricate herself from Mitch's case. She groveled and begged until Sasha granted her request.

Rylie climbed back into bed, placing her hand on her stomach, trying to ease the knot that had slowly begun to build in the pit of her stomach. She knew, without a doubt, that Mitch would move on, forgetting her existence in a moment. She breathed deeply, trying to reassure herself that this would mean she could resume her normal, everyday life. No entanglements.

But even that thought now depressed her.

CHAPTER EIGHT

By some sheer act of mercy, Rylie's Saturday morning Krav Maga class went relatively smoothly, even though she was slogging through it with the limited sleep she'd gotten the night before. Her four regular students showed up, as well as two new participants, who all had the same deer in the headlights look. She got excited to see their expressions change over the class hour as the intensity of the workout brought them the same unexpected exhilaration she had felt the first time she practiced it.

Finishing up at five minutes before the hour, she spent time after class meeting with the newbies, discussing the program dynamics and reviewing the specifics, costs, and their goals. She was always curious to find out what others wanted out of self-defense, as it was a different and unique experience for each individual. She learned that not everyone came out of fear and self-loathing. Damaged beyond repair.

With her bag and gear packed, Rylie walked out the gym door, waving a goodbye to Kip, who was at the front with a client, and headed to her car. She spoke with Sasha the night before and promised to swing by and pick her up before heading to Logan to see Mark off to Africa. As if she knew she was thinking about her, Rylie's phone chirped with a new text from Sasha.

Where are you?

Rylie sat down in her front seat and typed a quick message back.

BRT…leaving class now.

Hurry up.

Rylie chuckled to herself at her friend's impatience. Sasha was a lot of things – a fashion plate, a doctor, an over-sexed woman. But patient, she was not.

Within fifteen minutes she was out front of Sasha's Beacon Hill brownstone, watching Sasha fly down the steps, her short, gauzy skirt billowing in the breeze. She was impeccably dressed, day or night, and always a little bit wild. There were times Rylie felt a tinge of jealousy at her obvious talent for accessorizing, wishing she herself could put something together other than T-shirts and jeans. She'd certainly improved over the years, with constant nagging and counsel from Sasha. At least she'd even gotten to the point of rotating the earrings she wore on a daily basis – which was a vast improvement. She had her limitations, she knew, regardless of Sasha's constant badgering.

Jumping in the car, Sasha leaned over and gave Rylie a quick peck on the cheek, slapped on her seatbelt and pulled down the visor to reapply her lipstick in the mirror, all within a matter of seconds. Sasha was efficient, to say the least, if not a bit anal about her lipstick application.

Satisfied with her painted pouty lips, Sasha smacked her lips together and adjusted herself in the seat to turn to Rylie.

"So…do I need to drag it out of you?" she asked, not beating around the bush with a formal greeting.

Rylie gave her a quick look over her shoulder, pulling into the fairly vacant street traffic.

"Drag what out?"

Sasha's mouth quirked up in a knowing smile. "Oh gee, let me think. Maybe I'd like to know what the hell happened between you and Mitch Camden that sent you flying over the freaking ledge yesterday? That man is a Greek god and you're a pussy for not being able to handle it." That was Sasha…never one to mince words or filter her thoughts.

Rylie knew to expect the first degree from Sasha, but debated whether to come clean and share every detail. Knowing her friend would eventually figure it out and make her spill everything, she decided she'd share most of it and leave out some of the more savory parts.

Rylie loosened and then tightened her grip on the steering wheel before responding, really uncertain of how to explain it to her. "I don't know, Sash. Maybe I am…or was a bit overwhelmed by his…"

"By his what? His incredible hotness? His virility? His huge cock?"

Rylie couldn't help but choke out a laugh at her friend's bold choice of words. Recalling the heated moments she'd spent with Mitch over the last week, she considered what it was that had her fleeing for the hills.

"No – it's not that," she said, shaking her head, trying to find the words that made her weak. "It's his intimidatingly smooth arrogance and self-confidence."

Sasha looked at her as if Rylie had two heads.

"Really? He was too confident in his masculinity? Most women would wet themselves over a man like Mitch. He's wealthy, smart, insanely gorgeous, and from what I hear, one of the most eligible bachelors in Boston."

She grew quiet and contemplative for a moment, looking intently over Rylie's profile. Rylie felt uncomfortable in her examination, as if she were mentally sussing out the details. But instead, her tone was laced with apologetic worry.

"Ry, did he try something on you? You know if he did, I will personally kick his ass. I will never allow a client to intimidate my employees, physically or verbally. You know this."

Rylie could feel Sasha's eyes boring into her scalp, like little daggers digging to get inside her brain. Sasha was intensely fierce when it came to protecting her friend, especially in light of her history.

Rylie shook her head emphatically.

"No – God no! At least not in the way you mean," she said, hesitating slightly, her face heating up like a torch. "Mitch…he…well, I guess, kissed me…" She stopped, taking a quick glance over to Sasha, waiting for the reaction to her admission. "More than once."

"Oh, holy shit. And did you kiss him back?"

Rylie shook her head with her admission.

"Oh my God! I'm so proud of you! Please tell me you at least liked it, otherwise there is something seriously wrong with you."

Rylie knew her friend was only joking, because she had an amused smile on her face. But considering it had been five years since she'd enjoyed a man's touch, her statement still held a lot of truth. She had worried that maybe the damage done to her had been irreparable. That she'd never feel safe again with a man. Never want to open herself up to the possibility of getting too close. Protecting her heart and her body from the pain and anguish.

"Yes, I liked it. A little too much," she whispered guiltily. "But I crossed the line, Sasha. My judgment was impaired and I couldn't do my job effectively. I couldn't touch him without feeling something and it was unprofessional. That is NOT who I am. I've worked hard to get where I am. My reputation…in fact, your clinic's reputation is at stake. And the only way I can prevent that irreprehensible behavior from occurring in the future is to stop working with him altogether." She looked at her friend sheepishly. "I know that's the coward's way out…but it was impossible to resist him and do my job effectively."

Sasha took a breath and blew it out, straightening out her skirt and repositioning herself back toward the front of the car. Her disposition went from enthusiastic to somber.

"Well, Ry, I hate to tell you this, but you're going to have to face your fears. You can't always get what you want."

"What does that mean? I thought you were able to work it out so that I could transfer him to Carmen next week?" Rylie could hear the sudden panic rising in her voice, feel it creep up in her throat as it clawed to escape. She felt the walls closing in on her.

"Listen. I did check Carmen's schedule and she said she could pick up the three days next week and I emailed Mitch to let him know. Then he sent me an email not twenty minutes later informing me he has a business trip out of town and needs a therapist able to travel…" Rylie knew what was coming next.

Sasha played with her skirt, a sign of nervousness that Rylie rarely saw from her.

"Ry, you know Carmen's a single mom and can't travel because of her kids. And I certainly can't leave my patients and upcoming surgical procedures. So it's up to you....plus, he offered to donate money for the addition to the clinic."

Rylie had just pulled into the parking ramp at Logan International and sat there in stunned silence. She felt shell-shocked. Anxiety bubbled up from the pit of her stomach and rippled through her body. The telltale signs of a full-blown panic attack were taking shape, the tightening of her chest, the short, choppy breaths that had Rylie gulping for air. She swallowed thickly and turned to face Sasha.

"He bribed you? Oh my God – what does that make me, his paid prostitute and you're my pimp?" Rylie's face burned red. This could not be happening. All she wanted to do was get away from him and the strange hold he seemed to have over her. Her brain and body warred with her, the mixed feelings having an internal sword fight. She didn't want to be near him, yet that's the only place she wanted to be.

Rylie glared at her friend and then took a steadying breath.

"And just where exactly will you be sending me on this business trip of his?"

Sasha gestured a 'Ta-Da' with her hands, bestowing a congratulatory smile at her friend. With her voice two-octaves higher than normal, she exclaimed, "Miami!"

****

Rylie put on a good face as they met up with Mark and his family inside the terminal. Sasha had started gushing tears the moment she saw him, as they all hugged and said their goodbyes. Before he went into the security line, Mark pulled Rylie aside to hug her and speak with her privately.

"Hey sweetie, it's only going to be a year. I promise I'll Skype you weekly," Mark said, pulling her close in a bear-hug. "You can keep me updated and fill me in on all the outlandish details of Sasha's love life – that slut!"

Rylie laughed, but a tear slipped from the corner of her eye, making her way down her cheek. She would miss him immensely and was worried for his safety being so far from civilization.

"And the offer holds – you can come visit me anytime you want. I may look all brave and manly on the outside, but between you and me, I'm scared shitless."

Rylie hugged him tighter. She was so proud of Mark, accomplishing what he set out to do. He was pursuing his dream by joining Doctors-Without-Borders and would be in Ghana for the next twelve months. He was so brave and confident, despite his admission to the contrary. She wished she could be more like him, to prove with actions that she could be strong and courageous. To recapture the fire that had been stolen from her.

"Then don't go," she choked out. "I'll miss you so much."

"Ah, sweets. It'll be okay. You're in good hands here. And from the sounds of it, you may have someone to keep you entertained during my absence."

Rylie pulled back from his grip and looked up into his caring face, giving him an inquisitive look. Mark shrugged his shoulders and gestured innocently.

"What? You think I haven't heard about the sparks flying already between you and Mitch Camden?" Damn that Sasha. Could never keep her mouth shut.

Mark chuckled and ruffled Rylie's hair. She turned to where Sasha stood and gave her an evil look.

"No, Ry, it wasn't Sash. I made that call the other night at the bar. Mitch was asking me a lot of questions about who you were, what you did, etcetera, etcetera. And it became pretty obvious when I saw you talking with him, even though you may not admit it to yourself, that there was something brewing there. You two looked rather chummy." He pulled away from her and stepped back, his hand coming up underneath her chin. His eyes held her stare, as she blinked back tears. "Just promise me one thing."

Rylie cocked her head. "What? I've already promised to Skype your ugly face every week."

"Ha! So true," he laughed, but his smile quickly faded.

"Just promise me to be careful. I've known Mitch practically my whole life. He's an awesome guy and comes from a great family. But with women, well, he's a notorious heartbreaker. He's not looking to settle down. He's good for a fling, I'm sure. I just don't want to see you hurt."

Rylie grabbed hold of his shoulders and he brought his head down to touch her forehead. "First off," she started indignantly. "I'm not involved with, nor will I be involved with, Mitch Camden. He's a client, for God's sake. And second, I think he's an arrogant ass."

Mark laughed harder as he leaned in. "My dear sweet Rylie, you just keep telling yourself that." He pushed himself off, patted her head and then turned to rejoin the rest of the group, who were now huddled around Sasha, the constant center of attention.

Waving their farewells, Sasha looped her arm around Rylie's as they exited the main concourse. They walked in silence, arm in arm, until they reached the car in the lot. Standing outside, Rylie looked out over the rooftop to her friend, who she could tell was trying ardently to mask her sorrow with an overly bright smile.

Sasha and Mark had been best friends since their freshman year in college and were thick as thieves. They shared a small apartment all through med school and had been each other's confidants through countless hook-ups and break-ups over the years. For some of their longer-term significant others, their friendship was more than cause for jealousy, even though neither Mark or Sasha had ever expressed a love more than friendship for one another. They were just connected, with a deep and true, unromantic love for one another.

Sasha let out a sigh. "I guess it'll just be the two Amigas from now on," she said, throwing her hands up on the roof of the car with a *thunk*. "Which means you're going to have to up your rowdiness factor, Rylie Hemmons. Starting right now. We need to go to O'Leary's and get shitfaced!"

Rylie tried to think of a quick excuse to get her out of a night of Sasha drowning her sorrows and getting hit on by a dozen men. Nothing seemed to come to mind because she really had no life outside of Sasha and her antics. So she said yes to what would inevitably be a night of Sasha ditching her for a one-night stand with a hot, single man.

Rylie never envied or begrudged Sasha for her seductive persuasion over the opposite sex. In fact, she found it entertaining how easily Sasha could ensnare and beguile a man with just a wink and a laugh. It could also have something to do with Sasha's magnetic personality, and maybe even more how well she was endowed.

Turning down Sasha's street, Rylie grimaced. "Hey, before we go out tonight, you need to tell me how the hell you got me trapped in this Miami business. I'm still pissed at you, by the way."

"Oh, pfft," Sasha waved, jumping out of the parked car and heading to the door of her brownstone. "That reminds me, I need to lend you some of my barely-there ensembles for your trip. I have just the one-piece for you," she declared, looking Rylie up and down. "Remember that little red suit I got when I went to Jamaica last year? Oh girl, you are going to have him eating out of the palm of your hand! Ooh, and don't forget that slinky silver dress I bought at Bergdorf's in New York. If he doesn't get a full-blown hard on when he sees you in that dress, I don't know what it will take." And just like that, Sasha was back to her happy, lovable, if not a little nutty, self. It even made Rylie crack a smile as they entered the front door.

"If you recall, I think I mentioned that I don't want anything to do with him *or* him eating out of the palm of my hand. Have you not been listening to me over the last week? He makes me so mad I want to scream. I don't want to sleep with the guy!"

Sasha turned to her as she entered her bedroom closet. Hands on her hips, she shifted her stance from one foot to the other. She cocked an eyebrow.

"Well honey, as the saying goes…you can either fight or fuck." She grabbed a Louis Vuitton bag and began filling it with what seemed to be two-dozen bathing suits, skirts, dresses and heeled sandals. "And fucking is just more fun…"

CHAPTER NINE

The remainder of the weekend went by in a blur, with her Saturday night out with Sasha culminating in nothing more than Sasha passing out on her couch by two a.m. Rylie spent Sunday doing the domestic chores that demanded her attention, watching Sunday afternoon football on TV and packing. She'd decided against spending the entire day with her father, instead needing some quiet time to herself. The upcoming week would be difficult and she needed some time to come to grips with where she'd be going and who she'd be with.

The only interesting things that had occurred were two emails she received, via way of Sasha. One was an invite to be Sasha's date to a charity fundraiser for Doctors-Without- Borders. Rylie had no idea why Sash invited her to accompany her when she could have gotten any gorgeous single guy of her choosing to attend. She supposed it was in support of Mark's efforts, so she would go along with it. But God, it sounded like torture. She didn't like to get dressed up and having to small talk over cocktails with wealthy-as-fuck people. It was so not her scene, but she placed the event date of November first on her calendar. She scowled thinking of the formal wear she'd be expected to wear.

The other item in her Inbox that sparked her interest was an email from Mitch's administrative assistant, Georgina Packard, who provided her the details of the upcoming trip to Miami. A car was to pick her up from her apartment first thing that Tuesday morning, taking her to Logan where she'd be flying American Airlines in First Class down to Miami International. The two details that appeared to be missing were her hotel accommodations and what kind of gym amenities it would provide. She would need this information in order to prepare Mitch's planned exercises for each day of the trip. She typed a very quick and formal email back to Georgina, who was hopefully in-the-know about her boss's arrangements.

Within ten minutes she had a response back, but it didn't come from Georgina Packard. The email address was from Camden Ventures, but it was an email directly from Mitch. He was apparently now in possession of her email address.

So much for privacy.

To: Rylie Hemmons
From: Mitchell Camden
Date: October 10
RE: Your Itinerary

Dear Miss Hemmons,

It pleases me greatly to know you'll be continuing in my rehabilitation and will be accompanying me to Miami. I can only assume you'll provide me with the same level of exceptional therapy I've come to expect from you.

To answer your question, you will not be staying in a hotel but in a private home that I've rented. I can assure you that it is fully stocked with all the necessary equipment you may need, as well as a pool, sauna and hot tub. Which I hope we can put to good use, for my therapy, of course.

I look forward to your exquisite care and your magical hands. Please contact me directly with any questions or concerns.

Yours Truly,
Mitch

PS: Please bring evening attire.

OMG!

Rylie was speechless as she finished reading the email a second time. Her level of anxiety had reached a tipping point after hearing about the Miami trip, but now it was full-scale panic as she'd learned she'd be isolated with Mitch in a rented house, and not in a hotel as she had originally expected.

She wished she had Sasha's confidence and could just go with the flow and not feel so self-conscious about the sleeping arrangements. And what about his comment on the evening attire? Her stomach was in knots as she looked over at the pile of clothes that she'd dumped out on her bed when she returned from Sasha's. The skimpy, one-shoulder sequined cocktail dress and silver Christian Louboutin three-inch sandals all but screamed, "Fuck Me!"

Rylie swallowed hard. She'd be fooling herself if she didn't admit to wanting Mitch to find her desirable when she wore it. She wanted to see his expression as he perused her body from head to toe, licking his lips to prove his hungry appetite for her.

Right there. That pissed her off. Thinking this way was not going to make the trip any easier. She could not afford to have these thoughts or feelings jumbling up her head. She had to remain professional and follow the rules on this trip. No dopey-ass commentary or fantasies from this point forward, she resolved.

Rylie typed out a response indicating she'd see him on Tuesday and sent it off. There, now that that was done and out of the way, she could go for her run and head over to her father's house for another night of football.

****

Mitch had been laser-focused on completing his required exercises over the weekend. He was nothing but obsessed with getting back to full-speed as soon as feasibly possible. In fact, he'd become comfortable walking without the aid of the crutch. He wondered if Rylie would be proud of the progress he'd made in just one week. The knee brace was still securely worn, but his range and motion had improved considerably, allowing him to bend and squat with a higher degree of confidence. And truth be told, he felt his balls begin to reappear, his male ego taking a beating over the past few weeks having to rely on the aid of those fucking walking sticks.

With his therapy going well and most of his projects on track, his thoughts became consumed with the upcoming trip and spending time with Rylie. She was constantly invading his thoughts throughout the week and he smiled to himself as he conjured up the image of her reading his email the day before. Knowing what he now knew of her and her fiery little temper, he could envision her huffy response. Her hands would be drawn to her hips, her mouth scrunched in a haughty gesture and it was more likely than not that some choice curse words would have been flying. He laughed at the image he procured in his head. If only he could have told her in person, he would have grabbed hold of those hips and sucked off those potty-words from her lips with his mouth, making her forget all about her hostility toward him.

For some reason, her combative reactions to his moves turned him on like no one's business. Of course he wanted to sleep with her. Why wouldn't he? She was smart, beautiful and had the most perfect ass he'd ever seen. But there was more to it with her. She held his interest in a way no one else had before. Maybe it was the chase. She didn't throw herself at him like most of the women he was with or dated. Nah, she was a challenge to his ego with a Capital C. And his hopes were to get the time to really know her while they were in Miami together.

The Coral Gables home he had rented for the Miami trip belonged to his Yale-friend-turned-investment banker, and was a four bedroom, four-and-a-half bath waterfront Mediterranean Villa, complete with a sixty-five foot double-decker luxury yacht anchored off the private dock overlooking Biscayne Bay. With the yacht at his disposal, Mitch had already planned a day of sailing and snorkeling out to Key Biscayne. He enjoyed nothing more than being outdoors in the great wide-open. When he yearned for relaxation, all he needed was the earth, the sky and the water to find his nirvana. Although he would be forced to forego the jet skiing due to the condition of his knee, he figured the snorkeling would be a pleasurable way to enjoy the warm waters of the Bay during his visit.

He was uncertain of Rylie's interest in the water, or boats for that matter, but he was betting that the romantic dinner he had planned on board the yacht would get her interested in something else.

Hopefully him.

CHAPTER TEN

The black Towne Car had pulled up and was waiting outside Rylie's apartment at exactly nine a.m. Tuesday morning. Rylie came out of her apartment door and a well-suited chauffer gladly accepted the two Louis Vuitton bags from her, and placed them in the opened trunk.

"Good morning, Miss Hemmons. I'm Lenny your driver," he cheerfully introduced himself. She half expected him to break into the *Zip-a-Dee-Doo-Dah* song for as big as the smile he was giving her. God she despised happy people this early in the morning, especially before she had coffee. "Is this everything for you?"

Lenny appeared to be in his late fifties, a tad on the short side and a little paunch in the middle, but gave Rylie a warm and eager smile as he loaded her bags and opened the door for her. Settling in on the black leather seat, a wave of disappointment hit her as she found the car to be empty. She had thought, maybe even slightly hoped, that she might find Mitch waiting for her, but then came to the conclusion he may have already headed to Miami. After all, this was a business trip for him and he may have pressing matters to attend to before she arrived.

Leaning her head back on the car seat, she let out a breath that she'd been holding in before she got in the car. At least now she could close her eyes and relax before her trip. She'd never really enjoyed the thought of flying. It wasn't a fear so much as a severe form of paranoia and dread. The feeling stalked her any time she had to get on a plane, which was only twice before. She'd worry over whether the pilot had too much to drink the night before, or if they had gotten enough sleep, or whether the mechanics thoroughly checked all the nuts and bolts. And don't even get her on the topic of weather disturbances. The first sign of turbulence, she began praying the *Our Father* and gripped the seat rests so tightly her fingers would go numb.

Thankfully, Sasha came to the rescue once again on this trip. Not only had she supplied all of the luggage and most of the clothing for the entire three-day trip, but she also prescribed some Valium for Rylie to take right before take-off. Just one little teeny, tiny pill would help soothe her nerves and calm her potential anxiety. There was no way in hell she was going to have a nervous breakdown in from of Mitch Camden!

"Miss Hemmons, we'll be arriving at the airport in less than twenty minutes," Lenny said from behind the wheel, as he shot a glance over his shoulder at Rylie. "We just have one stop on our way."

"Oh, all right. That works for me. Thanks for letting me know."

Rylie continued to look out the car window at the passing cars and people on the streets, not really paying much attention to where Lenny was taking her. A few minutes later, the car pulled up alongside a tall historic brick building in what appeared to be near the Boston Common area. Rylie glanced out the window, noticing a coffee shop sign above the entryway into the building. Confused over the stop, she rolled down the back window a crack to get a better look up and down the street, watching Lenny get out of the car. Her eyes followed him in the rearview window until he stood next to a man out on the sidewalk. There, standing outside the door, holding two cups of coffee in each hand and his bags at his side, was Mitch.

The sight of him, dressed casually in form-fitting jeans that hugged him in all the right places and a long-sleeved T-shirt, had her catching her breath. This is exactly what she secretly hoped for, but really hadn't wanted. A warm sensation erupted throughout her body, creating a tight knot in her stomach, which was both tense and exhilarating. She looked down at her hands, which were fisted on her legs, clammy and shaking ever-so slightly.

Get ahold of yourself, you wuss.

Rylie had spent the last week psyching herself up, planning out exactly how she would keep her distance and remaining firmly within the professional lines she'd drawn when it came to the purpose of this trip. She could not think about Mitch in any other manner than as her client. Her patient. Her livelihood. She would avoid staring at him and ogling his firm, muscular legs, or his chiseled abs. Or his beautiful, panty-dropping smile. No, she would need to think of him only a job.

Rylie nervously adjusted herself against the back of the seat, silently reassuring herself that she could handle this, and then checked herself in the rearview mirror. Her hair was hanging loosely past her shoulders, her eyes seemed bright, although she could see the dark circles of wariness underneath. She turned to look out the window, as Lenny spoke animatedly to Mitch out on the sidewalk, their laughter erupting over something Mitch said. She smiled slightly at the sound of his laugh. As Lenny picked up the bags and opened the back door, Mitch caught her eye as he walked toward the car to join her in the backseat.

Immediately the car was filled with his clean, brisk scent, a slight hint of the spicy aftershave he must have used that morning. She breathed in and sighed longingly, but caught herself before Mitch had a chance to notice. He smelled delicious and utterly edible. She quickly worked to push that thought, and any of all thoughts of her eating him, out of her head. *Gah.*

Mitch sat back into the seat and handed her a to-go cup of steaming hot coffee. "Careful, it's hot." He smiled at her as he turned to place his seatbelt around his hips low and tight. She wondered if he meant it as a dimly veiled innuendo. Why did she even have to go there? He turned again to catch Rylie staring at his lap, a slightly bemused look on his face. Her eyes met his and she felt her face warm.

"You blush as bright as the sun," he remarked. "I like that. And I hope I got your coffee how you like it, too. Two sugar cubes and a dash a cream, right?"

Stunned into an awkward silence, she turned her head to take a sip of the coffee, then remembered her manners. "Mmm…thank you for the coffee. It's just how I take it." She considered for a moment how in the world he'd know that bit of information. Her head swung back around to find his eyes on her. "Wait, how would you possibly know that? That freaks me out."

"I have my ways. There are a number of things I know about you, IQ. I'm an inquisitive mind and I need to know these little insights about the people I work with. It's a way of building trust."

"Trust, huh? How exactly do you build trust like this? You could've just asked me instead of being so creepy."

Mitch nodded his head. "Fair point. I can see how you'd think it was a bit intrusive of me. But that's just my method and how I work. And it's not like I had to do any stalking because your receptionist Claire was extremely helpful in answering my questions," he chuckled, taking a sip of his coffee. "Yes, she's very helpful in that department."

Rylie grunted over hearing the name of the clinic receptionist. She'd never been a big fan of Claire and found her to be ditzy and a little too flirty with the male clients. In fact, Sasha had mentioned a recent example of Claire's impropriety when she asked one of their married clients if he was a swinger. Yeah, not the sharpest tool in the shed. Luckily the client had played along and was a good sport, but Sasha had to put her on notice.

She let out a frustrated sigh, shaking her head in disgust. "Geez, it's so nice to know my privacy is in such good hands. I'll have to chat with my motor-mouthed assistant when I get back. But that's beside the point. Mitch, if you're so interested in me…or rather, if you're interested in building my trust, why don't you just come right out and ask me directly?"

She internally reprimanded herself for even asking that question. She shouldn't even care why. This was supposed to be strictly business and she didn't want him to get to know her any more than he already did. All she should care about was building the trust and rapport that comes with being his physical therapist. His recovery was partially in her hands and he had to trust her to know what she was doing and have his best interests in mind as she devised her therapy plans. That's all. Nothing more should be required. At least, that's what she kept telling herself.

"Well, I would have if you hadn't chosen to run and hide from me. I think you made it pretty clear after calling me an asshole, which I take exception to, that you weren't interested in building any kind of relationship with me, either personal or professional. So I had no other choice, really. Am I wrong?" He tilted his head toward her, his hair swaying over his forehead. She had the sudden urge to run her fingertips through it.

How he was able to turn the blame on her after he was in the wrong, was beyond comprehension, but Rylie felt the guilt boiling up to the surface, ready to gush like a geyser.

Before she could respond, Mitch turned to face her, his knee bent up on the seat, brushing up against her leg. A burst of heat sparked up Rylie's leg, as if someone had struck a match using her body to light the fuse.

His hand came down to gently rest on her knee. "Listen, Ry. It should be fairly apparent that I'm more than a little attracted to you. I think you're the sexiest woman I've ever met. Every time you've touched me, I get turned on. I can't help it and I'm not ashamed to admit it. But I am sorry if I made you feel uncomfortable. I get it – you need to keep boundaries in your line of work and I'm making that difficult," he reached over to grab Rylie's hand and place it in his, leaving them resting above her knee. She looked at his lips as they curved up into his trademark smile and the dimple in his chin that beckoned her to inch closer. Instead, she shifted further away from him, as if he were a threat. In a way, he was.

"So here's my plan. I'm going to dazzle you over the next three days. I want to prove to you that I'm not the asshole you think I am.

After our trip, when we return to Boston, I will play nice and continue my therapy with Carmen, instead of you – but if all goes well, you'll find out you want me as much as I want you and we'll see where it goes from there. What do you think?"

Bringing her hand up to his mouth, he turned it over, palm up, and kissed the center. Rylie, surprised with Mitch's gesture, jerked her arm back and twisted her fingers together in her lap.

She felt trapped in the small, confining space in the backseat with Mitch far too close for comfort. And he was being utterly open and honest about his intentions. That wasn't what Rylie had expected and it was throwing her off her game, creating cracks in the walls she was trying to erect. It definitely had her wondering more about his ethics and whether he really wasn't as much of a player as Mark had led her to believe. But then again, maybe he was really just a wolf in sheep's clothing.

His plan did have her seriously considering the possibility of letting her guard down just a little to see what would happen over the next three days. Why couldn't she have some fun and stop being such a worrywart over her code of ethics and career? Her brain was telling her to resist – don't give in, never give up! Don't let him close and you won't get hurt, physically or emotionally. But her heart, and her body, ached for him. She wanted him to make a move and take her right now in the backseat and make her forget all about her moral standards. Forget about the fears that wrapped her tight in a cocoon of self-loathing and despair.

Nope. Not going to happen. Those fences she had built were meant to protect her from feeling these things. To keep her safe. Her body stiffened and she sat up ramrod straight.

"I think you're full of yourself and have a pretty damn big ego. I guess I should be flattered, because I'm sure most women would jump at the chance to be wined and dined and swept off to paradise for a three-day affair. But I'm not most women, Mitch. I'm me. And I've worked hard to establish my career and I'm not willing to tarnish my reputation with a fling with a gorgeous client. Maybe that means nothing to you, but it does to me."

The car slowed and came to a stop curbside at the American Airlines departures terminal. Lenny had exited the car and came around to open both doors for Rylie and Mitch. Grabbing her handbag and carry-on, she walked over to stand next to Mitch who was directing Lenny where to put the bags. Turning to Rylie, he gave her one of his lazy, melt-your-heart smiles.

"So, you think I'm gorgeous, huh?"

Rylie snorted and stifled a laugh. "That's all you heard from what I just said? Really, your ego is insufferable."

He chuckled and gestured her forward, placing his hand on the small of her back to lead her in to the concourse. "At least that's a start. I can work with maybe. And Rylie…"

She stopped and turned to look at him over her shoulder. Mitch was inches from her and she could feel the heat from his body. His lips twisted in his disarming smile. "I know you're not like most women. That's what I like about you. You're not only incredibly beautiful, but you're genuinely intriguing. You're a challenge to my ego. And I'm going to have a helluva great time finding a way to overcome that challenge."

His arm came up and around her shoulders to escort her through security. "Miss Hemmons, are you ready for this?"

Rylie swallowed hard, trying to absorb what he had just said and wondered if he was asking if she was ready for the flight and trip or for him and his fool's plan.

"I honestly have no idea."

CHAPTER ELEVEN

The flight from Boston to Miami was a three hour and twenty minute flight. Just enough time for Mitch to work on some projects that required his attention, respond to the emails that were marked High Priority by Georgina, and to watch Rylie as she slept in the seat next to him.

It almost pained him to sit in such close proximity to Rylie and be unable to reach out and caress her soft, sun-kissed skin and her long, silky amber tresses. During their therapy appointments, she had worn her hair pulled back and out of the way, but today she wore it down, allowing the locks to cascade down her back. He could smell the lavender and honeysuckle scent from her shampoo and it was all he could do to restrain himself from running his fingers through her hair, inhaling her sweet fragrance.

Rylie had fallen asleep almost instantaneously once they had boarded the plane, which he found amusing. Traveling as often as he did, Mitch could never fully relax on a flight and frequently had materials to review or presentations to prepare for, so sleeping wasn't an option. As he watched Rylie breathing quietly, her chest rising and falling in a soft rhythmic pattern, he reflected on what she mentioned prior to their flight about the nervousness she experienced when flying.

They had just boarded and found their seats in the second row of First Class when Rylie pulled out a small vial of pills and a bottle of water. Mitch eyed her dubiously.

Rylie shrugged and swallowed a small white tablet. "What? I have a fear of flying and one Valium helps calm my nerves so I don't freak out and make a fool of myself."

"Fear of flying? I guess it surprises me to know you fear *anything*."

"Yeah, I'm one tough bitch," she snickered, swallowing the pill and replacing the lid on the water bottle. "Let's just say I've conquered most all my other fears, but flying in a big-ass tin can is not one of them. Too many what-ifs and unknowns. And let's face it, the law of averages is bound to catch up with you one day."

Mitch scratched his head and looked at her nonplussed. "And I certainly didn't figure you to be a Debbie Downer. I suppose you'll tell me next that I might very well get infected with some mutating disease if I use the head on the airplane, too?"

Rylie laughed and shrugged her shoulders. "Roll the dice and take your chances…but don't say I didn't warn you!"

Her sedative kicked in about twenty minutes later, prior to even taking off. Mitch had secretly hoped they'd have time for conversation during the flight, but found that watching her sleep proved to be much more entertaining and arousing.

Her side profile was model perfect, with her heart-shaped face offset by high cheekbones that narrowed down to a classic chin. The gentle slope of her nose culminated in a graceful button tip and her mouth, her full, sensuous lips that were a perpetual glossy pink and were at the moment slightly parted as her head leaned against the window.

Yes, she was beautiful and sexy. Mitch had had beautiful and sexy women before but they never held his interest for long, not that it really mattered, since he was not interested in getting into any form of a relationship. Rylie captivated him. He liked the steel she projected and her spine, never taking shit from anyone. And she was funny, with a biting humor and sharp tongue. She bickered, gave him lip and could be down-right crass with him, but never to the point of crossing the line. In fact, it surprised him that she was so uptight about her professional boundaries. He understood her logic, but it was frustrating that she was denying the attraction between them. She almost seemed to be scared of getting close. It seemed illogical, knowing her tough exterior.

A sudden jolt of turbulence had Rylie nearly jumping out of her seat, her hands grabbing tightly onto the armrests, her body jerking upright. He watched as her heavy eyelids opened half-mast, as she slowly recognized her surroundings and breathed a sigh of relief. Mitch took the opportunity to raise the armrest between them and patted his lap, giving Rylie permission to lay down.

Too drowsy to protest, she placed her head down across Mitch's lap and sank her face into the warm denim material. Mitch knew this would be a bad idea, knowing he'd be hard in seconds, but it felt too good to change direction now. And he was well aware that this was a one-time event, knowing full well if she hadn't been blissed out on her little dose of heaven, her head would be nowhere near his leg.

Adjusting himself slightly, he leaned back in his seat and with nowhere else for his hands to go, he placed one hand on Rylie's head. Brushing away a few strands that had fallen across her face, Mitch slowly began to stroke her hair, which was fanned out in silky wisps across his leg, weaving his fingers in and around, trailing from her scalp down to her mid-back. His hand stopped just shy of the bottom of her cream colored top, which had come loose from the black leggings she wore. Unable to stop it, his hand skimmed down to the curve of her hips, where it rested and his eyes scanned to view a scrap of baby blue lace peeking out from her waistband.

Fuuuck.

Before his thoughts even caught up with him, his fingers began to toy with the lace, agilely grazing the soft backside, just inches from her firm ass. He continued his leisurely play until Rylie let out a soft mewling sound. His fingers stilled momentarily, until she snuggled closer to him, her breasts pressing up against his hard leg. He stiffened, feeling the uncomfortable bulge straining against his jean zipper.

Mitch cursed under his breath as he considered his options. One, he could very carefully move her off his lap and back up into her seat, where he'd be freed from the agony of her face planted securely near his dick. *Unlikely– his dick definitely liked her presence there.*

Okay, idea number two. He'd leave her head on his lap and he would try to conjure up memories of his grandmother baking him cookies when he was in Boy Scouts. Yes, that's it. Thinking of Grandma would help reduce the temptation of touching the sleeping beauty on his lap and keep his thoughts wholesome and pure. But it wouldn't eliminate them entirely. Grandma or no Grandma, Rylie's sprawled body lying across his lap, snug and tight, had his hands itching to roam.

That left option number three. He could endure the torture and enjoy the secret thrill of knowing that Rylie was wearing the sexiest lace panties he'd ever seen and with the hope that he would see more of it in the not-so-distant future. Yes, he decided. He would sit and suffer in silence, with his hard-on the size of Florida with no hope of relief, and relish in the sheer fact that she was there with him.

He smiled at the thought. Last week, had she had her way, she never would have set eyes on him again. She ran from him. Ran from the inevitable. But he wouldn't lose the fight. He found a way to get her back, if only for a few days, and under cleverly disguised pretenses. Now they were on their way to Miami and he planned to take full advantage of their time together. He had no doubt he'd be seeing those lace panties soon enough…

****

"Please return all tray tables and seats to their upright position and prepare for landing." The flight attendant announced loudly over the microphone.

Rylie slowly stirred awake, her head still in a fog. Her eyes flicked open, blinking once and then twice, as she lifted her head trying to recall where she was. Planting her hands on something very hard and very firm, she pushed herself to a sitting position. Realization struck her like a lightning bolt. Her eyes directed to the spot on Mitch's lap where she'd just been napping, a small wet stain graced the leg of his jeans, just south of his crotch.

His laugh had her jerking her head back to look at him. "For the record, that wet spot is your drool…definitely not me."

Rylie was mortified as she looked at him in horror. She had no recollection of falling asleep or how she ended up laying on his lap or even how long she'd been sleeping, but the drool spot she conveniently left for him was a visual demarcation of her embarrassment.

Mitch returned the armrest down to its original place and pushed his seat forward. Using his shirtsleeve, he rubbed his jeans where she had just inhabited, trying to erase the damp spot.

"I have to say, that was the sweetest two hours of torture I've ever endured."

Rylie's cheeks flushed a bright pink. "Oh my God, I feel like a complete dumbass. Why didn't you just wake me up or push me off?"

He gave her a speculative look, his eyebrows raised in question. "Why would I want to do that? Any man with a chance to have a beautiful woman on his lap would do the same thing. My little friend here feels a bit deceived, however," Mitch chuckled as he bent his head to aim at his crotch. "When a woman's mouth is that close, he normally thinks he's getting some dessert. But don't worry – he won't hold it against you…well, not unless he gets lucky." His tone was joking, but she could hear the desire twisting through his words.

Rylie's blush deepened as she looked away and covered her face in her hands, groaning audibly. "Are you seriously trying to embarrass me or just get under my skin with your not-so-subtle sexual commentary?"

Mitch stood up to grab their bags from the overhead bins and handed Rylie her carry-on. "Neither, really. I was just hoping it might turn you on. That would make us even right about now."

She glared at him as she accepted her bag and placed it on her shoulder. Okay, so maybe the feel of his thick, muscular thighs did have her obsessing over the thought of running her hands up and down his legs, which would make any hot-blooded woman lust out. And it wasn't like all his references to his over-eager dick didn't have her body heating up just a little bit. She wasn't dead. She would never admit it to him, but it was kind of hot.

She shook her head, trying to make her scowl look more realistic than it felt. "Not a chance. Maybe your charm and blatant sexual innuendo's work on other women, but you'll have to try harder than that for me." She silently kicked herself as soon as she let the words fly. Why the hell would she say that? It offered the possibility of him having a chance to get with her. Did she want that potential growing between them?

Mitch turned back to look at her as they departed the plane. A gleam in his eye told her exactly what he was thinking.

"Well then. It's a good thing I work *very hard* for the things I want, IQ. Sounds like I might have a chance with you after all, since I'm pulling out all the stops this week."

Mitch ducked his head as he exited the plane and smiled back at Rylie.

"Oh, and by the way. I like the blue panties you're wearing."

Rylie nearly tripped over her feet as she saw the devilish grin and his dimple appear and then disappear as he walked ahead of her and off the plane.

Holy shit. How did he know the color of her underwear?

CHAPTER TWELVE

The embarrassment that Rylie felt was soon replaced with awe as she and Mitch made their way along Miami Highway One in the white BMW Z4 convertible Mitch had rented. The Atlantic Ocean was a swirling mass of blue and green, the warm Florida sun sparkling across the water, waves and sand.

Salty ocean air wafted through the car as they continued south along Biscayne Boulevard en route to Coral Gables. Rylie couldn't help but smile as she felt the warm breeze hit her face and whip her hair behind her, a waving silk flag of chestnut streaming in every direction. She stole a glance over at Mitch, his eyes hidden behind a dark pair of Ray-Ban aviators and a baseball cap shadowing his face. What she could see as she covertly glanced at his profile was the golden-hued stubble that blanketed his jaw and his mouth that was upturned in a gentle smile. He was obviously enjoying the drive. He looked sexy and relaxed.

They rode in a comfortable silence through south Miami for close to twenty minutes until they drove past a sign welcoming them to Coral Gables. As they drove the palm tree lined streets, Rylie was captivated by the sheer opulence and majesty of the multi-million dollar mansions they passed. Turning down Harbor Point, Mitch maneuvered around twists and turns until they came to a gated entry, not unlike his own home back in Boston. Leaning out of the car, Mitch entered the code and the large wrought-iron doors opened to a long winding driveway. As he stretched out over the car door, his T-shirt lifted to expose his sleek lower back. Rylie swallowed hard, willing herself to look away.

At the end of the drive sat the largest and most beautiful Mediterranean-style, red-shingled roof mansion she had ever seen. Her jaw dropped as she turned to look Mitch, who had just put the car in park and gotten out to stretch his legs.

"Please tell me you don't own this place."

Mitch grinned, stripping off his shades to look up at the home looming in front of them. Shaking his head, he picked up a bag from the trunk and slipped it over his shoulder.

"I wish. She's a beauty," he smirked, pointedly directing his response to Rylie as he said it. "The house belongs to my old college buddy, Richard. He bought his place a few years ago and is now in the midst of a divorce. I won't go into details, but let's just say he did a lot of *entertaining* down here without his wife, who later became aware of all of his transgressions. Now he has to sell the house as a part of the divorce. He only put it up on the market a few weeks ago, but said I could crash here during my trip, since it's not in use."

"Too bad for him, the scumbag. But on the bright side, his loss is our gain, I'd say." She reached into the trunk and pulled out her bags and headed into the front entry behind Mitch, who entered yet another code into the key box.

His comments about his friend had her wondering about Mitch's past and whether he had been married. She only knew he wasn't married now, but that didn't mean there hadn't been a woman in his life before this. In fact, aside from his penchant for flirting, she had no idea whether he was a serial dater, a monogamous lover, or just a one-night stand kind of man. She shouldn't care, really. But even so, her curiosity was piqued and a small spark of jealously ignited in her belly. *Stupid, stupid, stupid.*

The gate door led into a small Mediterranean courtyard laden with a Grecian-style ornate fountain and ivy snaking up the sides of the walls. Mitch unlocked the glass double doors as he gestured for Rylie to lead the way. She stopped short as she entered, causing Mitch to nearly plow into her backside when she stopped just inside the foyer. She stood in complete astonishment as she soaked in the scenery around her. A one-eighty degree view of the ocean spanned the room, which was decorated in bright white furniture, accented with gold and red pillows and rugs. The entire back of the home was wall-to-wall windows, and sliding glass doors leading out to the pool and patio.

Letting her bags drop to the floor, she walked toward the back and opened the sliding door, stepping out to the patio. White covered lounge chairs circled the underground pool, which was shaped like a club card, and led to a Jacuzzi that overlooked a private dock oceanside. A very large yacht, docked on the slip, bobbed up and down as the waves caressed its bows. The water was so crystal blue, and the sunlight glittered off the expanse of ocean like thousands of diamonds on display. Her hand came up to shield her eyes from the brightness.

Rylie exhaled as she took in the magnificence of her surroundings. "Holy shit, Camden. I think I may be in the market for a new home. You think your friend will give me a good deal?"

Mitch had sidled up behind her, making it obvious that he was admiring both the view of the water and Rylie's backside.

"I'm sure he'd be willing to consider a lower price if I put in a good word for you." He slid his arm around her waist, his hand moving down to lightly rest on the curve of her hip. He let out a roar of laughter when she jerked away from his grip with lightning fast speed.

"I was just testing the waters," he joked, shrugging his shoulders in feigned innocence. "And speaking of waters, get a load of the yacht. She's a sixty-five foot *Marquis* that Rich bought a few years back. He took me out on it the last time I came down for a visit. Wait until you see inside. It has three staterooms, two heads, a fly-bridge, state-of-the-art galley, an upper and lower deck…she's impressive."

Rylie found it amusing how excited Mitch seemed to get over the description of the boat. She'd been out on her uncle's fishing boat in the past, but never on a luxury yacht like the one in front of her. Curious as to the name of the boat, she walked to the stern to find out its name. *Pussy Whipped.* Well, that explained a lot.

"It's a wonder his wife didn't catch on a little sooner to his extra-curricular activities."

Mitch chuckled and shook his head. "Rich was always a cad, even in college. He never had less than a few women at the same time. There's no way Belinda wasn't aware of what she was getting into when she married him. And if she didn't, well…at least now she's a much wiser and wealthier woman."

Rylie couldn't help her look of dismay. "So you condone that sort of behavior from married men?"

"Wait, what? Of course not. How did you possibly deduct that from what I just said? I was just stating a fact about Rich and Belinda. I have nothing to do with my friend's adulterous ways. He and I are nothing alike," he emphasized. "I believe in monogamy and honesty when I'm in a relationship, if you must know."

She looked at Mitch and then back at the boat, giving it one final assessment. She didn't mean to accuse Mitch of the same thing, but it did help to reveal his feelings on faithfulness and honesty in a relationship. It didn't change anything, but it did quiet that jealousy monster that popped up earlier.

"Good to know…thanks for sharing." Rylie flung her hair back and turned to walk back to the house. "So, since I am here to work, I think it might be a good idea to take advantage of the pool for your therapy today. Want to give it a try?"

Mitch's face drew up in a broad, playful smile.

"With or without our suits?"

****

Feeling entirely too self-conscious, Rylie stepped out on her second floor bedroom balcony, clad in her blue Nike one piece, a towel wrapped securely around her waist. Although she had brought two other suits that belonged to Sasha, she chose to wear the more functional suit while working with Mitch on his exercises. Even though it covered all of her torso and chest, it was still revealing enough, hugging every curve of her body and accentuating her cleavage, which she was currently trying to contain with her arms strapped tightly across her chest.

From her perch above, she could see Mitch sitting by the side of the pool, lazily swinging his lower legs back and forth, creating small circular whirlpools. His long, lean and very muscular torso was exposed to her. She felt like a voyeur from her hidden spot high above, watching him with interest as he tested the waters. He was clearly enjoying the sun's rays, as it cast its light across his body, lighting him up in a warm glow. As he bent over the side to scoop some water up in his cupped hand, she noticed the way his back muscles tightened and released. She could practically feel them strain, taught and tense, as she ran her hands up and down their length. He was a beautiful Adonis.

Turning to leave, Rylie stubbed her toe against an ill-placed planter with some sort of fragrant floral arrangement and let out a small curse. She stood stock still, hoping he didn't hear her muffled cry. She timidly peered back to find Mitch looking up at her with an amused grin, his eyes shaded by his hand.

"Liking the view from up there, Rapunzel?"

She smiled tightly, feeling chagrined that she was caught watching him.

"How could I not? The ocean is magnificent!" she chirped, easing out of her discomfort. He was now watching her intently, his eyes grazing over her body. She coughed to clear her throat, which had dried up with his seductive perusal. "I'll be right down."

Maneuvering herself around and away from the vicious planter, she stepped back into the room and made her way down the stairway to the doors leading to the back patio. This place was paradise. The beautiful surroundings and the tropical atmosphere enveloped her senses, melting away the stress and embarrassment from moments before. She inhaled, closing her eyes to let the warm air infiltrate her thoughts, calming her like a drug. She needed to let go of this stupid fear that gripped her like a vice, twisting and pressing her down, like the hands of her assailant. This stranglehold had controlled her life over the last five years and it wasn't a way to live. She couldn't be that person any longer. She needed her freedom.

Her career and her friends and family had been her life preserver all this time, giving her shelter and protection, but preventing her from breaking out of the chains she'd so tightly clung to. As she considered the way she was feeling toward Mitch, she realized she should feel lucky to be in this position, where she could work for and in the company of a gorgeous man in a tropical paradise, away from the stress and triviality of the real world. She should enjoy his flirtatious remarks and playful antics, instead of remaining bitter and angry over what she couldn't have. Why couldn't she just let loose a little bit and enjoy the moment? Revel in his flirtatious and salacious nature?

Mitch seemed genuinely interested in her and hadn't done anything to prove otherwise. So why not just go with the flow…let the cards fall where they may? Be a carefree Rylie and not let the tough and rigid Rylie get in the way of fun. She smiled to herself, nodding in agreement at her decision, as she stepped out into the hot sunlight and caught sight of Mitch lying flat out against the colorful tiles of the pool deck.

Taking a deep breath, she took three quick steps forward, letting the towel drop to the floor and literally plunged in. The waves from her entry splashed up and across his legs and chest, startling him to an upright position.

"Shit! Give a guy some warning next time."

Rylie sprang back up, arching her head back and slipping her hands through her wet hair to smooth it back and out of her face. Water dripped from her long, dark lashes and the waves she made with her spirited entry lapped against her body. She gave Mitch a buoyant smile.

"You just going to sit there all day and stare at me or get in here and do this thing?"

"I was just waiting on you, IQ," he winked, sliding down the edge and submerging into the pool's depths. "Looks like you're back to your old bossy and sassy ways."

She caught herself rolling her eyes and grinned. Swimming over to the edge of the pool, she grabbed a bag she'd brought out earlier and pulled out some water weights, a kick board and small weighted balls.

"Sex toys?"

Smirking, she threw one of the balls to the end of the pool. It sunk to the bottom. "Don't you wish…now, go fetch."

He gave her a WTF look.

"Oh come on, Mitch. Didn't you ever play this game as a kid where you'd sink a bunch of toys in the water and then race to retrieve them? My brother and I used to have these competitions with his toy soldiers to see who could grab the most the fastest. Of course, we also ended up with a lot of head injuries after we'd slam our heads together by trying to beat the other to the bottom of the pool. But hey…I won't try that on you today," she laughed and then swooshed her hands through the water toward the other end. "Now, get your ass moving. You need to work and activate your quad muscles. Aquatic therapy is the best, most non-impact method of rebuilding the strength. You're going to do this ten times or until I say otherwise."

Mitch stood there for a moment a bit dumbfounded, tilting his head to the side and eying her speculatively.

"I have to say, IQ. I do enjoy this bossy side of you. And I like the idea of a little one-on-one competition. You up for a challenge?"

"Aren't you afraid I'll kick your ass?" she teased, shoving him lightly in his shoulder.

"I'd have to say I wouldn't mind losing to you a damn bit."

Rylie enjoyed the banter they had going, and found that by letting herself enjoy the moment, she felt happy. That feeling had long eluded her when it came to being around a man. Whatever it was with Mitch, whether it was his charm or sex appeal, just got to her and made her feel…wanted.

"Challenge accepted. But not until you've completed five pick-ups. That way, I can wear you out and beat your ass with ease."

Swimming back over to the other side of the pool, she pulled herself out of the water and onto the ledge. Grabbing the remaining balls in her hand, she threw them all in. "Ready, set, go!"

****

It was as if someone flipped a switch in Rylie, who was now suddenly joking and laughing with Mitch, freely sharing stories about her childhood and playing around in the pool, clearly relaxed and happy. To Mitch, the biggest turn-on was an easy flirtation with a beautiful woman who could just as casually lob over some "*That's what she said*" one-liners just as quickly as he could. This new Rylie was even more beautiful, with her brown sugar eyes glittering every time she laughed and smiled.

The afternoon in the pool proved to be both fun and functional. She did do what she said she was going to do and beat him three out of five times in the dive-and-catch race, but he got her back the final round. She'd thrown the ball to the end of the pool, counting to three and both speeding off, kicking and flailing towards the goal. About half way down the length of the pool, Mitch knew he was losing his lead and allowed her to swim past him. He stood in admiration as he watched the way her legs kicked gracefully behind her and her lithe body maneuvered through the water.

The tight blue Lycra suit clung to her body in every perfect curve. It fit snug between her creamy thighs, wrapping around her small waist and around the perfect shape of her ass. Her breasts were round and supple, more than a handful, he anticipated. Her nipples formed against the material, crying out to be pinched and tweaked between his competent fingers, and bathed by his tongue. He shook his head to clear his thoughts, realizing it may be a lost cause. Just being in her presence made him ache to be inside of her, to feel her underneath him. But he knew he had to take this slow. For some reason, she was protective of the boundaries she'd created and seemed firm on the rules she'd set between them. But rules were meant to be broken.

A few seconds later, Rylie popped out of the water, hand raised in the air, clutching her red ball in victory. "Eat it, Camden – I win again! Michael Phelps can kiss my ass."

Mitch couldn't help himself as he waded through the water, grabbing the top of her head with both hands and dunking her. Immediately letting go, she came up sputtering and laughing, protesting and calling him names.

"You're such a poor sport!" she gasped, making a show of coughing out the water she'd taken in. "You can't stand it that I'm just that good and kicked your ass." She pushed the strands of wet hair out of her face, sticking her tongue out at him in defiance.

He took a few steps closer, closing the distance between them, the water coming up past their chests. "I'm the loser? So says you. Even though you're the one prancing around in here with that perfect little ass of yours willing me to lose just so I can watch it and your beautiful body swim past me. I think you wanted me to lose just for that reason."

Water dripped off her chin down to the cliff of her breasts, as he watched her reaction, which had turned from joking to heated desire. In one quick fluid movement, Mitch had his arm securely wrapped around Rylie's waist, pulling her up against him. Her small gasp had him wanting to take her in the pool, pushing aside her suit and filling her in one smooth movement.

"You know what I do with poor winners, don't you?" he asked, a slight growl in his tone added for emphasis.

She blinked, her lips parting ready to say something, but instead she licked her lips.

He was tempted to take them. To possess them. To feast on her mouth like she was his only form of nourishment. To hell with the consequences.

Instead, he dunked her again and waded to the side of the pool as he hopped out. He was too close to losing it and had to get some distance from her, at least for now.

Grabbing one of the towels from the chaise lounge, he dried off and wrapped it around his waist. Taking the other towel, he unfolded it and with outstretched arms, invited her up. She was staring at him with a dumbfounded look, making him feel like a jerk. Nothing he could do about that right now if he wanted to keep sane.

"We should think about getting showered and dressed. We have a thing tonight with my business clients." Slipping the towel around her shoulders, Mitch backed away to avoid any further contact with her wet and slick body. "Tonight's casual, T-shirt and shorts if you want. Did you bring a cocktail dress for tomorrow night, like I suggested?"

"I wouldn't exactly call that a suggestion, more like an order," she snorted and rolled her eyes. "But yes, I did bring a dress."

Rylie took the towel, drying herself off as Mitch stared intently, watching her hands as she moved the towel up and down the length of her body and then over her head to dry her hair. Shaking it loose, it fell in wet, long waves down her back. It was all he could do to keep himself from grabbing a fistful of hair and yanking her into his arms and kissing her speechless.

"Are you going to tell me where we're going and who we'll be meeting? I'm not exactly sure why you're even taking me anywhere, because I'm not here as your date. And I'm certainly not your for-hire escort, Mr. Camden."

He was amused at how easily she could get riled up and huffy over something she thought was a slight. No, he didn't think of her as a paid escort, of course not. But a date? Hell, yes. That is definitely what he wanted and it peeved him that she made it sound so unwanted.

"So we have to put labels on this? Well then, let me tell you this," he said with a swell of annoyance, pressing in close to her, his mouth mere inches from her lips. It would take nothing for him to capture her mouth and lose himself in her.

"If you were here as my *date*, you wouldn't still be standing here in that dripping wet suit. I'd be getting you hot and wet in a whole different manner – with my hands, and mouth and tongue. And I have never, nor will I ever, need a paid escort of any kind. So, now that we're clear on those matters…I suggest you go get your ass ready."

With that he turned and walked toward the house, leaving her gaping after him.

CHAPTER THIRTEEN

The Miami sun was beginning to set, leaving a golden orange glow hovering over the city. Mitch still hadn't told her where they were headed, but they were driving towards the metropolis of Miami. It was still hot and sticky, a not-so-balmy eighty-five degrees, so Rylie had settled on a pair of white shorts and a blue tank top, very casual as he'd suggested, paired with some slip-on sandals. She'd pulled her hair back into a ponytail, mostly to get it off her neck, which was now beaded with sweat from the coastal humidity.

She was still a little more than miffed at Mitch for how he ended things out by the pool earlier. For once she'd let her guard down just a little and was beginning to enjoy the easy banter they had going on, joking and laughing together. But then he had to go and say something to remind her of what an asshole he could be, so Neanderthal and caveman like. The ego that man had was off the charts. She was not, nor would she ever be, one of his play toys that he could use and throw away after he'd gotten what he wanted. If it's one thing she knew more assuredly about herself was that she would always demand respect from a man. She would not be treated in any other manner.

Yet, for all the testosterone-filled aspects of his words earlier, he'd done nothing else to give her any indication that he was anything but respectful to women. He opened doors for her. He complimented her, although it was usually with a tint of sexual overtones. He also seemed to appreciate the level of her abilities as it related to her profession. So what was it that he did that always got under her skin? Was it the way he looked at her, the way his eyes seemed to drink her in, making her light up on the inside?

She figured this had to be the case, as he opened her car door for her to get in as they got ready to leave for the evening. Mitch had said nothing to her when she came out of her room to find him waiting for her near the kitchen. He'd simply given her a look and walked her out to the car. The only exception was the little hiss he emitted as she slid down into the leather car seat. He'd given her a long appreciative glance up and down her legs, a pained expression on his face. Good. He should feel a bit uncomfortable.

She playfully posed. "It might last longer if you took a picture."

He let out a little whistle and smiled a cheeky grin. "Be careful what you ask for. I just might."

They continued driving for a considerable distance, past downtown Miami and then into North Miami, as traffic slowed to a screeching halt on I-95. Swarms of cars, trucks and every other sized vehicle with flags and banners streaming from their windows, passengers yelling and cheering, as they all seemed to be heading in the same direction. She turned to Mitch, pulling at the front of his T-shirt to get a look at the logo, as his plan finally came into view for her.

"You're taking me to a Dolphins game?" she asked.

"Am I? Because this isn't a date, you know." He grinned his lopsided smile and motioned with his head to a bag down by her feet on the car floor. "Open it up. That's for you."

A gift? Well that was an unexpected surprise. Not something a typical asshole would do. Pulling the plain brown paper bag up to her lap, she opened it and pulled out an aqua and orange colored V-neck T-shirt with the Miami Dolphins logo on the front.

"I know you're a die-hard Patriots fan, but maybe tonight, since the Fins are playing the Jets, you can root for Miami." He shrugged nonchalantly, the edge of his mouth quirking up, indicating his mirth.

Rylie felt her body tingling with a joy and excitement she'd never felt before – the butterflies knotting themselves in a tiny spin cycle in her stomach. She'd never been surprised like this by anyone, not her brother or her father, or any of her friends, past or present. Even though it was only a T-shirt, for some reason it made her feel special and cared for. And it clearly showed that Mitch had a sweet side, even if he had practically admitted only wanting to get into her pants.

Rylie bit back a smile that was threatening to take over her face. She was in foreign territory and wasn't sure what the protocol was for a gift like this.

Leaning over the gear shift, she planted a sweet, chaste kiss on Mitch's cheek. He jerked back slightly, seemingly caught off guard by the display of affection.

"Thanks," she whispered in his ear, her voice thick with genuine gratitude. "This is kick ass."

"You're welcome," he grinned, looking over at Rylie, who was nearly squirming in her seat with excitement. "I wonder what you'll do when I tell you where our seats are? I'm sure it will be worth more than a kiss on the cheek," he mused, pulling into the parking lot and showing a pass to the parking attendant. She slapped him lightly on his arm.

"Don't get your hopes up, Camden…but where exactly are our seats?"

He hummed to himself and played coy, pulling into a parking spot and turning off the engine. "Do you know who the owners of the Miami Dolphins are?"

Rylie searched her recollection and nodded her head. "Yeah, I think it's a collection of several celebrities. Gloria Estefan, Marc Anthony, J-Lo and maybe even the Williams' sisters. And, oh yeah, Jimmy Buffett. Why?"

"You might just want to be careful not to sit in any of their assigned seats tonight, since we'll be in the owner's box."

Rylie's mouth dropped wide open. She was in complete and utter awe at the idea of watching a game in the owner's suite. "Holy shit – are you kidding me? H-How in the hell did you score that?"

Stepping out, Mitch walked around the car to open Rylie's passenger door, lending his hand to help her out. Keeping a tight hold on her hand, he pulled her close, lowering his head a few inches to meet her eye level.

"Let's just say I have friends in all the right places, IQ." Bringing her knuckles up to his mouth, he gave them a kiss, his eyes never leaving hers. He then turned her hand over, where he placed a kiss on the inside of her wrist, his tongue licking the same spot. "And I'm very glad I get the chance to pull in some favors for someone as beautiful as you."

She pulled her hand back, trying to look piqued as she moved ahead of him toward the stadium, but his compliment and his very hot mouth had affected her more than she would ever let on. Inside, she swooned. If the liquid heat that rushed between her thighs and low in her belly was any indication, Mitch Camden could definitely charm his way into her pants. And all it took was football tickets.

****

The suite was stocked full of free-flowing booze, a banquet of food, lively conversation with regular bursts of whoops and hollers, and of course, celebrities galore. Everywhere Rylie turned she'd end up face-to-face with a famous personality. Jay-Z and Bey popped in, along with their entourage in tow. Marc Anthony and a beautiful model came and went, barely saying a word through their enormous show of PDA. Gloria Estefan and her family were there. Gloria was full of smiles and constantly humming a beautiful tune in the midst of the chaos, her husband by her side the entire time.

Rylie was completely star struck. She wanted to be respectful of their privacy and space, but she so badly wanted to introduce herself to all of them, and tell them what a big fan she was of each of them. But she also was a guest of Mitch's and would not be making a fool out of herself in his presence. It didn't stop her from texting Dylan, though, and rubbing it in where she was and who she was with.

Filling up her plate at the buffet, she turned to see Mitch taking a sip of his beer, chatting with a man she hadn't met. He was talking to him, but his gaze was on her, as he smiled and raised his glass in a toast to her, beckoning her over to them. As she headed in his direction, she couldn't help but wonder how someone like Mitch would have these types of connections. Mitch was certainly an extremely bright and successful man, as well as rich and utterly handsome, but that didn't necessarily parlay into gaining access into the private parties of the rich and famous.

As if reading her mind, Mitch brought her in on the conversation and introduced her to the man he was speaking to.

"Rylie Hemmons, let me introduce you to Randall Tully. He's a business partner of mine. You can thank him for the exclusive back-stage access to tonight's game."

Transferring her plate to her left hand, she raised her right to shake his outstretched hand, which he brought to his mouth to kiss. "Miss Hemmons, so nice to meet you."

The difference between his kiss and the one Mitch had given her out in the parking lot was night and day. With Mitch, his kiss acted as the spark to her flame. He could start fires with the way he consumed her. As for Randall Tully, he turned her skin cold.

"Mr. Tully, it's a pleasure. I can't tell you what a big fan I am of football. And this is the first time I've been in a suite like this!"

"Please, call me Tully," he stated, holding on to her hand a little longer than necessary, sending a cold shiver up her arm. "I'm so glad that you could join us tonight. It's refreshing to have such a beautiful woman here who knows a thing or two about the sport."

Rylie saw Mitch scowl slightly at Tully's hand-holding and decided she'd play a little. She could tell he seemed annoyed, but she didn't know why. She hadn't done or said anything that would cause him to be irritated. It was then that she realized that she actually enjoyed the feeling she got from Mitch's interest. The way he looked at her, like she was something beautiful. He seemed to notice her, even in a room full of beautiful and interesting people, his eyes were always pinned on her.

While not particularly practiced in the art of flirting, she wanted to see what a little could do to Mitch's attention. "Tully," she cooed, trying her best not to sound ludicrous. "This is so much fun! It's really too kind of you to invite us into this private suite. You're much too generous. So how do you and Mitch know one another?" She flipped her hand through her hair, drawing a silent question from Mitch, his eyebrow quirked up.

Tully looked over to Mitch and gave him a little elbow to the arm. "Mitch and I are business partners. He's a genius when it comes to land development projects. In fact, we're currently working on one down here in Miami that will be a first ever of its kind."

It was obvious by his uncomfortable stance that Mitch didn't like being flattered or praised, but joined in to explain more about the project. "I met Tully and his partner John Albertson, or Albie, as we call him, through a mutual acquaintance. They were looking to renovate an area down here and establish it as an eco-friendly, all green and sustainable project, so they contacted me. It's been about three years in the making and we're just starting the ground breaking this week. That's why I'm down here."

Rylie nodded, flashing a bright smile. "Sounds interesting. I'd love to learn more about it," she said, directing her statement to Mitch. Tully, however, pounced on the opportunity.

"I'd be more than happy to show you around the site while you're here. When would be a good time for you, Rylie?"

Caught a little off guard, not realizing her mistake, she looked helplessly at Mitch, who was finishing off his beer. Taking a swig, he shrugged his shoulders and gave her a conniving smile. Great, she could tell she was now on her own after her little charade and was on the hook to try and get out of it. She didn't know Tully, and the feeling she got from him was a bit like that of a predator. Shiny on the outside, but slimy on the inside.

"Oh – well, I'm not really sure. I don't actually have any free time scheduled, since I am working and on Mitch's time. Mitch?" Rylie glared at Mitch now, giving him a pleading stare, looking for a way out. She didn't realize the type of game she'd gotten into, being a pawn between two equally competitive men. And from the looks of it, Mitch was going to make her work for it.

Grabbing another beer off the counter, Mitch opened the top and took a long drag. Before he could step in to intercede, Tully was off again.

"Well I could take you out tomorrow for lunch. Mitch has some meetings with the contractors and city council members, don't you Mitch?"

For a brief moment, Rylie thought Mitch looked like he would break the bottle with the force in which he gripped the neck. Gradually he loosened his hold and the tension eased from his fingers and he again shrugged his shoulders.

"Yeah, sure. If that's what Rylie wants, that's fine. As long as I get what I'm paying for, the rest of her free time is up to her."

Rylie jerked her head to give him an evil glare. How dare he make her sound like a prostitute! She was not *Pretty Woman*, for God's sake. And just like that, he was now back to asshole status, just as she was beginning to think Mitch was such a gentleman. She glared at him with as much intensity as she could muster.

Tully took full advantage of the opportunity. "Great, it's settled then." Taking her hand, he placed it to his lips again and then ran his fingers down the length of her arm in a very sexual gesture. She shivered, trying to ignore the disgust factor that emanated from his touch. "I'll see you, darling, tomorrow at ten. I'm looking forward to it."

Rylie tried to smile, but nearly bit through her tongue with the anger bubbling up from the depths of her being. Her words were strangled in her throat and she just nodded as the crowd cheered wildly at a play on the field, as Tully excused himself to watch the action.

She was seething as she went back to the bar and grabbed another beer. Sensing that Mitch was standing behind her, she stepped back and forcefully elbowed him in the chest.

"Ouch – what the hell was that for?" he asked, rubbing the spot where her elbow had slammed into him.

"Seriously? That thing you said to Tully" she whispered in a frantic hush. "You made it sound like I am some kind of a whore and you are paying for my *services*." She brushed past him, hissing an "asshole" under her breath and walked towards the outer terrace to watch the action on the field.

Mitch followed her to the stairs, gingerly limping down each step. Sitting down in the leather stadium chair next to her, he watched the anger slowly dissipate from her furrowed brow.

Placing his beer bottle in the seat holder, he ran his fingers through his hair and let out a loud sigh. "Shit. I'm sorry if it sounded like I was implying something other than the truth, but I got pissed off at how you were flirting with him. You were making googlie eyes at Tully and I didn't like it. Apparently I was little jealous…and I didn't like it."

A laugh erupted from Rylie, as the rest of the stadium cheered at an interception that had just been made by the Dolphins.

"Googlie eyes?" she asked, giggling harder. "I wouldn't even know what googlie eyes are, much less be able to make them! But seriously, you left me hanging out to dry back there. I don't know who the hell this Tully guy is, but he was looking at me like I'm his favorite candy. It was kind of creepy. And now I have to be expected to hang with him tomorrow? That's just great."

"I know, I'm sorry. I'll see if I can rearrange some of my meetings tomorrow so you won't have to go alone."

Mitch leaned over in his seat, his arm coming up behind Rylie's head, his breath coming out in a hot puff in her ear. "I can't say I blame the man, though," he said, his voice low and thick. "You are as sweet as candy."

Rylie turned to face him, as he gave her a sexy, lopsided grin. His smile made her stomach do backflips and it turned her on to hear him say it. But there was no way she'd ever admit it to him. Instead, she did the only thing that came naturally in a situation like this. Rylie shoved him with her shoulder and then turned to punch him in the arm.

CHAPTER FOURTEEN

The bright morning sun poured in through the plantation shutters that covered the windows in her bedroom. As her eyes adjusted to the glaring light, she could smell the aroma of French Roast wafting from her open window, coming from somewhere below. Pushing back the covers, she got out of bed and stepped over to the balcony, opening the shutters to listen to the sounds coming from below. Some sort of rhythmic Calypso or Merengue music played softly from outside. Never having tried Salsa or Zumba dance, much to Sasha's dismay, she wasn't quite sure which of the musical genres it came from, but she found the up tempo rhythm got her blood pumping.

Stepping back into the bedroom, Rylie decided she'd need to shower and brush her teeth before joining Mitch downstairs. She assumed he was still in the house, since they had decided the previous night that they'd conduct his therapy session at eight before he left for his offsite meetings. She glanced at the clock on her night table, which indicated it was six-thirty.

She'd slept well, after finally falling asleep the night before. The game had ended in a loss for the Dolphins, and Rylie had carried that heavy feeling of loss with her as they drove back to Biscayne Bay. She had ridden a roller coaster of emotions throughout the evening, starting from surprised and excited when she learned about the football game and the luxury suite, moving into irritated and annoyed with the stupid male games being played between Tully and Mitch, and finally culminating in sense of loss, from something deep within her that she couldn't quite articulate when the evening came to an end.

Mitch had seemed reserved and reticent on their way home to the rental, saying only a few words to her the entire ride back. He had avoided any physical contact with her the remainder of the game, she'd noticed, which had not been his M.O. since the day she met him. The ten thousand square-foot home vibrated with an emptiness and a quiet so loud it hurt her ears when they entered, even with the lights illuminating the beautifully decorated rooms.

"Do you have everything you need tonight?" he asked softly, placing his keys on the hall table as they stepped into the foyer.

Rylie shook her head. "Yeah, I'm good thanks. Well, maybe I'll just go get a glass of water before I head to bed." She started toward the kitchen when his hand came out unexpectedly to lightly grab her wrist. Even though it was barely a second, the touch ignited her.

"No, I'll get it for you," he said softly, a tinge of apology wrapped around his words. "I think I saw some cold bottles in the fridge."

"Thanks."

Standing in the hallway waiting for him to return, it became very apparent just how alone in the house they were together. Just the two of them. No one else. No one to prevent anything happening between two consenting adults.

She swallowed a hard, nervous gulp of air as he returned with the bottle. Would he try to make a move on her tonight? If so, would she let him? God, he was so confusing. One minute he was playing with her, telling her in no uncertain terms that he wanted her, and then the next minute he's stoic and silent, almost resentful toward her being there. But that was crazy, right?

He gave her a look of concern. "You okay?"

"Oh, yeah…it's just been a really long day. I'm tired and think I'll head to bed."

He seemed to ponder her response, shifting from one leg to the other. "Of course. Do you need me to wake you tomorrow morning?"

She suddenly had the image of him rolling over in her bed, waking her with his hand caressing her face and his mouth making a wet path up and down her body. It was exactly for that reason that she had to make her escape and head to her bedroom, to get away from him and this insane attraction.

Rylie ran a hand through her hair, which she'd taken out of the ponytail when they got home and told him that she didn't need to be awakened, she had her iPhone alarm. And honestly, she was an early riser and woke with even the little bit of sunlight.

"You have gorgeous hair," Mitch said, as he stepped toward her and twisted a few silky strands in his hand. "I like it when you wear it down."

Did the air conditioning just shut off, because damn it was hot in here!

Rylie felt the heat rise as if an inferno streaked through her body. She unscrewed the cap of her water bottle and took an ice-cold gulp, noticing the small shake of her hand as she did.

After a very long minute, Mitch let go of her hair and stood back. His hazel eyes turned dark and heavy with desire.

He inched closer. Rylie felt the heat from his body transferring to hers. He spoke low and arrogantly. "Just so you know…I'm not going to kiss you good night."

She blinked. "Oh," she whispered, disappointed. "Okay."

"Do you want to know why?" he asked, arching an eyebrow.

"Um…sure. Why?" She was feeling a bit out of breath. Her mouth was dry and parched, despite the water she just drank. She wanted to taste him on her.

"Because if I kiss you goodnight, Rylie, you won't want it to end," he said, his finger coming up to softly brush her cheek. "You'd want more. You'd want me to take you to your bed to fuck you. With my fingers, and then my tongue…and then with me inside of you. You'd want me to make you come and you'd scream my name each time you did. And believe me, I would do that to you. I'd make you come *all* night long. But if I did that, you wouldn't get any sleep, because it would be All. Night. Long. And since I know you're very tired tonight, after a very long day, I'm only thinking of your well-being. That's why I'm not going to kiss you goodnight."

He grabbed the bottle from her trembling hand, as she stood there with a glossy-eyed look on her face, to take a long drink. Replacing the cap, Mitch handed it back to her, placing it back in her hands.

His fingers wrapped around hers, wet from the bottle's condensation. She shivered from the extreme sensation between the hot and cold. His words had the heat building and pooling between her legs. Simply from the words he said and nothing more. They were naughty and dirty and turned her on like no one's business. This whole sexual reverse psychology really worked on her. Because if she didn't think she wanted it before, she sure as hell wanted him now.

She felt something hard behind her. He had somehow backed her up against the wall as he'd been talking and his body leaned into her, his hands placed on the wall on the sides of her head. His lips, still cold and wet from the water, came down to barely touch the shell of her ear.

"So goodnight, IQ. I hope you get some rest tonight, because you're going to need it for what I have planned for you for the remainder of our trip." Pushing himself away, Mitch turned to head to his room, leaving Rylie staring after him, out of breath and panting as if she'd run a marathon.

For obvious reasons, Rylie couldn't fall asleep as quickly as she'd hoped and sleep eluded her. She tossed and turned, annoyed with herself and with Mitch, because she *had* wanted him to kiss her. She longed for the taste of him again. For his tongue to slide into her mouth, to kiss her until she was writhing with need. And he knew that, the bastard. So instead of giving her what he knew she wanted, he smugly left her with a low torturous ache pulsing between her legs, wishing for a different ending to the night.

If only cold showers could work on women as effectively as they did for men, then she wouldn't have been laying there drenched in sweat with thoughts of Mitch's teasing smile and the satisfied look on his face when he left her, running through her head. She imagined she would see that very same grin as he was coming apart inside of her. *Gah.*

The ache between her legs became unbearable and all she could think about was how it would feel for Mitch's stubbled jaw to outline a path down *there*. For his fingers to press deep inside of her, finding that perfect spot where he'd push and stroke her until she was writhing with ecstasy. Rylie flipped over to her stomach, letting out a groan of frustration, her pillow drowning out her sounds.

Her hands pushed down through the tangle of sheets, feeling the warmth between her thighs. Mitch's words came flooding back to her, sensual and hot. *You'd want me to take you to your bed to fuck you. With my fingers, and my tongue.* Rylie's own fingers slid beneath the fabric of her panties, moving over the soft, delicate skin.

With me inside you. You'd want me to make you come and you'd call out my name each time you did. She felt hot and slick, feeling his words on her body, caressing her. She imagined Mitch's fingers touching her, sinking deep within her. His lips replacing his fingers, sucking on her as she started to feel the pending eruption.

Applying pressure at the juncture of her smooth folds, her fingers circled in a rhythmic cadence, as she panted breathlessly in the darkness of the room. Her hips ground against her hand, her heart pounding faster, the tension building from deep within her core. Her breath caught with the anticipation of what was to come, as she finally began to unravel, the sensation ripping through her body like a cord being pulled and let loose.

She let out a muffled groan against the pillow, as her much needed release sent her floating back down into the bed. As her eyes began to finally close with the pull of sleep, her last thought before drifting off was wanting what she just had, but with Mitch. And somehow she knew that it would be a hundred times more explosive and intense with his hands and mouth at her service.

Now in the morning light, dressed in a pair of khaki shorts and a white tank, Rylie blushed as she recalled the manner in which she fell asleep the previous night and felt a tinge of nerves, curious if Mitch might see it written all over her face. Would he know he had such an effect on her that she had to take matters into her own hands? That he left her wanting for something she knew she couldn't have?

Her mind then considered the possibility that maybe he had also been in the same boat as she last night and maybe he got himself off, too. Her face flushed with the image of Mitch jerking off in the room down the hall from hers, feeling the same explosion she did in her release. She bit her lip to keep herself from smiling as she stepped out onto the terrace, where Mitch was sitting at a patio table, coffee and breakfast set for two.

His eyes roamed up her body and his trademark grin, dimple and all, told her he was glad to see her and that however the night ended between them last night was in the past.

"Well don't you look all relaxed and happy this morning, IQ. Glad to see you got some rest." Mitch put down the iPhone he'd been reading and poured her some coffee. "Help yourself to whatever you'd like. I can also make you whatever you want for breakfast."

She was surprised by his gesture. "You can cook?"

"Come on now. Every bachelor should at the very least know how to scramble some eggs and fry up some bacon. But my true specialty is Apple Bourbon French Toast. That's the best damn breakfast you'll ever taste." He set down the coffee carafe and placed a napkin on her lap, his fingers barely grazing her exposed thigh. But it was enough to send her a jolt of electricity and to sit up straight.

"I'll believe it when I see it," she laughed, grabbing a bagel and slathering it with cream cheese. "But it does sound pretty good."

"Trust me, it's heaven. You'll find out soon enough."

She twisted in her chair, feeling a bit uncomfortable from the weight of his words and the promise of things to come. Maybe she was just reading into it now, but it seemed like everything he said was prepping her for something bigger. More intimate.

She choked down a bite of bagel and took a sip of orange juice, berating herself for thinking anything of the sort. She tried to get her thoughts on something other than Mitch and scanned the scenery out in front of her, the ocean and bay glistening in the morning sun. A few sailboats lined the horizon, with their colorful sails hoisted high, and a cruise ship inched further from land out in the far off distance. She loved the water and smell of the ocean air. It made her head hum with satisfaction.

Mitch followed her gaze and seemed to know what she was thinking.

"I grew up on the water. Learned to sail by the time I was ten. My father would take me out, teach me how to appreciate the ocean and learn how never to underestimate the volatility and unpredictability of its nature."

"You know how to sail?" she asked, now more curious than ever to learn more about him.

"Yep. In fact, I thought we could go out on the yacht later today and out to Key Biscayne after my meetings and after your, uh, *tour* with Tully."

Rylie frowned at the mention of the tour, but then did a happy dance in her chair. "Oh, I'd love that. So, were you able to move some of your appointments? I feel bad you'd have to do that for me," she said, wearing an expression of guilt. "I'm sure it'll be just fine. I teach Krav Maga classes, for God's sake. I'm pretty sure I can handle a frisky little perv like Tully if he gets out of hand."

Mitch put down his coffee and raised his eyebrow at her. "You teach, *what*?"

"Krav Maga. It's a self-defense martial arts class. I started close to three years ago. I love it – it's such a rush."

Mitch nodded his head in admiration. "Well I'm glad I didn't try anything funny out on you last night, then. And I'll make sure to announce my presence if we're ever caught in the dark so you don't think I'm a would-be assailant."

Rylie's eyes dropped to the table, trying to avoid the terror that rose from those words. Dark. Assailant. It was stupid that she could get that easily flustered at the mention of that. She didn't want him to see the vulnerability they caused or her embarrassment over being such a freaking pussy.

Wanting to void any further discussion about the specifics for her reasons for taking up Krav, she quickly jumped up and started clearing the table. Noticing the time on his phone, she mentally calculated the time they'd have to work out before he had to leave.

"It's nearly eight. We should get started with your exercises so you can get to your meetings."

"Sure. And yes, to answer your question, I was able to reschedule one of my meetings and pushed the city council to eleven today. So I should be able to meet up with you and Tully at lunch, right after your tour. Then we can make our escape out on the yacht."

She picked up the tray of fruit and bagels and started toward the kitchen. "That sounds good. Why don't you go jump in the pool and start your warm-up. I'll be right back out."

****

While Mitch's knee was becoming less painful as he continued to work with Rylie, the pain she was causing him elsewhere intensified the more time he spent around her. The amount of effort he exerted trying to keep his distance and his dick in check was wearing him out. His body hummed with every touch of her hand or brush of her body against his. His body was coiled so tightly, he felt he might explode at any given moment. In fact, since last night, he did explode not once, but twice.

The words and sentiment he spoke to Rylie last night after the game were meant to turn her on and leave her desperate for him, hopefully sending her into his arms sooner rather than later. Instead, his plan backfired, because her reaction to him in the hallway got him so hot and his dick so hard, he had to rub one out as soon as he hit his room. And although it was probably his imagination, he thought at some point in the night, he heard her moaning and, God, that was hotter than fuck. He envisioned her spread eagle on her bed, naked with the moonlight cascading shadows across her body, her hands nestled between her legs, touching herself as she got off. And that right there was a fantasy of his come true, which led him to jerking off again.

And then to see her emerge from her bedroom, her hair still damp and in a loose bun on the top of her head, biting those lush lips of hers and a blush bursting on her face, he wanted to grab her by the hips and pull her to him, running his hands over every inch of her perfect body. But that was all stuff of fantasies, because he couldn't touch her. At least not right this minute.

Mitch couldn't recall ever having to work this hard *not* to touch a woman. His usual encounters with the opposite sex were normally fast, hot and over within a matter of days. There was never a reason to take it slow or proceed with caution. He found women who were willing and understood his no-strings-attached guidelines.

It was different with Rylie. He could feel her desire for him when they touched and saw it written all over her face when she looked at him, her eyes filled with an unspoken need. He knew it burned just as deep and constant with her as it did for him, yet he held back, respecting her need to keep the professional boundaries clearly drawn. But it was damn near killing him. He wanted nothing more than to watch her desire grow under his skillful touch until she was panting breathlessly, begging for him to satisfy her hungry need.

He had nearly succumbed to that very urge during their morning session right after breakfast. As usual, his thoughts while working out with Rylie were never on the grueling exercises, but the close proximity of her wet body to his. She was once again wearing the skintight modest suit, which wasn't all that revealing, but that made no difference to Mitch and his imagination. She was a goddess in anything she wore.

Rylie stood facing him, their bodies inches from one another, demonstrating the correct posture for a squat he was to do across the pool's length. Leaning in, she placed her hands on both of his hips, pressing him down into the water, into the squat position. Mitch's breath caught in his throat as her breasts briefly grazed his chest as she leaned down to him. Her reaction was immediate, as her taught nipples strained against his bare torso, creating a friction so hot all the water in the pool couldn't extinguish the burn.

Realizing her error, she stepped back, but not before his hands caught her from behind, reaching to cup the bottom of her ass and bringing her entire body flush against him. Feeling her body tighten under his grip, he hesitated a moment, searching her eyes for an answer to his silent question. She responded with trepidation, almost in slow motion, as she moved her hands between their bodies to touch his bare chest, sliding around his neck. She licked her pink lips, her pupils growing wide and dark. That was all the answer he needed to take possession of her mouth.

His kiss was hot and demanding. His tongue entered her mouth, greedily taking its fill. Every stroke and sweep of her mouth was a banquet feast and he was more than ready to dive into the main course. Mitch rocked his hips against hers, his hardened length grinding against her, rubbing feverishly where he most wanted entrance.

His teeth nipping along her lower lip, Mitch's hand began to draw a path from the curve of her butt, up her spine and around her front until he palmed the soft swell of her breast.

Her nipples tightened into hard buds as she let out a lusty breath against his mouth. His fingers found the strap of her suit, maneuvering it down over her shoulders, until her ample breast spilled out of the wet material. His thumb brushed lightly over her nipple, an audible gasp coming from Rylie's mouth.

Mitch stepped back to admire. "Perfect," he whispered, bending down to take her nipple between his lips. "And I knew you'd taste sweet."

Rylie's hands were now clenching Mitch's hair, sending a flood of erotic tension through him, as he sucked her nipple with feverish intensity. Mitch grabbed her butt again and pushed her up against the side of the pool, as Rylie's legs wrapped around his waist, bringing their bodies even closer.

"Mitch…this is such a bad idea…" Rylie cried out in anguish and desperation.

Mitch raised his mouth to hers again, thrusting his tongue inside to quiet her thoughts. His fingers continued to pluck the hardened flesh of her nipples, his own erect flesh pulsing against her sex.

"I think this is the best idea I've ever had," he rasped. "I want you so much, Rylie."

Mitch's hand glided over her breasts, down her flat, hard stomach, to the juncture of her thighs. His fingers teased its subject through the tight material before sliding underneath, delicately pressing the warm flesh apart, feeling the slick heat between her folds.

Damn, she felt so good.

Rylie threw her head back with a gasp, but not in ecstasy, in protest.

"No, Mitch. I…I can't."

Pushing hard against him and abruptly dropping her legs, Rylie turned to lift herself up and over the lip of the pool. Mitch grabbed hold of her waist and pulled her back to him, her backside pressed firmly against his chest. They were both breathing heavy.

Wrapping his arms around her middle, Mitch pressed his face against her neck, trying to steady both of them and help to make sense of the thoughts swirling around in his mind. "Come on, Ry…you know this is going to happen. You don't have to be afraid."

"What makes you think I'm afraid?" she hissed. "Maybe I just don't want this."

She wiggled to get free as Mitch slowly loosened his grip, realizing it was a lost cause for the moment.

"I think that's bullshit. You do want it – you want me. You're just afraid to admit it for some reason," he said, more forcefully than he meant. "And I don't understand why."

He watched her get out of the pool, readjust her suit back up over her body and take a towel to dry off.

"Rylie, please," he said more softly this time. "Whatever it is, we can work through it. If it's because I'm your client, well, that can be easily remedied. You can fire me or better yet, I'll fire myself," he tried to smile, his eyes pleading with her to look at him. "I want you more than anything. Why won't you give this a chance?"

Rylie stood poolside for a few minutes, looking out at the direction of the ocean, quietly reflecting over the situation before finally responding.

"I think our session is over for today. I'm going to go workout before the tour, so I'll see you later. No need to join us for lunch. I'll be fine without you."

Mitch slowly walked up the pool steps and grabbed the towel from the chair. Exasperated and completely vexed by the turn of events and her rejection, he didn't want to press the subject any further with Rylie. She'd made it clear it wasn't going to go any further, so he was through with punishing himself by thinking otherwise.

If she wanted it strictly business, then that's what she would get, even if it killed him.

"I'm still going to try to make lunch," he mumbled. "And we're still going out on the yacht. You can bet on that."

Rylie nodded in understanding, not with any real confirmation, and then she darted in the house without looking back.

Mitch watched her until she disappeared and took a long breath. She completely and utterly confused him. He thought that based on her response to their kiss, she was ready to let go, to pursue this attraction heating up between the two of them. But once again, just when he felt he was hitting the point of no return, she pulled back, looking started and bewildered. As if she had no idea how she'd gotten her legs wrapped around his body or was in his arms half naked. And whatever it was that brought her hurdling back to earth, crashing through the atmosphere until she hit, it was likely something he couldn't do anything about. And that just pissed him off more.

It would be a very long, long day.

CHAPTER FIFTEEN

Rylie's legs burned as she finished her brutal five-mile run along the Biscayne Bay neighborhood and beach. The sun was hot and blistering, making sweat bead and drip down her neck and back, plastering against her humid skin.

With each breath and every stride she chastised herself for her stupidity over her behavior that morning with Mitch. Why the hell did she act this way around him? Why couldn't she just give in and let it happen naturally? She wanted nothing more than to wrap herself around him and let him penetrate her body and her soul, but her brain kept putting the brakes on.

Yes, she was scared. The feelings that erupted inside her when she was with Mitch were too enormous for her to comprehend. It wasn't just a craving or a sexual desire for him. Without putting a name to it, she felt the beginning of something blooming within her, something that had been long dead and buried.

And if she was being completely honest with herself, she was using her occupational code as a means to avoid the real root of the problem. Of course she didn't want her lack of judgment to affect her reputation in her chosen profession, but it was more than that. What it boiled down to was the thought of losing her heart to Mitch and he, in turn, leaving her heart shattered and broken. Just like when her mother left. A heartbreak she never wanted to live through again.

The damage that had been done to Rylie and her family was indescribable. They were left feeling victimized and vulnerable, not to mention lacking control over their lives. And even after all this time, her father would never open up and talk about the pain she had caused him. He busied himself in the day-to-day responsibilities of taking care of her and her brother, burying the pain and avoiding any long-term relationships with other women.

She saw what it did to him. He had been an empty shell for twenty-two years, hollow on the inside and he'd allowed his self-worth and spirit to be crushed by a selfish woman who didn't give a damn about her own family. And now, as she looked at her own life at age twenty-eight, Rylie saw that very same resentment and fear crowding her heart so completely, leaving barely a sliver of room for anything close to love.

She's promised herself, especially after her attack, that she would never become a victim again. No one would take away her will or control. And that's exactly what happened when you succumbed to the advances of a man. You lost your voice and your reasoning in the heat of the moment. And afterward? The inevitable would happen. Mitch would take what he wanted and then leave her with a gaping hole in her heart. Not.Going.To.Happen.

Rylie stretched her muscle-cramped legs out in front of her on the yoga mat in the Olympic-sized workout room. Her calves ached and her quads were on fire from her run and she was looking forward to using the Jacuzzi after she cooled down. Reaching for her toes, she grabbed hold of her feet to bend down, releasing the tension in her back. Her phone, which was on the iPod player cranking out the newest *KONGOS* album, began to ring. Jumping up to grab it, the caller ID displayed Sasha's picture. Smiling, she clicked the Answer button.

"Hey Sash."

"Hey girly…is it HOT in paradise?" she asked, stifling a laugh.

Rylie giggled at Sasha's over-emphasis on the word hot, knowing intuitively her comment meant more than the temperature in Miami.

"Tell me all about what's been going on…give me all the juicy details. Have you fucked him yet? Oh God, I bet it was incredible!" she gasped over the line. "And have you worn the red suit yet? He probably came in his shorts the minute he saw you in that thing. That suit accentuates every single curve of your gorgeous body and your flat, perfect abs and your awesome ass. You might be my best friend, but I still can hate you for looking so much better in my clothes than I do."

Sasha continued to pepper her with questions, one after another without pause, as Rylie would every now and again give her an "uh-huh" and "yes, no, maybe" response.

Rylie thought about the red monokini Sasha had packed for her, which she hadn't had the chance to wear yet. She had planned on wearing it on the yacht that afternoon, since the other suit she had was too functional and was still drip-drying in her bathroom shower. But now she didn't plan on going out with Mitch. She'd pretty much screwed that pooch on that invitation.

Although technically it was a one-piece suit, it had to have been the sexiest suit she'd ever worn. It was a deep red demi-cup bikini top that tied at the neck, connected to the bottom with side cut-out hourglass material, with string bikini bottoms. To say it was revealing was an understatement, even though it covered much of her abs and belly button. From the back it looked just like she was wearing a string bikini, but the front? Ooh-la-la.

"I haven't worn it yet, but we were planning on going out on the yacht this afternoon to swim and snorkel. But now I don't know if that will happen."

"What does that mean? What happened? Trouble in paradise already? You haven't even fucked him yet – what could possibly have gone wrong?"

Rylie filled her in on what happened in the pool earlier and how he seemed pretty frustrated when he left the house. Her friend was not the slightest bit deterred by what Rylie had shared with her or her concern over potentially damaging their relationship before it even started.

"My dear, Rylie. You know what they call that level of frustration? It's called foreplay. It's obvious he wants to get in your pants, right?"

"Yes, I think that's fairly obvious."

"And you've been a royal cock tease and bitch up to now, stringing him along, right?"

"Well, I guess, but not on purpose. I just haven't allowed him to do anything more than kiss me. And…well, touch me."

Sasha was silent for a moment, clearly ruminating over the situation, like Angela Landsbury trying to solve a murder case on *Murder She Wrote*.

"This is perfect. Sounds like he's already good and wound up tight from all your teasing, which means you've got his cock by a string. So here's what you're going to do later today. You're going to flirt like crazy with this Tully guy at lunch. Make Mitch so jealous, he'll lead you into the bathroom stall, shove you up against the wall and fuck the shit out of you, before dessert is even ordered."

Rylie was flabbergasted at her friend's visual, but it did sound like it had merit. That is, if he even ended up showing up to lunch.

Sasha continued, giving her friend the step-by-step on how to ensure her yacht adventure turned out to be a sexcapade on the high seas.

"Once you're on that boat, all you need to do is strut your sexy self around in that red suit and he's going to forget all about your fickle tirades from before. Trust me, this will work," Sasha exclaimed excitedly. "And when it does, and you've experienced the best sex of your life, you're going text me to tell me how BIG he is. Or better yet, just send me pictures!"

Rylie choked out a loud laugh, giggling uncontrollably into the phone.

"Only one problem, Sash. What if he doesn't show up for lunch?"

"He will, girl. He will."

****

Mitch's meetings seemed never-ending, boring as hell, and the last place on earth he wanted to be. His concentration was shot to hell and his mind hadn't been on anything that the other parties were saying. He was distracted beyond belief.

He glanced down at his watch, which now stated eleven-fifty a.m., the end of his meeting with the city council nowhere in sight. Mitch silently groaned with the knowledge that he wouldn't make it to the restaurant before Tully and Rylie began lunch. His only hope was intruding somewhere before the end.

Recalling how greasy Tully acted the day before when he was pawing over Rylie at the game made Mitch bite back a wave of anger. He'd known Tully for years and seen him with plenty of women, often while they were out carousing for the same entertaining pleasures. He never thought of Tully as a sleaze-ball, just a typical single man in his mid-thirties with money to spend and a libido that went with it. The *Wolf of Wall Street* in Miami, no doubt. A flare of jealousy erupted as Mitch thought about Rylie alone with Tully. Was she laughing at his jokes? Were their knees touching underneath the linen covered table? Was Tully's arm draped possessively over Rylie's shoulders, his fingers brushing the fine hairs on the back of her neck?

Brooding about the what-ifs was just about killing him. Closing his laptop, Mitch pushed his chair back and stood.

Reaching out to shake their hands, he swung his bag over his shoulder, stepping toward three of the council members.

"Harold, Joleen, Debra," he said politely. "I'm sorry to rush off, but I have a lunch meeting I must attend that I'm already late for. I'll be back in the office on Friday and I'll look forward to hearing your decision on our building plans. Until then, I appreciate your time. Thank you."

If the others in the meeting were surprised over his abrupt conclusion, they didn't show it. They all shook hands and nodded their goodbyes with the promise to reconvene and give him their decision soon.

Mitch nearly bolted out the building doors and down to the parking ramp, jamming the key into the ignition and squealing out of his parking space. By his calculation, he would make it to the restaurant by twelve forty-five, assuming he didn't hit traffic.

His heartbeat raced in anticipation of joining Rylie and Tully for lunch and potentially interrupting any plans they were making to see each other again. He didn't think Tully was Rylie's type, but that wouldn't prevent him from pulling out all the stops to wine and dine her. Similar to what he was trying to do this week. He laughed at the irony.

He had no right to think or act the way he did over Rylie. Hell, if she wanted to date Tully, more power to her. But he would damn well make sure she knew what she would be missing out on if she didn't pick him.

Throwing the car in park, he opened the door and handed the keys at the valet, who was eagerly waiting at the curb. "I won't be long," he said, taking long strides into the Oceanside restaurant.

Whipping off his sunglasses, he scanned the room filled with dozens of diners. A young hostess wearing a tight fitting black dress stepped around the podium and in front him. "Can I help you, sir? Do you have a reservation or are you meeting someone here?"

"Yes, I'm meeting someone. Randall Tully? He's here with a woman." Mitch nearly said *my woman*, but caught himself.

Hostess girl looked over her computer screen and hummed. "Ah, yes. Here they are. Mr. Tully and his guest are sitting out on the deck. Let me take you there."

Mitch rudely pushed past her, heading to the back of the restaurant facing the water. "No, that's okay. I can find them. Thanks, though." He handed her a five-dollar bill and stalked away toward the patio.

The sun was bright and the glare off the water had him squinting and averting his eyes from the onslaught of light. Temporarily blinded, he halted his forward movement. He couldn't see them, but he absolutely, without a doubt, heard the commotion that came from the table to the right, shaded in the corner of the deck.

"I asked you to get your hand off my leg, Mr. Tully. That didn't give you liberty to move your hand further up my thigh. If you don't remove your hand this minute, I'll be prompted to move it for you."

Two seconds later, Mitch heard a deep, agonizing curse. "FUUUUUCKKK!"

Mitch heard the loud noise of chair legs scraping against the deck floor, the sound of knives and forks being jostled on the table and then a slam of a hand on the table top.

Her voice was full of fury and hell fire. "That was the sound of me breaking your fingers, Mr. Tully. You should go ice that as soon as possible. And keep that in mind the next time a woman asks you to stop."

Mitch snickered quietly, as he stepped back under the deck's awning just as Rylie appeared around the corner, smacking directly into his chest.

Looking up at him, Mitch saw the reddened features of Rylie's face, her eyes turning nearly black with fury and her mouth creased tightly in a thin line.

"Asshole," she spit. "Please get me out of here…now."

She didn't have to ask him twice.

CHAPTER SIXTEEN

Rylie and Mitch packed a cooler of full of snacks, along with some beer and wine, and headed out onto the yacht for their afternoon excursion. After the less than thrilling morning meetings Mitch had endured and the lunch groping Rylie experienced, they both decided the boat was the best place for them to forget their troubles. Rylie had acquiesced and given in to the sound of a relaxing day out on the water.

"I know it's rude to ask," she said as they climbed on board. "But how much do you think a boat like this is worth?" Rylie had asked out of sheer curiosity.

Mitch scratched at the stubble on his chin as he placed the cooler and towels onto the deck, taking in the luxury of the vessel. "I'd guess at least a million, if not more."

Rylie's mouth dropped open, mouthing an "O". She'd never known anyone who could afford a million-dollar yacht. Her people were blue-collar from the streets of Boston and even Jenny Caldwell, her friend from junior high who married a dot-commer who struck it rich, probably didn't own a boat as big or as luxurious as this one.

As Mitch stood at the fly bridge helm, working the navigational equipment and preparing for their departure, Rylie went down below to change and take a tour of the entire boat. The yacht was unlike anything Rylie had ever seen.

Three levels, from the galley below to the fly bridge at the top of the boat, came equipped with three gorgeously appointed staterooms, each with its own bath and marble countertops. There was custom cherry cabinetry in the full-size salon and the galley was covered with marble floors. Two full size decks on both the bow and the stern, with a spiral staircase that connected the space between the floors.

Stepping inside what she presumed was the Master stateroom, she put down her bag and sat at the edge of the California king-size bed, giving it a little bounce. Mitch appeared in the small doorway, his body filling the door frame completely. Rylie's face flushed a bright red over being busted testing out the bed.

A smile twitched on his lips. "Is it too firm or too soft or just right, Goldilocks?"

Rylie waved her hand dismissively, indicating he was full of it. Feeling the weight of his stare upon her, she sprung to her feet, losing her balance as the boat rocked side-to-side, nearly toppling her back into the bed. Mitch's hands shot out faster than her own, grabbing her by the waist to steady her on her feet, bringing her back to an upright position.

"Whoa there, beautiful – be careful. You need to get your sea legs under you." Letting go of her as quickly as he had reached for her, Mitch stepped back into the doorway, his eyes sweeping a path up and down her body. Rylie saw his darkened expression and felt the heat centered in her belly. That always seemed to happen these days.

"Thanks. I wasn't expecting the sudden movement." Rylie smiled and bit down on her lip. "So…you should probably go back up to the helm and steer the ship, sailor. And I'm going to change into my suit."

He gave her a wink and an appreciative smile. "I won't argue with that. I thought we could go snorkeling when we get out to Key Biscayne, if you want. I found all sorts of water sports paraphernalia in the hull. Or we can take the dinghy up to the beach – there's a beautiful lighthouse at Cape Florida State Park. Or we can just hang on the boat – whatever you want to do."

Rylie flushed with excitement. So many options. She thought the snorkeling sounded perfect and told him so.

"Excellent, we should be far enough out in about thirty minutes and I'll drop anchor. So go ahead and get changed and take your pick where you'd like to lounge above deck," he said, using a sweeping motion with his hands. "Aft or bow, there's plenty of perfect spots to select from."

Rylie toyed nervously with the bottom of her nautical striped tank top, feeling the cabin grow increasingly smaller. "Sounds good. I'll see you up there in a bit."

Mitch turned to walk out the door but then stopped just past the threshold, swinging back around.

"And Rylie. You haven't mentioned it yet, but I hope you'll fill me in later on what exactly happened earlier with Tully. Whatever it was, I'm sure he deserved what you gave him…but damn, I was impressed with what I heard. You were badass. I'm glad I haven't done anything to piss you off."

Rylie stifled a giggle, grabbing her bag from the bed and moving towards the Master suite bathroom. "Not yet, at least…"

She snickered as he turned and shut the door, leaving her alone again. She walked into the large bathroom, complete with full size marble floors and walled shower. It was bigger than her own bathroom in her apartment. Looking down at the skimpy suit in her hands, she began to bite her lip, feeling overly anxious about putting on the swimsuit that Sasha had loaned her to wear. It left very little to the imagination. While she had worn bikinis in the past, she had never felt particularly sexy or beautiful in them. She'd always been taller than most, including guys, and she was gangly through her teens and a bit on the sporty side to be considered a beautiful woman. But when she was around Mitch, all of that changed.

Around Mitch, Rylie felt wanton and desirable. He made her want to dress up in tight clothes, in short skirts, and run around in a string bikini, flaunting her body at him because she knew he appreciated it. He'd already indicated several times that he wanted her, but she'd botched it up royally, running away each time like a scared school girl. But damn if she didn't want that to change. Her body said one thing, but her stupid head always mucked things up. This time, she planned on taking Sasha's advice and let it all go. Take control of her desire and get something she wanted.

Shimmying out of her shorts and panties, she pulled on the suit over the length of her body. She could do this, she thought confidently, as she turned to look at herself in the mirror. Wowza! *Damn she looked good.*

Placing her hands under her breasts, she plumbed them up, turning sideways to view her backside. The red suit looked amazing, hugging every toned inch of her upper body. She felt like she was staring at a completely different person. Not the tomboy from last week, but a sexy, thrill-seeking harlot. Oh yeah, it was on.

She ran her hands down the sides of her waist, feeling the exposed skin in the cut-out of the suit, pressing further down over the curves of her hips where the bottoms were fastened with flimsy ties. If she had to make one guess, it was that she might very well take Mitch's breath away. And that, she decided, was exactly what she wanted to do.

Stealing one last look in the mirror, she grabbed a towel and some sunscreen and headed up the steps to the helm. Not finding Mitch in the lower helm, she climbed another set of wooden stairs to the fly bridge, where he was sitting in the Captain's chair, his focus toward the front of the boat, looking at ease and relaxed as he navigated the waters.

"Hey Captain, I'm going to lay out on the sun pad. It looks pretty comfortable out there and it appears that's where the most sun is hitting right now," she said, stepping up behind Mitch and pointing toward the area right in front of the fly bridge helm. "Would you do me a favor? If I fall asleep, just wake me up when we anchor."

Mitch turned his head to look at her and stopped cold. The expression of desire that ran over his face told Rylie everything she needed to know. He appeared at a loss for words.

"Cat got your tongue?" she teased, taking full advantage of his dazed mental state.

Mitch stood there motionless for a few seconds before gesturing with his finger for Rylie to twirl around. "Please…let me see the entire package."

Rylie indulged his curiosity and pivoted on her heels, turning in a slow circle. He let out a long, satisfying whistle. "Holy hell. That is the hottest thing I've ever seen. You. Are. Gorgeous." He enunciated each syllable in a staccato clip, the desire in his tone unmistakable.

Still not used to his compliments, Rylie blushed again, wrapping a towel quickly around her waist. Just as she started to head out to the front, Mitch grabbed the towel and it came undone, falling to the floor.

"Come on now. You can't give me a peep show and then go all modest on me. At least let me ogle you for a little while longer."

Picking up the towel from the floor, she stuck out her tongue and wiggled her ass as she walked out on to the deck. "Fine. Ogle all you want."

****

Shit.

She was trying to kill him.

The torture he endured watching her lying out on the lounge chair in front of him the last hour had his cock rock hard and saluting. With every movement she made, flipping over from her front to her back, rubbing lotion over her long, sexy legs or adjusting her cleavage in the fucking fantastic suit she wore, he thought he'd lose it. His eyes wandered over every part of her shapely body and he thought of every spot he would rub his tongue and hands.

He was harder than he'd ever been. All he could think about doing was walking over to that lounge chair, spreading her legs wide and anchoring himself deep inside her wet, tight body. His dick twitched at the thought.

He had to find something to do right now before he went fucking crazy. They were close enough to the island now where he could drop anchor, so that's what he did. Flipping a switch on the control panel, he felt a jerk and then heard the metal sounds of the anchor making its way to the bottom of the bay. Satisfied that they were secure, he turned off the motor and went to the front to wake Rylie.

He stood over her, watching her rest peacefully, her breathing a nice easy rhythm. Her face held the same beautiful look, just like the one she wore when her head was on his lap on the plane. Her hair was spread out over her shoulders, billowing over her breasts.

Before his brain even registered his actions, he placed his hands on the back of her neck, nudging her slightly forward in the chair. She stirred, but didn't fully wake, mumbling something incoherent. He let out a shallow breath and then let his hand move down under the curve of her bottom, scooting her forward, allowing room behind her for him to sit down. Mitch swung his leg over the side of the lounge chair and sat back, nestling his body between her and the back of the chair.

This was heaven. With her bare back pressed tightly against him, her ass was secured snugly against his erection. Exactly what the doctor ordered. She sighed and laid her head back into the contour of his neck, allowing his face to have access to her neck and shoulders.

With feather light touches, Mitch's fingertips brushed softly down the side of her arm, tracing figure eight patterns along her warm skin. Rylie let out a long sigh before her eyes flew open and she tensed against him.

Mitch let out a low and languid whisper against her ear. "Shh…let me make you feel good."

He released a warm breath against her neck and his lips began to trace the curve of her ear, as he felt her slowly ease up and melt against him. Rylie's hands moved to his thighs, her fingers moving in the same pattern as he had traced down her arm.

He groaned in pleasure. It hurt so good.

His lips resumed their play as he kissed a path just below her ear, teasing the soft skin with nips and laps of his tongue. His teeth grabbed to bite her earlobe and a moan escaped, her head rolling back to give him more access.

Mitch continued to kiss and suck up and down her neck, his hands now moving to the front of her neck, caressing down her throat until he reached the swell of Rylie's lush breasts. Slipping his hand underneath the material of her suit, he cupped her right breast, the pad of his thumb rubbing against the taut skin of her nipple. It turned into a hard pebble under his touch and Rylie jerked in response, as she sucked in a shallow breath.

"You feel so good. Do you know how you make me feel?" he whispered, his lips pressing against the back of her neck.

"Yes," was all she could say in response, as she dug her nails into his legs.

Feeling encouraged by her gauging fingers, he continued to work the nipple, circling it and coaxing it into a hard, tight peak. He wanted to work her into a frenzy and bring her to the brink of desire, to drown out any conflicting thoughts.

His hand moved slowly down her stomach, feeling the warm flesh of her abs, where the hourglass material was non-existent. In this position, he was helpless to do anything except touch her with his hands, but he wanted nothing more than to trace the lines of her cut-out with his tongue. Just the thought had his erection pulsing hard against Rylie's back.

He continued his descent down her body until both hands were marking their territory along her inner thighs. Rylie moaned in anticipation, bucking just slightly under his touch. She felt so good – her skin warmed from the sun, burning with intensity under his touch. He stroked her thighs, and with each movement, his hand would brush lightly against her hot center, where he could feel the heat pooling. She was already wet and ready for him in just a few short minutes. This woman was incredible.

His fingers settled on their final destination, as Mitch made small circles on the exterior of her suit, teasing and playing, fast and then slow. Palming her, Rylie rocked hard against his hand, grinding for release.

"Do you want me to make you come?"

"Yes…please," she breathed, her voice ragged.

Her demanding plea nearly sent him over the edge. He slid his fingers under the material, feeling the soft skin underneath his fingertips and the slick heat of her sex. He growled in appreciation.

Opening the smooth folds, his thumb skimmed across her center, as he began to stroke her wildly. Curling a finger inside her center heat, he found her wet and damp, ready for her to take him.

He continued to circle her heat and added a second finger inside of her, pumping them in and out, increasing his pace for a few strokes and slowing it down again, her breathing catching as he did. His fingers agilely giving the promise of exquisite release.

"I'm so close….I'm…Please, don't stop!" she cried hoarsely, riding his hand fast and hard. He couldn't stop even if he wanted to. His entire being was now focused on making her explode in pleasure. Her hands flew behind her head, grabbing Mitch's hair and pulling it tight. He growled at the sensation, of her animalistic grip and her molten desire.

He could feel when she was on the verge of letting go as her body strained against him, tense and wild. Her hands dug into his scalp with an even deeper pull, as her body jerked around his fingers, sending a hoarse cry from her throat.

Her body slowly relaxed, as his fingers remained inside, stroking her heat as she came down from her climax. Rylie released her grip from his hair and stretched lazily against him, pushing his finger deeper. She let out a lusty laugh, as she jerked in response.

Mitch smiled against her neck, breathing in the sweet smell of her hair.

"You feel amazing. I wish I could have seen your face when you came."

Rylie slowly shifted her body to look at him, pressing her stomach against his erection. Groaning, he moved his hands from between her legs up the side of her body.

"You can see me now," she purred, giving him a seductive look. "How do you think it was?"

Taking her face between his hands, be bent his head to plant a soft kiss on the bridge of her nose. Wisps of her dark hair had come loose from the makeshift bun she'd made at the top of her head. She looked beautiful in her afterglow. "I hope it was as good as you look."

Rylie ran her hands up his chest, her fingers entwining in his soft golden chest hair. Finding his nipple, she circled the flesh, her tongue darting out to taste.

His lashes lowered, watching her erotic play, as warmth spread across his body. His eyes narrowed, taking in the raw pleasure of this simple gesture. Rylie's eyes flashed up toward him, a mischievous gleam in her eyes. She studied him for a moment, as if considering a question he might have asked. Her hand swept down over his chest, over his stomach and down to the waistband of his swim trunks. His muscles tensed, as he took in a deep breath. His body warred with his mind. His hope was that she would stop, and yet he wanted nothing more than for her to keep going.

Her hand met his hardened arousal, palming his length, giving him a tight squeeze and stroking her thumb against his tip through his trunks.

Mitch shifted restlessly under her weight.

"Rylie?"

"Hmm?" she murmured, her gaze moving from his shorts, up his abdomen to his eyes.

"What are you doing?" he asked, as his eyes moved down to see her nipples pucker against her bikini top.

"If I have to explain, then I'm not doing a very good job at it," she laughed, her lashes fluttering and her hands continuing their assault on his body.

He groaned, knowing exactly where this would go if he didn't stop it now. With all the willpower he could muster, he pulled at her hand that was still on his erection, giving it a rough tug and then bringing her hand up to meet his lips. Pressing a wet kiss to her palm, he moved her up to a sitting position, giving her a husky chuckle.

"There is nothing I want more…but not right now. This day is all for you and snorkeling awaits."

She gave him a bewildered look, probably confused by his sudden refusal. And damn if he didn't think he'd lost his mind. Mitch bent down to kiss her, sliding his hands back around the nape of her neck, a deep rumble emerging from his chest. "You taste so good, I want to devour you."

"Mmm…"

Mitch hovered above her, his mouth and tongue roaming the depths of her mouth. He was demanding, taking her lower lip between his teeth, biting down just hard enough to elicit a moan. That one sound had him wanting more, wanting to taste and explore, as his hand found her breast, pushing the silky material of her bikini top away, exposing the perfect lush globe. Releasing her mouth, Mitch bent down and took her breast into his mouth, rubbing his tongue over its soft, ivory flesh. She arched in his mouth, muttering something he couldn't quite make out.

Holy hell, how quickly she could have him gasping for air. He palmed her breasts, rolling his thumb over her nipples as they hardened with his touch.

He had to stop this torture before he flipped her on her back and ripped that suit off her body, plunging into her hot, wet depths.

Cursing under his breath, he released his hold and gave her a gentle push forward. Rylie, breathing heavy, looked up in surprise.

"What? Did I do something wrong?"

"No, of course not. That's hardly my problem…"

She moved her legs underneath her butt, sitting back on her heels and turned towards him. "Then what is it? Why don't you want to finish what you started?"

He sighed, pushing the material of her suit back into its rightful place, letting his hands remain on top of her shoulders.

"Rylie…less than six hours ago, you made it very clear, and in no uncertain terms, that *this* wasn't want you wanted," he said, his hand pointing out the gap between them. "I apologize for my lack of self-control just now, but I couldn't stop myself. You looked so fucking sexy lying here and you were driving me crazy. I was powerless to leave you alone. But I don't want to move too fast, because I don't want you to regret that decision."

Rylie's head hung low, her back rounded down in a dejected posture, frowning at the truth in his statement.

Mitch placed his finger underneath her chin to nudge her head back up to look him in the eyes. Her warm brown eyes held hurt and rejection, which wasn't what he wanted to see. He didn't want her to feel criticized by his words. That was the last thing he wanted to do.

"I already know with one-hundred-percent certainty that I want you, Rylie. You have to know that. You have kept me up at nights over these last few weeks thinking about you. My concentration is shot to hell because all I do is fantasize about being with you. All I can think about is how it will feel to be inside of you." Mitch reached over to gently touch the side of her face.

Rylie pressed her cheek into his palm. She was so beautiful. Equal parts heaven and hell. Pain and pleasure.

Her eyes closed, avoiding his stare. "I'm sorry I've made a mess of things. I'm an idiot…" she began to say, as he placed his fingertips to her lips.

"Shh…stop that. You haven't messed anything up. In fact, I think you've done something that's never happened to me before."

"What's that?"

Mitch chuckled, wiggling his eyebrows suggestively. "Resisted my deadly charms."

She threw her head back and laughed. "You're such an arrogant asshole," she said, affection apparent in her tone. "I pity the women who do fall so easily for your wicked sexy charms. You probably turned them inside out with just a kiss and then left them hanging out to dry when you moved on to the next one."

"Wow – you certainly have a low opinion of me."

Although, she was spot on with her assessment. His past romantic affairs were never very long-running and that's the way he'd always wanted it. He got in, he got out. No one got hurt. That's exactly how he liked it and what he needed.

Mitch kept his facial expression light, but he felt the sting in the truth that she voiced and the opinion she formed about him. Was he that much of a lowlife and cad? Would it hurt his chances at being with her?

She shifted uncomfortably. "Oh, come on. You're not an innocent by-stander, Camden. You're a love 'em and leave 'em kind of guy. Just admit it."

The truth hurt. It had never been said straight to his face. He felt like he was being blamed and punished for his lifestyle and he didn't like to hear it. Especially not from Rylie.

"While that may be true, I've never taken anything that wasn't freely given to me. It takes two to tango and everyone I've been with knows what to expect with me. And speaking of tango," he said, trying to direct the conversation elsewhere and away from his sexual encounters.

"What the hell happened between you and Tully earlier? Did you really break his fingers?"

Rylie grimaced, flicking her hand in the air. "Oh, that. I only broke *one* of his fingers, but it was his own fault for being a total douche. And I gave him ample warning, but the idiot wouldn't stop. He kept trying to touch me, leaving me no other choice but to put a stop to it," she shook her bent head, indicating her irritation. "I'm not normally in the habit of exerting physical force."

Mitch sat in awe, his rage tempered somewhat as she recounted the events that led to Tully's much deserved ass-kicking. He watched this beautiful woman tell the story as if it didn't faze her in the slightest. She was tough and courageous and incredibly sexy. What more could a man want? The thought nearly knocked the wind of him.

"The first thirty minutes of our lunch were fine – just idle chit chat, basic get-to-know-you conversation. But then he asked me if I also practiced massage, and would I like to give him a massage? And then he suggested that a happy ending massage was exactly what he was looking for and his hands got gropey with my legs. I finally said enough was enough and told him so. I think you were there for the finale, right?"

His anger at Tully's behavior grew, imagining his hands roaming all over Rylie's legs. His unwanted touching making her feel violated. "That motherfucker. He had no right. And you had every right to do what you did, Rylie. I'm sorry that happened and I wish I could have been there to protect you. I had just arrived when I overheard his whiny-ass hysterics. What exactly did you do to him?"

"Here, I'll show you." She reached out to grab his hand and when he hesitated, she said, "Don't be a chicken. I won't hurt you."

Rylie laid out her hand, as Mitch tentatively placed his hand in hers. The touch was full of intensity and there was a moment when they just stared into each other's gaze. Trust. Desire. Longing. To Mitch, it meant complication and risk.

Placing her hand over his wrist, she demonstrated the move. "It's a fairly basic self-defense move. When an assailant has grabbed you, you just reach for the thumb or pinky and just pull it back, hard and quick. Major amount of pain with minimal effort." Rylie's hand pulled up lightly on his pinky, giving him a visual of her technique.

Mitch pulled his hand back out of her grip and rubbed his fingers. "Seems barbaric. How exactly did you learn about these techniques? Or more importantly, why?"

"It's a long story," she said, purposefully evading the question. "Right now, I'm getting pretty warm and want to get into that water. You ready to snorkel?" She jumped off the chair to stand and grabbed his hand to help him up.

He didn't know why she was reluctant to tell him, but it was obvious she was hiding something. Something in her past was clearly the catalyst for her knowledge and use of self-defense. He would eventually find out. But for now, the day was about enjoying some fun together.

"Let's do this."

CHAPTER SEVENTEEN

The remainder of the afternoon, Rylie and Mitch swam and played in the warm, salty water, snorkeling through Biscayne National underwater park, a large offshore barrier reef, one of the largest coral reefs in the world.

Rylie was entranced by the beauty and color of the underwater world, as they snorkeled just outside the bay. Mitch brought along an underwater camera and snapped pictures throughout their swim. Colorful, neon sea life surrounded them, as they submerged themselves in the quiet, peaceful heaven on earth.

The entire afternoon was an experience that Rylie would never forget. It was as close to paradise as she'd ever been, starting with the mind blowing orgasm Mitch had given her earlier on the boat. She'd never felt that wanton and alive in a man's arms before or even thought she was capable of coming undone under a man's touch. But Mitch had shown her what her body could do and the pleasure she could receive if she was just willing to accept it. Her body still yearned for another release his experienced fingers had given her. He'd touched nearly every part of her, yet she still wasn't close to being satisfied. His touch turned her into a junkie, her body jonesing for another hit of the lusty drug he had given her earlier.

Rylie loosened up during their afternoon, striking sexy poses in the water as Mitch snapped her picture. She felt relaxed again in a man's presence for the first time in a long time. Ever since her attack, she had stayed away from any sexual relationship. Her time with Skeet was so brief, it couldn't even be clocked on the radar as a fling. He probably tried to kiss her, but she couldn't even remember that clearly. She became an ice cube, tense and rigid, when a man even tried touching her – until Mitch came along. He had the power to melt her into warm puddles of sensual desire.

Rylie looked behind as she felt something tap her leg. Mitch was pointing up, indicating he was heading back to the boat. She gave him a thumbs up and kicked her way to the water's break. Once above water, she pulled off her snorkel mask and blow tube, slicking her wet hair out of her face. Drops of salt water hung from Rylie's lashes, as she closed her eyes to wipe them clear. Opening them once again, she was startled to see Mitch inches from her face, a smoldering look in his deep, hazel eyes.

Grabbing her around the waist, he pulled her against him. She gasped in surprise as she felt his hard erection straining against her stomach. He groaned gutturally, as he placed his mouth upon hers, his tongue seeking entrance.

"You looked incredible down there," he said against the side of her mouth before his roving tongue moved down her neck, licking and sucking. A hand moved down between her legs and she gave an instant jerk, her sex throbbing in delight. His fingers circled the exterior, rubbing against the already swollen flesh as she pressed herself against his hand. "And you feel absolutely incredible down *here*."

She whimpered, wrapping her legs around him, wanting to feel his erection against her most sensitive spot. She'd never known she could be this fully turned on so quickly, so easily by just a few words and touches. If the sound he made was any indication, he was finding the same erotic pleasure in their movements. So caught up in her lust, she didn't realize what Mitch was doing until her head went underwater. He'd sunk them both under, bobbing back up in two short seconds.

Rylie came up spitting and coughing, as she let out a throaty laugh, swimming away from him toward the boat.

"I think you need to be schooled in the best methods for getting a woman wet...because that, Camden, is not one of them!" she said with laughter, as she reached for the ladder to climb up to the boat's deck. Half way up, she turned back, using her toes to splash him in the face.

Mitch grabbed hold of her leg and pulled her back in. "Oh really? And what makes you such an expert on the subject matter, IQ?" He wrapped his arm around her waist, bringing his lips to her ear, playfully nipping. "I think you should tell me who's made you wet before so I know who my competition is."

Rylie pushed against his shoulder and tried to ascend the ladder again, this time making it to the top and grabbing a towel on the bench. Looking down at Mitch, she held out her arm to help him up, but gave him a finger wave, shooting him a warning look to avoid any funny business.

Stepping back from the platform, Rylie made room for Mitch, her eyes drinking in the sight of his golden body, soaking wet and good enough to eat. His body was gorgeous. Smooth, yet hard, in every place imaginable. His broad shoulders and muscular pecs were perfectly sculpted, with a light smattering of hair on his long arms and chest. Rylie found that utterly sexy. Her eyes continued their journey down his lean torso, over his ripped abdomen to the sexy, secret trail that ran from his navel down past the top of his swim trunks. She licked her lips and made a mental note to explore that region at a later time.

Mitch towel dried and sat down on the padded bench on the back of the deck. Giving Rylie a long look, he snapped the towel against her leg.

"So, are you going to tell me or am I going to have to drag it out of you?"

"Tell you what?"

"About my competition. You know – is there anyone or anything I should know about your love life before I ask you out?"

Rylie snorted at the question and the implied proposition. "As if it's any of your business…but I haven't dated for a long time. And if you must know, Mr. Nosy Pants, I doubt you have any competition in the sex department when it comes to me," Rylie looked down at her hands, feeling a bit shy and nervous about what she was just going to admit. "In fact, um – that was the first orgasm a guy has ever given me."

Rylie was too nervous to look up, but dared a quick peek and saw an utterly stunned, yet proud of himself smirk on Mitch's face.

"How is that even possible? I mean, I know I'm very, *very* good in that department…but fuck."

"Humble much, are we?"

Mitch laughed. "Hey now – you're the one giving me the ammunition here. But seriously – you've honestly never had an orgasm with anyone before?"

She shook her head. "Nope."

"But you have with yourself?"

She blushed, giving Mitch the answer he sought.

"Holy shit, that's hot," he said, pressing his hands down his legs. "That gives me a lot to work with here. I think I'm speechless."

"Why does it surprise you? You make me feel like I'm a leper or from another planet or something. I've just never dated much and I've only had one serious boyfriend before and that was back in college. I don't know, maybe I'm just a late bloomer."

Rylie watched the question appear on Mitch's face before he even asked. "So, when was the last time you, uh, had sex?"

Groaning, she shook her head in exasperation. "Ugh – I knew I shouldn't have brought this subject up. This is embarrassing. I can't tell you that!"

"Why not? You just told me you get yourself off. Why is this any different?"

She tried to think of a good retort and came up short. When was the last time she had sex? She'd never been in to one-night-stands or hook ups. She believed that sex should be with someone you cared about, someone who made you feel good about yourself and someone who respected you. Maybe even someone you loved. She thought she'd loved Erik in college, but looking back at it now, it was more likely just a deep friendship with him. Yes, they had sex and experimented a little, but she never felt on fire with him. Lukewarm at best. And over the last several years, she was just trying to figure out where she fit in the world and getting her career started. And then she was attacked.

She thought about Mitch's question again. "Like I said, I've only had one serious boyfriend and I don't sleep around. I guess the last time I had sex was over five years ago. Nothing to write home to Mom about." Rylie lay back on the dry towel covering the lounge chair and pulled a hat down over her face, partly to shield herself from the hot rays, but more to avoid the intense stare Mitch was giving her at the moment.

"Hmm...." he said, contemplatively. "Hmm."

"What does that mean? *Hmm?*"

He reached down over her body and gently stroked the soft flesh of her leg, starting at her ankle, working his way up to the edge of her suit. Rylie shivered.

"It just gives me something to think about, that's all. Now that I know this about you..." he stopped abruptly, his lips coming down between her legs, his tongue sliding up the inside of her thigh. "I'm going to have to up my game a bit."

Pulling himself back up into a sitting position, Mitch took out his watch and looked at the time. "But right now, I need to get us back to shore so we can get ready for our evening out. We're attending a cocktail party with some of my clients and others from the local industry."

Rylie groaned over the idea of a cocktail party and was about to complain when he shut her down.

"Don't worry, Tully won't be in attendance, not to my knowledge, anyway. I think you'll like this crowd. I'll make damn sure you enjoy yourself. That's a promise."

Mitch patted her on the knees and leaned down to kiss the top of her head, hat and all. "I'm not afraid of seeing Tully again. I'm just not that into formal parties. I'm not very good at social interactions."

"I guess I'll just have to find a way to entertain you tonight, won't I?" He gave her a salacious grin and moved back inside.

Rylie watched Mitch head back to the helm and start the engine, feeling the jerk of the anchor being raised from the bottom depths. It was a little like the pull she was feeling with Mitch. He was somehow loosening that anchor that kept a hold of her feelings for so long, tightly submerged in the bottom of her heart. Her new fear was what might happen once she let go of that life preserver she'd been holding on to for so long. Would she sink or swim?

CHAPTER EIGHTEEN

Mitch was used to waiting for women to get ready for dates. And they always made him wait. His mother had schooled him on never rushing a woman when she was getting ready. It was like telling Picasso or Rembrandt to "just throw some paint on the canvas and move on," she'd say. "You can't rush perfection." So he learned to bide his time, have a drink and wait patiently.

When Rylie emerged from her guestroom promptly at seven-thirty, he was more than a little surprised. She was not only on time, but the very definition of perfection. He was thrown off balance even more so as she walked toward him, her long, tanned bare legs heightened further by silver strapped three-inch heels. The hem of her dress came up well above her knees, displaying a beautiful pair of toned gams. Her lush, silky brown hair fell in thick waves down her back, displaying two glittery hoops dangling from her ears. Her dress was a one-shouldered, silver sequined cut-out mini-dress that hugged her body and every luscious curve from her shoulder to her thigh.

His mouth went dry, as his first thought was whether she was panty-less beneath the form-fitting material. His jaw dropped as she stopped in front of him and pirouetted, giving him a 360-degree view of her mouth-watering body. His hands reached out, stopping her movement, as he traced the cut-out on the back of the dress, which exposed the side of her waist and a hint of her toned oblique.

All his plans to go out for the evening completely vanished from his thoughts, as he considered the fastest means of getting her out of that dress and into his bed.

"Well?" she asked, hands on hips. "Is there some sort of rating scale for this sort of attire? It's not exactly my normal look, so it would be helpful to know where I fall on the one-to-ten scale."

There was no scale where she was concerned. She crushed it. She was out of the fucking ballpark. "Rylie – you are off the fucking charts. You are absolutely…stunning. Holy shit, I can't even breathe. I think I need to sit down before I pass out."

She laughed and shoved him lightly in the chest, as he mockingly fanning himself and then took her wrist, pulling her into his body.

"I hope you brought some extra lipstick with you."

Before she could ask why, he took possession of her mouth, quickly parting her lips and finding entrance to her hot warmth. His lips left hers suddenly, Rylie pouting in response. "I won't be able to keep my mouth off of yours tonight, so you may have to reapply a few times."

She smiled against his mouth and her hands wrapped around his back, moving lower to cup his ass to give him a hard squeeze.

"As long as I can do this to you every time you kiss me, I'm good. I have to admit, I've wanted to do that since the very first time you came into the clinic," she said huskily.

"Oh really?"

She blushed, her teeth gripping her bottom lip. The one he wanted to bite and suck on while he was buried deep inside her.

"Yeah. You have a really nice ass, Mr. Camden."

"Well, by all means then, carry on. My ass is at your disposal day or night. I will, however, hold you to that promise and I'll expect these hands on my ass later." He chuckled, grabbing her hand and leading her out the door to the car.

The party was in full swing as they entered Pearl Champagne Lounge in Miami Beach. Mitch escorted Rylie into the violet lighted club, watching her eyes light up as they made their way past the chic, all-white décor and crystal chandeliers, toward the private VIP room and wrap-around terrace overlooking the Atlantic. Go-Go dancing waitresses dressed in crystal encrusted bikini tops, tiny satin white booty shorts and feathered head dresses, gracefully weaved through the guests, passing around hors d'oeuvres and champagne flutes to the hundreds of party goers.

Mitch grabbed two glasses from the tray, handing one to Rylie. She saluted him her thanks, as they continued to make their way through the throngs of revelers, on their way out the doors.

The music was loud, a thumping mix of techno and hip-hop, and a parade of beautiful, scantily clad women made their way around the lounge. One stopped in front of Mitch, giving him a jiggle of her breasts and then grabbing his crotch. He politely, but assertively, removed her hand from his groin and laughed.

"You never know what you're going to get in Miami." His eyes moved to Rylie's face, watching her eyes sparkle in the neon lights. Her dress caught the flashing strobe lights and glittered an ethereal glow. An angel in his midst.

Mitch continued to watch Rylie as she scanned the room and party, her face telling him without words what she was thinking. The party had a burlesque vibe, a little raunchy and over-the-top. He wondered if she'd ever been to anything like this before. Recalling their conversation from earlier, he highly doubted it. He was in awe over the innocence she still possessed. She wasn't a virgin, but with such limited encounters, she didn't have much experience. It only heightened Mitch's desire to guide and instruct her on what she might find pleasurable, and how to pleasure him. She seemed reserved, but willing to explore, which had his lust spiking even higher. He promised himself he'd take his time and not rush things, leaving it to her to make the next move and avoid any potential regrets on her end. But once she gave him the go-ahead, it was going to be full-throttle, no going back.

Removing the champagne glass from her hand and placing it on the table, Mitch led her out onto the crowded dance floor. The music, which had been a thumping techno beat, had now slowed down to a smooth, sexy rhythm, perfect for slow dancing.

Rylie looked up into his eyes warily. "Mitch, I don't dance. I have no rhythm and I'm not exactly graceful. I'm like a giraffe in a ballet."

He smiled silently at her self-deprecating description, but just pulled her close so that the top of her head fit underneath his chin. He gathered her arms, bringing one up to his shoulder and the other nestled in his palm. His other hand wrapped securely around her waist, pulling her in snugly to his chest. He breathed in the sweet scent of her shampoo and felt her breathing even out against him.

They swayed to the music, Mitch lost in the sensation of their bodies moving together, fitting perfectly with one another. He could feel her heartbeat and her pulse, which beat wildly against his heart. It felt good, holding her in his arms like this. He wanted this woman with every cell of his being. Not just sexually, although that was predominantly how it started. There was something else about her that called to him, spoke to his soul. Captured his attention and drove his mind to distraction.

"Can I ask you something?" Rylie whispered, bending her head back to look into Mitch's eyes.

Mitch shook his head, taken out of his reverie. "Of course."

"Do you wine and dine all the women you date like this?"

Shit. Truth be told, he didn't. He'd honestly not had to go through the trouble with other women. Sure, he treated them with respect and showed them a good time. But had he ever gone to the same lengths to attract a woman before like he was doing now with Rylie? The answer was no. She was a first. A beautiful challenge.

"Do you think this is a date?" he teased, but the look on her face had him bursting out in hysterics. It was a cross between sheer embarrassment and terror.

Trying to back pedal, she said, "I didn't mean to imply this was a date, or anything. Well, I don't know…I guess it does feel a little like a date. Oh God. I feel so stupid now." She bent her head in shame. He had to put the poor girl out of her misery.

Placing his hand underneath her chin, he gently lifted her face back up to him. "Hey, I'm just messing with you. I would definitely consider this a date. And no, I don't pull out all the stops with just anyone. You are special, Rylie. Beyond incredible and I'm honored you're here with me, even though I did have to coerce you to come to Miami."

There was no place in the world he'd rather be than right there with her in his arms at this moment. He bent his head to hers, dropping his mouth to hers, touching her plump, kissable mouth to his lips. Brushing gently at first, reveling in the softness, the sweetness, the feel of his lips and tongue dancing with hers. She was delectable and his body wanted more. He had to pull apart before he couldn't stop.

"Do you want to get out of here?" he asked, breathing hard.

"Yes."

Sweeping her off the dance floor, Mitch's head turned at the sound of a loud commotion. A group of people, who seemed to be looking around in confusion, seemed to part, making a path for whatever or whomever was coming out their way. For some reason, Mitch felt his stomach clench and the hairs on the back of his neck stand up, at the same moment he got a clear view of Tully making his way through the crowd. Behind him were two uniformed Miami Metro police officers. Instinctively, Mitch put his arm around Rylie's waist and pulled her close.

Tully's eye flashed to Mitch's and then zeroed in on Rylie.

"There she is! That's the one," Tully yelled, pointing a bandaged hand directly at Rylie, who was standing in his path looking dazed and confused. "Officers, that's the woman who assaulted me today. I want her arrested."

The two officers looked at one another briefly and then down to Tully, who was a full head shorter than they were. The Latino officer, who was on the left, spoke to Tully calmly and with authority.

"Sir? Are you saying this woman here," pointing again to Rylie, who had yet to move and whose expression had shock and horror written all over it. "…that this young woman assaulted you today, broke your hand and your ribs and beat up your face?" The officer shook his head in disbelief. "That's a lot of damage for one female to do to a…*man*." The officer hesitated momentarily, a smirk toying at his lips, waiting for his words to sink in. The other officer had to turn his head away, the grin and mirth on his face too revealing.

"Yes, that's exactly what I'm saying. And I have witnesses that will corroborate my story. Now do your fucking job and arrest her!"

Mitch stepped in front of Rylie, his arm going around his back to protectively move her behind him. He took two steps forward.

"Excuse me, officers. My name is Mitch Camden," he stated, handing one of the officers his business card. "I was a witness today at the restaurant. I'm not sure what exactly Mr. Tully has told you happened or who really is to blame for all that bodily damage, but let me assure you, it was not Rylie Hemmons." He gave Tully a disgusted look.

Tully twitched and squirmed, looking like a toddler preparing for a full tantrum. "That is not true! Mitch was not there today. He's lying."

Mitch wanted to reach out and grab Tully by the neck and cut off his air supply. What a prick. How did he not see this before now?

Mitch cocked his head to the side. "*Really*, Tull? What the fuck are you trying to pull here? I was there and heard exactly what went down at the end of your lunch today. I was standing just outside on the deck and heard Rylie assert not just once, but twice, asking you to get your fucking hands off of her. She specifically warned you that she would break your fingers if you didn't. And when you didn't respectfully comply, and continued to grope her, she did what most women wouldn't have the guts to do. She broke your finger and then calmly walked away."

Mitch looked up at the two officers and stated matter-of-factly. "Rylie did not do anything other than defend herself against this asshole's molesting hands."

The officers looked from Mitch, to Rylie and then back again to Tully. One took out a notepad and asked Rylie to step over with him so he could get her statement. The other pulled Tully aside. Mitch listened in as he gave Tully the riot act.

"Mr. Tully, if this is true, and your so-called witnesses testify to what Mr. Camden just recounted, it seems to me that Ms. Hemmons had every right to fend you off. If I were you, Mr. Tully, I'd drop this bullshit now, because it's not only a waste of our time, but it's making you look like a world-class pussy."

Tully stood there fuming, his hands bunched up in fists and his face in a tight and angry expression. Mitch watched him turn around and stomp off and out of the party.

The Latino officer, Lieutenant Lopez, came back over to speak with Mitch. "I don't know about you, but I'd have to say that guy has a Little Man's complex," he chuckled, taking his notepad to scribble some additional notes. "You apparently know him well?"

Mitch rubbed his hand over his face. "Yeah, at least I thought I did. I've been doing business with the guy for years, but I've never seen him act like this." Mitch turned his concern back over to Rylie, as he noticed the other officer was just wrapping up his questions with her. "What's going to happen now?"

"Depending on the information Ms. Hemmons provides us, and if she chooses to press charges, we will investigate it further. I'm thinking Mr. Tully will drop his charges. He's obviously pissed about being beat up and wanted someone to blame other than himself."

Rylie and the second officer returned to join Mitch and Lieutenant Lopez. Rylie appeared shaken up, but no worse for wear, her face wearing a confounded expression. Mitch put his arm around her shoulders and pulled her to him. She smiled a weary smile as she took the business card the officer handed her.

"Here's my contact number, Miss Hemmons, if you can think of anything else to add or if he bothers you again. We have your number in case we need to get in touch with you further. Sorry for the interruption of your evening. I hope you can enjoy the rest of your party."

Rylie nodded her head and placed the card in her clutch. "Thank you, Officer Jens and Lieutenant Lopez. I appreciate it. I hope we won't have a repeat of this in the future." Turning to Mitch, she laughed. "Miami really knows how to show a girl a good time!"

As the officers turned to leave, Mitch pulled Rylie tight against him, one hand wrapped around her waist and the other on the back of her head. His mouth was at her ear.

"I'm so sorry, Rylie," he said in a whispered plea. "I had no idea Tully was capable of that kind of crap. Effective immediately, my association with him no longer exists."

Rylie looked up at Mitch, her eyes full of guilt and shame.

"Oh no. Please don't let what happened here ruin your business partnership. You have a lot riding on this deal. I would feel horrible if I had anything to do with you losing money or this project."

Mitch kissed her lips softly, tasting a hint of strawberry and champagne on her breath.

"Rylie, knowing what I now know about Randall Tully, there is no way I'd ever continue to do business with him. Ever. Do you understand?" His hands reached out to cradle Rylie's face, as he laid a kiss on her forehead.

Rylie raised up on her tip-toes and kissed his cheek and smiled. "Thanks. You're a pretty decent guy for being such an impossible asshole," she joked, grabbing his hand and leading him toward the bar. "Now I think I'm in need of a drink after that little episode."

"One drink, coming right up."

****

Rylie laid her head back on the headrest as Mitch drove them back to the beach house from the party. The warm feel of the ocean breeze caressed her face as the convertible sped along the Oceanside road with the top down. She also was feeling pretty good and buzzed, accentuating said warm feelings of contentment.

After the shock had worn off from Tully's confrontation, the remainder of the evening was filled with more dancing, mingling, dinner, and more than a few champagne cocktails. She was feeling the tingling effects of a nice buzz and was relaxed, as Mitch remained by her side the entire night. His hand was either holding hers or wrapped around her tightly. A warm, satisfied feeling swept over her at one point as they danced to a slow, sexy Enrique Iglesias song and she lifted her head to see him smiling down at her.

Oh – what that smile did to her. She couldn't think about anything else as she was transfixed in his gaze, sending molten heat flowing through her body, landing squarely between her thighs. She wanted him to take her out on the beach and do *very* bad, bad things to her. She wanted to feel the rough texture of the sand against her naked body, a contrast to the smooth abs and chest pressed snug against her.

Rylie was itching for Mitch to touch her and had finally come to the conclusion tonight that she wanted to sleep with him. Her only problem now was how to let him know what she wanted. She'd never made the first move before, always leaving it up to the guy and usually their hasty efforts at foreplay. And she certainly wasn't vocal about her needs or desires. Would she just ask Mitch to make love to her or demand it? What if he liked it rough and dirty? She'd never experimented with much of anything out of the norm, that simple vanilla kind of sex. But the way he made her feel, she was willing to try just about anything, as long as instruction was included.

She'd finally come to a decision about what she wanted from him as he parked the car outside the house and walked over to open her door.

Dropping his hand to her, she took hold and stood up, losing her balance. Wobbling on her heels, she grabbed his shoulders to steady herself.

"A little tipsy, are we?"

"Nah," she slurred, a tiny hiccup escaping. "It must be the heels. I don't usually wear these things." She tried to bend down to illustrate her sure footedness, but toppled again into his arms.

"Okay. Whatever you say. Let's go inside and get you some water so you can get to bed."

Rylie giggled and repeated. "Get me to bed…*suuuurre*. That's exactly what I was thinking."

Mitch gave her a speculative glance, assisting her with the removal of her shoes and holding her elbow as she entered the house.

Whoa. The room was definitely spinning a bit more than it should. Maybe she should just get some water and lay down for a while to get her bearings before she started on her mission – *The Seduction of Mitch.* Rylie giggled to herself and found a chair to sit down, as Mitch handed her the glass of water.

"Here – you need to drink this. Champagne has a way of sneaking up on you."

Rylie hiccupped again and drank thirstily. Finishing the glass, she fumbled with it before setting it down. Looking back up at Mitch, she found him leaning against the kitchen wall, arms crossed, watching her with a bemused look.

"Whatcha doing way over there, Camden? I think you should be over here by me," she demanded, pointing to the space in front of her.

Another hiccup. *Dammit.*

"I'm keeping my distance, IQ. You are way too sexy for your own good and a little too drunk, which is a really bad combination. And you're very, *very* tempting. Distance is our friend right now."

"Well I disagree. How am I supposed to seduce you if you're way over there," she said, throwing a flailing hand in the air toward him and then back at her. "And I'm way over here?"

Mitch chuckled and pushed off against the wall to pick up her glass and refill it for her. Reaching out to her, Rylie shook her head in disapproval.

"I don't want more water."

"Then what do you want?"

Rylie chewed on her lower lip, realizing it was now or never. "I want what you promised me last night. You said you wanted to fuck me." She tried to stand, but her legs gave way. Mitch was right there to catch her, his hands holding her up under her arms.

Mitch let out a noise that sounded like air deflating from a tire. "Dammit, Rylie. I've been waiting so long to hear that from you. But not tonight when you're drunk. You need to go to bed to sleep this off. I want you completely stone-cold sober when I take you."

She sucked in a shaky breath, getting ready to argue and plead her case, but her eyelids began to droop and her body felt laden with brick and mortar. Mitch carefully assisted her to the guestroom where he adroitly removed her dress and gently laid her on the bed. Rylie lay there, exposed to Mitch in just her pink lace strapless bra and lace thong, looking up at him with a forlorn expression.

Closing her eyes, she mumbled, her head falling back onto the soft pillow.

"Okay, maybe later."

CHAPTER NINETEEN

She woke up thirsty, thirstier than she'd ever been. She pushed herself to an upright position, a feeling of dizziness fluttering through her brain. Gaining her balance, she peeked over at the clock on the bedside table which read two-thirty. *Holy cow*. She must have passed out as soon as they got home. She was kicking herself for drinking so much champagne. Why didn't she just stick with her usual beer? Champagne, that conniving backstabber.

Rylie quietly got out of bed, gingerly walking into the bathroom, turning on the dimmer switch to a soft glow. She turned on the water faucet as a glass and a note next to it caught her attention.

"*Drink this*" the note read. Mitch.

Well, that was thoughtful. And after the stupidity she pulled earlier with her oh-so-smooth hot shot seductive moves, he should have made a laughing stock out of her. As her brother would say at a time like this, "Smooth move, Ex-lax." God, she felt like a fool.

She fished back into her memory at her actions earlier in the evening, trying to determine how embarrassed she should feel at the moment. Let's see. There was the unbelievable turn of events at the party with Tully and two local police. Yeah, that was priceless. Nearly getting arrested by Mitch's business associate. Very classy.

And then there was the moment she practically fell down drunk into his arms when she was trying to ever so coolly and seductively get out of his convertible. She was uncoordinated even on the best of days, but with a few glasses, or five, of bubbly, she was a downright circus freak.

And the coup de grace? The icing on the cake? The way her not-so-smooth and charming maneuvers failed to get Mitch to take her to bed. Epic fail. He was probably wracking his brain at this moment trying to figure out a way to end this thing before it even started. She was a joke. A great story he could tell his friends about the time "this incredibly stupid drunk girl came on to me and then passed out before anything got under way."

Finishing the water and handling her bio needs, Rylie pulled on the T-shirt that was on the end of the bed. She looked down at the bra and panties she still wore and had a faint recollection of Mitch slipping off her dress and shoes and laying her down on her bed. His hands had caressed her arms, as the material slid down her limbs. A ripple of sensual heat fluttered through her now, reawakening the aching need that had been building over the course of the last week.

Straining to hear if Mitch was up and awake, she opened the door and stepped out into the hallway. Holding her breath, she walked across the hall to Mitch's room, listening for any indication of life on the other side of the door.

Looking down at her feet, hesitantly shifting from one foot to the other, she debated whether she should knock. Weighing the merits of making any more of a fool of herself, she at least wanted to apologize for her ridiculously moronic behavior earlier. She'd rather hide her face until she left tomorrow and avoid the awkwardness of this whole thing, but she had to grow a pair and deal with her mess.

Knocking softly, she waited. Nothing.

Taking a chance, she turned the knob and opened the door, peeking her head through the crack as her eyes adjusted to the dark.

"Mitch? Are you asleep?"

Silence. Just as she was about to turn and leave, she noticed the curtains were pulled back and the patio door open. Taking a breath, she propelled herself forward with all the courage she could muster, and stepped out into the warm, humid air. Mitch was in a lounge chair, legs stretched out in front of him, a cognac sifter in his hand, staring out into the night. He looked relaxed and so incredibly sexy.

"Hey," she whispered.

Turning his head slightly, she could see the outline of his smile in the dark.

"Hey, yourself. You feeling better? You'll likely have a killer headache in the morning."

Rylie took the remaining steps toward his chair and stood over him.

"Thank you for taking care of me."

"No problem."

She stood there, unsure of how to proceed. All she knew was that he was more intoxicating than any drink in the world. He smelled so good, musky and spicy, like a worn leather.

"I'm really sorry for making such a mess of tonight. For Tully and getting accidentally drunk and…for making a fool of myself."

Mitch took a sip of his drink and slowly placed it down on the ground. Inching his hips and legs toward the side of the chair, he extended his hands to her.

"Come here."

His command flooded her body with heat. His words held such promise – forgiveness, kindness, redemption and sweet, sweet seduction.

Her feet moved in accordance to his request, bringing her within touching distance of his body. His hand darted out and grabbed her wrist, yanking her down so that she was sitting on the edge of the chair, her back to his chest.

He leaned into her, his mouth at her ear, the sound of his voice as smooth as the scent of Scotch on his breath.

"None of that was your fault, Rylie. I shouldn't have put you in that situation," he murmured into her neck, as his lips came down to lightly brush her skin.

And just like that, her worry over her transgressions evaporated and her body took over. In a move that shocked and surprised even her, she pulled the T-shirt over her head, dropping it to the patio floor and swung a leg over Mitch's body. Straddling his lap, her hands went to his chest, as her ass wiggled across his groin.

"Just so you know, I have three rules…"

"Rules?" he asked, his voice soft and low, a hint of curiosity, but displaying no other surprise over the direction of the conversation.

"Yes, rules. Number one – I don't want to hear flowery terms of endearment in the heat of the moment. Call me by my name is okay, but no pet names."

"So no IQ?"

"Not when you're trying to make me come." She smiled wickedly.

Mitch stifled a laugh and gave her a check off signal with his hand. "Got it. Next?"

"Rule number two – no kinky stuff. I'm not interested in that."

"Absolutely. Not my thing, either," he said, nuzzling his nose between her breasts, his tongue licking the flesh licentiously. "And number three?"

Rylie grabbed Mitch's hands and brought them to her lace covered breasts. She arched into his palms, enjoying the intense pleasure and heat of his palm.

"Rule number three is…" she inhaled sharply, trying to catch her breath.

"What?" he pleaded, his thumb circling her nipples through the material.

She was hesitant, but wanted to be honest with him before they went further. She wasn't experienced like most of the women he had been with.

"I need you to help me – show me what to do – what you like. I want you to teach me everything."

Mitch's hands left her breasts and he combed his fingers through the silky strands of Rylie's hair, a low growl emerging from his chest. He tugged her mouth down to his, capturing it with his lips.

"It will be my pleasure." His voice came out in a husky rumble. "Are you ready for lesson one?"

Rylie nodded her head. "Yes."

"Unbutton my shirt."

Rylie tugged the shirt from his pants and began to slowly unbutton his dress shirt with shaking fingers, as they skimmed across the exposed flesh of his chest with each undone button. The shirt lay open, as her eyes took in the exposed beauty of his golden chest. Her hands began to roam, charting a course down below, wanting to feel his steely length.

Mitch's head fell back with a moan, and then came back up, his face nuzzling her breasts. His hands reached behind her, stilling for a moment as he looked up to meet her intense gaze with an imploring expression. "May I?"

Her heart was torn open with his gentlemanly request. Rylie bit her lip and shook her head in confirmation. She had never wanted anything more than to feel his hands covering her naked, swollen breasts. The clasp came undone, as Mitch let it drop to the floor, his hands gently brushing the skin of her arms, his fingers igniting a trail of heat with his touch.

His hands brushed over her lush curves, his thumbs flicking over her hardened nipples and she arched up, beseeching him for more.

He bent down, taking a nipple into his mouth and he began to suck. "Everything about you makes me so fucking hot."

Rylie sighed from sheer pleasure of his mouth, her hands sliding through his hair, yanking him closer as the sensations intensified. She groaned from the exquisite torture as she looked down to watch him, her breasts pressed into his palms as he explored her with his tongue. He smiled up at her with pure male satisfaction.

Her hands resumed their course lower, as she pressed her hand firmly against his erection. "I want to touch you," she said with a shaky voice.

Rylie felt his arousal pulse against her, as his hands went to his pants, lacing his fingers with hers.

"Unzip me…" His voice was deep with desire.

Rylie did as instructed, unzipping his tailored pants, tugging them down past his hips and feet, throwing them in a heap to the ground. She could see the outlined silhouette of his hardened shape straining against the material of his dark gray boxer briefs. She slid her fingers underneath the elastic waistband, pulling them down, his erection springing free.

Rylie felt wildly out of control as she gazed upon his impressive length. A maddening hunger and power coursed through her and the need to touch him took over. Her fingers trailed down through the mesh of hair, as she locked her hand around his hard and thick length. He felt like smooth marble. Mitch thrummed in her hand, as her own sex clenched in a heady response. She grazed a fingertip lightly over the tip, flicking a drop of moisture from his head.

A guttural groan surged from the depths of Mitch's chest, as his hand took possession of hers. "Grab the base tight…now stroke," he instructed, moving her gripped hand up and down his erection. "Oh, shit, that feels so good."

Rylie was coming apart at the seams as she watched Mitch's expression and heard the need in his voice. His head fell back against the chair, as his hands slid up and down her thighs with the same pace and rhythm. She moved wantonly against his leg in the same motion, feeling wet and slick, aching for something just beyond her reach.

Breathless, Mitch took hold of her hand, unwrapping it from his cock. "Unless you want this tutorial over before it begins, I need you to stop this wicked pleasure." His hands reached behind her, cupping her ass and pulling her up into his arms as he stood.

Rylie gave a surprised gasp. "Wh– what are you doing?"

"I'm taking you into my bed so I can continue with your lessons."

She caught her breath in response, wrapping her legs around him as she'd done so many times in the water over the last couple days. This time, she wanted nothing between them – she wanted to feel his nakedness crushing against her; inside her.

He gently laid her on the bed, Rylie landing with a soft thud, as he tore off his shirt sending it flying in a heap on the floor. Rylie stared at him for several beats as he stood over her, every part of his body now on display for her pleasure. All she had left between them was her panties. Did he want her to take them off for him? Her hand went to her belly, splaying it across her abdomen. Mitch stared at her like he was a starving man and she was his buffet.

"Rylie, you are so fucking beautiful," he growled, bending over her, as he began to trace an invisible line that started from her ankle, up the inside of her thigh. "So gorgeous." His fingers traced the edge of her lace panties, as she sucked in a breath. He continued the same movement on the opposite leg.

"Spread your legs for me."

She did as he asked, lifting her head off the mattress to see what he was going to do. Her nipples were puckered and hard, as he reached out to touch them, playfully circling the pink peaks, as he moved in between her legs. A shiver ran down her spine, as gooseflesh traveled her body from her arms to her toes.

His interest diverted, his hands trailed along the sensitive skin, his tongue following the same path. It was obvious that Mitch was taking his time, in no particular hurry, leisurely enjoying the foreplay. Rylie, on the other hand, wasn't sure she was capable of waiting. It felt like she'd been waiting all her life for this moment. And she wanted it all now.

"Please," she whimpered. "I want you."

He gave her a wicked grin, as his tongue circled her belly button, then dipped in and darted back out. His mouth continued to move south and Rylie moaned, her hips writhing up against him.

She cried out a tortured noise. "Oh God…"

"Lesson number two, Ry, is about patience. All good things take time."

Mitch smiled as a warm puff of his peaty, smoky Scotch breath came out against her pelvis. His fingers were now poised at the edge of her lace panties, as they swirled and teased the sensitive spot between her legs. Her heart sped up as she nearly came undone in anticipation for what was next.

Not ready to give in to Rylie's pleas and demands, he placed soft kisses across her lower abdomen, sucking and nipping up and down her torso. Rylie could feel the heat pooling between her legs, the aching throb of her sex, her desire reaching a breaking point.

Mitch ran his finger along the lace edge, inching his pinkies under the material so he could slide it down past her hips, slowly moving it down past her ankles. Returning to her awaiting sex, his finger slid down between her satiny folds. Rylie nearly came unhinged as he slipped a finger deep inside her, as she arched up into his hand. With his thumb pushing against her center, he began circling her, his finger moving in and out at the same time, creating a burning need for her release. She was so close to reaching the edge, poised at the precipice. She clawed at the bed, trying desperately to find purchase, gripping the covers tight in her fists, as she rocked against him, whimpering out unintelligible pleas.

Didn't he know she was so close? Just a few…more…strokes and she would be there, screaming in agony and pleasure. She thrashed and moved, feeling his fingers curl around her tight center.

"I…oh God….I'm there...Mitch…" she screamed, as an explosion rocked her entire body. Her climax was an enormous fireball, bursting into flames, ripping through her with no mercy. Mitch continued to stroke her as she came down from her release, as she slowly let go of the sheets that were bundled tightly in her fists.

Mitch moved up between her legs and poised his hard tip at her entrance, nudging and teasing. "You are so wet – it's killing me," he said, reaching over to a side table where he grabbed a condom.

Rylie reached between their bodies and grabbed his erection, as he groaned. She reached for the wrapper in his hand.

"I want to put it on you." Her hands left him momentarily, taking the packet and ripping it open. "Show me how."

Mitch took her hands in his and held them over the tip, securing it on the top and then let her go.

"Roll it all the way down – hard," he hissed. She did as he instructed, feeling pleased as he groaned against her touch.

"Please, Mitch. I want to feel *you* inside of me." Rylie squeezed his hardened cock between her legs, positioning him at her entrance as Mitch pushed inside to bury himself deep within her.

"Holy fuck, Ry – you feel so good."

She let out a moan, of both pleasure and pain, as he slowly eased himself in and out, sinking in deep. It had definitely been awhile, so she had to get accustomed again to the feeling. Her hands slid up and down his back, as she felt his muscles tightening.

"Are you okay? Am I hurting you?"

"Ohh, yes – this is so good." On the downward motion of her hands, she grasped his butt tightly, pulling him in deeper.

He moved, in and out, thrusting harder and faster. His breathing became ragged, tiny beads of sweat forming where their bodies were joined.

"Wrap your legs around me tight, baby."

She complied, as she moaned when she felt him thrust in even deeper, plunging in and out in a steady, sensual rhythm. They rocked together, touching, licking, sucking, as the familiar tension began to build once more.

She could feel the pleasure climb again, that ache low in her belly, working its way through, slithering down to her core. Mitch continued to pump in and out, nipping at her ear, his tongue sliding in and out. Slipping his hand down between their joined bodies, his fingers sought her heat. One touch, just a flick, had her cursing out expletives, as she clenched around him, screaming her release, at the same time his body jerked and then stilled as he emptied himself into her with a shudder.

Moments went by with neither of them saying anything, their rapid breathing getting back under control. Mitch remained inside her, as he lifted his head to look into her eyes. He placed a kiss on her forehead, then her cheeks, her nose and then finally a long, stirring one on her mouth. Sucking her bottom lip, he bit lightly before letting go. Rylie couldn't say a word. Her body was in nirvana, completely and utterly satiated.

She felt Mitch twitch inside her, as she giggled from the sensation and cocked her eyebrow at him.

"What? You think it's funny that you just made me come and I want to do it all over again?" He tweaked her nose, as he pulsed inside her again. "You won't think it's so funny when you're sore tomorrow." As he said it, he slowly eased out of her, moving off to the side to discard the condom in the trash.

"I want you to make me sore…I want to feel you all day long." He rolled over to face her, lifting her head to rest on his arm. She reached a hand out to trace his stubbled jaw. "Mitch…"

His hand caressed her shoulder and ran it down the curve of her hip. "Mmm…hmm?"

"How was I as your student?"

He laughed at the audacity of her question. "Oh, young grasshopper...you were brilliant. However, I think we'll need to keep up with your lessons. Practice makes perfect."

She slapped him on his stomach, but smiled as she got up from the bed to go into the bathroom. Mitch's hand darted out and grabbed her wrist, stalling her momentarily. He dropped her hand and lightly touched the curve of her ass, rolling over it and down her leg.

"Did I mention that I think you're gorgeous?"

"Hmm, if you did, I must have been in the middle of something," she snickered. "But that's sweet. And don't let this go to your head, because I know your ego is already as big as the continent, but you're pretty gorgeous yourself."

She reached down and kissed his nipple, lingering there to allow her tongue to trace the dime size center. Heading back into the bathroom, she turned on the soft recessed lighting and looked longingly at herself in the mirror.

Her entire body was flushed a soft pink hue. She touched her sensitive breasts that had been thoroughly ravaged, sucked, touched and kissed. Her hand trailed down her stomach until it reached her silky center. She sighed, remembering the erotic sensations and two orgasms Mitch had given her over the last few hours. Had she ever felt that way before? She'd never experienced a man taking the time to be that in tune with her body, to leisurely touch every inch of her and to ensure her needs were so completely satisfied before his own. To patiently teach her how to pleasure and be pleasured?

Rylie smiled at her reflection in the mirror, wondering what Sasha would say when she found out about tonight. And just like that, the panic seeped in. Her mouth dried up and she felt like she had swallowed sandpaper. The old familiar grip of fear and anxiety welled up in the pit of her stomach, gripping her like an overgrown vine.

Mitch was a man who got what he wanted, when he wanted it and now that he'd slept with her, would likely find her irrelevant and obsolete. He was a man who liked the challenge of the chase and now that he'd fulfilled his need, she would be completely useless. He was bound to leave her. It was only a matter of time.

She turned off the faucet and dried her hands with the hand towel as Mitch knocked lightly on the door. "Hey, can I come in?"

Still naked, she turned around, feeling exposed and self-conscious, looking for something to cover herself with. Before she could reach the towel rack, he stepped in, taking two long strides to reach her and encircle her in his arms.

"You interested in skinny dipping?"

"What? Like now?"

"Yes, now." He let his eyes roam over her body. "Looks like you're already prepped for it – we just need to grab some towels, unless you had other plans on what you want to do with me." His lips moved down to caress the small crevice at the base of her throat, as her head tipped back granting him access. She hummed, the vibration against his mouth making him growl.

"I'm up for a dip…and maybe something else, too." She turned on a bright smile, placing her earlier thoughts in the back of her mind for later.

"That's what I was hoping to hear."

Taking her hand, he led her into the bedroom, opening the patio door to walk out to the pool. The air still held a slight humidity in it, covering their naked bodies with a sheen of moisture. Jumping in the pool, Mitch dove underneath, coming up for air and raising his arms to reach for her. She took a step forward and plunged in. Maybe that was the only way to get over this thing with Mitch…dive into the deep end and hope she could hold her breath until he gave up.

As soon as she hit the water, Mitch was there in front of her, his hands scooping her up under her butt.

"If you asked me what my favorite part of your body was, I'd have to say it's your ass," he said, caressing her butt in his hands. "Followed by your legs as a close second. They were the first thing I noticed about you the night at the bar. But it was your high and mighty smack down of me that had me wanting to get to know you more. Do you know how beautiful you are when you give a good beat-down? Damn, that was hot. Is that an inherited trait?"

Rylie stilled in his arms as she considered his question. She shouldn't have been surprised with such a personal question after the night they just shared, but talking about her family put her on uncomfortable ground. He already knew about her dad and Dylan, but opening up about her mother was a bit unnerving and wasn't something she often did.

"It might be, maybe it's from my mother's side. My dad and brother are pretty laid back and easy going. They rarely get ruffled about anything and always seem to be calming me down. Maybe I've always felt I had something to prove, given I was the only female in the household."

"Where's your mother?"

Rylie squirmed in his arms, trying to find a backdoor strategy out of the conversation they were having, hoping to move on to something else. His arms tightened further around her body, his hand roaming up and down the length of her legs.

"My mother left us when I was four." Shrugging nonchalantly, she pulled out of his arms and swam in the opposite direction.

The pool lights cast a warm glow across the water, as she made her way to the end of the pool. Mitch quickly following suit, coming up behind her to press his lips to her ear.

"Well that's shitty. Did you ever hear from her again?"

"Nope. She left a note for my dad and he thought she went out to California or something. He said she was full of wanderlust and never wanted to be tied down in life."

Mitch pulled her to him tightly, his arms holding her reassuringly. "I'm sure she loved you and your brother, but just had her own issues and didn't know how to deal. It wasn't you, you know." Mitch slid his arm around her, turning her around to face him.

She gave him a half-hearted nod. "Of course I know that. She was a selfish, heartless bitch and she didn't deserve us. But it still hurts to know she didn't love us enough to stay."

"Rylie, it's not right what she did, and you may never know why she left. But the end result is it shaped you into who you are today. You are a beautiful, smart and ambitious woman, and I can tell you've used that fucked-up life lesson to build your character. It's that character that I've enjoyed getting to know…and I'd like to get to know more of you. Starting with these long legs of yours," he chuckled, running his hand up the back of her leg. "Definitely one of your best traits."

Mitch grinned his lopsided smile, as his dimple peeked out. This close to him, she couldn't stop herself this time from leaning in and sucking on it.

"What do you think your best trait is? And if you say it's your dick, I'll smack you," she laughed playfully.

"Let's see…my best trait? Well, I finally got you into my bed, so it must be my power of persuasion." Licking the soft outside of her ear, his tongue surged in and made her cry out. "But to keep you in my bed, I may need to work a little harder."

Nudging his leg between hers, Mitch pushed her gently against the side of the pool, his hand coming up between their bodies.

"I also have a helluva lot of stamina. I hope you don't need any sleep tonight, because I plan to be relentless."

CHAPTER TWENTY

Rylie gasped, as Mitch's fingers began to trace circles around her sex as he moved his tongue in an identical pattern, plunging in and out of her mouth. He couldn't pull his eyes away from her, her naked body wet and glistening in the moonlight. His cock lengthened against her, as she moved her hand to cover him, running her fingers against his erection. Mitch swallowed thickly, his desire overwhelmingly strong for her mouth to replace her hands. But first, he had other things he wanted to do.

He slid his finger between the wet opening of her legs, his mouth capturing hers, running his tongue across her teeth. His mouth watered in his need to taste her, to feel her come apart under his tongue. "I want to taste you on my tongue."

He slipped his tongue inside her mouth before he moved her toward the pool steps. Taking her hand in his, he directed her to the pool house, where a warmly lit room awaited.

He led her over to the cushioned wicker chaise lounge, laying her down, his hand brushing down the length of her. Taking her legs by the knees, he pressed them open, one on each side of the chair. Bending down on his knees, careful of his injury site, he hovered over her, his lips seeking the wet and heated flesh, placing soft, feather light kisses inside her inner thigh. He licked his way farther up her body. Her thighs quivered as she tried without success to remove his head from between her legs.

Mitch just shook his head. "You're not going shy on me now."

He placed his hands on the inside of both her thighs, his thumbs caressing the soft skin, still wet from the pool. Peeking up, he could see the sensual curve of her breasts, as she propped herself up on her elbows to look down at him.

"You like what you see?"

She bit her lip, pensively nodding yes.

"I've never actually…well, you know…had a guy go down on me. I'm not sure if I'll like it."

He shook with the laughter that bubbled out of him.

"Oh you'll like it," he murmured, licking his lips before his tongue darted out to touch the inside of her thigh, mere inches from her heat. "I'll make sure of that. And feel free to watch." He smiled salaciously against her hot, wet core.

Mitch's cock twitched at the torment she was causing him with her honest admission of uncertainty. The idea of being her first at anything was unbelievably erotic and made him feel like a fucking king.

He moved one hand to cup her ass and the other gently pushed her knees up one at a time. Deft fingers dipped into her heated center, finding her agonizingly wet, as his mouth moved over her sweet flesh. The sound that escaped her when his tongue met her slick center had him ready to explode. Her hips arched up to meet his mouth, as her hands reached blindly to grab his hair.

His lips turned up into a smile, as he blew a light breath against her sex, then circled it with his tongue.

"Oh my God, Mitch…" she cried breathlessly. "Don't stop…please."

There was no way he could. Her aroused scent and the taste of her had him nearly coming against the cushions of the chair. His fingers slipped into her wet opening, as she contracted around him, groaning with every back and forth he gave her. She struggled and shifted beneath him, her hands gripping the throw pillows near her head, as he continued his gentle sucking.

He knew she was close, her hands finding their way back to his head to dig into his scalp, her tiny pleas getting louder and more exaggerated with every flick of his tongue. His long fingers stroked her passage, until she tightened around him, stilling momentarily as her body surrendered in a loud cry of ecstasy.

His fingers remained buried inside, allowing her to ride the remaining waves of pleasure, continuing to lightly stroke her down from her high. He lifted his head to watch her movements, her body flushed with a sensual afterglow. All he wanted to do at that moment was to bury himself deep inside of her and make her come over and over again.

Rylie slowly recovered, her arms releasing Mitch from her grip and crossing over her bared breasts. Sighing contentedly, she lifted herself to a sitting position, as Mitch came up to sit next to her, his hands lightly rubbing her back.

"That was unbelievable…wow," she murmured, leaning into his chest and kissing the inside of his neck. Her hand moved at a leisurely pace down his chest and torso, fingering the treasure trail leading to his engorged arousal. "My turn to repay the favor."

"I'm completely at your mercy."

Licking her lips, Rylie grabbed hold of his stubbled cheeks and kissed him hot and wild. Her hands quickly left his face and pressed against his chest, pushing him back on the lounge chair.

"I'm not particularly practiced at the art of seduction, so you'll need to tell me what you like, okay?" she stated innocently, conveying both her eagerness and desire to please him.

He smiled down at her as she licked her way down his abdomen, circling his navel and flicking the tip of his cock. He groaned in anticipation. He was hungry and starving for her mouth and she was clearly setting out to kill him.

"Whatever you do will be perfect. Just *don't* be gentle." As he finished stating his request, Rylie covered him completely with her wet mouth, her hand claiming the base of his length, stroking up and down his rigid shaft. His guttural moan told her whatever she was doing was working. She began to find her rhythm, sucking, licking, sheathing her teeth over him, each stroke bringing out sounds of pleasure from Mitch's mouth.

Mitch's hands slipped in to her hair, his fingers sliding through the luscious strands, as he looked down to see her beautiful mouth covering him, her hair fanning out over him.

Fuuuck. He loved seeing her in control, taking the reins and being completely unaware of how she could make or break him. He began to move with her and asked her to increase her speed. He wanted to make it last, to relish in the hot wetness of her mouth, but he was so close to going off.

Knowing he was ready to climax, Mitch pulled her mouth away. She looked up at him, her lips swollen and plump, questioning his action. "I'm going to come, Ry…"

He pulled her up so that her breasts lay against his arousal, pressing into the center of her cleavage as his hot release thickly covered her chest. She moved with him as he continued to pulse hot across her smooth body.

"Rylie," he groaned out, as the intense pleasure of his release crashed through his body. As he came, and came, and came. Arms wrapped tightly around Rylie, his breathing slowly returning to a normal rate, his hands stroking her hair as she rested comfortably on top of him.

Mitch kissed the top of her head. "If I haven't mentioned it already, that mouth of yours, when it's not talking smack, is so damn hot. That was mind-blowing."

She laughed, looking up at him with a teasing smile. "Huh, I always thought they called that something else."

"Very funny, smart-ass," he chuckled, smacking her on her ass. "Are you ready for some sleep before the sun comes up?" Her reply came in the form of a yawn.

CHAPTER TWENTY-ONE

Rylie felt a contended thrill waking in Mitch's arms, the gentle pressure of his hand laid across her breasts, his breath coming out in elongated puffs against her hair. It was as if all the fight had left her, as her guarded walls slowly crumbled in the night, shattering in a million pieces, washed out to sea.

This feeling was wholly unfamiliar to her – a euphoric, happy bliss that cradled her, just as Mitch was doing to her now. She'd never felt this before, on the verge of something so deep, just as he'd been in her last night. She sighed thinking of their night together. How it started out so disastrously with Tully's angry bullying, and her self-imposed drunken state, to a surreal night of lovemaking like she'd never before experienced. She had no idea how erotic and enjoyable sex could be when your lover is focused on giving you such sexual gratification. Mitch was so willing to give, and so easy to please in return.

Mitch gave her the confidence to experiment and to feel seductive, and not in a manner that made her feel used or dirty. He turned her on and made it okay for her to let go and enjoy her sexuality. Just thinking about the sex they had last night brought back the familiar ache between her thighs, the same one she'd felt over the last three days with him. An ache that, although momentarily satisfied during sex, returned even stronger and with more desperation each time. How could she possibly live without this after they returned home?

They hadn't discussed it. This thing between them. She was pretty sure it was just temporary – a three-day affair in a tropical paradise. Mitch never once mentioned a girlfriend or wanting a relationship. She didn't even know whether he was exclusive when he slept with a woman, or if he had a different partner every night of the week. The thought made her dizzy and sick to her stomach. She knew he wasn't married or living with someone, but that didn't speak to his sex life or dating status. What did she mean to him? Would they be together again when they returned to Boston?

The anxiety gripped at her again and she felt like a caged animal. Rylie quietly got out of bed to return to her own bedroom across the hall, turning to look at Mitch's sleeping form once more before shutting the door to his room. He was so gorgeous, his tanned and chiseled body resting peacefully, the sheets tangled up around his legs. A part of her wanted to slip back into bed next to him and wrap her arms around him, letting her hands stroke him awake.

She sighed, willing herself to let go of those thoughts and begin to distance herself from him. She had to make herself forget last night. Return to the way things were before so it wouldn't hurt so much when the inevitable happened. He would leave her.

She was too keyed up now to go back to bed and her euphoric bubble literally burst with the morning-after weight of the world on her shoulders. Deciding a run and workout would be the answer, she dressed in her tank, running shorts and shoes, and dashed out into the blazing heat and sunlight, ready to leave her worries on the road.

As usual, the pavement under her feet quieted the thoughts running through her head. She had to get a grip on the emotional toll this was creating in her, the war inside her mind…and her heart. She nearly stumbled in the middle of the street as a thought took shape in her brain. It was not possible. They'd had great, mind-blowing sex, and it was more than she ever imagined. But it certainly didn't translate to the L word. Maybe lust, but anything more was inconceivable.

"No effing way," she said aloud to herself, shaking her head and jumping at the sound of the car horn that blared at her in the intersection.

Moving onto the sidewalk, Rylie bent down to her toes, stretching her back and limbs. If she didn't get a grip on where her mind was leading her, she would be an utter mess by the time she got back home to Mitch.

Turning down the drive, she slowed her pace as she mentally kicked herself for being such a pussy and emotional wreck after just one night. Why she was getting caught up in something that was just a fuck was beyond her. Running up to the patio in the back, she drew up short when she saw Mitch sitting on the veranda, shirtless in only shorts and flip-flops, looking at her with an intensity too dark to name.

"Where the hell have you been?" he bellowed. Shit, he seemed angry. Why was he mad at her?

He bounded to his feet, stalking toward her, looking like a wild, feral cat. "Can you even imagine what I thought when I woke to find you not in my bed beside me, but also nowhere on the fucking property?"

She swallowed thickly. Holy cow, he was mad. Having finally reached her, Mitch placed his hands on her hips and jerked her toward him, burying his head in her neck.

"I was going crazy with worry. Common courtesy would have suggested you leave a note or text of some kind."

All she could think to say was, "Oh."

Mitch yanked his head back up with an incredulous look. "Oh? Just Oh? Jesus, Rylie. You were only accosted yesterday by a lunatic man, who then sent the police after you. What if he tried something else? I was out of my mind terrified that something had happened to you this morning."

Rylie stood there frozen, absolutely stunned into silence. She had no idea he would have been worried about her and the thought of leaving a note had never even occurred to her. His concerned outrage over her actions shamed her and she immediately felt guilty and apologetic.

"I…I'm…sorry, Mitch," she stammered, caught off guard by his reaction. "I didn't do it on purpose. I just needed a run and some time alone. I didn't realize…well, it slipped my mind to let you know."

He appeared somewhat mollified by her apology and swatted her butt as he followed her into the kitchen.

"Well, don't leave me without a word next time. Got it?"

She tried to bring her heart rate down a notch and needed to rehydrate. Opening the refrigerator door, she bent down to get a bottled water.

"Hey Mitch, do you want –" She was unable to continue her question as he grabbed hold of her hips from behind, his erection pressed against her backside.

"Why yes, thank you…I do want…" Turning her around to face him, he grabbed the water and unscrewed the cap, taking a gulp and moving his lips to her mouth. She opened for him, as the cold water poured from his mouth into hers, a waterfall of wet lust. Rylie was caught by surprise, but quickly gave in to his cold, almost punishing kiss. He pressed her up against the stainless steel fridge, flicking her hardened nipples through her sports bra, her body immediately responding, wanting and needing more of what he sought. But her rational side took hold.

"Mitch, wait," she said, tearing her mouth from his and pushing his chest away. "I need a shower."

Mitch backed away and looked her over, taking her hand in his and pulling her toward his bedroom.

"Then by all means, you'll get a shower," he smiled back at her, his lips upturned in a seductive, devilish grin. "And I'll get to live out my fantasy."

The marbled bathroom floor was cool on her toes, as she carefully stripped out of her bra, running shorts and panties. Mitch was a step ahead of her and was already naked, standing under the shower's spray. The marbled shower stall came equipped with a massive overhead rain shower-head and six side sprayers.

She stepped in, admiring the view. "This shower is pretty decadent. I may never want to get out."

"I can arrange for that. Come here, let's get you wet."

Rylie quirked her eyebrows at him. "That should be an easy task for you, considering how well you did last night." She laughed, reaching behind him to grab his ass.

"Hmm…I like where this is heading." Taking the lemon and sage scented shower gel, he squeezed some in his palm, returning his hand to just in front of her body. "Any particular place you'd like me to start?"

She liked the way Mitch gave her the reins to lead wherever their sexual play took them. It made her feel in control and empowered, driving them in the direction she wanted to take it, with a little co-piloting from him. Rylie licked her lips and placed her hands on both of her breasts.

"Here."

The corner of Mitch's mouth twitched up into a crooked grin. Bending over just slightly, his tongue came out to flick the hardened peaks of her nipples, taking one at a time into his mouth. Once he withdrew from the first, he covered it with his hand, lathering them until they were silky and slippery with suds.

"Mmm…they are quite dirty. They definitely need some attention." Placing his hands on her hips, Mitch turned her around to face the marbled wall, her hands moving in front of her to lean against the hard, cold surface. Returning his hands to each sensitive breast, he continued his seduction of caressing and rubbing, as she felt the familiar ache begin building between her legs, every touch creating a rush of wet, hot heat.

His mouth came to her ear, his rigid length pressed up against her lower back, thrusting in a slow, sensual manner. She turned her head to the side, meeting his mouth, her tongue greeting his in an erotic welcome, as he captured her mouth in a demanding kiss.

"Where else would you like me to wash?" he asked in a hushed whisper against her mouth.

She pulled at his wrist, sliding his hand over her abs and down to her inner thigh.

"Touch me here."

Her legs were shaky, both from the run and the excited tension that was escalating through her body. She moaned softly as Mitch complied, his warm long fingers taking a drag of silky flesh, moving upward from just above her knee, stopping short of the spot aching for his touch. In an involuntary movement, she thrust her body forward, into his hand.

Frustrated with his teasing, her body begged him to touch her where it counted.

"I take it that wasn't the spot?" he snickered, gliding his hands around her waist to cup her ass. Squeezing, he opened her legs slightly, pressing her center against the streaming jet of water coming from the sidewall shower-head. Mitch continued with the pleasure, his hand snaking down underneath her ass and through her legs to the front, where his fingers melodically massaged her most sensitive flesh, hot and swollen with need.

Locking her in, his chest tight against her back, his thighs and cock slammed hard against her backside, he moved in measured cadence, as Rylie rocked in tempo along with him.

"I'm so close," her voice shook, her body trembling. "It's so intense…"

"Just let go. I want to feel you come."

Rylie was overwhelmed with the erotic contrast of the cold wall against her breasts, the hot water pulsing against her sex, and Mitch's strong fingers bringing her to the edge of oblivion. It was a tidal wave of pleasure, as he slid two fingers inside of her, pushing in and sliding out, her hips rocking back and forth in time.

"Oh…ohh," she gasped, closing her eyes as the dam burst open, flooding her with the strongest current of pleasure she'd ever felt before. She cried out, her hands wildly straining to hold on to the slick shower stall as she came with an intensity so strong she thought she'd collapse.

Her legs felt like Jello. "Oh my God, Mitch." She stammered, falling back into his arms, breathing heavy.

Mitch brushed her wet tangled hair out of her face and kissed the side of her neck. Breathing in her scented skin, his lips moved down her spine, his hand lingering between her legs, as she trembled with pleasure.

Without notice, he spun her around to face him, his lips at belly button level, hands between her legs, spreading them wide.

His eyes stared up at her, wild with need. "I need to inspect my work," he said in a husky tone.

Rylie nearly lost it as his tongue slid across the silky rise of her heated center. Sucking. Licking. Tasting. Drinking her in. Throwing her hands into his hair, she tossed her head back in ecstasy, the waves of sensation crashing against her, bringing her to the edge of an erotic breakdown. She was so lost in the movement, the texture of his tongue, the rub of his scruff against her inner thighs. It was too much. It was sensory overload and she was coming apart again. As if he knew she couldn't handle any more, he abruptly stopped to stand up, grabbing her face in his hands.

"I need to be inside you. Now." Turning off the water, he pulled her out of the shower and into the bedroom, turning her away from him when they reached the bed, bending her over, her arms stretched out in front.

"I want to fuck you from behind," he said gruffly, a statement, not a question.

Mitch positioned himself behind her, one hand on her lower back and the other reaching for her breast. There was a momentary pause and a rip of the condom packet and then he was back.

"Put me inside you," he instructed.

Rylie eagerly obliged as she reached between her legs, finding his erect flesh and bringing it to her wet entrance. Mitch grunted as she circled her hips against him.

"I don't want to be gentle."

She breathed heavily, looking back over her shoulder at him. "Then don't be."

With an urgent need, Mitch dove into her as she let out a hoarse cry. He was thick and hard, filling her completely. His hands held on to her hips as he found a rhythm, pacing himself in time with her. In this position, Rylie would have normally felt a loss of control, unable to touch him or put her mouth on him. It was so deep this way, as he slid in and out of her, making her quiver as she came closer to another orgasm.

Mitch continued to stroke her breasts, his thumb rubbing across her sensitive nipples, sending ripples of pleasure down to her belly.

Mitch took one of her hands and brought it to her entrance, interlocking his fingers with hers, sliding them back and forth across her slick flesh.

"Do you feel that? How good we are together?" he mumbled, his face pressing against her back.

She could feel them getting close, climbing the peak together. Freeing her fingers, he brought his hands back to her hips, as he gained momentum, pushing deeper and faster into her, telling her over and over again how good she felt. Rylie felt her orgasm crest, just as Mitch bellowed out his own release, emptying himself inside her.

Mitch pulled out and fell back onto the bed next to Rylie, who stretched out and flopped on her stomach. "How do you do that to me?"

She smiled, turning to her side, her hair in a tangled mess. "Do what to you?"

"Make me lose control," he clipped, running a hand through his hair. "I keep telling myself to hold it together, make it last, and then I hear you moan and feel how tight you are, and I just…lose it." His hand reached over to brush a strand of hair over her shoulder, stroking down to her ribs and then to the underside of her breast. "And these beauties don't help matters much."

Rylie laughed as his mouth made its way to the tip of her nipple, taking it between his lips and sucking.

"Stop it," she giggled, shoving him off of her. "It's your fault for starting all of this in the first place, you perv. Had you just kept your mouth shut and your hands off, this never would have happened."

Mitch's facial expression looked as if he were injured. "What?" he whimpered, his bottom lip pouting. "You blame me for getting you off? If there's any blame to be had, it's all on you."

She looked at him incredulously. "How in the world is it my fault, Camden?"

Mitch sat up and propped himself up on his elbow, his hands roaming and caressing her bare arm. "You're a temptress, that's why. Because you're so freaking hot, I couldn't stop thinking about you from the moment we met. At first I thought it was just the pain in my knee keeping me up at night, but then I realized, it was just you. Your God damn sexy body, and your brutal insults…and your beautiful eyes…" He leaned over to kiss her eyelids.

"And your luscious lips…" He kissed her lightly, biting her bottom lip.

"And your sexy mouth…" His tongue surged inside her mouth.

"You kept me up many, many nights thinking about what it would be like to kiss you. To touch you. To be inside you."

Rylie rolled back over to her stomach, lifting herself onto her elbows. Turning her head to him, she braced herself for the answer to the lingering question on her mind.

"And now that you've had me? Now what?"

He inched closer, his hand on the curve of her back, gliding it over the slope of her ass and then down her legs.

"Now I just want more. Much, much more."

****

Mitch left after having eaten breakfast and showering, needing to attend one final meeting in Miami before they left for the airport that afternoon. Rylie busied herself with the chore of cleaning the breakfast dishes, a shower and packing her bag. By noon she was on the verge of boredom as she sat out on the veranda with an iced tea and her Kindle, trying to get into one of the new *James Patterson* thrillers when she heard an incoming text notification. Picking up her phone from the table, she saw that the sound didn't originate from her phone. There were no unread text messages on her phone. She heard the sound again and followed it into the open door to Mitch's bedroom.

Scanning the room hoping to spot it, his iPhone didn't appear. It wasn't on the nightstand, nor the large cherry dresser along the wall. Stepping into the bathroom, she looked around the counter and in the drawers, but nothing. Turning back to the bedroom, she noticed the rumpled sheets and comforter hanging off the edge of the bed. Her body flooded with heat, as she recalled their morning together before he left. He was insatiable and drove her wild with just a word or a touch.

Lifting the comforter and blankets from the floor, she bent over to check under the bed. There it was, lying face down, a telltale sign of their utter recklessness and abandon the night before when she had her way with him.

Scooping the phone up, she glanced at the black screen as she turned it over in her hand. Pulling herself to a standing position, she held the phone in her palm, which grew clammy and weighty with an uncontrollable curiosity to see what the text said.

She shook her head in defiance of her thoughts. She would not snoop to read his text. That was an invasion of his privacy.

But what if he needed to know something urgently and she was the only one who could respond? That made sense in her head, even though she had no other means of getting in touch with him if the message was urgent.

Conflicted over the conundrum, she had made the decision to just let it go and not check the message. She was about to set it on the bureau when another text came through, lighting up the screen with all the unread messages.

Message One: *Hey Shithead. You haven't called back on the contracts. Need ASAP. Thx. Jax.*

Hmm…seemed like an urgent business matter. But again, she had no way of reaching Mitch and didn't even know when he'd be back. She thought he'd mumbled something about one or two o'clock as he walked out the door earlier, but she'd been lost in his kisses to pay much attention. Hopefully this could wait until then.

Her eyes moved next to the message just below the first. Reading it once through, her brow furrowed, as anger rose like bile up her throat.

Message Two: *Hey M – it's Elle. Can't wait to see you! Looking forward to you in a tux. It's been far too long. XOXO*

WTF?

Who the hell was Elle and why was she going to see him in a tux?

This was exactly what she knew would happen. How stupid could she be? To expect that Mitch didn't have anyone else in his life or after one three-day affair with her he'd just drop everyone else he was seeing or sleeping with to be with her? *Idiot*!

Of course he was seeing other women. Why wouldn't he? He was an extremely handsome, sexy, eligible bachelor with money and influence. He ran in social circles she only knew from tabloid magazines. He hobnobbed with celebrities. She meant nothing to him but an easy fuck. And she now hated herself for dropping her guard and jumping in with both feet. Now she was falling and would end up at the bottom of the ravine she'd never wanted to be in and didn't have the first clue how to climb the fuck out.

Turning on her heels, she walked out of the room and started to gather her belongings. She could play this out in one of two ways. Stay there until Mitch returned, head back to Boston and part ways, no harm, no foul. Or, she could check for an earlier flight, call a cab and leave Miami as fast as she could. Good riddance.

She decided on the latter.

This time, however, she didn't fail to forget common courtesy, which Mitch was obviously a stickler on, and left him a note on the table, right next to his forgotten phone.

CHAPTER TWENTY-TWO

Mitch was practically humming as he got into the car to head back to the beach house. All his meetings successfully completed and all his Miami business all but wrapped up, save a faxed contract to a waiting Jackson – he was nearly giddy as he thought about getting back to Rylie. Apparently the scientific studies on sex and the after effects were correct, he mused. It really did boost physical energy and emotional vitality, because he was buzzing with energy all morning, even with the pitiful amount of sleep from the previous night.

He hated leaving her earlier this morning as she lay in his arms, her body radiating a warm post-coital glow. She'd fallen asleep with her head across his chest, breathing softly and smelling of the lemon and sage body wash he'd used on her in the shower.

The sheer will it took for him to get out of bed and leave her was nothing short of superhero strength – of which he didn't think he possessed. As soon as he left for his meetings, the only thing he could think about was speeding up time and slipping back into bed with her the minute he returned. He'd been so completely lost by the morning's pleasures, that he'd forgotten his phone and hadn't realized it until he was halfway to his meeting location.

What was it about Rylie that had him so head over heels for her? She was gorgeous, no doubt. She wasn't like other women he had dated, who were superficial and trivial in their looks or style. Rylie was a natural beauty, unfettered by materialistic needs – comfortable in her own skin. She was street smart, and tough – the result of growing up in a two-male household. Yet she was naïve and uncertain in her sexuality, but honest in her approach to it. She gave as much as she took and was eager to learn and explore. She didn't play games or say one thing but mean the other. How refreshing.

He couldn't get enough of her and wanted to learn more about who she was and what she wanted in life. Had he ever considered that with others he'd slept with? Was there ever any interest in anything other than sex with them?

Mitch chewed on that question as he pulled up into the driveway. He laughed at himself to think that in less than a month, Rylie had swallowed him whole and she didn't even know it. She had no idea how completely absorbed he was in her – how much he wanted her and how easily she could chew him up and spit him out, leaving him with a gaping wound.

Shaking off the thought, Mitch walked in the front door, placing his bag on the floor and keys on the hall table.

"Hey, IQ…I'm home," he called out to a silent room, a small echo reverberating down the hallway. "I need to make up for my absence…" He'd had fantasies all morning and was already hard thinking about getting her where he wanted her.

Hearing no response, he walked back into the guestroom and opened the door. The bed was neatly made and there was no visible sign to indicate she was ever even there. Moving across the hallway to his room, he stepped in, walking out to the patio and calling for her again.

Empty.

Maybe she was down in the workout room. Heading out the bedroom door, he passed the kitchen where the sight of his phone on the table caught his attention.

Good. Thank God he hadn't lost it somewhere. Picking up the phone to check for any messages, he noticed a yellow sticky note folded neatly next to it.

Curious, he unfolded it, reading the note twice before letting out a loud *What the fuck*?

Mitch,

Thanks for the great time. I had fun. I had to head back to Boston sooner than expected. I'll call you.

Ry

Mitch stood there stunned – floored by what he'd just read. What the hell is this all about? What was she thinking just leaving a note and taking off on her own back to Boston? What the hell would possess her to do something like that?

He picked up his phone, ready to call her and saw the number of messages and texts he had received since that morning. He quickly flipped through them, checking for any that came from Rylie. Her contact information was already programmed into his phone, but nothing popped up with her number. Just a few from Jax and one from Elle. He'd have to deal with them later.

Feeling frustrated, confused by her abrupt departure and more than a bit pissed off, Mitch tried calling her phone. It went directly to voicemail. *Shit.* Now what? Just sit here like a fucking idiot and wait? No way. She wasn't getting way that easy.

He quickly dialed Georgina, who was able to get him on an earlier flight, but made a fuss over the fact that he had to leave immediately in order the make it. Throwing his clothes together in his bag, he locked up the house and headed to Miami International, all the while wondering what the hell happened to send Rylie packing that fast.

With the small exception of Tully's antics, he thought the last three days with Rylie had been amazing. They'd spent time getting to know one another, enjoying the calming beauty of the ocean and the scintillating sites that Miami had to offer. He'd tried not to push too hard, to allow her space and time to decide if she wanted him. He was crazy for the girl, but gave her complete control over whether or not to proceed. And thank God she did, otherwise he would've gone nuts. His insatiable desire for her was nearly killing him. The night of the football game was torture. Watching her enthralled in the action of the game was an incredible turn-on, but not as much as seeing her in the tight fitting T-shirt and her long, lean legs in the short shorts she wore. And then their afternoon on the boat was even better than any fantasy he'd ever had. He thought she had enjoyed herself just as much as he had, leading to their overwhelming sex throughout the previous night and into this morning.

And then she just disappears on him. What was up with this girl? Most women he'd been with got clingy after sleeping together, but no one he'd ever just up and walked away. Or ran away.

Mitch got to the gate a few minutes prior to them shutting the door. He had First Class again and as he sat down and snapped his seatbelt closed, he was reminded of Rylie's head on his lap a few days earlier. Closing his eyes and drawing in a long breath, he pictured how beautiful she was sleeping peacefully across his legs, the feel of her against his body. He had to find her and ask her what was going on in her head to make her leave so abruptly.

And then it occurred to him. Maybe she didn't feel the same way he did about their time together. Rylie hadn't been the one to instigate things between them – it was always he who pressed the subject. Maybe she was just sick of fighting him off and gave in finally, deciding after-the-fact that it wasn't what she wanted after all.

Whatever it was with her, he had to find out. And he'd be willing to accept her decision, even if she didn't want anything further to do with him. It would feel like a blow to the gut, but he'd understand and would walk away gracefully. He'd dealt with loss on a massive level. He could certainly handle having Rylie tell him it was over before it even started. He wouldn't like it though. And as usual, he'd see it as a challenge, knowing he couldn't just walk away without a fight. He fought for what he wanted. And dammit, he wanted her.

****

Sasha was at the airport waiting when Rylie arrived in Boston. She'd called en route to the Miami airport requesting a pick-up and begged her not to be armed with questions. Sasha agreed, but her promise lasted only a mere five minutes.

Pulling onto the highway, Sasha glanced slyly over at Rylie. "Well, at least it looks like you got some sun. You have a nice glow about you." Her sweet smile didn't hide the real meaning in her statement.

Rylie stared out of the passenger window, lost in her thoughts. "Uh-huh."

"Or maybe the glow is from something else," she snickered. "Maybe it was hot, dirty sex on the beach. Maybe Mr. Miami Vice had his way with you, every which way from Sunday, and you've turned into a sex-starved zombie."

"Uh-huh," she murmured.

Sasha burst into a roaring fit of laughter, bringing Rylie's attention back to earth, swinging her head to look over at her friend, who had obviously just gone crazy.

"What's so funny?"

"Shitballs, girl. You have no freaking clue, do you?"

Rylie had no idea what she was talking about and the expression on her face likely told her so.

"Ry, whatever happened down in Miami has turned your brain to mush. Now, you can either bury your deepest, darkest secrets until they eat away at you like flesh-eating bacteria…"

"Oh gross."

"Or you can unload and tell your best friend about everything that happened, all the juicy and gory details. And then I can smack you and tell you how stupid you are for leaving that gorgeous man down in Miami."

Slamming on the brakes at a red light, Sasha's face lit up in a broad, 'you-know- I'm-right' smile, her thumb drumming an impatient beat on the steering wheel.

"Nothing happened."

Sasha's hand flew out and smacked Rylie's head, catching her off guard. Rylie grimaced and rubbed the side of her face that stung.

"Owww! What the hell was that for?" It was obvious her friend had really lost her mind. She was going off on her like a mad woman.

"I'm sorry, but that's bullshit! I know you. It's written all over your gorgeous, lying, sack-of-shit face. And I mean that with all due love and respect." Sasha placed a hand out to grab hold of Rylie's, interlocking her fingers with hers.

"Rylie," she said softly this time. "Tell me what's going on. I've never seen you like this. I promise not to pass judgment or criticize. Just tell me what has you so messed up that you're fleeing the scene of the crime."

Rylie was all at once flooded with emotion. Tears threatened to come pouring out, as they welled up in the corner of her eyes. She felt ridiculously helpless, confused and outright crazy insane. What the hell *was* going on with her?

"I...I don't even know where to start. I'm so confused. This whole thing is insane. I'm messed up and don't know what to do."

And then it happened – the levy broke. Tears that had been damming up had now begun pouring out of her eyes. She was a blubbering idiot. Sasha's mouth gaped open, as she pulled over to the side of the road to stop the car, obviously at a loss for words. Grabbing Kleenex out of her purse, she handed a fistful to Rylie, who bent her head in shame, as the tears streamed down her face.

Trying to form words in the midst of her sobs, Rylie began her story of all the whirlwind events that transpired in Miami. Every single, sordid detail.

Sasha nodded her head, not uttering so much as a peep, as Rylie continued to share what happened between her and Mitch over the past three days. It took nearly fifteen minutes, with a few stops and starts to blow her nose and wipe her eyes, until she'd completely finished her recap. Sasha continued to observe her friend in silence, every once in a while patting her knee or handing her another Kleenex.

Sitting in silence, with the sounds of the city and cars whizzing by their parked car, Sasha comforted her friend in her time of need. And then without notice, she slapped her upside the head once more.

"Good Lord, you're a freaking idiot!" she lectured.

Rylie barreled back against the side of her seat, her head pressed to the window, looking out for any further sucker punches. "What the hell! You said you wouldn't pass judgment or criticize. What do you call that?"

"That was honesty, not criticism. And you're damn lucky you have a friend like me who has such values. Now, are you ready to hear the rest of the truth?"

Rylie stared at her wide-eyed and in shock. She had just poured out her guts to Sasha, revealing her most hidden feelings and she goes all psycho bitch from hell on her. No, she really didn't want to hear the truth, because she already knew it. She was already fully aware she was a chicken shit and was running scared, away from something that could possibly be real and special, all because she was afraid she'd get hurt. Or worse, because she didn't know how to feel about it. The future unknown was too much for her to deal with.

Sasha's features grew soft, pulling Rylie into her arms over the center console and into a hug. "You know I love you and I only want the best for you."

Rylie nodded in agreement, sniffling into her used tissue, still a little wary of her friend's fast reflexes.

"Here's the deal. You ran away from Mitch before giving him a chance because you're scared. You're scared that you might give him your heart and then be left holding the pieces, just like what happened when you were a kid and your mom left," she said, placing her hand under Rylie's chin and bringing it up to look her in the eyes. "But let me tell you something...and really listen to what I'm saying. Just because your mother left you, your dad and Dylan, doesn't mean that other people will leave you, too. Normal people do not just walk away from those they love."

"I know that," she whispered with a small hiccup.

"You can't close yourself off forever, Rylie. At some point, you're going to meet someone who totally rocks your world. Someone you can't stop thinking about and can't get enough of. A guy who you not only want, but *need...*"

She searched Rylie's face for a telltale sign that she'd hit the mark, but Rylie just sank further into her seat. "Whether that's Mitch or not, I couldn't say. But what I can tell you is that it's obvious that you do have feelings for him. And based on the strings he's pulled to be with you, it's obvious he has a thing for you, too. So why not just let it happen and see where it goes from here? Go out and get to know him - enjoy his company. And for the love of all that's holy, have great sex! You're young, hot and single. Go out and live life like you mean it."

Rylie stared at Sasha in silence, mulling over her little speech. And then she burst into laughter.

"That was quite a speech, Coach. I feel all motivated and shit."

Sasha flung her ebony curls over her shoulder and chuckled. "You know it. Do I need to slap you again?"

CHAPTER TWENTY-THREE

A week had passed since Mitch returned to Boston. One excruciatingly long and taxing week; full of meetings, disagreements, negotiations, the obligatory Sunday dinner with his parents, several physical therapy appointments with his new therapist, Carmen, formal social engagements and zero Rylie encounters. A week from hell.

That's not to say that he hadn't tried reaching her. Mitch texted her twice upon his return from Miami, called her twice, the second time leaving a rambling and long-winded message for her, asking – no, begging her to call him back. He told her that he only wanted an explanation as to what happened to her and to see that she was all right. He said he only wanted to see her one more time, maybe dinner? Or maybe lunch. Hell, he'd settle on coffee, whatever she wanted. He just had to see her. But he heard nothing in return. No text, no email and no returned phone call. He was living in hell. Aside from acting like a creepy stalker and going to her place of business, he was out of options in how to get her to talk to him.

He may have mentioned this to his mother one night at their family dinner, one that was always a bit awkward because his mother insisted on setting a place for Matthew. It initially freaked him and his father out and they wondered if they should mention it to her. But after it continued for six months, they all just got used to the idea that Matthew would always be a part of them and even if he wasn't there face-to-face, he was present in their lives.

Their conversation had started off as it normally did – how was work? What was new in his business? How was Jax? Was Mitch seeing anyone? The last question was always a singular "no, mother," in order to stop the prying and meddling that was bound to occur if she got a whiff of any potential women in his life. As he was now her only heir, she wanted nothing more than to see him happily married and with children as soon as it was possible. But this time, his response was different. He had the overwhelming urge to mention Rylie and their trip, the time they shared together and then her abrupt departure. He thought he'd shocked his mother at first, but she smiled warmly and with the wisdom of a woman who knew a little bit about the female psyche. She quickly ascertained that their common denominator was their family friend Mark, therefore, he should reach out to him and find a way to get her back.

Damn, his mother was one smart woman.

That's exactly what he found himself doing after returning home that night. Opening up his laptop and logging into Skype, he swirled his whiskey sifter in one hand, and clicked the button to dial Mark, who was half-way around the world in Africa. Through the miracles of modern technology, he was able to see and speak with him over Skype. Mark seemed a little worse for wear, but happy to hear from him.

"Holy shit, if it isn't Mitch Camden!" Mark had exclaimed, looking a little worn out and ragged, a scruffy reddish/brown beard covering his jaw. "What's up buddy? To what do I owe this pleasure? How's the knee doing?"

Mitch rubbed his knee, as it throbbed at the mention of his recovery. "The knee is doing great, thanks for asking. I had the best surgeon in Boston and some amazing therapists in the process," he said, the compliment referring to Mark and his team. "So how are you doing, bro? How's Africa?"

He could see Mark's facial expression grow weary and sad, his eyes welling up ever so slightly. "Eh, you know. It's a different world down here," he said quietly, rubbing his eyes, as if to get an image out of his head. "A lot of disease, poverty, hunger…families torn apart. I'd be lying if I said it was a cake walk. But it's also the most amazing experience I've ever had and I'm glad I'm here. I do miss the States, though. And the comforts of home. I miss my family and my friends.

Speaking of friends…" he paused, giving Mitch an inquisitive look. "Have you continued with your physical therapy? And you've been working with Rylie?"

Mitch gave him a lopsided grin. Oh yeah, he'd seen a lot of her recently. And he wanted more. So much more. "Yes, Doctor. I have, thanks for asking. And my therapy is going well. I haven't been on crutches for a few weeks now and the pain is almost non-existent. I'd been doing some water therapy with Rylie…or at least, I was."

"Oh yeah? That's great. Rylie is an amazing therapist and really knows her clients' needs. She's truly one of the best I've worked with. And she's also a great person, but I suspect you already know that."

Mitch's smile faded as he hesitantly replied.

"Yeah, man, I do. Rylie is pretty damn great."

"But…something's going on? What is it? Is she okay?" Mark's voice rose up an octave, filled with panic.

"Yeah, man. She's fine. Or at least I think she is. The last time I saw her, she was – she came with me on a business trip to Miami…"

Mark's expression turned dark and protective. "What the fuck did you do to her, Mitch?"

"Whoa, whoa…I didn't do anything. Dude, I've been trying to get ahold of her since we got back. She was the one who left me high and dry in Miami and now won't return any of my calls. I've been trying to see her for over a week…I want to…well, I want to…be with her. But she's not making it very easy to do."

Through the staticky internet connection, Mitch could see Mark throw his head back in laughter. His anger spiked.

"You find this funny, bro?"

Mark shook his head and his laughter subsided. "Yes, I do find it funny. Now that I've seen third world problems, I find your first world tales of unrequited love pretty goddamn funny. And so are you. You're acting like a love sick puppy. Mitch Camden, god of women, who's never had to chase down a woman before, is now chasing after the one woman who has resisted his charms. That's freaking hilarious!"

"Laugh it up, shithead. I'm so glad I could provide you some entertainment in your absence. And what makes you think she resisted my charms?"

Mark's smile ended, replaced with a menacing glare, pursing his lips together in thought. "You better not have fucking laid a hand on her, dickwad. I may be half way across the world, but I will kick your ass the next time I see you if you did."

Mitch sat back in his desk chair and ran his hands through his hair. He wasn't sure if he was getting a protective brother vibe from Mark, or if what he saw from him fell in the "I've wanted her for a long time, back the hell off" category. Either way, he could appreciate his feelings toward her. He felt the same way.

"Mark, this is serious. I could use your help here. And considering I did lend you some pretty sizeable financial support in your endeavors to save the world, I think you could at the very least help a brother out."

"You got me there. And I do appreciate your support you know. You and your family have invested a lot and I can tell you it's made a huge investment in the lives of these people, so thank you."

"Bro, you're a better man than most and I'm in awe at what you're doing. And we'll be sending you additional support in the next few weeks after the charity event my mother is hosting next weekend. It should prove to be very helpful."

"Okay, so tell me what I can do for you. How can I help you out with your little Rylie problem? She's a stubborn woman, so I don't know what advice I can offer to you, so don't expect too much. I'll do my best."

They chatted for another ten minutes, considered a few options and scenarios that might sway Rylie into meeting with Mitch again. Whatever he did, Mark warned Mitch to tread lightly and not go in with barrels a' blazing. Coming on too strong or attempting to push her in a corner would only force Rylie to go on the defensive. And they both agreed that she knew how to attack when cornered.

"Mark, you're a good man. Thanks for the advice. I'll let you know how it goes. And keep yourself safe, you hear me? We need your skilled hands back here in Boston."

"You bet. And Mitch…take good care of her. I love that girl."

Ah, so that's how it is. Yeah, he got that. "I will. Take care, bro."

The internet connection went dark, as Mark disconnected from the conversation, leaving Mitch mulling over their conversation and the words of advice Mark had offered up to him. He knew Mark was sincere in his concern for Rylie and he wondered if Rylie ever felt the same way for him? Had it only been a one-sided romantic love? Or did part of Rylie also love Mark more than platonically?

He shook off the question and considered his next move. He needed to get Rylie in a place where she didn't feel vulnerable or challenged. Somewhere she'd feel relaxed and could hold a conversation without feeling trapped. Based on the insights and information Mark threw out, he knew the exact place, but just had to figure out the time.

****

It had gone from brisk to downright cold in New England since she'd returned from Miami. Boston October's were unpredictable; one day it could be in the sixties and the next it could dip below freezing, with inches of snowfall. Now heading into November, however, there was a light drizzle and it was a balmy forty-three degrees. Cool enough for Rylie to wear a long-sleeved Nike running hoodie and a pair of pink, printed running tights.

She was a creature of habit and loved her morning runs, regardless of the weather conditions or her moods. As of late, her mood had been far from cheerful, much to Sasha and her family's chagrin and disapproval. She'd hoped the excessive running that she'd been doing over the last week would have improved that and would help vanquish Mitch from her ever-present thoughts. It hadn't helped yet, but there was always hope that today was the day.

She ran her normal route along the Charles River, stopping several times to stretch out her calves and muscles, enjoying the view of the Harvard rowing team making their way through the cold, smooth waters. She shook her head to clear the thought of the warm Atlantic waters that she and Mitch snorkeled in and the way she felt wrapped in his arms. It was exactly those kind of memories that would not help her cause.

She thought about the immature behavior she demonstrated over the past week, avoiding his attempts to reach her. She was acting like a stupid, childish girl to run and hide from him. It was her only defense mechanism at this point, having no other means of dealing with the emotional turmoil he caused her. On one hand, she wanted to be with him and felt so incredibly contented when they were together. She actually liked him. He was funny, smart, beautiful and fun to be with.

And on the other hand, she didn't want to get too close where she'd lose herself in him. Her heart wasn't capable of going through something like that again, even if in a different context. And even if there wasn't anything going on with Mitch and the Elle woman he received a text from, she didn't want to get her heart broken. She couldn't handle that.

So where did that leave her?

It left her empty. She felt hollow; sullen; irritable; and uptight.

Sasha was right about one thing. She was in her mid-twenties and needed to live life, otherwise she would soon become a grumpy and cynical old woman who looked back on her life with regret and looked at the future with pessimism.

Finishing up her run, she walked into The Cambridge Cup coffee house to get her daily coffee fix. The line was longer than normal, even though it was still fairly early on a Sunday morning. She grew impatient with the customers ahead of her that were having difficulties with their orders, as she irritably tapped her running shoe in a restless beat against the tiled floors.

A velvety rich voice broke into her agitated thoughts, nearly sending her flying forward into the couple in front of her.

"I've got a table in the corner and an extra-large cup of steaming hot Americano waiting for you already, if you'd like to join me."

Pivoting around on her heels, she stared up into the golden tanned face of the man she'd been running from over the last week, but whom she desperately wanted to run to.

"Wha – what are you doing here?" she stammered like an idiot.

"I wanted to have coffee with a beautiful woman."

Rylie's face flushed hot, looking up into his smoldering eyes.

"Actually, I take that back," he said, as she gave him a look of confusion. "I wanted to have coffee with the most beautiful woman I've ever met. And I was told she might be here today. And lucky me…here you are."

He smiled down at her and the space between them seemed to have shrunk. Her body felt like it was being drawn in by some sort of magnetic pull, drawing them together. Rylie could barely breathe being so close to him again. Perhaps sensing her uneasiness, Mitch stepped back, pointing the way to his table.

"I know I've caught you off guard, and I'm sorry for that," he continued, as he placed his hand lightly on Rylie's lower back, guiding her around to his table to sit. "But you left me no other choice. I needed to see you. To talk to you. Will you talk to me?"

He sat down across from her at the small café table made for two and took the lid off her coffee cup, emptying in two packets of sugar and stirring it with a stir stick.

"Cream?"

She nodded in response, taken aback by his presence and how much of a gentleman he could be. He poured the cream and placed the lid back on the cup, handing it to her.

"Thank you," she squeaked.

"You're welcome. And thanks for not bolting." He took a sip of his coffee and sat back, crossing one leg over the other. He appeared to be waiting for her to start the conversation. She wasn't being obstinate, but she honestly didn't know where to begin. She simply sat there, taking him all in, her pulse beating in surprise and shock.

He was dressed casually in a charcoal gray Helly Hansen sailing jacket and jeans and appeared comfortable in the silence that stretched out between them. He blew on the hot liquid in his cup and then took another sip of his coffee.

Finally, when she couldn't stand the silence any longer, she spoke. A little more curtly than she had meant.

"You came here looking for me. So what do you want to talk about?"

He raised his brows and grinned. She gnawed on her lip, scanning his facial expression which indicated a piqued interest.

"Oh, I don't know. Maybe I hoped you could suggest who I should play in my fantasy football league this week? Or maybe what exercises I should be doing for my knee, since my therapist didn't leave me with my daily instructions before she left Miami? Or perhaps we could talk about why I can't get you off my mind and I've lost all semblance of concentration?" He set down his cup and leaned in toward her. "We can start with whichever question you'd like."

Rylie made an audible gulp, her rattled nerves vaulting through her body.

She decided to go with the easiest question. Something she had confidence to explain. "If I were you, I'd play Marshawn Lynch from the Seahawks this week. They're playing strong and are assured a win and he's a running back on fire. And if you need a QB in your line-up, Drew Brees is a sure pick for TD points."

He nodded, his lips upturned in a small smile. She loved his smile. She loved his lips. Shit, she loved what his mouth could do to her. *Gah.*

She grabbed a napkin and borrowed a pen from the guy sitting at the table next to them. Making a few notes on the makeshift writing tablet, she slid the napkin across the table to Mitch, watching his confused expression.

"Sounds like your therapist is an ass and left you with no instructions for your continued therapy. So here are three exercises you can do this week at home to keep strengthening your knee."

He smiled as he read through them, laughing when he came to the fourth.

"You said there were three, but I see there's a fourth listed here."

"Yep," she nodded affirmatively.

"I don't think the fourth is going to help my knee very much."

"Probably not...but it will help me say what I need to say."

She sighed deeply, placing her elbows on the table and her head in her hands. After a second, she looked back up at Mitch, who was watching her intently. She'd never been very good at apologies. Wasn't a very often occurrence in a household of men, who would typically just grumble a "sorry" or "my bad" when they fucked up.

So here she was, sitting across from a man she knew intimately well, who was looking to make amends, and she was the one who had to "man up" and take ownership for her mistakes. She owed him that. She needed to gain his forgiveness.

"The fourth is my advice for how to deal with me. You need to have patience and be willing to run after me and accept my apologies...because I am an idiot," she dipped her head again, feeling regret and guilt. Mitch's hand came out and under her chin, lifting it gently to meet his eyes.

"Ry…don't do that. Don't ever hang your head in shame. Whatever you were feeling or whatever drove you away is not your fault. If anything, it was probably me. I pushed you too far and too fast. What can I say, I'm a Type A personality?" he shrugged and then placed his hands on the table, opening them up for her to take hold of him. She tentatively reached forward, laying them down on his. He squeezed them gently; reassuringly.

His voice was soft and sympathetic. "Will you tell me what happened? What did I do to make you run off that way?"

"Mitch, it's not you…" she laughed at how cheesy and cliché her words sounded. "It's me. It's my history. It's the circumstances. It's just that I'm not equipped to handle this kind of stuff."

"Stuff?"

"Yeah, you know. Relationship stuff…or whatever label you want to use to describe our little fling. I got caught up in it and it was off-the-radar intense. As they say, if you can't stand the heat, get out of the kitchen. So that's what I did."

He nodded thoughtfully at her explanation.

"And then, well, I don't know. I wasn't sure what you'd want from me after that, or if you would be coming back to Boston to your girlfriend."

He shook his head vehemently in denial.

"Ry, I do not have a girlfriend. I'm not seeing anyone. And if I was, I would have been open and told you about it. And I certainly wouldn't have slept with you if I did. That's not the kind of man I am."

Her thoughts raced back to the text she saw on his phone that last day in Miami. If he didn't have a girlfriend, who was Elle to him? And why would he lie to her right now if he was being so open about his relationship status? She swallowed her questions, partly because she was too scared to ask for the entire truth and partly because she didn't really want to know. Call it passive-aggressive denial. That was exactly who she was.

Mitch scooted his chair closer to her, so their shoulders were touching. He grabbed her hand with both of his, bringing it to his lips, brushing them across her knuckle before kissing it fully. Tingles shot up her arm, sensations flooding through her body, echoing a tune of their time spent together.

"Rylie, can I ask you something?" he asked, dropping her hand in her lap.

She smiled hesitantly. "Sure."

"Go out with me…on a date. Since *technically* our time in Miami was strictly business and professionally motivated."

Rylie snorted.

"Well, the majority of our trip was business and the rest was all my pleasure," he replied with a devilish grin. "But you weren't there as my date. So, I'd like to take you out this week on an official date. We go wherever you want. Do whatever you want to do. My only ask is that you set aside any and all preconceived notions about me and just have fun. You up for that?"

Fun. She could hear Sasha giving her the first degree about how she should go out and have more fun. Live a little! Fine – okay. Why the hell not?

Rylie nodded her head in agreement, downing the final gulp of her nearly cold coffee, as well as her anxiety.

"Okay. But just so you know…I don't put out on a first date," she snickered. "Maybe first base, if you play nice."

The rain had moved from a light drizzle to a downpour since she'd gone into the coffee shop earlier, and they were soaked as soon as they walked outside together. Mitch took her hand as she jumped across a puddle, as they made their way across the street. At the corner, he took off his jacket and held it above their heads, sheltering them from the downpour. He leaned in and placed a kiss on her forehead.

"Don't worry, I can play nice. You'll see…"

CHAPTER TWENTY-FOUR

After trying to coordinate schedules and come to agreement on which night of the week would work the best for their first date, they agreed on Wednesday night. Rylie had thrown out the typical Friday or Saturday evening, but Mitch admitted he was too eager to see her again and couldn't wait that long.

Taking time out for lunch, Rylie and Sasha had just ordered their soup and salads at the sub shop across from the clinic and sat down at a table. Pulling out a few napkins, Sasha gave a handful to Rylie.

"Where did you decide to go tonight?" Sasha asked, wiping the crumbs left from the previous table's occupant and pushing them on to the floor. Rylie gave her a look of disgust. "What? If they don't have time to come over and clean off our table, I have no qualms about messing up their floor." She wiped her hands in a show of defiance.

Rylie rolled her eyes at her beautiful and vocal friend. They were so opposite in so many ways, but somehow clicked as friends. She'd always secretly hoped that Sasha and Dylan would end up dating and falling in love, even though the thought of Dylan's sex life made her stomach turn. That's not something she ever wanted to know about. Hearing about Sasha's anonymous exploits was sometimes even more than she could handle. But it would have been a nice thought if she'd have become her sister.

"Mitch is taking me on a brewery tour and to dinner."

"A man who knows a way to your heart – food and beer. Very nice. And how about afterward?" she smirked, winking at Rylie as she took a bite of her salad.

Rylie held up her hands. "Who knows? Maybe a walk around the harbor, or visiting the elderly in the nursing home or baking some bread…"

Sasha kicked her under the table. "You know what I mean, bitch," she laughed. "I'm asking if you're going to have hot and dirty sex…because one of us has to get some this week. I'm in a drought."

"Living vicariously through me and my sex life. Now that's a first," Rylie joked, pushing her plate to the side and taking a drink of her iced tea. "I actually told Mitch that I wanted to take it slow."

Sasha's mouth dropped open. "Sweet Baby Jesus – why in the world would you want to do that? That man is sex on two legs! And you've already tested the goods, so what's the point in waiting?"

"Has your mouth always been this filthy? Good grief. And yes, I know we've already gone down that road," she lowered her voice a little, turning in both directions to make sure the tables next to her weren't interested in their conversation. "I just want to make sure it's not just all about the physical attraction. I know we already have the chemistry – I just want to see if we have a connection elsewhere."

"Sounds boring as hell, but whatever." Sasha flung her hand in the air in annoyance.

"Mitch's a really smart man, Sash. And he's investing in and constructing some pretty amazing state-of-the-art eco-friendly buildings. He's a visionary and a very progressive thinker. I like that about him."

Sasha moved her hand in a flapping motion, the universal sign for 'blah, blah, blah.'

"Yeah, snore. If things were that hot in Miami, do you really believe you'll be able to contain it now that you're back home? Puleeez. You're kidding yourself, Ry. Why not just admit it and let it happen? Although, I do admire your sincerity in the matter."

They walked outside the restaurant and entered the busy street, full of afternoon traffic and pedestrians, bundling up against the cold rain. Deep down, Rylie knew there was truth in what Sasha was saying. She probably was kidding herself to expect she'd be able to control herself around Mitch tonight and not want to tear off his clothes and see his beautiful, naked body. He'd give her one of his charming smiles and she'd melt into a puddle at his feet. Good Lord, she was a pathetic mess.

They headed back into the clinic to finish up the remainder of the day's clients. Picking up her charts as she entered the office door, Sasha turned back to Rylie.

"I realize you're all smitten and stuff right now, but don't forget you've already promised to be my date at this charity event on Saturday night. So don't go making any plans with Loverboy, because I've got dibs."

"Oh, that's right, it's this weekend. It did actually skip my mind so thanks for the reminder. Do we need to go shopping or do I just get to raid your closet?"

"I have the perfect dress for you! Do you remember my client Stefanie Trieger? She's a designer and works for Zac Posen. She had some samples from last season and gave me three of them. They are absolutely fab – and we are going to look so freaking hot!"

If the dress was anything like the little number Sasha sent down with her to Miami, she had no doubt it would be killer. Truth be told, Rylie was actually excited about the possibility of dressing up again. She had felt so sexy when she wore the silver sequined dress the night of the party. Or it might have had something to do with the way Mitch looked at her that night.

Rylie hugged her friend, who was taken by surprise and nearly fell over. "We'll have a girl's day. How about I make appointments at that spa you go to and we can get our hair and nails done, too?"

"Whoa – what happened to the real Rylie?" she asked, feigning surprise and looking her up and down and behind her, as she stood in front of her with an amused look. "Did aliens land and take over your brain? This is a first."

Sasha grabbed hold of Rylie's arms and started spinning her around in glee.

"Good grief, get over yourself. Maybe your girly-girl ways are finally rubbing off on me a little, but don't get too excited. I'm still watching football with the guys tomorrow night."

Sasha laughed and twirled around once more. "My wish has finally come true! I actually have a 'girl' friend now! Woohoo!"

****

By the time five-thirty rolled around and Rylie was finishing up her daily paperwork, the butterflies and nerves began to jumble in her stomach. She couldn't wait to go out with Mitch, but now she was getting cold feet. She hadn't thought about it like that while in Miami, only because she thought it was just a fling. But now that it had taken a different turn, the vibe was weightier.

She went directly home, showered and changed into her favorite pair of jeans and was deciding on what top to wear when her door buzzer sounded off from downstairs. Crap, he wasn't supposed to be there until seven and a glance at the clock showed it was six thirty. She hastily threw a sweatshirt over her head and ran out to the living room, where she pressed the Talk button.

"Hello?"

"Yes, this is Carlson Floral. We have a delivery for Ms. Rylie Hemmons."

What? A delivery? She wasn't expecting that. Checking out her front window, she saw the distinct red and white Carlson Floral van parked out on the street in front of her building. Thank God it was a delivery and not a very early Mitch. She rushed back over and buzzed him in.

Feeling like a caged animal, she paced back and forth in front of her door, waiting for the guy to make his way to the third floor. The knock on her door had her swinging it open in excitement to find the man holding the biggest, most ginormous bouquet she had ever seen. Not even at Aunt Cynthia's funeral had she seen anything quite this breathtaking. She took a step toward him and wondered how in the world she'd even get it through the door.

"Please sign here," the man said, shoving a clipboard and pen in her hand. She dutifully scribbled her initials and handed it back, exchanging it for the flowers in his hands. "Thanks, Miss. Have a nice day."

Rushing them over to the table, she set them down and found the card. Her breathing had accelerated and her pulse raced, and with shaking hands she looked down to see what she assumed was Mitch's handwriting.

Looking forward to beer and your beauty tonight.

Oh Wow. She was a goner.

Rylie was not, nor had ever been, a gooey hearts and flowers kind of girl. There was never any need to be. She was no nonsense and practical. Romance was nothing she'd ever needed nor wanted. But holy hell…this was unreal. The bouquet took up nearly all the space on her small kitchen nook table. She didn't know much about floral arrangements, but this had to have cost a small fortune. And the smell…the aroma was downright intoxicating.

Just then her phone vibrated and a text appeared from Mitch.

I can't wait to see you.

Double Wow.

She wondered if he had already been outside waiting and saw the delivery van pull up. She stalked back over to the window to covertly look around, but didn't see his yellow Tesla.

Knowing she only had another thirty minutes to get ready, she went back into her bedroom and put on a tank and a navy cropped sweater, and pulled on her favorite black riding boots. She brushed her hair and left it down and loose, remembering Mitch liked it that way. She brushed her teeth, applied a light berry tint to her lips, a few strokes of mascara to her lashes and she was ready.

Seven o'clock on the nose, Rylie's door buzzed. She was conflicted as to whether she should let Mitch up to her apartment or just meet him downstairs. She chose the latter, grabbing her coat and keys and barreled down the three flights of stairs to the front door of her building.

Mitch had his back to the door and turned around as she stepped over the threshold. Her breath caught when he smiled, greeting her with his lust-worthy dimple.

"Hello gorgeous," he purred in his sexy baritone. "And may I say you look stunning." Mitch reached out his hand to grab hold of Rylie's, but she abruptly pulled back and stopped him. His head swiveled back around.

Stepping in front of him so her eyes were level with his, she placed her hands on his face, getting a zing of exhilaration from the texture of his five o'clock scruff against her hands.

"I have to properly thank you for the flowers."

He quirked his eyebrows, but couldn't get out his next thought as her lips came up to meet his in what started out as a tender kiss, but grew immediately hot with pent up desire. Mitch groaned against her mouth, as she let her tongue roam and stake her claim. His hands wrapped around her, soon slithering up her back under her unbuttoned coat. The feel of his cool hands across her warm back had her shivering with desire. Maybe she should have had him come up to her apartment first. Then again, she wasn't so sure she could have kept things on track if they'd been anywhere else.

Quickly realizing that they were out in the open in front of her building, Rylie pulled herself away, dazed and breathless – shocked by her own wanton behavior.

Mitch stepped back a few paces and shook his head. "That is not how I normally begin first dates. But damn, if that's the beginning, I can't wait til the end."

Rylie blushed, shoving some loose strands behind her ears.

"I don't normally start them off that way, either, but things with you aren't exactly typical."

He chuckled, placing his warm arm around Rylie's shoulders and walking her to the car. "So how has your week been so far?"

She settled into the car seat and waited to respond until he was buckled in. "It was good. Long. Torturous."

"You're not kidding. I had back-to-back meetings and contract negotiations every day this week so far. I swear Jax was about to clock me because I was so unfocused." He turned to give her a quick look. "All I could do was fantasize about you."

"I'm glad I wasn't the only one," she said, sighing deeply. If only he knew the truth. She had turned into a wanton and horny woman. She'd fantasized about Mitch in every position she knew existed, and even got pretty creative with others. She'd catch herself during the middle of a therapy session, staring off into space, picturing Mitch running his hands up and down her spine. Covering her body with hot, sultry kisses, her mouth taking shape, just as someone would give her a questionable look and ask her if everything was okay, because she looked a little flushed.

Mitch interrupted her this time. "I know you want to take this slow, like a true first date – but I'm just warning you in advance that if you kiss me like that again, the way you just did, all bets are off."

His admission only had her wanting him even more and rethinking her need to pace things with Mitch. She'd already had dessert – and it was sinfully delicious – so why go through the hassle of starving herself?

"Well, I know you enjoy challenges. Am I right?"

"Of course – it's what I do for a living – I like to take risks and I like a good challenge. But I'm not a fan of denying myself pleasure," he added.

She stifled a laugh. "Or getting what you want, when you want."

"That, too. So where are you going with this?"

"I was thinking we could use the old baseball scoring analogy – each time you see me this week, you get to move to a new base. You know, first, second, third...home."

He gave her a sly grin. "Mmm-hmm. Could be fun."

"But if you try stealing any bases, well, you lose."

Mitch scratched his head. "Exactly how would I lose? Seems like a win-win either way," he chuckled, placing a hand on her knee. She slapped at his hand.

"Okay – I'm in. But the same holds for you, too. We'll see if you're up for the challenge," he chuckled, running his hand up and down the length of her thigh. "It's been awhile since Junior High. Remind me what the bases are again?"

She laughed, biting her lip, knowing he was probably pulling her leg. "You're so old you don't remember? It's the four 'Fs' – French, Feel, Finger and…well, you know the last one." She blushed, feeling the heat rush to her face.

"Ahh…I think I'm going to enjoy this game. So tonight is only French kissing, huh?'

"Yep."

"Good thing I've been to France and know some really, *really* good foreign techniques," he smirked, pulling into the brewery parking lot. "So you better prepare yourself for tonight's end of the date closer…"

CHAPTER TWENTY-FIVE

Mitch had stayed true to his word and over the course of the first two dates had played along with Rylie's challenge, even though it nearly killed him to be with her and be unable to take her to bed.

Sitting in Camden Ventures board room on a long Friday afternoon, he listened to one of his accountants discuss the tax implications of his current project, but his mind was actually on the previous night with Rylie. They'd gone out to dinner and afterward wound up walking around Harvard Square, hand in hand, a slight chill in the air so that she held herself close to stay warm.

She spoke with a quiet reserve about her brother and her dad, but he could sense the love and deep respect she had for them both. He had shared with her about growing up in the Camden household, the relationship and bonds he had with his brother, mother and father. The loss the family experienced when his younger brother, Matthew, died.

They talked in easy companionship throughout the evening and ended their night in her apartment for a nightcap. Her back was to him as she stood at the kitchen counter pouring two Scotches in lowball glasses. Mitch moved in behind her, pressing her tightly to him, her body fitting him perfectly. Encircling her waist with his hands, his lips came to her ear, his tongue tracing the delicate curve of her jawline. Her breath hitched, as her body relaxed against him.

His voice came out low and smooth. "So what's on the agenda for tonight, IQ?"

Rylie slowly turned in his arms, handing him his drink and smiling a sheepish grin.

"No agenda…what did you have in mind?"

He swirled his glass and took a sip, never taking his eyes of her. "I'm thinking about undressing you, laying you down on this floor, pouring the remainder of my Scotch over your body and licking it off."

Her mouth gaped open and he could tell she was a little unnerved to hear his suggestion, but came back quickly with her response.

"That sounds devious and a little depraved," she commented, licking her lips. She leaned in, raising on her toes just slightly and pressed a hot kiss to his lips. She tasted of the sweet, earthy flavor of the Scotch, mixed with her own intoxicating essence. He growled, pulling her tighter so that he could feel her nipples tighten against his chest. She wiggled her body, her hips circling against his already hardened arousal.

His hand moved underneath her rear and hoisted her up on the counter. Setting his drink down momentarily, Mitch nudged her legs open so he could stand in between their warmth. Focused now on the buttons of her shirt, he slowly and painstakingly unbuttoned her shirt, his hands lingering on each button, brushing the buttery soft skin of her supple breasts and toned abs as he made his way down her torso.

Rylie's head was thrown back against the dark cherry wood cabinets, the lush swell of her breasts arching up toward him, awaiting his touch. He palmed the fleshy mounds and rubbed his tongue over her nipples until they hardened. She pressed further into his open mouth, releasing a moan that was hungry and starving for him. Unclasping her lace bra, it fell off her shoulders and down onto the floor. Mitch grabbed the glass and slowly trickled the warm amber liquid across her hot flesh. Holding her with one hand behind her back, his mouth came down to claim her, tongue lapping up the drops of liquid that rained down her breasts. His lips caught her nipple, sucking and teasing it, as it grew taut.

"This counts as feeling you up, right?" he said into her breasts.

"Oh yeah, I'd say that," she moaned, arching even harder into his mouth. He let go of her nipple and moved over to the other, to ensure equal attention. She gasped as he took her into his mouth again, her legs wrapping around his hips and forcibly thrusting her pelvis into his.

Mitch pulled back from his thorough and seductive assault of her body into a punishing kiss. He was breathing hard as he spoke against her mouth.

"Are you trying to get me to lose this challenge, IQ?"

She pulled back sharply, her eyes burning with passion.

"Yes. I mean, no," she gasped. "You just make it feel so good. I just need more of you." Her hand went to the hard plane of his erection, stroking him through his jeans.

"You're killing me. You know that, right?" he grunted against her as she continued her grip on his length. "I can't get enough of you quick enough…but I'm not backing down from this challenge. And you can't give up that easy."

It took every ounce of his will to pull her hand away from his body as he slowly backed away, giving himself the needed distance. "We made this deal and we're going to stick to it. It's the damn principle of the thing."

He looked into her face, which was crestfallen, her bare breasts still laid out in front of him, tempting him to return to their flavorful banquet. He placed his hands around her and lifted her off the counter, gently setting her on her feet. Her body was still warm and flushed, as he handed her back her shirt from off the floor.

She looked like she was going to hall off and deck him, as she jerked it from his hands and began to button it up. Or worse, might decide to go all Krav Maga on his ass.

"Well you're a buzzkill, Camden. Isn't it normally a woman who's the dick tease?"

Mitch laughed, knowing she had a point, silently cursing himself as he looked over the beautiful woman in front of him. He tried to remember the last time he would have stopped himself from taking what he wanted and what was freely being offered to him. He couldn't get enough of Rylie, but it was so much more than that now. She had penetrated his thoughts, day in and day out since he'd met her, and he couldn't stop wanting her. But it felt deeper; stronger. An insatiable hunger and longing that he hadn't felt with anyone before her. He had visions of them together, climbing a mountain in Peru, or diving in the Caribbean, or sitting on the porch watching the sunset.

Mitch cupped the sides of her face and brought her lips to his, gently sucking on her mouth, trying to tell her without words how he felt about her.

"I hope you know how much I want you, Rylie. You make me crazy with desire and there is nothing I'd like more than to strip off the rest of your clothes and take you to your bedroom and spend all night making you mine. But I'm also a man of my word and believe in holding to agreements that I make." His hands made their way down to her hips, holding her in place in front of him. "I like you, Rylie, and I want to take things slow with you."

Rylie's expression visibly shifted from anger to admiration. Then she socked him in the gut with her fist.

"Well that's all admirable and shit," she hissed, taking her glass and her bra and walking into the living room. "Thanks for getting me all hot and bothered and leading me on." Turning slowly back to face Mitch, who was still rubbing the spot in his abs where she hit him, she gave him an earnest look. "But I do appreciate you keeping your word. Not a lot of guys would do that."

They spent the rest of the evening playing three riveting games of Domino's, which Rylie beat his pants off of two of them, and he left her with a kiss and another promise to challenge her again soon.

"…he apparently lost a couple hundred grand in some scam and that's why he was so badly beaten." Something hitting him along the side of his face brought Mitch's attention back to the present. "Dude, are you even listening to me?" Jackson asked, giving Mitch a look of irritation from across the board room table.

Mitch turned around away from the office window, in which he'd been staring out and half listening to his colleagues talk about the

Miami deal, while thinking about Rylie, and looked at his very frustrated partner.

"Sorry…what were you talking about?"

"I was talking about Tully and how he wound up with broken ribs, a busted nose and a black eye down in Miami. He apparently bamboozled some investors in some sort of Ponzi scam and one of them was Juan Carlos Perez, a Cuban drug lord. Let's just say Juan Carlos took matters into his hands the old-fashioned way," he said, illustrating his point by socking his fist into his hand. "So what's up with you? Our discussions not as interesting as your fantasies these days?"

Mitch knew he wouldn't be able to cover up his day dreaming from his very perceptive friend, so he just shrugged his shoulders and flipped him off.

Jackson laughed and shook his head. "So when am I going to meet this lovely lady who has your dick firmly in her grasp?"

"I'm making her dinner tonight at my place, so not tonight," he grinned and raised his eyebrows in a suggestive manner. "And tomorrow night is the charity gala, so I'm not seeing her and she has plans already, too. But maybe I can bring her over to your place to watch football on Sunday."

"You going to tell her about your arranged date for the event tomorrow night?"

"Hmm. Hadn't really thought about it, since it's just a favor to my parents and not a date. Although I doubt she's the jealous type, I see no need in getting into specifics when it's nothing of consequence. It's not like I'm going on my own volition."

"Yeah, you're probably right. What she doesn't know won't hurt her."

CHAPTER TWENTY-SIX

"So you're telling me that you spent the entire night at Mitch's place, in his bed and you two didn't fuck?" Sasha looked incredulously at her friend, who was sitting next to her at the nail salon having her nails painted a silver metallic color. "What the hell is wrong with you?"

Rylie blushed as she looked up at the nail technician who had a big smirk on her face. "Nothing is wrong with either one of us," she whispered harshly to her friend. "It was a perfect night. He made me dinner, we had a bottle of wine, watched some high school football on TV and then went to bed. And it's not like we didn't do *anything*...just not *that*."

Sasha made a scoffing snort and put her hands under the dryer. "I just don't get it."

Rylie gave her a modest shrug. "Just because you have no have self-control what-so-ever doesn't mean the rest of us don't. I like the fact that he's willing to take his time with me. It feels...right. It raises the stakes and the intensity. In fact, it's hot. And I mean really, *really* hot." She fanned her painted hand in front of her face, trying to tamp down the blush she felt creeping up on her face.

Her cheeks stained red as Rylie recalled the night before with Mitch. She hadn't driven to his house anticipating spending the night in his bed, fully clothed. She had worn her sexiest lace and silk bra and panties, secretly hoping he would finally give in and forfeit the bet. As it so happened, he did thoroughly enjoy seeing her in them and told her so with his hands, his mouth and his body.

They had just finished with the dinner clean-up and sat down to watch the local high school rivalry match-up on Friday night football, snuggling on the couch, Karma laying at their feet.

Rylie nestled against him, her hand on his muscled leg and her head resting on his chest, his arm wrapped securely around her shoulders.

She knew where she wanted the evening to go and decided to make the first move, as she began to slowly stroke up and down his leg, making figure eights with her fingers, feeling his muscled quads clench with each touch. She couldn't see his face, but felt his breath against the top of her head, his breathing accelerating every time her hand moved back up toward his crotch. She could sense his growing excitement and feel the heat burning through his jeans. She knew what to expect to find the moment she reached down and placed her hands firmly against his zippered jeans. Her heart rate spiked, the exhilarating zing rushing through her veins, the power of taking control surging through her own body. Placing her hand against his zipper, she tugged open the button and slowly unzipped his jeans. Mitch sucked in a sharp breath.

"What are you doing?" he inquired, his voice sexy and gruff.

Without so much as a word, she slid off the couch, grabbing the material at his hips and yanking them down with her. From her vantage point between his legs, she peeked up and saw the dark glow of desire in Mitch's eyes, his eyelids hooded with lust, his lips parted slightly. He looked beautiful and dangerously sexy.

"Batter up," she teased, yanking her shirt off to expose the lace bra she was wearing. Mitch groaned with anticipation, his hands reaching out to touch her. Brushing him away, she took hold of his wrists and placed his hands on the side of the couch. "I'm up first."

Running her hands up the hard planes of his legs and thighs, she followed with her tongue, licking his inner thighs, careful to avoid his tender knee cap. Sitting back up on her knees, she leaned over and kissed the trail from his navel to the waist band of his boxer briefs, his erection pressing hard against the material. Her hands stroked the hardened plane, as Mitch moaned, his eyes never leaving her face.

"Third base has never felt so good."

A thrill shot through her body, as it tightened and responded to his sensual words, causing moisture to flood between her own legs. She wanted nothing more than to make him feel the same way – to push him to the edge of reason.

Pulling his shorts down to free his erection, Rylie gripped the base of his arousal tightly in her fist, reveling in the smooth, but hard texture. She felt him swell in her hand, as she stroked and worshipped his hardened length. A drop of moisture appeared on the tip, inviting her tongue to taste him. She loved how he tasted a heady mixture of salty and sweet – all male. She closed her eyes as she opened her mouth to take him in, sliding her tongue from his tip to his base, enjoying the feel of him between her lips.

Her eyes fluttered opened as he let out a deep groan, his head landing back against the couch and his hands coming to rest on her head, fingers plunging into her thick hair. Her desire grew deliciously intense as she watched his expression of contentment and satisfaction, knowing she was responsible for his pleasure and ecstasy. She continued to suck and pull, guiding him in and out of her hot and wet mouth, feeling her own body respond, the urgency amping up to an intensity she was very familiar with. She thought about his mouth on her and his fingers curling inside of her, as she began moving her mouth faster and faster around him.

She was aroused beyond belief, her own sex throbbing for his touch. She moaned at the thought, just as she felt Mitch tighten and tense, his hands gripping her hair. She knew he was close and that his release would come hard and fast. This time, she wanted to feel and taste all of him as he came. Closing her eyes, she felt a thrill, an empowerment of strength as she held him in her mouth and hands. She'd never felt so in control of another person's fulfillment.

"I'm there, Rylie. Fuuucck…I'm there," he said, as his breath hitched as his body jerked, releasing a hot, thick stream deep into Rylie's throat. She swallowed quickly, feeling a buzz of contentment as she looked up into Mitch's face.

He is so incredibly beautiful.

The thought popped into her head as she looked up into the lazy smile that flashed on his face, as he opened his eyes and gazed down into hers.

Releasing him from her mouth and grip, she wiped her hand across her mouth and slid up his body. Curling her hands around his head, she leaned over to kiss behind his ear, continuing down his jaw line until she met his lips. In one fluid movement, Mitch wrapped his arms around her and flipped her on her back on the soft leather couch, bringing his half-naked body to cover hers.

Pulling his head back from hers to look down into her face, his hazel eyes glistened in the faint glow of the TV light.

"That was perfect half-time entertainment," he murmured, crushing his mouth to hers. "*That* was amazing…Now I think it's my turn to tie up the game and even the score." A sexy grin appeared across his mouth, as he slowly planted feather-light kisses down her neck, sending shivers down her spine. His hands made their way down to her breasts, as he kissed and nipped the soft flesh, teasing her with his fingers. Her body was screaming for him to touch her and she told him so as she arched up in a soft whimper.

Mitch chuckled, his finger tracing the lace bra covering her supple breast. "A little impatient, are we?"

"Mmm…I'm so ready," she said, squirming against him. "It could be a quick inning."

He chuckled, as his hands started to work on her bra. "We'll just see about that."

Releasing her bra, allowing her breasts to lay naked before him, Mitch took a sharp inhale and exhaled. His mouth grasped her nipple, pulling it into a hardened peak, while his hand pressed her breast further into his mouth. His hot mouth covered her, his tongue laving back and forth across the tips of her nipples.

She was burning up, her body careening into a wall of ecstasy. Her thoughts muddled with only one thing on her mind – the excruciatingly wonderful torture Mitch was giving her. She wanted more – everything. All at once.

Mitch ran his fingers down the side of her body, skimming her hot flesh, making his way down to where she wanted him most. He reached down and unbuttoned her jeans, pulling them open and down past her hips. She arched her hips off the couch to help, as he shimmied the denim down her legs, quickly returning his hands to her panties. His hand cupped her, his thumb brushing her sensitive spot, dipping in and under the lace trim and darting back out again. Teasing her mercilessly.

She could barely take it. "Are you trying to drive me crazy?" she asked, biting down on her lip as she let out a groan of frustration.

He snickered, stilling his hand on her inner thigh, where he'd been tracing an erotic path. "And if I am? What are you going to do about it? I could just stop…" His hand left her leg and he pushed himself up to a sitting position.

She gave him a look of disgruntled horror. "You wouldn't…dare."

Taking her hand, he brought it to his mouth, grabbing her fingers and licking them before placing them between her legs. "There's more than one way to skin a cat," he mused, guiding her fingers underneath her panties. "Pun intended."

He applied pressure, using her fingertips, stroking between the wet folds, circling the aroused flesh.

"Hmm…you were right. You are ready. So wet and ready."

Gripping the lace panties in his fist, he yanked them down and off her legs, his face replacing where the lace had just been. She moaned loudly, feeling his breath on her sex, as he dropped her hand to the side of the couch and replaced it with his tongue.

Rylie grabbed hold of his hair and arched against his mouth, which had taken possession of her body's most sensitive spot.

His tongue circled and teased, flicking over and over the delicate and responsive nub, bringing her closer and closer to fulfillment. Her hips ground into the supple leather underneath her, circling and arching in a rhythm against him. Her cries and whimpers grew louder, more demanding as her world and the light around her grew dim, her only focus on her impending orgasm. And then the world ceased to exist as she reached the peak and sublimely rode the wave of fulfillment.

Later that night, Rylie lay naked wrapped in a tight cocoon of Mitch's warm, strong arms, Karma once again at the foot of the bed. They had moved into his bedroom and talked for a while about their lives, their dreams and their families. The intimacy she felt with Mitch was something she'd never had or experienced with anyone else and she shared details about her mother that she had only shared before with Sasha. It dawned on her as she snuggled in the comfort of his arms, how much she had come to trust him. She felt safe. Admired. Loved?

That feeling scared her to no end. Mitch had made it clear and in no uncertain terms that he enjoyed being with her and definitely desired her, but had never made mention of a long-term relationship. She had no idea where this was going and wasn't the type of girl to ask or push him with ultimatums. In fact, she didn't even know what it was she wanted from him. The feelings he invoked in her were strong, no doubt. And she thought about him constantly when she wasn't with him and wanted nothing more than to be in his bed. But that didn't translate into love, did it?

As if he were reading her mind, Mitch brushed his lips over the top of her ear and asked "What are you thinking about?"

She turned onto her shoulder to look at him, a stream of light shining across his forehead and eyes, reflecting in his dark hazel irises. She placed her hand on his jawline, running it down to his chin, feeling the brittles prickle against her palm.

"Isn't that a chick kind of question to ask?"

Mitch chuckled, taking her hand in his and bringing it to his mouth for a kiss. "I guess so. You must bring out the sensitive side of me. But don't evade the question. What were you thinking about just now?"

"Your dick."

He boomed with laughter, causing Karma to whine and pop her head up on the edge of the bed. "I can imagine how it could occupy your mind so completely, considering its impressive size and skill," he joked, pressing his growing erection snugly between the V of her legs.

"Ha! Well, now you know how my mind works. And how about you," she asked, her hand finding the topic of their conversion and stroking its length. "What were you thinking about?"

A part of her was a bit nervous as to what he might say. She wondered if he was thinking about how fast he could get her out of his bed and on to his next conquest. Even though they had the conversation the other day in the coffee shop about his current dating status, there was still a small nagging voice in the back of her head that was throwing up warning flags to BE CAREFUL!

She stiffened a little as he pulled her closer to him, her brain clouding over her body's naturally fiery response to his touch.

Mitch cleared his throat before answering. "I was actually wondering what plans you had for the, oh – let's say – rest of your life?"

She couldn't contain her laughter, as she snorted loudly. But when she looked at him again and saw the seriousness written all over his face, she shifted in his arms uncomfortably.

"Um – are you joking?"

"No."

"Well, that's heavy," she commented, trying to roll further to the other side of the bed.

Mitch grabbed her arms and pulled her over on top of him, opening her legs so she could straddle him in a sitting position. Rylie was feeling overly exposed and vulnerable, and tried covering her breasts by crossing her arms, but he quickly took hold of her wrists and brought them down to his chest.

"I mean it, Ry. Being with you…what you do to me…well, what I mean to say. Ah, shit. This is coming out all wrong." He closed his eyes and sighed heavily, taking a deep breath before trying again. "I'm in love with you, Ry. You are the most incredible, sexy, gorgeous, amazing woman I've ever been with. I want more. I want more of you, all the time."

Rylie exhaled a breath she hadn't realized she was holding in. This was big. Huge. Unbelievably huge. She was literally at a loss for words, unable to respond to the weight he'd just laid on her. What did he mean by wanting more? More of what?

She was thankful for the darkness that surrounded them so he couldn't see the expression on her face. He would have seen a look of sheer terror, mixed with unfettered joy. How weird of a combination was that?

Mitch placed his hands on the sides of her face and brought her down to just an inch from his, where he held her and stared into her eyes. He then placed the sweetest, softest kiss on her lips.

"I didn't mean to freak you out –"

"You didn't…I'm not…" she swallowed hard. "Freaked out. Maybe just surprised, that's all. You caught me off guard." She took his hands and slid her fingers between his. "I want more of you, too. But I think we should figure out what that means to each other. We might have different versions of what *more* looks like."

Mitch's devilish grin came about one second before he flipped Rylie over onto her back and covered her with his own body. Threading his fingers through her hair and just before swallowing her lips in a hot kiss, he said, "I'll show you *more* right now…then we can talk *more* about it later."

CHAPTER TWENTY-SEVEN

"You've got a stupid grin on your face and I know it's not because we're going to this charity event tonight," Jackson said, shaking his head at the expense of his friend, who was straightening his bow tie in the hall mirror. "And it certainly has nothing to do with your date, either."

Mitch grimaced at the thought of spending the next five to six hours with the newly single Elle on his arm – a huge favor to his mother who was hosting the event. After his mother called him several times over the week to remind him of his promise and to be 'nice' to 'poor Ellie,' Elle had also called and left three messages for him, sounding needy and desperate. While not the least bit interested, he finally called her back to make arrangements for their night. He made sure to mention several times that they were 'just friends' and he was dating someone. And, oh how he wished that someone was going to be with him tonight instead of Elle.

Although he had not specified what his plans entailed for the evening earlier that morning before Rylie left, he promised to call her when he got home. She mentioned she was going to some party with Sasha, but had indicated it wouldn't be a late night, either. In fact, he was hoping he would be able to make it an early night and drop Elle off at her home as soon as possible so he could see Rylie afterward without it appearing to be a booty call.

"So what if I'm smiling? Don't see what it's got to do with you, ya prick."

Jackson took a sip of his beer and cocked his eyebrow at Mitch, who had been fussing with his tie for over five minutes.

"Must be having some severe withdrawals from your sexy therapist lady to put you in that kind of mood. So what's going on there? Things must be pretty serious if you've invited her over tomorrow night."

Mitch finished with his tie and turned to grab the beer from Jackson's hand, taking a long swig before handing it back.

"Yeah. She's pretty great. You'll like her."

"I'm sure I will. It's obvious she has your dick tied up in knots, so that's saying something."

Mitch ignored his friend's comments and opened the hallway closet to get his outer jacket, folding it over his arm and grabbing his keys. A limo was parked and waiting outside his house, ready to pick up their dates and head downtown to the Boston Harbor Hotel on the waterfront. He had been with his mother and her co-chair, Charlene, the day they visited the site a year earlier, when he helped her pull some strings with the hotel manager to coordinate the planning of the event. It was a beautiful location and he knew if he could just get over the fact that he wasn't going to be with Rylie, he'd have a good time.

On their way to pick up Elle and Jackson's date for the evening, Deirdre, they popped open the chilled bottle of champagne and toasted themselves on another new project they'd signed earlier in the week. They'd also received a copy of *Architecture Today* in which they were both interviewed and a full story written on their last years' string of successful projects.

"Here's to being the new "Eco-Kings!" Jackson toasted, clinking his glass to Mitch's.

Mitch smiled at the sound of their new media nickname and toasted back to his friend and partner. "And to the best partner a guy could have. Thanks buddy. I couldn't have done it without you."

The limo had pulled up to their first stop, which was Elle's house. Mitch opened the door and stepped out, leaning back in to whisper. "Looks like she at least walked away from the marriage with a pretty damn nice house," he said, whistling as he looked at the gated entrance of the three-story brownstone and headed to the front door.

Ringing the door buzzer, he heard the sounds of little feet scampering across the hardwood floors, giggles and some laughter. Elle's voice from behind the door made a shrill, "Shhh – go back to bed you two," and then she swung the door open.

He had to admit, she did look stunning in a long flowing yellow gown and her matching blond hair coifed in a high chignon. She smiled then, and although beautiful, under closer inspection, her face held a desperate and harsh quality to it. Her features were pinched and tight, perhaps from too much work or just being angry all the time. He smiled back and held out his hand to shake hers, which was already outstretched in greeting.

"Mitch, darling, it's been far too long," she exclaimed in the same shrill voice, as she came in for the two-cheek debutante kiss. "You look absolutely handsome! Definitely not the scrawny kid who used to push me down in the sandbox."

He laughed at the memory, not only because it was true, but because he remembered why he'd push her down. Her voice always held that same grating, fingernails-down-a-chalkboard quality and it drove him crazy. Even then. He took a quick breath and smiled.

"You look lovely, too. So glad we could escort one another tonight. I know my mother was appreciative." Stepping in the foyer, he helped her with her coat as she grabbed her clutch from the hall table. Rattling off a few snippy instructions to her nanny, who looked like a timid house mouse, she turned to him and gestured toward the door.

"I'm ready if you are."

Mitch held the door and allowed her to step out, as he followed close behind. No, he was indeed not ready for the rest of the evening, but he'd made a promise and would have to get through it. Thank the good Lord the limo had plenty of booze and it was an open bar the rest of the night.

****

The party and silent auction were in full swing by the time Sasha and Rylie had arrived at the hotel, fashionably late, of course. And more than a little tipsy. Sasha had made sure that they had plenty of cocktails pre-party at her townhouse as they got ready for the evening.

The hotel was one of the oldest and most historic in the city, with the ballroom doors and windows looking out over the scenic Boston harbor. The room was beautifully lit from the glittering crystal chandeliers above, with a soft blue candescent light streaming down from the elegant coffered ceilings.

Booze was flowing from every corner of the room and the servers were making their way through the crowd with mouth-watering hors d'oeuvres held high on silver trays. Rylie's stomach growled as someone passed in front of her smelling like bacon wrapped prawns. Her mouth watered. She and Sasha had only had coffee and donuts before their spa treatments earlier in the day and didn't have time to eat before they got dressed and ready, so she was famished as the trays of food continued to pass her by.

"I need to get something to eat, like now," she growled, pulling at Sasha's arm as they entered the ballroom.

Sasha pulled her arm away as she instantly reached for two glasses of champagne from the server in front of her. Handing one to Rylie, she took a sip and smiled. "First, we drink some bubbly. It will make everything taste delicious. Then we need to go find Mark's parents. They should be around here somewhere. And please be on the look-out for any hot, eligible men…I need one like you need food. My vibrator just isn't cutting it anymore."

Rylie shook her head in disgust and then furtively glanced around to make sure they weren't in earshot of anyone overhearing what she just said.

"Good grief, Sash. Keep it down, will you? We're in a pretty swanky place tonight where the mention of a V word might just get us kicked out."

Her volume picked up a notch. "Which V word? Vibrator? Vagina? Vulva?"

An older gentleman and two white-haired women standing in a close circle within a few feet of them were clearly not amused by her antics and turned around with up-turned noses, giving Sasha the death glare. Sasha shrugged and took a swig of her drink.

Rylie was beyond mortified. "Oh my God," she winced, yanking Sasha away in the opposite direction of their uptight audience. "Shush. Please remember to use your inside voice tonight and refrain from that kind of language and I promise you I'll try to help find you a man. Okay?"

Sasha squealed in delight and gave Rylie a quick hug. "I won't be choosy tonight, as long as he's tall, rich and extremely gorgeous. Oh, and of course, he has to have a big co–," Rylie slammed her hand over her friend's mouth to shut her up before she could finish her sentence. Sasha's eyes were blazing, as Rylie leaned in to whisper in her ear.

"Next time I'll use soap," she said in as menacing of a voice as possible. She loosened up her fingers, but gave her a look that said, "*Are you going to behave now?*" Sasha nodded her head as Rylie released her hand from Sasha's red lips. Opening her clutch, she grabbed a lipstick tube and handed it to Sasha. "Here, go fix your make-up. You're all smudged now."

During Sasha's absence, Rylie walked around the ballroom, admiring all the beautifully dressed men and women. She'd only been to one other affair that was quite this decadent, but felt this time that she fit the part. The dress that Sasha had loaned her was a crushed red velvet that fit tightly over her curves. The halter cowl-neck draped in the front, revealing a peek-a-boo cut-out for her cleavage and was backless, displaying just enough skin to be sinfully sexy. Her only thought when she had put it on and looked at herself in the mirror was how it would feel if Mitch were there with her, his hand placed gently on her exposed back, stroking up and down her spine.

God, she thought Sasha was bad always talking about sex, but now it was all that she could ever think about. Finishing up her glass of champagne, she replaced her empty one with a full one as the server swung around and then went in search of a plate of food.

Milling through the crowd, she overheard laughter and stories being shared in the small groups of people formed throughout the room. She smiled at the strangers that passed her or glanced her way, always hopeful no one would stop to make small talk. She was already feeling giddy from the first glass of champagne and began to sip the other when she spotted a couple across the room and the woman's dress caught her eye.

The first thing she noticed, and what drew her attention to her, was the beautiful, silky canary yellow dress that was covering the woman's lithe body. Her first instinct was to want to run her hands down the material because it looked so very soft…as smooth and creamy as butter.

The next thing she noticed, even though the couple had their backs to her, was how brilliantly happy the woman seemed. Her smile was a mile wide and she continued to look adoringly at her date. One of her yoga-toned arms was wrapped possessively around her date's arm, as she laughed and smiled up at him, and the other one was on his back, stroking his broad shoulders.

Even though the lights were dim, and she practically halfway across the room, the man looked extremely handsome and they seemed to make a very attractive couple. The other couple talking with them was laughing at something the man said and they were clinking their glasses in a toast. They seemed charmed and enjoying the moment.

Her eyes were still on the group when a server came by to offer Rylie some food. Already past her point of famished, she took a napkin and two little medallions of meat and thanked the hostess, just as someone from across the room called out "Mitch." Her head jerked up at his name, just as she popped the appetizer in her mouth and glanced up.

Their eyes met, first in recognition.

And then in shock.

Rylie almost spewed out the half chewed up appetizer had she not just swallowed it down, a choking sensation caught in her throat as she did.

She couldn't breathe.

She couldn't think.

She had to get out of there.

It finally registered that the couple, the beautiful canary-like blonde woman and the handsome man, was Mitch. With some other woman. And now he was staring at her, over the shoulder of the man that had called out his name. Spinning around on her heel, her dress caught underneath her and nearly sent her toppling into Sasha, who had conveniently reappeared right behind her again.

Grinning widely, she helped Rylie get upright. "Be careful, Ry. We know what high heels and too much champagne do to you," she giggled, obviously feeling the effects from her own two glasses. And then she looked into Rylie's face. "Whoa, girl. What's the matter? Are you okay?"

"Sasha, don't ask me any questions. Just get me the fuck out of here. Now."

****

Sasha looked around helplessly before running out to try and catch up to Rylie, who was now halfway to the ballroom doors. It was then that she heard Rylie's name being called by a very low, sonorous voice.

Turning in the direction in which it came, she did a double-take when she came face-to-face with Mitch Camden.

"Mitch! What on earth are you doing here?" she smiled, her voice indicating she was a little confused, concerned and curious all at once.

"Sasha. Good to see you," he said, without smiling or even really looking in her direction. His eyes were darting around the crowd trying to search out the direction in which Rylie had run off. He gently placed his hands on Sasha's shoulders and brought his head down to hers. "I just saw Rylie and she saw me, but it's not good. She ran off. Sasha, I need your help in finding her before she leaves. Please…"

Mitch felt like the wind had been knocked out of him. He was gasping for air like a drowning man. And he felt like drowning. When he saw Rylie's expression of horror, her eyes darting from Elle to him to back to Elle, he knew right then that he had fucked up royally. And now he saw the same expression on Sasha's curious face, as Elle came gliding gracefully up behind Mitch, placing her hands on his arms.

"Mitch, darling. Is everything all right with you? You just ran off like the building was on fire."

His tone was forceful, leaving no room for question as he shrugged off her hands. "Please return to the party, Elle, and get your hands off me." He watched as she huffed and skulked away, while Sasha still stood there mystified as to what was happening. "Please, Sasha. I need to get to her and explain that what she saw wasn't what she thought she saw."

Sasha's eyes blazed in repugnance. "Oh really? And what do you think she saw, exactly?"

It was obvious that he would need to get through Sasha first before he'd ever be able to explain it to Rylie.

"I think she misinterpreted what she saw between me and Elle. I'm not *here* with her. I'm *here* as a favor to my mother, who asked me to bring Elle. I'm not here on my own accord and she's not my date. But

I think Rylie may have seen Elle's very possessive and aggressive hands on me, leading her to believe a different story."

Sasha's eyes grew dark and assessing. Her hands went to her hips, clearly in her judging stance. Mitch would have told her to "fuck off, I need to go after her," but knew his only chance was through the voice of reason of her best friend.

His voice grew soft and his hands were shaking, his eyes pleading with her to help him rectify the situation and find Rylie. After several minutes, she finally exhaled and nodded her head in agreement.

"Fine. I'll help you. But you have a lot of explaining to do. You should've come clean before tonight and told her about Elle. It was a douche thing to do and now you're going to have to pay for it."

All he could do was agree with her. "I know."

They both darted off into the main reception foyer, trying to yell for Rylie over the booming music from inside the ballroom. A half dozen people turned to see what the ruckus was about, giving each other sideways glances and staring at Sasha and Mitch as if they were both missing their heads.

Returning from the grand staircase, where she didn't see any sign of her, Sasha ran back to the ballroom doors to find Mitch standing there, frantically typing in his phone. That reminded Sasha about the keys to the car, which were in her clutch. She opened it up and dangled them in joyous triumph, flashing him a gigantic smile.

"She can't get far without these! Her purse was too small for them so I put them in mine for safe-keeping." When he gave her a look of confusion, she threw up her hands in exasperation. "That means she must still be around here somewhere, nimrod."

"Great. I'm going to check the perimeter and the terrace, you go downstairs and check the atrium." As he gave her directions, Jax came stalking out into the hallway toward them.

"What the fuck is going on?" he inquired, first looking at Mitch and then centering his attention on Sasha, who was small and petite next to both of their large towering frames. "And who the hell are you?"

"Jackson Koda, meet Dr. Sasha Lee, Rylie's friend and boss." They both quickly shook hands and nodded their greetings. "Rylie was here, Jax. She saw me with Elle and I think assumed I was *with* Elle. It probably didn't look good in her eyes, but now she's run off and we need to find her."

"Okay, tell us what to do."

"You two go downstairs and check the lobby and bar and out on the street. She could've jumped in a cab. I'm heading out to the terrace. Text me if you find her."

"Will do. You're coming with me, Shorty." Jax directed Sasha. "Let's go."

CHAPTER TWENTY-EIGHT

Yep, she did it again.

She was running away from all of her stupid, girly feelings and the humiliation she felt when she saw Mitch with another woman. A woman who he said he didn't have. He told her not once, but twice, that he wasn't with anyone, that he didn't have a girlfriend. And yet she witnessed it with her own two eyes. Clear as day and more painful than a thousand paper cuts to her heart.

The moment she jumped in the waiting cab and fled for home, she put her plan in place. She'd dialed up Mark, told him she was coming and then told him she'd call him as soon as she got to the airport. Then she went online the moment she got to her apartment to purchase her ticket. Throwing as few items of clothing and necessary toiletries in her suitcase as she could, she grabbed her passport and walked out the door.

The only slight, teeny, tiny problem interfering with her hasty plan was that she lacked her car and car keys. But she knew they'd be in good hands with Sasha until she returned. And then, of course, there was an issue with Sasha and her job.

The worst thing that could happen was that Sasha could fire her ass for leaving without notice. No, the worst thing was that Sasha could kick her ass for leaving. Either case, she was going to hear an earful the next time she spoke with her. Which could be any moment, because according to her phone display, she'd received four calls from Sasha and two texts. And then there was the ten she saw from Mitch.

She feared the inevitable. She knew there was no getting out of talking to Sasha, but maybe she could delay it until she hit another continent. Mitch was another matter altogether. She didn't owe him shit. He was a user, a playboy, a liar and a cheat. And not necessarily in that particular order.

As the cab drove her to Logan, her thoughts drifted again to what she witnessed and experienced that night. A night that was supposed to be filled with fun and friendship that had turned on a dime to humiliation and anger.

God she was so angry. She should've stayed and punched him in the balls. She should have stayed behind and railed on him for making her feel like a piece of worthless shit. And for what? What reason did he possibly have for lying to her like that?

One moment he tells her he loves her and is buying her flowers and talking about their future, and the next he's practically flaunting the canary woman in his face! Well, okay, maybe not to that extreme, but it hurt, nonetheless.

The pain was excruciating. She knew it would hurt. Now she finally understood what her father felt when her selfish-ass mother up and left them. It felt like her heart had been hollowed out with a spoon, yanked out with forceps, and then covered with igniter fluid and scorched in a burning pile of coals.

Her solution was to get the fuck out of Dodge. To put the five thousand or so miles of distance between them, at least for a little while, so she could forget about the asshat who used her and made her feel cheap and dirty.

When she arrived at the airport, she called Mark again to let him know her flight details and when to expect her. This time, instead of sounding excited, he sounded determined to keep her away.

"Rylie. I'd like nothing more than for you to come visit me. For you to see what's going on in the world and to help out. But it's obvious you're not in the right frame of mind right now. You're upset. You're not thinking straight. Come on, you don't have to do this now."

"What the fuck, Mark? You didn't put stipulations on this when you asked me to come before. I'd even endured all the needles and vaccinations a month ago knowing I'd be coming to visit you. I thought you would want to see me. I thought you loved me..."

She could hear the words she spoke, but knew she was saying them for someone else. Someone else who had told her he loved her, but obviously didn't want to give up his lifestyle to accommodate her.

"You know it's true, Ry. I do love you. But you're just using that as an excuse to escape your pain. You need to stay there and deal with whatever shit's going on with you and Camden."

She was pissed that he brought Mitch up in their conversation. How dare he even speak his name. She wanted to eradicate him from her mind. Obliterate her thoughts and feelings altogether.

"I can't. I need to leave."

There was a long pause on the other end of the line. Several moments had passed and Mark hadn't said a word. Rylie was lost in her own thoughts as she sat limply in the airport terminal chair, just outside of security.

"I think you'd be making a big mistake if you left right now, Rylie. Sasha will skin you alive the next time she sees you if you get on that plane. You can't do that to her or your career. She may be your friend, but she has a business to run. She can't have employees running off without notice."

They finished their conversation when Mark was interrupted to handle a medical emergency and had left her sitting in the airport terminal in a conflicted state. Her flight wasn't set to leave for another two hours and she promised she would call him before she boarded.

Her heart ached. She was putting her job and career in jeopardy if she just upped and left. Even though she highly doubted Sasha would ever call in her chips, but there was always a chance. Her head throbbed with the onslaught of a stress headache. Rylie crouched low in the seat, letting her head hit the back of the chair. She closed her eyes to shield herself from the harsh lights of the terminal, wanting to black out and erase everything from the previous four hours.

****

Mitch was nearly out of his mind thinking through the scene that Rylie had witnessed and what she must have seen between he and Elle. He had put up with Elle's unstoppable flirting for hours and kept his impatience under control every time she let out her whiny, high-pitched laugh, or continued to paw him at every inopportune moment. But when he realized Rylie was there and saw the pain and crude awareness that went through her eyes, it nearly brought him to his knees.

There is no way he'd ever meant to hurt her. All he wanted was a chance to turn back time and explain to her about Elle and the reason he was with her at this event. Why hadn't he just told her the truth in the first place, so she knew she could trust him?

You're a dumb shit, that's why.

This was a mess and he didn't know what the hell he was doing.

And there she was, running away from him yet a third time. They would definitely need to sit down and talk through that little quirk of hers. If they were going to have a life together, she would need to know that she couldn't just run off at the drop of a hat when things got tough or difficult. My God, she was so stubborn. But he loved that about her.

He loved her.

Now he just needed to find her more than ever so she could stop running and he could be the man she needed. An honest and truthful man.

After he, Sasha and Jax had spent over an hour searching the hotel for Rylie and continually calling her cell phone, they had nearly given up, until a phone call from Mark interrupted their search. He hightailed it out of there and to the airport, where he now stood looking down over the sleeping form of the woman he loved.

"I know what you think you saw…" he started softly, watching Rylie's body jerk to life in front of him. He knew what he would see when she opened her eyes. Anger. Hatred. He could deal with anything right now, except defeat.

As soon as he said the words out loud, Rylie's eyes snapped open and she whipped her head up to give him an icy cold glare.

"You don't know shit, asshole."

"I'll give you that one. Yes, I'm an asshole. I plead guilty on all accounts." Mitch dropped to his good knee in front of Rylie, his hands instinctively moving to touch her. Needing to connect on some physical level. "I'm an asshole because I wasn't upfront and completely truthful with you about tonight. Rylie, I never, in a million years, would do anything to hurt you. Please believe that…this event has been planned for a long, long time. Did you know my mother is the co-chair?" He was playing the family card, hoping it would soften the blow a bit more. Her expression hadn't changed. Her glare was still an iceberg.

"Margo Camden, my mother, is a woman of many hobbies, but drumming up money for good causes and bleeding heart campaigns is where she excels."

Rylie scooted up in her chair, her back stick straight, still ready to defend herself. "What the hell does this have to do with anything, Mitch? What does it have to do with you and me and that canary girl you were with tonight?"

Mitch cocked his head to the side. "Canary girl?"

"Her dress made her look like a canary. I'm sure she's just as flighty."

He chuckled at her description. Without even knowing her, she was dead on.

"Her name is Eleanor Stanwood. Well, she has a married name, but I don't know what it is."

Rylie reared up, like a cat ready to fight. "You mean she's married?"

"No. No. She is the daughter of my mother's best friend, Betsy. My parents asked me well over a month ago, right after my surgery, to escort Elle tonight because she was just getting over a bad divorce and needed a night out. But then you happened," he paused, resisting the urge to reach out and touch her face. To hold her hand. To kiss her lips. To pull her in his arms.

"Jesus, Rylie. I don't know why I just didn't tell you upfront about this obligation tonight. If I had, none of this would have ever happened. In fact, after we got back from Miami, I should have just cancelled out on this night altogether. I'm a stupid, fucking idiot."

Rylie shifted slightly, pulling her knees up to her chest and wrapping her arms tight around her legs. "Yeah."

Mitch watched her with fear and trepidation, worried she would bolt at any moment and run through security before he could stop her. She sat there for several painful minutes, her chin resting on her knees, Mitch still on bended knee in front of her. Praying she would forgive him.

"So, I was about to leave for Africa," she began, letting out a long breath. Mitch's heart stopped, not wanting her to go further. Not willing to let this end here. "But I can't go now." Her voice was full of sadness and despair.

"Yeah?" he asked hesitantly, moving up to take the seat next to her. "Why is that?"

"Because, while you may be a stupid, fucking idiot, you look really hot in a tux. And if you hadn't been there tonight, dressed up like double-oh-seven, I wouldn't have had the opportunity to tell you that I think you look really hot in a tux."

Mitch sat there dumbfounded and at a loss for words, a jolt of happiness bubbling up from deep within. Even in the midst of her anger and the pain he'd caused her, she was still the sweetest, god-damned beautiful woman he'd ever met.

"Rylie," he whispered, taking one of her hands from around her legs and pressing it to his mouth. "I love you. And if I hadn't come tonight and you hadn't been here, I wouldn't have had the chance to tell you I love you and that I want only you."

Mitch stood up slowly, taking her hands into his and bringing her up against him, so she could feel the beating of his heart. His hands wrapped around her waist, holding on to her for dear life. His fingers traced an infinity symbol along her back, as she shivered and arched into him, reaching up to touch his lips with hers.

She pulled back and forced her chin up to look at him, a smile beginning to take shape on her beautiful mouth.

"But I'd rather you take me home so I can get you out of this tux and finish our game. I think the bases are loaded."

EPILOGUE

Scoring the Super Bowl tickets was the easy part. Getting Rylie to New Orleans on Super Bowl weekend, without her growing suspicious of his plans, was a feat near impossible. But by some pure dumb luck and the help of Rylie's best friend, Sasha, Mitch was able to keep his surprise a secret and get Rylie to the airport without her questioning his plans.

He had spent the last three and a half months getting to know Rylie in every possible way. He finally me her father Dan and her brother Dylan and spent nearly every Thursday night when he was in town at Dan's house watching football and cheering on Rylie's beloved Patriots. He finally felt that he'd won Dan over when he brought over a signed Philadelphia Eagles jersey of the late Hall of Famer, Reggie White. He still felt like he got the stink-eye from Dylan, but that seemed to soften when he offered up his Tesla to drive while he was out on town one week on business.

His knee was back to fighting strength and he was now able to resume the life of adventure and activity, which now included Rylie. While she was never overly impressed with his jet-setting life, she did seem to enjoy the same levels of highs and thrills he did from his adventures. They went scuba diving in Cabo San Lucas after the Christmas holidays, where Jax suggested they go instead of their annual ski trip. Sasha even came along so they could be a foursome, although it seemed all she and Jax did was argue like the Odd Couple, Oscar and Felix. He was pretty certain nothing was happening between those two.

They'd also planned an upcoming trip in March to go visit Mark in Africa. While there, they were going to provide their assistance using their talents – Rylie assisting children recovering from lifesaving surgeries and Mitch aiding in the design and building of a new hospital annex.

And now here he was, not only ready to take the woman he loved to her first Super Bowl game, but also ready to propose to her while there. He'd thought of hundreds of other methods of getting down on one knee, which would be rather ironic, in and of itself. But recalling just how ecstatic and exhilarated she was when they went to the Dolphin's game in Miami, he knew this would be the perfect opportunity.

And even if her beloved team didn't win the highly coveted Championship ring, well at the very least, she would walk away with a pretty big one on her finger.

THE END

ABOUT THE AUTHOR

Sierra Hill decided to write her first full-length romance after a corporate acquisition led her to a stint of unemployment, offering her some quality writing time. She has always been an aspiring writer and feels incredibly blessed to be living her dream.

Sierra is a huge alternative music fan and enjoys attending as many live concerts as often as possible, even going on the road when her favorite band Pearl Jam is on tour. She frequently indulges on what some might consider an unhealthy dose of reading, dark chocolate goodies and too much coffee.

Sierra resides in the Seattle area with her husband of eighteen-years and her long-haired, German shepherd. She is currently busy working on her next book.

Please enjoy the following excerpt from the novella, *The Reunion*, coming soon!

CHAPTER ONE

~April~

Delaney Cooper's ten year high school reunion invitation sat on her kitchen table, silently taunting her with a sarcastic 'neener-neener' finger-wagging sneer.

It came in the mail the day before, forwarded from her parent's house in Madison, along with a host of other mail. Bills, brochures, coupons, political advertisements – the usual weeks' worth of garbage laid out as a reminder of the monotony that was her life. She'd sifted through the stack after she returned home the night before, her customary Pinot in her hand, a half-eaten bag of Tostitos on the counter and her favorite Sirius XM radio station playing in the background.

How appropriate that Adele's "*Someone Like You*" was wafting softly through the speakers, her songbird voice singing something about "Regrets and mistakes, they're memories made" as she had opened up the envelope, the one with the George Washington High School insignia in the upper left hand corner. Her hands trembled and her memory was flooded with images from those formative years. Mostly images from those she had taken of her classmates. Photographs for the yearbook. Photos depicting all the fabulous fun everyone was having during their senior year. Homecoming. Spring Break. Prom. Sports competitions. Cheer squad. Graduation.

All pictures of *other* people having fun.

Many women panic over the impending social gathering ten years after the best years of their lives. They might worry about losing the twenty pounds they'd put on since high school, or about getting back into shape post-baby, or wanting a boob job before the big event.

But not, Laney. Her panic didn't stem from a concern over any physical imperfection, although she could do without the extra padding added to her toosh. No, her anxiety was born from the distinct possibility of coming face-to-face with the boy – now man – that she had quietly crushed on throughout high school. The boy who was so far out of her league he should've been from another planet. The boy who stole her heart and carelessly tossed it away like it was his leftover lunch from the school cafeteria. The boy who, the night after graduation, took her virginity, thereby giving her the best night of her life and a dream of something she hoped would remain forever.

Forever, however, ended three weeks later when Evan Stansfield enlisted in the Navy and married Tanya Jansen.

It was silly, really, to think she ever had a chance with Evan. How foolish she was to think that, because he was everything she wasn't. Fierce. Wild. Funny. Outgoing. Incredibly gorgeous in his bad boy hotness. Every guy wanted to be his friend and every girl wanted him for herself. He was on the homecoming court three years running and was named Homecoming King their senior year. He dated only the most popular, sought after girls in school and was never lonesome for a date. Evan oozed charm and charisma, which seemed to pour out of every cell of his body, making him so damn likeable that no one could resist. Not even Laney.

And yet for some reason, still unknown to Laney after all these years, Evan had wanted her, even for the briefest of moments.

In an effort to begin saving for the future business she wanted to start after college, she'd taken a job at a local bar and grill her senior year. She knew, even then, that her career aspirations were to become a photographer and that she would someday open up her own studio. She loved to be behind the lens – capturing those rare and beautiful moments in the lives of others when they exuded happiness, joy and sometimes pain. She felt it and understood it and lived vicariously through it.

However, she'd found out on her first day at Lucky Lucy's Sports Bar, that she wasn't cut out to be a waitress. It was a disaster. She spilled a bowl of minestrone soup on a patron's lap, a business man who from the looks of it was not at all interested in hearing her pleading sobs of apology. She also broke a pitcher of beer when it slipped out of her hands and shattered on the already sticky and beer-splattered floor. She nearly broke out in hives when a group of college guys at one of her tables started shamelessly flirting with her, throwing out sexual innuendo and references that left her face blotchy and red.

Running into the back of the kitchen, her eyes brimming over with hot, messy tears, she sank down on her knees and balled. There was no way she could continue trying to be something she wasn't, where she had to be sociable and thick skinned. No, she was not suited to be a waitress, but better equipped to wash dishes, out of the way of others, back in the corners of the world where she could quietly go about her existence, invisible and out of sight.

Laney was sitting on her butt, her back against the cold tiled wall, her head bent to her knees in misery, when she felt a hand placed gently on her shoulder. Her head jerked up in shock, a startled look appearing on her face. The look turned to bewilderment as she stared into the stormy blue eyes of Evan Stansfield.

His eyes expressed concern. "Hey, are you okay?"

Her insides went wonky and her flesh became clammy. Her body went from extreme cold to equator hot simultaneously. The distant sounds of the bar area, laughter, dishes clanking, music blaring, barely registered as she tried to wrap her head around the reason Evan was crouched next to her. She couldn't quite grasp what he was saying to her, as if she were underwater. Everything was garbled and muffled. When she just sat there, for what probably was an eternity, her mouth gaping open at him, he let out a laugh.

"Well, I know I'm a sight to behold, but you're looking at me like I have two heads or something. Or do I have some spinach stuck in my teeth? Oh geez, do I have something nasty hanging from my nose?" He swatted a finger underneath his perfectly shaped nose.

She giggled at the audacity of Evan's self-deprecating humor. Could this gorgeous guy – this unattainable god of women, actually be trying to cheer her up? *No Way*!

Evan kneeled at her side, handing her a dish towel to wipe her tears. She gladly accepted it, sniffling away her tears.

She looked up sheepishly. "Um…thanks. You don't have to, you know…try and make me feel better."

"Oh, well actually, I was just going to let you know Table Eight needed some more coffee," he said, turning his head in the direction of the restaurant. Laney's expression was one of mortification.

Evan let out a loud, boisterous laugh.

"I'm just kidding. But do you honestly think I wouldn't be compelled to help out a pretty girl in distress?" His thumb came out to wipe away an errant tear that had trailed down along her chin. His touch had her flinching.

"Whoa – jumpy much? Sorry…it's supposed to be good luck to snag a tear before it rolls off someone's face. So anyway, are you gonna tell me what has you sitting back here in the corner crying your eyes out?" His eyes made a quick detour to her chest where her gold name tag was pinned askew. "*Laney*?"

The sound of her name coming from his beautiful mouth had created a memory to last a lifetime. She could die a happy girl now just from hearing those two syllables being spoken by the hot, kissable lips of one Evan Stansfield.

He stood up then, offering his hand to pull her up next to him. Smoothing her hands down the backside of her mini-skirt, she caught his eyes watching her movements, scanning her up and down. When his eyes returned to meet hers, he shrugged, unconcerned at being caught.

"What? So sue me. I'm not all that altruistic in my actions. A guy can't resist looking at a perfect ass." Then he gave her the most disarming, white toothed, wolfish smile she had ever seen. A smile that would have sent Little Red Riding Hood running for the hills.

"And let me tell you," he said conspiratorially, looking around the room as if he were in a spy movie. "If we weren't out here in the kitchen area with ten pairs of eyes on us, you'd better be damn sure my hands would have replaced yours in a heartbeat."

Laney gasped. Not only had he suggested she was pretty, but he'd also very bluntly told her he wanted to touch her ass. Swallowing down a thrill she could only describe as erotic embarrassment, she felt her face flush, the blood rising from the tips of her toes, up through her belly and to her cheeks.

Little did she know that it would not be the last time she would be enraptured by the smooth talking, blonde haired, blue eyed, knows-what-he-wants and how to get it, bad boy.

Laney sighed and shook her head, clearing the memories from a lifetime ago. She was a different person back then – an innocent girl, full of unrealistic dreams of being loved always and forever the boy who stole her heart. Dreams that would never be fulfilled.

Taking the silver embossed invite in both hands, she carefully and intentionally ripped it in half, tossing it, along with her memories, in the trash.

13078598R00163

Made in the USA
San Bernardino, CA
09 July 2014